BEING MRS DARCY

LUCY MARIN

Quills & Quartos
PUBLISHING

Edited by Jennifer Altman and Kristi Rawley

Cover by Cloudcat Designs

On the cover: *The Waning Honeymoon, George Henry Boughton*

ISBN: 978-1-951033-31-6 (ebook) and 978-1-951033-32-3 (paperback)

TABLE OF CONTENT

Prologue

It was done and, Elizabeth had been assured, done for the best. After at first arguing against it, she had accepted the inevitability, and now, as unfathomable as it was, she was Mrs Fitzwilliam Darcy. Just that morning, she had married him.

Never again to call myself Miss Elizabeth Bennet. Never again to call Longbourn my home.

The last was not such a hardship, thanks to her father.

The first stage of the journey from Hertfordshire to London passed in awkward silence. Elizabeth attempted two or three times to start a conversation with her new sister, but Georgiana's replies were perfunctory, and Elizabeth abandoned the task. Mr Darcy said nothing, but scowled each time she spoke, which contributed to her ill mood. His cousin, Viscount Bramwell—Sterling to his family—rode nearby. Elizabeth did not blame him for wishing to be away from them.

Am I not to speak to my new sister? Elizabeth wondered. *He is not inclined to conversation—ever—and I must conclude that neither is she. What a long journey this is going to be!*

Elizabeth's sense of dread grew with each successive mile they travelled, and increased tenfold when they entered Mayfair. It threatened to overcome her, but somehow she maintained her composure.

It will be well, Lizzy, it will be well. Remember what Aunt Gardiner wrote. He is a good man. I must find a way to believe that. Dear Lord, give me strength!

As uncomfortable, even distressing, as Longbourn had been these last weeks, it was familiar and there were people there she knew and understood and loved. Now she was entering the unknown, and by all indications it was an inhospitable one. Her heart raced each time it seemed they might stop. What would it be like to live among these people who did not care about her and could not exert themselves to even say a friendly word or two?

She vaguely remembered saying goodbye to the viscount, then, just a minute or two later, they reached Darcy House. Once Darcy was out of the carriage, he reached in and said his sister's name. Georgiana exited and immediately entered the house.

It was her turn. Taking a deep breath, Elizabeth placed her hand into her husband's, stepped down, and entered her new home. She could not affect a joyous demeanour, so she strove to act as she perceived Darcy was—restrained yet dignified.

Only the housekeeper and butler greeted them, and Elizabeth tried not to feel the slight; the entire household should be there to meet their new mistress. Darcy asked about his sister, and Mrs Northmore announced she had gone to her rooms. Elizabeth was taken aback by this very marked piece of rudeness, which was worse than the absent servants.

She said, "I believe she found the journey quite fatiguing."

"As did we all," Darcy replied. "Come. I shall show you to your rooms."

With a firm hand on her elbow, he led her upstairs and to a door. After a simple, "Mrs Darcy," he left her alone.

ELIZABETH AND DARCY DINED ALONE THAT EVENING. HE SAID nothing for the better part of the meal, and she longed for solitude.

There had been more than enough of today; tomorrow she would start on this new life into which she had been forced.

"How did you find your chambers?"

The sound of Darcy's voice startled Elizabeth. "F-fine. T-thank you."

"You will wish to make changes. Mrs Northmore can assist you. Your maid?"

"She seems very...fine."

He gave a curt nod.

Cautiously, Elizabeth asked, "Perhaps you would be so good as to tell me what you expect of the next few weeks. What I mean is, what family is in town, is there anything in particular you believe I should attend to?"

"Only the Romsleys and Sterling are in town, fortunately. Lady Romsley will accompany you to some appropriate modistes and warehouses to see that you acquire the items you need. I assume you will wish to...accustom yourself to the house. We shall not be home to callers. As soon as possible, we go to Pemberley."

Elizabeth nodded, and they resumed their silence.

After dinner, they spent a short time in a withdrawing room. With nothing to do and no conversation to be had, Elizabeth walked around, studying the features and furnishings. She ran her hand lightly across a mahogany table as her eyes wandered over the paintings that adorned the pea green walls. Her perusal was interrupted by Darcy who spoke in a clipped tone.

"It has been a long day. It is time to retire."

He escorted her out of the room and to her bedchamber. At the door, he bowed over her hand, and left.

HER NEW MAID, MISS DREWE HAD LAID OUT A LOVELY SILK GOWN for Elizabeth to wear and took pains to make her ready to receive her husband. The gown was white and one her mother had insisted on purchasing, despite the rather outrageous cost. As she looked at it, while Drewe undressed her, it morphed into the ugliest, almost terrifying, thing Elizabeth had ever seen. It was only with the greatest of effort that she stopped herself from snatching it up and tossing it into the fire.

But it was August, and too hot for a fire. It could not be destroyed, and this night, this new life as Mrs Darcy, could not be avoided.

Elizabeth did not know if Darcy intended to come to her. It was what was expected on a couple's wedding night, and it was within his rights to demand she acquiesce. But would he? He was unhappy about the marriage and despised her, as he had shown repeatedly in the six weeks of their acquaintance, but she believed men had strong, natural urges. There was also the important matter of an heir.

She dismissed Drewe as soon as possible and paced, nursing her anxiety. Would he come? Would he not? If he came, how could she bear it? What would she say? What would he say? She stopped every now and then to listen, thinking she heard him approaching her door. Her heart would pound in her chest, deafening her, her breath caught in her throat. When there was no knock and the door remained closed, she would sigh in relief and resume her pacing.

At length, Elizabeth concluded she was safe for the night; she would be spared that particular duty, his disgust for her and their marriage carrying *that* advantage at least.

As her wedding day came to an end, the reality of it all came crashing down on her. Never had she felt so alone, so friendless, and so hopeless. After uncounted hours, she collapsed on her bed—more luxurious than any she had ever known—and for the first time since rushing headlong to Georgiana Darcy's aid in Ramsgate, wept.

Chapter 1

Six weeks earlier, Ramsgate

The trouble began on a pleasant July night in Ramsgate. Elizabeth, her sister Jane, and their father had come to seek the sea's restorative powers for Jane, who had been ill in the spring. Having left Mrs Bennet and her three younger daughters behind in Hertfordshire, where Mr Bennet's estate was located, they passed the days peacefully, and Jane's health quickly improved.

Mr Bennet was convinced that constant exposure to Mrs Bennet's nerves had lengthened Jane's recovery. Mrs Bennet had pinned all her hopes for a rich son-in-law on her eldest daughter. Jane would make a brilliant match, saving them all from genteel poverty when, upon Mr Bennet's death, Longbourn passed into the hands of a distant, estranged cousin.

Elizabeth sat in the window of her bedchamber, enjoying the cool night air. Jane was abed, and Mr Bennet was downstairs reading. After several minutes, Elizabeth noticed a gentleman and lady hurrying towards each other from opposite ends of the street. They stopped under Elizabeth's window and began to speak in tones too low for her to hear had she wished to eavesdrop, which she did not. She momentarily wondered at the lady's brazenness before allowing her thoughts to wander.

A few minutes later, the man barked out, "No!"

Elizabeth looked down at them. The man spoke furiously, and, when the lady moved into the light cast by the streetlamp, Elizabeth was shocked by how young she appeared. *She cannot be older than Lydia!*

The man grabbed the girl by her arm, and Elizabeth could almost feel her trembling in fear. Her impulsive nature took control of her limbs, and she flew from the window, down the stairs, into the street, and to the girl's side.

"Pardon me, but may I offer you assistance? I live here," Elizabeth said, trying to appear calm.

The girl, who was perhaps fifteen or sixteen years old and very finely dressed, gave Elizabeth an imploring look; she seemed terribly frightened. Elizabeth judged the man to be at least ten years older and not so expensively attired.

"This does not concern you. Leave," he hissed.

The girl cried out as he tightened his grip on her arm. Tears fell down her cheeks, and her blue eyes begged Elizabeth for help.

"Let her go and I shall. With her!" Elizabeth retorted, taking the girl's hand into hers. She thought longingly of her father and wished she had called out to him before exiting the house.

Just then, Elizabeth's neighbours began returning home. First, a trio stopped to say a few words to her. Then, in the following minutes, several more parties spoke to Elizabeth about their evenings and asked after hers, eyeing her companions curiously. Elizabeth longed to be anywhere but on the street with two visibly unhappy strangers.

When at last the street was quiet again, the man demanded, "Stop interfering before you get us all into trouble! We are leaving. Now!"

The girl whimpered as he tried to pull her away, but Elizabeth refused to relinquish the girl's hand. "I will not let you take her!"

"Our affair is none of your business. We are engaged to be married. Consider this a lover's quarrel!"

The girl took a step backwards, and, out of the corner of her eye,

Elizabeth saw that her attention was caught by something—or someone—further down the street. The girl gasped and cried out, "Brother!"

When Elizabeth turned, she saw another gentleman rushing towards them.

The man standing next to Elizabeth swore and ran off.

When the girl's brother reached them, he exclaimed, "Georgiana! What in God's name? Was that—?"

At that moment, a new group of revellers entered the street and called out greetings. Elizabeth nodded and prayed they would not stop, but they did. One of them remarked on the man they had seen running away. Elizabeth remained as polite as possible; the girl and her brother remained silent. When at last the party moved on, one of them, a Mr Gnap, had the audacity to wink at Elizabeth and say, "I am guessing you would like to say a private good night to your...friends."

The street fell quiet, and Elizabeth felt the full weight of her situation. She was standing in the street, at night, with an angry man and a very distressed girl. She could only hope no one, herself included, would remember this night's events in the morning.

"I demand an explanation!" the gentleman said. He was tall and bore a resemblance to the girl, although he was much older. "Who are you, and what is your role in all of this?"

Elizabeth introduced herself and told him, as concisely as she could, what had happened.

"Is this true?" he asked his sister. "It was Wickham, was it not? You met him by design, Georgiana?"

Georgiana began to cry in earnest. "Y-y-yes."

Mr Bennet stepped out of the house. "Lizzy! Sir! Who are you, and what are you doing with my daughter?"

"Papa." Elizabeth gestured at him to lower his voice. "I can explain."

"I am Fitzwilliam Darcy. I suggest we leave the street as quickly as possible."

"Yes," Mr Bennet agreed. "Let us speak inside."

"I am taking my sister home," Mr Darcy said in a voice that would brook no disagreement. "I shall call in a day or two, sir. You have my word." He mentioned his direction and, without waiting for a reply, pulled Georgiana beside him and down the street.

Once safely inside the house, Elizabeth explained how she had come to be outside with two people wholly unknown to them. "She was so frightened, Papa, and that other man, the one you did not see, was angry and…so rough with her."

Mr Bennet frowned, seeming displeased by his daughter's actions. After questioning her closely about seeing their neighbours, he frowned and said, "Let us hope nothing comes of it. Perhaps they shall believe you were just saying good night to our guests. I shall be very interested to hear this Mr Darcy's explanation."

It quickly became apparent that those who had witnessed the unusual event would not soon forget. The next day, Mr Gnap stopped them on the street and said, "Had an…interesting evening, did you Miss Elizabeth? Who were your…friends? I did not catch their names." He winked at her as he said 'friends' and Elizabeth wanted to scream. When, two days later, Mrs Pogue, accompanied by a woman Elizabeth did not know, said to her, "I had no notion you knew Mr Darcy! I do not know him of course. One of the most sought-after bachelors of the *ton*. His uncle is an earl. But why ever was Miss Darcy so distressed? Did you argue? Was she ill?" Such meetings grew in number and Elizabeth even saw strangers staring at her and whispering to their companions. She caught two of their servants likewise talking about her, quickly scurrying away when she entered the room.

"There is nothing to worry about," she told herself repeatedly. "I did nothing wrong, and everyone's attention will soon turn to far more interesting topics."

A few days later, someone congratulated her on her betrothal.

When Elizabeth told her father about it, he was furious. "This is what comes of your impulsive behaviour!"

"Papa!"

"Enough, Elizabeth. These Darcys were nothing to us, and it should have stayed that way! Do you have any idea what you have done?"

Elizabeth could not understand her father and, rather than try to reason with him, left him to his anger. No doubt he would soon distract himself with a book.

Darcy had arrived in Ramsgate as a surprise for his sister, who was there on holiday with her companion, Mrs Younge. Soon after Georgiana retired for the night, he knocked at her door, wanting to ask about an excursion he thought she might enjoy. Receiving no answer, he opened the door to find his sister's chamber empty. He was not alarmed until he espied a note on the bed.

> *My dearest Georgiana,*
> *I dare not come to you with your brother there. We must talk about this unexpected development. Meet me tonight. Walk towards Spencer Square and I shall find you along your route. Our trusted friend will aid you as always.*
>
> *GW*

Darcy immediately set off after his sister, his fears compounded by his ignorance of Ramsgate, which delayed his finding her. He could think of nothing beyond the immediate consequences as he shepherded Georgiana back to their house with all due haste.

Once home, Georgiana threw herself upon the nearest settee. She sobbed loudly, while Darcy furiously demanded answers she was not capable of providing. He questioned Mrs Younge closely until she admitted she knew Wickham and gave up his direction.

"You will pack your belongings and leave my house by first light. If you have any sense of self-preservation, you will never speak of this, or utter the name Darcy again."

He sent a note to Wickham demanding his silence and immediate removal from Ramsgate. Darcy had in his possession the means to send Wickham to debtor's prison and used it as a bribe. He was sick with the knowledge that Wickham had preyed on his sister's naivety—likely as revenge on him—and vowed to do whatever was necessary to ensure word of the affair never spread; it would ruin Georgiana's reputation, and bring shame to their entire family.

As THE DAYS PASSED, DARCY EVER MORE DESPERATELY WANTED TO quit Ramsgate. Georgiana cried ceaselessly and refused to talk to him, and he wished for the wise counsel of someone not as affected as he was. The only person in whom he absolutely knew he could confide was his cousin, Colonel Fitzwilliam, who was Georgiana's other guardian and his dearest friend. But Tom was undertaking a mission for his general, and it would be at least a week before any purpose would be served by writing to him.

Two things delayed their departure. He still needed to call upon the Bennets. They were owed an explanation, and Miss Elizabeth Bennet his thanks. Then there was the gossip to consider. London society had taught Darcy that inconsequential events could easily become scandalous ones, and what had passed was hardly inconsequential. Until he understood what, if anything, was being said about Georgiana, he could not leave Ramsgate with a clear conscience.

When he could put it off no longer, and made his way to the Bennets' house, it was with a heavy heart and disturbed mind.

DARCY'S FIRST VISIT WAS NOT PROMISING. THE BENNETS WERE gentlefolk, although they were not of his social sphere, and he intended to have as little to do with them as possible. He was introduced to Miss Jane Bennet, who made a few inconsequential remarks while they waited for Elizabeth to join them. Mr Bennet only scowled, sighed heavily, and drummed his fingers on a book.

"May I enquire after your sister, Mr Darcy?" Elizabeth asked, as soon as she entered the room. "Is she well?"

"Yes." He had nothing more to say on that score.

Elizabeth opened her mouth to speak, but her father's voice stopped her.

"Mr Darcy, I believe you owe us an explanation."

Darcy told them he was his sister's guardian—their parents having both passed—and about Georgiana's holiday in Ramsgate, escorted by her companion, Mrs Younge, and his unexpected arrival. He explained his connexion to Wickham, who was the son of Pemberley's late steward. "My father bore the expense of his schooling, and he attended university with me. My father hoped Wickham would make the church his living, although it would not be an occupation to suit his character."

"No, I imagine not," Elizabeth muttered.

"Elizabeth," hissed Mr Bennet.

"During his last illness, my father expressed the wish that a valuable family living go to him. Wickham disclaimed all interest in it, and I gave him three thousand pounds in its place. Eighteen months ago, he came to me. The living was now available, and he wished me to present it to him. I refused.

"I have not seen him since. He and Mrs Younge, whom I have discovered are intimate friends, arranged for him to be here. He convinced my sister, who is a trusting, affectionate creature, that she was in love and they should elope. Mrs Younge informed him of my arrival, and he sent a note to my sister arranging to meet, which is how she came to be outside your house that night. Georgiana told him she wished to tell me of their engagement, which is to her credit. He reacted violently." He nodded at Elizabeth. "We are grateful you intervened."

Mr Bennet waved away anything else Darcy might have said on that score. When Elizabeth again opened her mouth to speak, Mr Bennet shot her an angry look.

"My daughters have had several uncomfortable experiences since Lizzy flew to your sister's defence."

"I understand there is...talk," Darcy replied, a sour taste in his mouth.

"What have you heard?" Mr Bennet demanded.

"Miss Elizabeth, my sister, and I are the subject of much speculation. The stories are confused, even contradictory. Miss Elizabeth was alone with two people at night outside of her house. Some believe it was friendly, if unusual; others talk about angry words being exchanged by the man and Miss Elizabeth. Georgiana was distressed, perhaps even the subject of the argument. There is speculation that there were two men involved in the...event, but at different times."

He asked Mr Bennet to tell him about the encounters his daughters had had. Darcy was not pleased with what he learnt, especially as the Bennets had heard the rumour of a betrothal between him and Elizabeth. He suspected they might take advantage of it to force his hand.

He took his leave soon after, saying, "I hope that in a day or two, talk will diminish, and people will move on to something of greater interest. However, we must be prepared for the possibility it will not."

"THE GOSSIP IS GETTING WORSE, NOT BETTER," DARCY TOLD THEM ON his next visit a week later. "It has spread beyond Ramsgate."

Mr Bennet said, "It is hard to imagine why anyone in Ramsgate would be interested in such nonsense, let alone anyone outside of it."

"How do you know this, Mr Darcy?" Elizabeth asked.

Darcy glanced at her—she was sitting with her sister—before turning again to Mr Bennet. "I received an express from my uncle, who is currently in London." He explained that the Earl of Romsley had heard reports that Georgiana or Darcy were caught in a compromising situation. The prevalent suspicions were that Miss Elizabeth Bennet and Miss Darcy were arguing either over a man who wanted to end a love affair with Elizabeth and transfer his affections to Georgiana, or because Georgiana was unhappy about her brother's engagement to a woman so much beneath them.

Darcy had accepted that something must be done to prevent the situation from spiralling further out of control. "I am afraid we are facing a very difficult dilemma. The gossip runs from the scandalous to the merely secretive. The least offensive is that Miss Elizabeth and I are engaged. Far more damaging is the speculation that Miss Elizabeth or my sister were attempting to elope with a strange man, or that I am attempting to make her my mistress."

Jane Bennet gasped.

"This will all die away with time," Mr Bennet said. "I have had enough. My daughters and I are leaving Ramsgate as soon as it can be arranged. You and your sister can sort out your problems on your own."

"I can assure you the matter will not be so easily resolved. Your name, your home, your description are all intimately linked to these tales," Mr Darcy replied.

"What are you suggesting, Mr Darcy?" Mr Bennet asked.

"I believe it is best for the reputations of both the Darcy and Bennet families if Miss Elizabeth and I…marry." His revulsion made it difficult to say the last word. The Bennets could not understand how disgusting the prospect was to him. He had thought on the matter for several days, and had, with his uncle's express, reached the conclusion there was nothing else to be done. Georgiana's absence—for she had not yet left the house—was not helping matters at all.

"You're mad," Elizabeth said, breaking the shocked silence which ensued from Darcy's pronouncement. "I have no wish to marry you."

"Believe me," Darcy retorted, "I have no wish to marry you either."

"I sincerely doubt my respectability or my family's have been impaired," Elizabeth replied.

"You are mistaken. Scandalous gossip is already circulating in London. Think of the damage this will do to you, your sisters, and your parents. This is the only way to end the speculation. Even then, given my position, it will take time and effort."

Elizabeth shook her head. "You are telling me the price I must pay for helping Miss Darcy is marriage to a man I hardly know?"

Jane Bennet sat with her face hidden by her hands, weeping. Darcy could find no pity for her.

Mr Bennet said, "Mr Darcy, let us step into the other room. We shall discuss this between ourselves."

"Papa!" Elizabeth stood.

"Not now, Elizabeth!"

Mr Bennet strode out of the room, closely followed by Darcy.

TWO HOURS PASSED BEFORE MR BENNET RETURNED ALONE; DARCY had departed without taking his leave of the ladies.

Mr Bennet announced, "You will marry Mr Darcy."

Elizabeth, who had been pacing, fell into a chair. She felt faint, and although she saw that Jane took her hand, could not feel it. Her voice hardly above a whisper, she said, "No, Papa! I cannot."

"You must live with the consequences of your actions. Marriage to such a man! It is your impulsiveness that created this! If you are unhappy with your fate, you have only yourself to blame!"

"Should I have refused to help a young girl in need? What would you have me do, Papa?"

"This will be the ruin of you, Elizabeth, but it is you alone or all of us. Why should I sacrifice your sisters' reputations because of something you did? How could I justify doing so? Would you have your sisters remain unwed—for what man would have them after this? Must Jane and Mary and Kitty and Lydia live in shame because of your selfishness?

"The *ton!*" He threw up his hands, his face pinched in disgust. "The way they behave, their immorality, and selfishness, their compete disregard for what is right, and for other people—you will now be thrown into their society, your care entrusted to a man who does not want you, who will never respect you. How could you have been so stupid, Elizabeth?"

Elizabeth's attempts to reason with her father were entirely without success.

Jane did her best to console Elizabeth, and counselled Elizabeth to make the best of the situation. "What we know about Mr Darcy is promising, Lizzy. He cares very deeply for his sister, and he must be an honourable man if he is willing to marry you to protect your reputation. It will turn out well. I know it will."

Elizabeth appreciated her sister's love and sympathy, but she had no such hope.

I, FITZWILLIAM DARCY OF PEMBERLEY, AM MARRYING AN UNKNOWN, undowered country Miss whose father's estate is entailed away to a distant cousin and who has relations in trade.

Darcy groaned and covered his eyes with one hand. He relaxed further into the leather armchair, pleased to be alone for the moment. While exceedingly grateful for Elizabeth's assistance to Georgiana, he was paying a dreadful price for her help. Elizabeth at least would benefit from their marriage. He would give her a distinguished name, exemplary connexions, and wealth far beyond what she had ever known. While she gained, he lost. His bride ought to be an accomplished lady, properly educated, wealthy, capable of being mistress to a grand estate, and possessing family connexions equal to his. Elizabeth Bennet was in every way lacking.

Georgiana did not react when Darcy explained the situation to her; they would escort the Bennets to Longbourn to be introduced to Mrs Bennet, an arrangement Mr Bennet had insisted upon.

Darcy was present when Mr Bennet announced it to his daughters.

"I am sure your mother and sisters will be delighted by our early return and with such a surprise for them."

Darcy hoped to never again hear such a sardonic tone. If Miss Elizabeth had inherited it, he would teach her not to use it.

When Mr Bennet said the wedding would be at the end of August, Elizabeth exclaimed, "August! But that is next month!"

"Very good, Elizabeth. We are all pleased to know you have not forgotten the order of the months."

Elizabeth's countenance reddened.

Darcy explained, "I am required at my estate in September, and will not be inclined to leave again once there." He wanted to get married, spend a week or two in London, and retreat to Pemberley as soon as possible. With luck, the gossip would fade before he felt compelled to bring Elizabeth back to town again. *And the sooner it is done, the less time I shall have to spend in the company of Mr Bennet. Please, God, let the daughter be unlike him, or at least young enough to change!*

Chapter 2

*A*s they approached Longbourn, Darcy saw Mrs Bennet and her daughters awaiting the returning travellers outside. Mrs Bennet's high-pitched voice grated on his nerves as she greeted her husband and older daughters, who exited their carriage a moment before he and Georgiana were forced to do the same.

"Georgiana, we shall not tell Mrs Bennet the truth of the situation. The fewer who know, the better. Our behaviour must show we are pleased to be here, and that the engagement is one of…affection."

She nodded.

As they left the carriage, Mrs Bennet said, "Who have you brought with you? I have never seen a finer carriage. Oh my dear Jane!"

"Mrs Bennet, let us go into the house," Mr Bennet said.

Mrs Bennet's incessant, inane chattering accompanied them into the parlour, where Mr Bennet performed the introductions. The room was small, the furniture outdated and worn, and there was far too much of it for the space to be comfortable.

"We made their acquaintance in Ramsgate. I shall spare you the details. The long and the short of it is that Mr Darcy is engaged to Elizabeth."

Mrs Bennet turned to her eldest daughter. "Oh Jane! I just knew —" She stopped abruptly, and stared at Mr Bennet, her mouth hanging open. "Lizzy?"

The sound went through Darcy like a sword. How could anyone live with such a noise? One of the daughters snorted and giggled. The one next to her also laughed but had the grace to cover her mouth.

"You heard me correctly. Elizabeth has gotten herself engaged. I believe we can sit now."

Darcy escorted Georgiana to a settee.

"Lizzy?" Mrs Bennet gaped at her second daughter.

"Yes, Lizzy!" Mr Bennet snapped.

"It is true, Mama." Elizabeth took a seat beside Georgiana.

It took several excruciating minutes to convince Mrs Bennet that Darcy was engaged to Elizabeth, not her elder sister. Mrs Bennet stared at him and at Georgiana, and he knew she was calculating his wealth.

Mrs Bennet said, "Well, I am sure you could not have chosen better. As you see, all my girls are very pretty. Jane especially. But then, Lizzy has qualities which make up for her lack of beauty, I suppose."

Darcy looked at Georgiana to see how she fared and caught a look of mortification on Elizabeth's face. *I suppose it shows she has some sense.*

"Mr Darcy," Mrs Bennet said, "do tell us about yourself. You took your sister to Ramsgate on holiday?"

He nodded once.

"Such a good brother. Did you hear, girls? Miss Darcy is a lucky girl to have such a brother, and now he is to be your brother, too."

"Perhaps we should say lucky Mr Darcy," Mr Bennet said, quirking an eyebrow, "to be gaining four such sisters."

"Yes indeed, Mr Bennet!" Mrs Bennet cried. "And do you have any other siblings, Mr Darcy?"

"I do not."

"Such a shame. A large family is a blessing, as long as there is money to see them all settled in life. I am sure you need have no such worries."

Jane said, "We were very fortunate with the weather on our journey home, were we not, Lizzy?"

"Yes, indeed," Elizabeth said with some enthusiasm. "The roads—"

"Oh, who cares about the roads!" Mrs Bennet cried before turning a sweet smile on Darcy. "And your parents?"

"We have lost them both."

"How dreadful for you! They would have loved my Lizzy."

Darcy did not respond.

Mrs Bennet continued, "Where are you from?"

"Derbyshire."

"Derbyshire." The youngest guffawed. "Where's that?"

"North, Lydia," the plain one—Mary he believed—muttered, her voice dripping with scorn.

Darcy wished himself far, far away. He had had some hope that, as deplorable as Elizabeth's situation in life was, at least the Bennets would be respectable. Mr Bennet's manner had not impressed him, but Darcy had prayed it was a consequence of the upsetting circumstances. Having met Mrs Bennet and the other daughters, he realised impropriety was the rule and not the exception.

Mrs Bennet said, "Miss Darcy, do tell us what your home is called and what it is like. How very grand it must be!"

"Mama," Elizabeth said, "Miss Darcy was, unfortunately, recently ill. I am afraid the journey has tired her."

Darcy was pleasantly surprised by Elizabeth's intervention, but it was forgotten in a minute as Mrs Bennet reprimanded Elizabeth for not telling her sooner. There then passed an awkward exchange during which Mr Bennet explained the Darcys would not stay for dinner, were spending the night at the inn in Meryton, and intended to depart for London early the next morning.

"But there are arrangements to make!" Mrs Bennet cried.

"Plans have been made, Mrs Bennet," her husband interjected. "They will be married at the end of August."

"August?" Mrs Bennet shrieked.

Darcy felt Georgiana start at the high pitch of Mrs Bennet's voice, and he suspected she was close to tears.

"How could you have made plans as you say without consulting me? My daughter is getting married, and I am to have no say about it?"

"Let us pray you are more fortunate with the other girls. Perhaps they will not need to marry with such haste."

Mrs Bennet's eyes flew to Elizabeth. Darcy was close to furious, and only the thought of the damage to his name and his sister's reputation should he abandon the Bennets kept him in his seat.

Elizabeth turned to Georgiana. "Miss Darcy, I am sure you would like to refresh yourself before the drive to Meryton. Come. Let me show you the way."

It was thus they escaped from Longbourn. Mr Bennet escorted Darcy outside to wait for Georgiana. They stood in silence until Elizabeth and Georgiana joined them, at which time Mr Bennet said a barely civil goodbye and left.

"I shall tell my mother the story we agreed upon," Elizabeth said.

Darcy nodded, but did not speak.

"My mother will expect you to write to me."

Darcy grimaced, her demand adding to his misery.

"Miss Darcy, I hope being with your family again is a comfort to you."

Georgiana remained silent.

"Miss Bennet." Suspecting they were being watched, Darcy took her hand as she rose from her curtsey and placed a kiss upon it.

ELIZABETH TOLD HER MOTHER AND SISTERS THAT SHE AND JANE MADE Miss Darcy's acquaintance one morning when they were walking by the sea. A sudden gust of wind had sent Miss Darcy's parasol flying. Elizabeth had chased it down and returned it to her. From that beginning, they had become friends. Mr Darcy was introduced to them when he joined his sister in Ramsgate, and Cupid had done the rest. It was romantic enough to satisfy Mrs Bennet, Lydia, and Kitty; Mary thought it was silly to choose a partner in life on such short acquaintance.

Soon after their return, Mr Bennet called Elizabeth into his book-room; he handed her a letter from her uncle, Mr Gardiner.

"Take it and be gone," he barked.

She went into the gardens to find a solitary spot to read the missive.

I write with news of a disturbing rumour. It is that Miss Elizabeth Bennet, lately on holiday in Ramsgate, is engaged to Mr Fitzwilliam Darcy, a very prominent gentleman from Derbyshire. I have been told that it is not a simple matter of two young people falling in love, or only shocking in the disparate situations of the two in question. There are hints something of a scandalous nature took place, or Mr Darcy's intentions towards the lady were not honourable, and he was forced into marriage once the affair became common knowledge.

There was more, but it mattered not to Elizabeth. If anything, it freed her to do what she longed to; she wrote to her aunt, explaining the truth and begging for advice.

I am so confused and anxious. I must find a way to reconcile myself to this situation. I dread what my marriage will be and am desperate for advice on how to make it as happy as it possibly can be. I always dreamt of being a good wife and, married to a man of my choice who I esteemed and respected, it did not seem a daunting task. We would learn how to be a married couple together, and our affection and desire to be united would guide us through any difficulties. Now, with such a start, how am I to face all the duties that come with being Mrs Darcy? I beg you to give me whatever advice you think will aid me in this uncertain time.

Mrs Bennet soon set about sharing the news of her daughter's splendid match. Elizabeth forced herself to smile as congratulations were offered, and to act as cheerful as she could when with others. When it became unbearable, she sought Jane's company and, more and more as the days crawled by, solitude. Jane worried excessively for her, and that, too, became a burden.

"Do not fear, Jane. I was not made to be unhappy, and I intend to do all I can to ensure I am not."

"Your sense and good nature will ensure you find happiness and love as Mr Darcy's wife."

Elizabeth prayed happiness was possible but did not expect love. She understood she had little to offer such a man, but she would do everything she possibly could to show she would be a good wife, a good mistress to his estates, and a good sister to Miss Darcy. That, she hoped, would earn her the respect of her new family, and perhaps, in time, a measure of their affection.

A week after their return, Elizabeth received a letter from Mr Darcy and a reply from Mrs Gardiner. She read Mr Darcy's letter first.

Miss Bennet,
I hope this letter finds you and your family well. Please give
the enclosed note to Mr Bennet.

FD

Elizabeth stared at the page, certain there had to be more to it. Once her mind accepted the evidence of her eyes, and she swallowed her frustration, she turned to her aunt's letter. Mrs Gardiner expressed astonishment at Elizabeth's situation and promised to keep her confidence.

I wish we could meet, but your father has requested we remain
at home. I suspect we shall not see you in London, either. Mr
Darcy may object to your coming to Gracechurch Street, or
receiving us at his home. You know why, Lizzy. My first piece
of advice is that you must abide by Mr Darcy's wishes and
decisions. A man, perhaps especially one of Mr Darcy's stand-
ing, will expect your compliance, and given the delicate nature
of your relationship, I believe you would do well to start by
appeasing him in such matters. The Darcys are very high.
Even without the scandalous rumours, his marriage to the

daughter of a country gentleman would elicit a great deal of talk. Until you have more opportunity to understand each other, it will be best not to challenge his decisions. Once he knows of your sense and intelligence, then you can ask for that which will add pleasure and comfort to your life.

I remember the Darcys from my years in Lambton. Your Mr Darcy's father was a good man and a fine master, and we have no reason to suspect your Mr Darcy is any different. I hope you will retire to Derbyshire soon after the wedding. Away from town, you will have occasion to learn about each other without so many eyes constantly upon you. Remember, he has been placed in an impossible situation just as you have been. You both need time to reconcile yourself to this.

Apply yourself to learning your duties as mistress of Pemberley, and of his house in town. As to your more particular duty, I shall offer words which I hope will ease your mind. Some anxiety in the best of circumstances is understandable. I pray Mr Darcy will permit you to grow accustomed to being his wife before he wishes to share your bed. When that changes, remember this: the marriage act, even in the absence of love, can be a wonderful and beneficial experience. Your marriage is a partnership, one in which you each have a role, duties to fulfil to your family, to those under your care, to each other, and, God willing, your children. It is a way to bind you to each other, and to take comfort in each other, regardless of the depth of your feelings. Let us hope you and Mr Darcy will learn to hold each other in affection, even to love each other. If you both wish to have a happy marriage, you can make it so.

EACH TIME SOMEONE CONGRATULATED ELIZABETH, AND SHE LIED BY omitting the truth or feigned joy when she felt none, a piece of Miss Elizabeth Bennet died away. At breakfast less than a week before the wedding, her father added to her growing dread. Mrs Bennet was in very high spirits as she talked about the exciting prospect of visiting Mrs Darcy, and Elizabeth's ability to introduce her sisters to rich men who would naturally be anxious to marry them.

"I shall not have you parading my daughters here and there, hoping some fool of a man offers to marry one of them. Elizabeth will be busy learning her place as Mrs Darcy. She will have no visitors— no, not even Jane—for…half a year. Then, perhaps, I shall reconsider."

Elizabeth was angry, but unsurprised by this latest mark of her father's spite. When he did speak to her, Mr Bennet continued to blame her for the situation, repeated his assertion that she had ruined herself, and several times expressed his dislike for fashionable society in the most vehement of terms. He would rather see his wife and daughters living in poverty than have Elizabeth married to such a man, he said. It seemed that any love he had had for her died the moment she went to Georgiana Darcy's assistance.

Mrs Gardiner wrote to tell Elizabeth what her friends in Derbyshire had to say about Mr Darcy.

In short, Mr Darcy is very highly regarded. He executes his duties with more than the common attention. We do not need to worry for your well-being. He will treat you fairly and in return you must do the same for him.

It brought her some comfort, yet she suspected Mr Darcy would be very sensible of his position of superiority in their marriage. Her wants and feelings and opinions would be of no consequence to a man who did not wish to know her, but who felt he must marry her.

Chapter 3

London, before the wedding

The evening of his return to town, Darcy shuffled through several letters his valet Quinn had left for him. Only the one from Tom held any interest, and he set the others aside for the moment. He skimmed through the contents, hoping for news of Tom's return to London.

> *I do not expect to be in London before the beginning of September. Do not await my arrival in town unless you have a particular reason to be there. I shall follow you to Derbyshire as soon as possible.*

Darcy was disappointed; he sorely needed Tom's counsel. He was struck by one other passage.

> *It was a good scheme of yours to send Georgiana to Ramsgate. She needs exposure to new people and places; it might*

cure her of her shyness. I am exceedingly glad you were able to join her for a time. That can only have added to her pleasure.

"How mistaken you are," Darcy whispered. "It was the worst idea I have ever had."

He remained slouched in his wing chair for a half an hour or more, thinking about his sister. Georgiana had fallen prey to the worst sort of conniving man. Wickham wore a handsome face and was charming, and Darcy had no doubt whatsoever that he had used those traits to exploit his sister, abetted by the conniving Mrs Younge. His dear, sweet little sister could not withstand their actions; she was too good, too naïve to understand how any person could behave with such malicious intent. *I should have protected her better. Good God, had something happened to her, had she not been rescued in time—!* He did not know how he could have borne to lose her.

After dinner, Darcy wrote to Tom about the events at Ramsgate and begged him to get to London as soon as he could.

"GOOD GOD, WHAT WAS SHE THINKING?" PHILIP FITZWILLIAM, THE Earl of Romsley, roared.

Darcy had just finished explaining the whole of Georgiana's affair with Wickham to his uncle and cousin Sterling. They sat in the earl's study, Darcy upon a red velvet covered Rococo fauteuil he had always found too hard to be comfortable. His mouth dry after his long recitation, he took a sip of the wine Sterling had pressed into his hands upon his arrival. It did nothing to wash away the bitter taste of his words.

"Are you certain that woman was not involved with Wickham somehow?" Sterling, Viscount Bramwell, asked.

Sterling was a widower, his wife Cassandra having died in childbed two years earlier. It had not been a happy marriage. His parents were anxious that he remarry; he refused to discuss the subject.

"I have no reason to suppose the Bennets are in any way connected to him."

Sterling said, "The Bennets could have started the rumours to force your hand. You said they are in a dire financial state." He yawned and adjusted the cuffs of his shirt.

"I do not believe there are any pressing concerns. However, the estate is small, and entailed away to a distant cousin. The daughters have insignificant dowries. It will be difficult for them to secure husbands of any consequence."

"Lovely. Make it clear from the outset that you will not have them all living with you, you will not support them, or advance the ambitions of any man fool enough to marry one of them. It is bad enough you will be saddled with one. You do not want to be forever throwing money after your in-laws."

"Bramwell is right. Make your position very plain. Let them know the limits of your charity." A furrow appeared between the earl's bushy eyebrows. "It would be best if we could find a way to get you out of this marriage."

"Without a marriage to satisfy the gossipmongers, the whole affair will be further scrutinised, and Georgiana's role may be uncovered. She was tricked, taken advantage of, but that will not matter. Any hint of scandal attached to her will not only ruin her reputation, it could do very real damage to mine, and affect your family as well as my Darcy relations. It is too much to leave to chance." After a short pause, Darcy added, "And there is Miss Bennet to consider."

Although visibly reluctant, Lord Romsley acquiesced. "Are the Bennets respectable?"

Darcy was slow to answer. "Mr Bennet's behaviour is not always as it should be. Mrs Bennet and the younger daughters are silly and vulgar. Mrs Bennet has a sister who lives in Meryton and is married to an attorney, and a brother who is married and lives somewhere in London. He is in trade."

Lord Romsley scowled. "That is unacceptable. Your wife cannot recognise tradespeople as members of her family. Refuse to allow Mrs Darcy to see them."

"She will have to become one of us. Leave behind the unfortunate Miss Elizabeth Bennet, and learn how to be Mrs Darcy, someone who is a credit to your name, or at least not a disgrace," Sterling said. "Is she at least pretty? A pretty face and a neat figure can help. I don't believe I need to explain my meaning."

"She is…tolerable, I suppose."

"You will have to find a way to think of her as more than tolerable." Sterling laughed. "At least until you have your heir."

Darcy ignored him.

The gentlemen discussed Darcy's plans, after which Darcy escaped Fitzwilliam House, having declined to stay for dinner.

APART FROM VISITING HIS SISTER DAILY, DARCY OCCUPIED HIS TIME with business affairs, attempting to banish thoughts of his marriage from his mind. Sterling allowed him a little more than a week before he insisted Darcy stop hiding.

"If you want to convince everyone your engagement is not scandalous, then you must act innocent. Nothing more scandalous than a remarkably poor choice of wife, that is." He grinned.

Darcy glared at him.

"Oh, do not try that on me, Cousin. If all the tittering masses spoke about is you choosing a penniless unknown instead of making the brilliant match they have been anticipating the past three years, you would be very well pleased. Come with me to the club. We shall visit the jewellers. Select a trinket for her. Someone will notice."

Knowing Sterling was correct, Darcy followed his advice.

He received an unpleasant, but inevitable, call from his uncle John Darcy and cousin Frederick Darcy, the two eldest members of his father's family. They quizzed him about his decision to marry, and his choice of bride. The visit did not end until Darcy agreed to host his relations at Pemberley in the autumn.

As the days passed, more and more congratulatory notes arrived, many asking endless questions about Elizabeth. He hated each one. His aunt Lady Catherine's latest missive, which told of her insult, and how deeply affected Anne was by his perfidy, had been especially trying. Darcy had crushed the paper with his hand and tossed it into the fireplace muttering, "I never promised to marry your daughter, madam."

Most provoking was a letter from Elizabeth.

I thought I understood you intend for us to remain in London for some weeks after the wedding, but my father claims not to know if this is correct, or if we go directly to Pemberley.

Did she wish to remain in town, or was it a hint she did not? It mattered not; their travel would be dictated by his needs, not her wishes.

And she had asked about his family. Did she expect him to write out his whole family history? He would not. It would take a great deal of effort to teach it to her, if indeed she truly cared to learn, which he doubted. *No doubt she is only truly interested in how much of my money she will get to spend. Good God, how am I to bear it?*

In two days, he returned to Hertfordshire to tie himself for life to Elizabeth Bennet. He did not believe it was possible to dread an event more than he did his wedding.

Chapter 4

The Bennets held a dinner party the day before the wedding, and it was as awful as Elizabeth feared it would be. Viscount Bramwell attended with his cousin, and Elizabeth tried to shield them from the worst of her family and neighbours' behaviour, but her mother and younger sisters would embarrass themselves, and her. During dinner, Mrs Bennet hardly stopped speaking long enough to eat.

"I shall soon see my other girls married just as advantageously. Mr Darcy has many rich friends, and Lizzy will introduce her sisters to them. His cousin you know, who is seated by Jane, is a viscount and heir to an earldom. If Lizzy can catch Mr Darcy, just imagine what my Jane will do!"

Elizabeth was mortified and could only imagine how such a display sunk her in Mr Darcy's opinion. *Not that his behaviour is above reproach! But he is rich, and I am not. That, I am convinced, is to him the essential point.* He was taciturn and plainly thought himself above his company.

After dinner, she suggested to Darcy that they take a turn in the gardens. They did not speak, and, after several minutes returned to the house. Before they entered, Darcy stopped her.

"You will be moving into a new society, one in which appearances are vitally important. With whom you consort, where you visit, where you shop, how you behave, all of it will be closely scrutinised. I expect you to apply yourself. The Darcy name is a much respected one, and I will not have anyone—including my wife or her family—threaten it."

Elizabeth entered the house without responding.

When Darcy took his leave of Elizabeth a short while later, she managed to say a curt, "Mr Darcy," but no more than that. She then excused herself and went upstairs. When Jane entered the room half an hour later, Elizabeth pretended to be asleep.

MR BENNET ALONE ESCORTED ELIZABETH TO THE CHURCH. SHE prayed he would remain silent; she did not need to be reminded of his anger at her, or his distaste for those of high society, on this of all days.

He spoke as soon as they were settled in the carriage. "I hardly know what to say to you, Elizabeth. Your marriage could be a disaster. You, of all women, do not need me to pretend otherwise. My advice is to do whatever you must to make your situation tolerable. He will not change for you. You will have to be the one to change. You must leave behind your friends, perhaps even your family. You are too intelligent to believe anything else is possible with such a man. I wish you happy, or if that is too lofty a goal—as I fear it is—content, or at least respectable."

Elizabeth said nothing. She would not take his hand as she stepped out of the carriage but could not refuse his arm as they entered the church, and he walked her to her destiny.

As Elizabeth exited the church on her new husband's arm a short while later, she found it remarkable that she could not remember saying her vows, or hearing Darcy say his. She knew she was married; everyone rushing to congratulate her assured her it was so.

The wedding breakfast seemed like a dream. She talked to people and ate, but nothing seemed tangible.

When she boarded the coach for the journey to London, a knot of fear settled in Elizabeth's belly. To be parted from all she knew and those who loved her, with so little hope for the future, was a fate sure to test her courage. She was not at all certain she was strong enough to prevail.

With little fanfare, the new Mrs Darcy left Longbourn.

AFTER CRYING HERSELF TO SLEEP ON HER WEDDING NIGHT, ELIZABETH began the next day by telling herself there was nothing to gain by succumbing to her anxieties and vowing to do everything in her power to find happiness in her new life.

With this resolution in place, she made her way to the breakfast room where she found Darcy and his sister. He looked pleased; she did not. Elizabeth greeted them cheerfully. Darcy acknowledged her with a nod. Georgiana ignored her. After Elizabeth's question regarding their well-being was met with silence, she held her tongue.

Several minutes later, Darcy said, "Colonel Fitzwilliam arrives this morning."

"I am sure you will be pleased to see him."

"Mm."

"Miss Darcy, has it been long since you last saw the colonel?" Elizabeth asked.

Georgiana pushed a piece of bacon back and forth on her plate.

"Some months," Darcy replied.

"I see." Elizabeth took a fortifying breath. "I was hoping to tour the house today."

"I have a great many things to attend to," Darcy said.

"Perhaps Miss Dar—"

"No." Georgiana stood and, without ceremony, left the room.

Darcy dropped his knife and fork onto his plate. "I shall be in my study." Just before exiting the room, he said, "Perhaps Mrs Northmore…"

Elizabeth's remaining breakfast was left untouched, and she pushed the plate away from her. *I understand my presence is disgusting to them, yet I am here, and I am not going away. We must learn to live together harmoniously. They must want that, too!*

A few minutes later, she sought Mrs Northmore's assistance. She did her best to absorb every bit of information the housekeeper imparted, from the provenance of the furniture and artwork to when each room was cleaned. Elizabeth had never expected to marry a man like Mr Darcy. Being his wife and mistress of his homes, so different from everything she was accustomed to, was a daunting task, and she doubted her abilities.

I can but try. And try I must and will! Courage, Lizzy!

Once the tour was completed, and she had been introduced to the servants, Elizabeth sat in the morning room near Darcy's study. She wanted her husband and sister to understand that she wished to spend time with them. It was a pretty, comfortable space. The paper on the walls was an ivory colour and the furniture covers a silvery blue, which Elizabeth found rather calming. She attended to her needle-work, occasionally hearing sounds that she hoped meant someone approached the room, but no one interrupted her solitude.

An hour later, a loud, urgent knock on the front door heralded Colonel Fitzwilliam's arrival.

TOM PACED, AND SPOKE QUICKLY, PULLING AT HIS HAIR. "GOOD GOD! Are you truly married? Georgiana almost eloped with Wickham?"

"Yes, to both."

Darcy handed him a glass of wine; Tom immediately drained half of it.

"I cannot believe it," Tom said. "How could she?"

"She is young, hardly more than a child. And you know how easily Wickham charms people."

"Do not offer excuses for Georgiana's behaviour! She knew better. How is she now?"

Darcy shrugged, and after a little conversation a footman was dispatched to fetch Georgiana.

Before she joined them, Tom said, "I cannot believe you are married. I shall not offer you platitudes. Whatever happens, you know I shall stand by your side."

Georgiana entered the room, and stood by the door, studying the tips of her shoes.

"Georgiana," Tom said. "I trust you are well."

She nodded.

Tom let out a grunt of frustration, took her by the arm, and forced her into a moss green armchair.

"What were you thinking?" he barked as he paced in front of her. "How could you be so stupid? The gossip that has been spread about you is ghastly. Did you know some people have been saying you and Miss Bennet were fighting over a man in the middle of the street like a couple of harlots? Have you thought for one minute about the consequences of your actions upon your brother, or upon the rest of us?"

He continued to lecture her for several minutes until Georgiana ran from the room, tears pouring down her face.

Darcy buried his face in his hands. "What do I do?"

"About Wickham and Mrs Younge? I will see that they are incapable of causing further mischief to any of us," Tom growled, his voice low and dangerous. "About Georgiana? I cannot even begin to —" He huffed and dropped onto the sofa next to Darcy. "About your marriage? I do not know. Tell me about her."

Darcy grunted, sat back, and looked at the ceiling. "There is nothing good to tell. Good God, Tom, her relations! I feel sick just thinking about them, knowing they are now my family. I will not recognise them, not more than I absolutely must. It is too horrible."

Tom insisted on hearing the particulars of his interactions with the Bennets, uttering sympathetic and reassuring words which did little to ease Darcy's distress.

MRS NORTHMORE ASKED ELIZABETH WHETHER THE COLONEL WAS staying to dinner. Glad to have some occupation beyond her needlework, Elizabeth said she would ask.

Raising a hand to knock at the door to Darcy's study, she heard him say, "How am I supposed to do that? I am married to someone I likely never would have met—we do not, *did* not travel in the same social circles. She is certainly someone I never would have considered."

The blood rushed out of Elizabeth's face, and her hand trembled. She was not surprised by his sentiments, but to hear him say it so plainly hurt. How could any of them ever be happy when he was disgusted by the mere thought of her? How could she ever gain acceptance as Mrs Darcy? Elizabeth took a fortifying breath. *No, Lizzy. You vowed to be optimistic. You knew it would not be easy.* In time, her situation would improve.

When she had regained her composure, she knocked and entered. Both men stood. Darcy performed the necessary introduction, after the colonel nudged him to do so.

Elizabeth said, "I have come to ask if Colonel Fitzwilliam is staying to dinner." She turned to the colonel. "You are most welcome, of course."

Darcy replied. "Yes. We still have matters to discuss. My cousin and I shall dine in here. I doubt Georgiana will wish to eat, but if you would be so good as to have a tray sent to her room."

There was a brief pause before Elizabeth said, "Of course." She turned to go, but Colonel Fitzwilliam stopped her.

"Mrs Darcy, I must thank you for your actions on what was, no doubt, a most disagreeable night. I shudder to think what would have become of Georgiana had you not intervened."

Elizabeth managed a small smile. She knew in her heart she would not act any differently, even knowing the consequences. At certain moments, however, and this was one, she wished she had been doing anything other than sitting in her bedroom window at the moment Georgiana and Wickham met.

At breakfast the next day, Darcy said, "My aunt and uncle come to meet you this morning. My aunt will escort you around town, take you shopping, and what have you. This will show everyone my family approves of the marriage."

"Lady Romsley's guidance will be very much appreciated." *Marriage is turning me into a liar, and it has only been two days.*

Later, preparing for the Fitzwilliams' call, Elizabeth found it difficult to banish her nerves. She knew how important it was to make a good impression on the Romsleys. She would be happier the more her new family tolerated and trusted her. In return, she would do her best to tolerate and trust them. *I must give them time to know me and ignore their...awkward manner until they do.*

When Lord and Lady Romsley and Colonel Fitzwilliam arrived, Darcy presented Elizabeth. She curtseyed, and the earl and countess nodded, but said nothing. The colonel did not address her at all.

"Georgiana is not down?" he asked Darcy.

"No."

Lady Romsley sighed and shook her head.

"Shall I have her informed of your arrival?" Elizabeth asked.

Speaking to Darcy, the colonel said, "I shall go fetch her."

"Tom," Lady Romsley warned.

"She should be here, not hiding away."

Elizabeth's suggestion that they sit was ignored, and there was an uncomfortable silence as the Romsleys and Darcy stared at her, and she tried not to notice their rudeness.

The silence was broken by Lady Romsley saying, "Come sit beside me."

Elizabeth took the demand to be directed at her. Once seated, she asked, "Would you care for something to drink, Lady Romsley? Lord Romsley?"

Lady Romsley accepted a glass of lemonade before she and the others resumed their close examination of Elizabeth.

At length, Lord Romsley stated, "You are from Hertfordshire."

"I am." Elizabeth smiled politely despite the gruffness of his tone. "My father's estate—"

"You have not been much in London?" Lady Romsley asked.

"Not very much, no. I have an aunt and uncle who live in London, and I have visited them as often as possible."

"Oh?" Lady Romsley looked at Darcy.

"The brother of Mrs Bennet."

"Oh, yes," Lady Romsley said with visible disdain. "Have you met them?"

"They did not attend the wedding," Elizabeth explained. "My father believed that the fewer people there, the better it would be."

She knew she was being provocative. After just a few minutes in Lord and Lady Romsley's company, she was quite ready to call them arrogant and very, very proud—not unlike Darcy, in other words. If she dared, she would tell them that she had no wish to be part of their family, and ask that they get on with deciding how they would trick society into believing she and Darcy had married for love, and that his relations were delighted with the match. Arguing with them would be a mistake, however, and so she held her tongue.

After Colonel Fitzwilliam and Georgiana entered the room, the conversation began in earnest. Lady Romsley questioned Elizabeth about her experiences and accomplishments and was clearly not pleased with the answers.

The most humiliating part of the visit was when Lady Romsley insisted on seeing Elizabeth's wardrobe. The countess examined each gown, pelisse, bonnet, and everything else she wore which could be seen by others. She pursed her lips and said little until Elizabeth assured her there was nothing more to be seen, silently adding...*unless your ladyship cares to examine my undergarments.*

"Your taste is not terrible, although you will need finer clothes now that you are Mrs Darcy," the countess said. She fingered a pink striped morning gown.

Elizabeth accepted this with a nod that just managed to be polite.

"While we are alone," Lady Romsley continued, "let me make something perfectly clear. I shall do my best to see you gain some measure of acceptance. It will be our actions—yours especially—which will determine what course the future takes."

"I am aware of that, Lady Romsley. I thank you for whatever assistance you can provide." The price of this meek speech was a piece of her dignity.

Lady Romsley fixed her gaze on Elizabeth. "I hope this ends far better than it seems it will now. Being Mrs Darcy is a great responsibility. I do not believe you understand that."

"I am aware of the seriousness of my situation."

"Given the wretched beginning to this marriage, any scandal attached to your name will be ruinous, not just of your reputation, but also my nephew's."

Elizabeth met Lady Romsley's eyes. "I am not in the habit of acting scandalously, and I do not intend to begin now."

"If you do, we will do everything we can to protect Darcy and this family, whatever the cost to you and yours."

Lady Romsley swept from the room, leaving Elizabeth to follow after taking a moment to calm herself.

WHEN THE PARTY HAD REASSEMBLED, THEY DISCUSSED THE COMING weeks. Tom would need to return to his general soon, and the Fitzwilliams were going into Worcestershire, where Romsley Hall was located. Darcy could not give an exact date for their departure to Derbyshire but said it would be as soon as possible. He sensed the tension between his aunt and wife, and assumed Elizabeth was to blame.

"When do you anticipate returning to London?" Lord Romsley asked.

"Not until the new year," Darcy replied.

"Good," Lady Romsley said. "You will have months before you have to face the *ton*. The society around Pemberley is not entirely inconsequential, however."

The question, of course, was whether Elizabeth could withstand the scrutiny of his Derbyshire neighbours. The society around Pemberley would be far superior, and more discerning, to what she had known around Longbourn.

"I shall endeavour to behave with all propriety."

Given the sarcasm in Elizabeth's tone, Darcy wished she had held her tongue. He would not countenance such rudeness from his wife.

Before she could say more, he announced, "I agreed to host the Darcys in November. Arrangements will be made once the ladies have written to Mrs Darcy."

"They will naturally expect to meet your wife, and it is right that you have them to Pemberley," Lady Romsley proclaimed. "We shall visit for the festive season. I shall then endeavour to prepare Mrs Darcy for your return to town."

"I shall see that invitations are sent to Marian and Catherine as well," Darcy said.

Lady Romsley nodded as Elizabeth said, "May I ask who they are?"

"My sisters," Tom replied as the countess said, "You will have to familiarise yourself with the family."

As the Fitzwilliams were preparing to leave, Lady Romsley told Darcy, "She is impertinent. Guard against it."

Chapter 5

My dearest Jane,
Let me assure you, dear sister, that I am well. Knowing you
would wish it, you will find herein an accounting of my life as
Mrs Darcy. I shall begin with the house.

*E*lizabeth spent some time describing her new home. She joked
about the challenge of learning all the servants' names and
her attempts to develop a good rapport with Mrs Northmore.

Miss Darcy and I have not yet learnt to be comfortable
together. To satisfy you, whose voice I can hear even now, I
shall add that I pray and trust that, with time and effort, I
shall be friends with both Miss Darcy and Mr Darcy, and I
shall continue to strive for that happy outcome.

I have now been out two mornings with Lady Romsley procuring additions to my wardrobe. Mrs Darcy, she assured me, needs better clothes and a great deal more of them than what she saw when she examined my wardrobe. Miss Darcy accompanied us on one of these mornings. I do not believe she got any pleasure from the excursion, but she did manage to secure a bonnet and a gown. Lady Romsley introduced me to two or three ladies.

We shall be in London another week or so. How I long to see my aunt, but it is impossible. Perhaps once I have demonstrated that I shall not disgrace the office to which I was so unceremoniously appointed, I shall be granted more liberty. Then, I pray, I shall at least be able to receive Mrs Gardiner, even if it is not possible for Mrs Darcy to call at so unfashionable an address as Gracechurch Street.

Do let me have news of you and my parents and sisters.

Your humble and resolute sister,
Elizabeth

ELIZABETH SIGHED AS SHE FOLDED THE SHEETS OF PAPER. Not wishing to cause her sister any distress, she purposely made light of her new life. She was more open when she wrote to Mrs Gardiner, and gave a faithful description of the events that had transpired since her last letter, which was before the wedding, and wrote,

Let me assure you that I am well. I remain confident that with time, and if I continue to follow your excellent advice, my situation will improve, but for now I must admit I am not happy. Mr Darcy does not treat me ill, although he and Miss Darcy provide little by way of companionship. They and the Fitzwilliams look upon me as an unwelcome stranger. I am relieved to report that my husband has made no demands of an intimate nature upon me. The reprieve is most welcome. I know it will not always be so, but with each day that I am Mrs

Darcy my courage increases, and I trust that by the time I must face the inevitable, I shall be able to do so with equanimity.

A WEEK AFTER THE WEDDING, DARCY HAD A MOST UNWELCOME visitor: Lady Catherine de Bourgh.

"Fitzwilliam! Never have I been treated in such an infamous manner! I have heard not a word from either you or my brother despite my many letters. I must hear you say it. Are you married?" She stood facing him, repeatedly striking the floor with her walking stick as she spoke.

"I am."

"How could you? Who, pray tell, is Miss Elizabeth Bennet? How did she make you forget everything you owed to your family, to me, to Anne!"

Darcy's failure to respond increased her ire.

"Do not think me ignorant of the disgusting innuendos which have followed you and this Miss Bennet from Ramsgate. Do not think me ignorant of her lack of fortune or family. This woman upon whom you have seen fit to bestow your name is a disgrace. For her, you insulted my daughter."

"I was never bound to Anne. Any disappointment she now feels is not of my making."

"Never bound to Anne? Your mother, God rest her soul, and I planned your marriage when you were in your cradles!"

The door opened to admit Elizabeth, the last person Darcy wanted to see.

"Is this her?" Lady Catherine demanded. "The hussy you chose over my Anne?"

Elizabeth made a noise of astonishment, and her mouth fell open.

"That is quite enough," Darcy barked. "It is time for you to leave."

Lady Catherine gasped. "You would speak to me in such a manner? I came here to demand answers! I have a right to them!"

"No, you do not," Darcy countered. "I have acted as I saw fit and without reference to you or anyone else for the simple reason that you have no say in what I do. Good day, madam."

"I have not finished with this," Lady Catherine vowed as she sailed out of the room.

"Who was that?" Elizabeth asked once they were alone.

Darcy turned his back to her. "No-one for you to concern yourself with."

Elizabeth repeated her question.

"I have no wish to discuss this," he hissed.

"I can well imagine you have no wish to discuss it," Elizabeth said, her voice quivering with impatience, "however I fear you must."

Darcy turned and glared at her. "I must?"

Elizabeth's cheeks flushed. "I entered the room to—"

"Why did you? You were not wanted."

"To tell you to lower your voices if you did not want the whole house to hear you. Who is Anne, and who was that woman? I have a right to know who is saying such disgusting things about me!"

Darcy growled in anger and frustration. "That was Lady Catherine, my aunt."

"Anne?"

"Her daughter."

"And?"

"Lady Catherine hoped I would marry her."

Elizabeth stared into a corner of the room, tapping her foot. Darcy watched, finding her behaviour peculiar, and felt his anger slowly ebb away.

At length, Elizabeth said, "Will she be difficult?"

"Lord Romsley will see she is not."

Elizabeth averted her eyes, her foot still tapping. Darcy was transfixed by the rhythmic movement of the tip of her slipper. She nodded, and her foot stopped.

"Very well."

Before Darcy knew it, he was alone again.

ELIZABETH SPENT SEVERAL MORNINGS SHOPPING WITH LADY ROMSLEY and sometimes Georgiana, making appropriate purchases, and, as

Lady Romsley said, being seen in an inconspicuous fashion. After an early, polite battle of wills, Elizabeth made Lady Romsley understand she would not be dictated to; she *would* have a say in what she wore. The excursions were tedious and exhausting. Every minute required pretending to be on easy terms with her new relations. She guarded every action, every facial expression, every word, and lived with the knowledge that many of the people they saw had heard salacious tales about her. Elizabeth did not believe she was suspicious by nature, but she could not ignore the number of times she saw ladies and gentlemen looking at her and whispering to their companions. She despised every moment of it.

Their final outing before the Darcys went into Derbyshire was marred by two middle-aged ladies who had lost the ability or desire to speak in hushed tones. Lady Romsley, Georgiana, and Elizabeth were in a busy warehouse examining a display of gloves when their attention was caught by the words 'Darcy' and 'Ramsgate.' Lady Romsley and Elizabeth stopped what they were doing and listened.

"They say she was his mistress and threatened to expose some perversion of his if he refused to marry her."

"I heard that she lured Miss Darcy to Ramsgate and presented herself as Mr Darcy's betrothed to force his hand. Miss Darcy was so horrified that she was ill for days. Look at her now. She still looks so dreadfully pale."

Georgiana gasped.

With as much dignity as she could muster, Elizabeth looked directly at the gossiping women. She said nothing, just stared at them, her eyebrows arched. After a long moment during which none of them spoke, Elizabeth turned back to the display of gloves, and picked up a pair in soft yellow. "I believe these will do nicely."

"Yes," Lady Romsley quickly agreed. "They will match your new pelisse very well."

THE FAMILY DINED TOGETHER AT FITZWILLIAM HOUSE THAT DAY. TOM was returning to Dorset two days hence while the other Fitzwilliams went into Worcestershire soon after. Tom greeted the Darcys upon their arrival and took Georgiana aside for a private conversation.

When they were alone and Georgiana saw that Tom was in a sympathetic humour, she spoke readily and at length about the ignominy of having Elizabeth as a sister. People stared at them when they were in public and it was intolerable. "Everyone can see that she does not belong among us. It is just as horrible when we are alone! How are we ever to be comfortable again with her here?"

It felt so good to finally say out loud everything that she had been thinking. Everyone had been so disagreeable since Ramsgate. None of them cared about what she had suffered, or what she felt, even though her life was ruined, and she had no hope of it improving as long as Elizabeth was among them. Georgiana had longed for a sister, but one who was her equal, not one who was in every way an embarrassment. Elizabeth did not behave as an elegant, fashionable lady should, did not dress properly, and her family was disgraceful.

Georgiana had been living such a wonderful life! At last, she had been finished with school, which she had hated. Studying music and art had been agreeable, and she had met one or two girls she quite liked, but there had been too many boring lessons to sit through, and too many girls she could never be friends with. They were envious of her. As they should be; she was Miss Darcy of Pemberley, after all.

Tom and Fitzwilliam had done just as they ought and set her up in her own establishment with a companion to amuse her. She had been a young lady of the *ton*, living the perfect life for one of her station. How Georgiana had enjoyed those months! The girls at school had longed to be in her position. So many of them were returning home to tiresome parents who would treat them like children and impose upon them endless rules and expectations, while she lived quite like an independent, grown up lady.

Then she had gone to Ramsgate and met George Wickham again. He had courted her and offered her love. She had believed him; why would she not? Her schoolmates would have been wild with jealousy had Georgiana married such a handsome gentleman, and her only fifteen! She, Georgiana Darcy, had attracted a fine, mature man, and would have been a wife with her very own home. Theirs had been such a romantic story!

But it had been a false dream. Wickham had left her heartbroken and humiliated. If anyone discovered the truth, she would be mortified. It was awful that her aunt and uncle and Sterling knew—she accepted that Fitzwilliam had to tell Tom—and insupportable that someone like Elizabeth, so far beneath her, did. Now Georgiana must suffer the embarrassment of calling such a woman sister and having to live with her brother instead of in her own establishment. She would be living under his supervision, with only Elizabeth for company. Not that Georgiana intended to spend time with Elizabeth unless it was absolutely unavoidable. She would ignore her and wait for the day that her relations sorted out how to get rid of her. Then everything could go back to the way it should be. Fitzwilliam would no longer be so unhappy, Sterling would stop saying such teasing things to her, Tom would never lecture her again, and, with no wife living with him, her brother would have to permit Georgiana to live apart from him once again.

Georgiana did not share these thoughts with her cousin, but rather dwelt on Elizabeth's unsuitability to be Mrs Darcy, and how uncomfortable it was to be the subject of speculation. When she had said all that she had to say, Tom spoke.

"I understand how difficult the situation is, but it will get better. Once you are at Pemberley, you will be more at ease. There, all three of you can learn to be friends. It will require effort, from Mrs Darcy most of all. You can help, Georgiana. Show her what she needs to know about being part of this family and our station in life."

To Georgiana, it sounded little better than torture. She could never be friends with someone like Elizabeth, and it was unreasonable to expect it of her. Tom would soon realise that. Until he did, she would simply remain silent on the matter.

THE FIRST TIME ANY OF HER NEW FAMILY SPOKE TO ELIZABETH SINCE entering Fitzwilliam House that day was at dinner.

"Mrs Darcy, are you looking forward to going into Derbyshire?" Lady Romsley asked.

Startled, Elizabeth ceased searching her ragout—which was quite delicious and tasted strongly of garlic and thyme—for another mushroom and said, "Yes."

"You will find Pemberley delightful."

Elizabeth smiled.

"Are we forever to call her 'Mrs Darcy'?" Viscount Bramwell asked.

"I beg your pardon?" Lady Romsley said.

"We rarely use such formality among the family, and it has become tiresome. It will be remarked upon eventually, mark my words. And so, my new cousin, I request you call me either Sterling or Bramwell. What shall we call you?"

"Elizabeth. Elizabeth would do." Only people who cared for her called her Lizzy.

"Elizabeth it is!" Sterling said. Evidently finished with her, he turned to his mother and said, "Did I tell you that I saw Sir John and Lady Serena when I was out yesterday?"

WITH EACH DAY THEY REMAINED IN LONDON, ELIZABETH FELT MORE and more confined and alone. Darcy had little time for her, and Georgiana kept to her room as much as possible. Elizabeth read, perused the household accounts, and did needlework. When these activities failed to engage her, she dreamt about changing her rooms, as she found the ornate décor more and more displeasing. The furniture, mostly of Restoration style, had elaborate, curving lines and was embellished with gold, the fabrics were vermillion, and the flower-patterned wallpaper was too busy for Elizabeth. *In short, there is nothing I like about it. Except perhaps the view from the window!*

She spoke to Mrs Northmore about it and arranged to have the work done while they were at Pemberley. *After all*, she told herself, *he did say I could. And I am convinced I would sleep better in a bed that was less ugly!*

What she longed to do was go for a long walk, but, although Hyde Park was nearby, she could only go if Darcy escorted her and he would not.

They were not at home to callers. They did see Colonel Fitzwilliam who came very early on the morning he was to travel south. He was closeted with Darcy for some time then spoke with Georgiana for a half an hour or so. His farewell to Elizabeth was polite, but not warm.

DARCY KNEW HE COULD SPEND MORE TIME WITH ELIZABETH, BUT HE preferred to be on his own. His mood had not been improved when Tom assured him the Darcys were still the subject of much speculation. Tom's other news—that Wickham was on his way to Africa and Mrs Younge had been encouraged to seek her fortunes in Canada—was more welcome.

Darcy received a not-unexpected call from his good friend, Charles Bingley; he could not refuse to see him since they had previously arranged to spend some weeks together that autumn, a scheme which was now abandoned. Bingley spoke of nothing other than his surprise at Darcy's marriage, wished him joy several times, and insisted that Darcy introduce him to Mrs Darcy.

"I shall be quite the popular chap about town if you do!" Bingley laughed.

With reluctance and trepidation, Darcy sent for Elizabeth, praying her manner would be as it should when meeting someone of Bingley's standing.

When she entered the room, Elizabeth smiled as though without a care in the world. It was an expression she wore frequently, and which told him how much she rejoiced in her new situation. He performed the introduction, keeping careful watch on his wife as she and Bingley exchanged a few words.

"Mrs Darcy, I cannot tell you how delighted I am to meet you!"

"Mr Bingley, I am very happy to meet you. My husband has spoken of you often."

Darcy was certain he had never mentioned Bingley to her, but it mattered not. Fortunately, after a few minutes of banal conversation, Elizabeth left them; she had given him no cause to blush as she greeted his friend, and he relaxed as he and Bingley sat to continue their conversation.

Bingley asked, "She is from Hertfordshire?"

"Near a town called Meryton."

A wide smile spread across Bingley's face. "I have just learnt of an estate for lease near there! I thought I would ride down one day this week to look it over."

Darcy felt aghast, although his countenance did not show it. "No."

"No?"

"No. Trust me on this—it would not suit you. The…the neighbourhood would not be to your liking." If Darcy had his wish, he would never set foot in Hertfordshire again—not near Longbourn, or Meryton, or anywhere else in the county. The thought of Bingley living near the Bennets was abhorrent. Mrs Bennet would have him married to one of her daughters before he knew what had happened. Darcy had no wish to see his friend suffer such a fate.

"Oh." Bingley's countenance fell.

"I am sure there are many other estates and ones in better—I mean in neighbourhoods which would suit you better."

"If you advise against it, naturally I will think of it no longer."

Less than five minutes later, Darcy succeeded in ushering Bingley out of the house.

Chapter 6

At the end of September, they bid farewell to London. Elizabeth longed for a good country walk but was apprehensive about the change. Derbyshire was a great distance away from her loved ones.

It took three long days to reach Pemberley. Darcy rode for part of the time; Elizabeth used these opportunities to try to engage her sister-in-law in conversation. She hoped that as Georgiana grew more accustomed to her presence, she would wish for them to develop a good rapport, so that they could be company to each other and aid one another in this time of change. But Georgiana would not even look in Elizabeth's direction.

If I did not know better, I would say she is deaf. The scenery is interesting, but cannot command all of her attention, hour after hour!

Elizabeth was pleased to find Darcy in an uncommonly garrulous mood during dinner their first night of the journey. The inn was fine, their private parlour comfortable, and the meal very good and welcomed after a long day in the carriage. He readily answered her questions about Pemberley and mentioned Lambton as the closest town of any significant size.

"I have heard it is very pleasant."

Darcy looked at her quizzically.

"My aunt was a girl in Lambton," Elizabeth explained. "I believe she lived there until she was fourteen."

"Does she still have family in the area?" Darcy asked slowly, clearly not pleased to be reminded of Elizabeth's low connexions.

"No," Elizabeth whispered. How she wished she had thought before she spoke!

A short while later, she asked, "Do you usually attend church when you are in the country?"

"Yes."

"What is the name of the pastor?"

"Llewellyn."

"Has he been there long?"

"Five years, perhaps."

Elizabeth nodded and tried to ignore the suspicion in his voice. "Is he young?"

"Thirty or thereabouts. Is there anyone else about whom you care to enquire?"

Elizabeth cleared her throat and prayed her voice sounded steady. "I do not believe I know the name of your steward."

"Potter. You are very curious this evening. I might ask why."

Elizabeth felt her cheeks flush. "I…I am simply trying to become familiar with my new home. I know so little of it."

After a moment, she realised she was tapping her foot, a habit her mother abhorred, but which appeared whenever she was particularly uncomfortable. She put one foot on top of the other to still it and cleared her throat again. "I thought it would be useful to know a little more and…and…This pudding is quite good, is it not?"

DARCY WAS ELATED WHEN THEY AT LAST REACHED PEMBERLEY. THE tight band of anger and anxiety which had him in its snare for weeks loosened. Staring at Elizabeth, Darcy thought, *If she did not under-*

stand what she gained by marrying me before, she will now. She could not have imagined calling such a place home.

Here, at Pemberley, Elizabeth's true character would be revealed. In the coming weeks, he could judge the sort of mistress, wife, and sister she would be. He prayed it would not be a terrible ordeal to manage her, that her weaknesses would be easy to amend or contain.

"It is growing late," he said. "I shall make a few introductions. We should quickly prepare to dine. Georgiana, you will remain with me."

The carriage stopped, and they stepped out. Darcy regarded Elizabeth, detecting a slight tension in her manner. He was glad; it showed, perhaps, that she understood that she could not simply walk into Pemberley and be as she had been when she was Miss Elizabeth Bennet.

AS THEY DROVE THROUGH THE ESTATE, ELIZABETH TOOK IN EVERY feature of her surroundings, waiting anxiously for a view of the house, and trying to control her nerves. When it came, she was pleased. The manor, a large white stone edifice, was magnificent and the lands around it were lush.

At the same time, with Pemberley now before her, Elizabeth felt the enormity of her task as she never had before. How would she ever learn to be mistress of such an estate, especially without a loving husband and sister to support her?

Darcy's eyes were upon her, but she would not look at him. At this moment, she feared his censorious stare would intimidate her more than she could bear. She fought to regain her confidence and courage before they reached the house and she had to appear before the servants as their new mistress.

Inside, Darcy introduced Elizabeth to the housekeeper, Mrs Reynolds, and the butler, Mr Hudson. The Darcys then walked down the line of servants so that they could welcome their new mistress. Elizabeth felt as though the servants, the housekeeper in particular, scrutinised her very carefully. Their curiosity was not surprising, but she was certain she detected disapproval.

Courage, Lizzy. You will find your way. It will simply...take time.

She hoped she had not just lied to herself.

WHEN ELIZABETH WOKE THE NEXT MORNING, IT TOOK HER A MOMENT to remember that she was now at Pemberley. She stretched her arms over her head and rolled her neck, seeking comfort for muscles made sore by the long carriage ride.

In the daylight, Elizabeth saw little she liked in the room's decorations. While her rooms in town were too dark, this bedchamber—and the accompanying sitting room—were too bright, with colours displeasing to the eye. The walnut William and Mary furniture was dark, heavy, and too embellished for Elizabeth's taste. There was also far too much of it, which would be easy to rectify at least.

I can only hope not to find too much of this style in the other rooms of the house. If so, I shall spend the next five years redecorating.

She ate the toast and tea Drewe brought, hardly tasting them in her haste, and announced her intention to take as long a walk as possible before breakfast. After that, she had a house and servants to get to know.

"It might rain, Mrs Darcy!"

"I shall not go far from the house, and if it starts to rain, I shall return."

She found her way to the gardens. The air was fresh; the scent of earth made damp by recent rain filled her nostrils, and Elizabeth felt a sense of freedom she had not experienced since leaving Hertfordshire. It was wonderful to stretch her legs and see the sights of the countryside. Before she was chased further away from the house by the sounds of gardeners at work, she walked along a stone path bordered by rich red chrysanthemums, purple asters, and bright orange marigolds. She saw the hint of a lake to one side—which she would explore another day—and walked towards a copse. As she passed by oak and beech trees, their leaves beginning to change to their autumn colours, she let her fingers linger on the rough bark and closed her eyes, listening to the gentle rustling of the wind.

She re-entered the house an hour later with her spirits nourished enough to face the day.

AFTER MAKING QUICK WORK OF HIS MORNING TOAST AND TEA, DARCY

strode out of the house and towards the stables. He was soon seated atop his favourite stallion and riding as fast as he could coax his horse to go. The abrasive action of the early morning air on his face as they flew across Pemberley's grounds washed away the weeks of anger and sadness, worry and frustration.

They stopped atop a small hill. Darcy looked around and saw fields full of sheep pulling at the grass, men and women out tending to the fields, and a few cottages here and there. It was such an ordinary sight, and it was comforting. No matter the disorder of his personal life, this was important. Pemberley was something that would endure, and it was for *this* that he had to remain strong. For the honour and duty of the Darcy family, he would find a way to make his marriage a success, to make Elizabeth as good a Mrs Darcy as she could possibly be, no matter how much effort he had to put into it. For this, he would have a true marriage to Elizabeth, one which produced an heir for the estate.

Thank God we are both still young. There is time, an abundance of time.

For the first time since the day he arrived in Ramsgate and found the note from Wickham telling Georgiana to meet him, he felt resolute. He was Fitzwilliam Darcy of Pemberley and he would prevail.

GEORGIANA WAS VERY GLAD TO FIND HERSELF AT PEMBERLEY WHEN she awoke that morning. The journey from town had been long, and she had been too much with her brother. And Elizabeth. After leisurely eating her toast while chatting with her maid, she spent some time at the pianoforte—she had not played in days—and then considered her situation. Of utmost importance was avoiding Elizabeth's company. Fitzwilliam and Tom had informed her that she would have to work on her languages and history—which was perhaps her least favourite of all subjects—since, in their opinion, she had left school without sufficient knowledge in these areas.

If she had disliked having to learn French or Italian or history as a schoolgirl, she detested it now, as a young lady who should be beyond all of that. She should be able to spend her time as she liked. She ought to be preparing to take her place among the *ton*.

Wickham had shown her that she would have no difficulties securing the affections of a handsome gentleman, so what did her understanding of history matter? Except, Wickham had... That did not matter.

Georgiana had been quite upset that her guardians had not thought to ask what she wanted to spend her time learning or doing, but everything was disordered at the moment with that woman among them, and Georgiana had no interest in risking another lecture by demanding she be allowed more freedom. They had insisted she would spend the coming months 'improving her mind,' and so she would have to act as though she accepted their orders. It was ridiculous that she had to account for every minute of her day. Just because Fitzwilliam was content to always be rushing here and there, busy with who knew what, did not mean she had to do the same. But what choice did she have? *Fitzwilliam is understandably in a disagreeable mood, and it would be best to let him believe I am busy doing as he and Tom asked. I must absolutely say that I have too much to do to spend time with* her. *I do not care how much Tom talked of me helping her; I will not.*

Expecting her brother to ask her how she intended to occupy her time when they met at breakfast, Georgiana was prepared. She had devised several excuses, and fervently hoped to prevent her brother demanding she keep Elizabeth company. When Fitzwilliam posed the dreaded question, she said, "I will practise my music, and I must spend some time on my studies. I have planned a course of reading, just as you, Tom, and I discussed." After her brother expressed his approval, she attended to her breakfast, content to ignore her companions, particularly the one who had no place amongst such good society.

WHEN THE PARTY SEPARATED, ELIZABETH DECIDED TO WANDER around the house on her own rather than ask Mrs Reynolds to show it to her. She quickly lost count of the morning rooms, withdrawing rooms, and dining rooms she viewed. In one parlour, she ran her fingers lightly across a beautiful pianoforte. She played, but not very well. There had always been something more exciting to do than practise.

Elizabeth wondered how much entertaining Mr Darcy did. The principal rooms had been recently redecorated. They were bright, elegant, and far from the fussy style of her chambers. Did he often have parties of friends to stay? How much of his time did he intend to spend at Pemberley now that he was a married man?

I suppose I shall find out when he believes it is necessary to tell me. I can only hope it is before guests are upon the doorstep!

When she had seen enough for the day, she returned to her rooms, sent for refreshments, and made herself comfortable upon a sofa. The day had been thus far blissfully free of upset or awkwardness. There was pleasure of a sort to be found in exploring a grand house. For the most part, she very much liked it, but some of the rooms did need refreshing, most notably her own.

I shall have to be happy with them for now. Perhaps the work can be done when we are in London for the Season. She sighed. *Perhaps by then I shall be confident enough to demand the expense!*

As a bride, she should naturally arrange her new home to her liking, but she was hesitant to do so, though she had asked for changes to her rooms in London. She had taken Darcy at his word when he said she should and had evidently displeased him by not seeking his advice on what to do.

"I will prove to them all that I can be a good wife and mistress, if they allow it. In fulfilling my duties, I shall be content. I *must* continue to believe that. Perhaps if I say it often enough, I will!"

Darcy had not yet shown her, by word or deed, that he wished to share her bed, and Elizabeth was not anxious to change the situation. Yet, she knew how much good it would do her standing within the family if she had a child, particularly a son, and how it would stem the speculation about their marriage. What a relief it would be to no longer worry about being the subject of gossip.

Elizabeth picked up a book. It was one she had brought with her from Longbourn and an old favourite. She longed for something new to read but did not feel the time was right to ask Darcy to show her the library. She was convinced he would refuse, or at the very least be unhappy, and she did not want a rejection, either overt or subtle. The day had been relatively pleasant thus far, and to ensure it ended in the same way, she would remain as unobtrusive as possible.

AFTER DINNER, DARCY ATTEMPTED TO COAX GEORGIANA INTO playing for them, but she demurred. He understood that she was not comfortable playing with Elizabeth there. She had always been shy with strangers, which had kept her from leaving school with a large group of friends, but she was also loving and warm with those she knew well. He had seen it time and again with his relations and with himself and Tom. It had been so that spring, before the ill-fated trip to Ramsgate, when he had called on her in town. She had been so happy to see him. They had sat together, her smiling and enthusiastically talking about what she would do while on holiday, and when he took her into Derbyshire for some weeks in the autumn. In time, he trusted that she would extend herself to being on better terms with his wife; it was simply too soon for it to be today. He would think on the matter no further at the moment. It had been a relatively satisfying day and he did not wish to spoil his easy mood.

I shall observe them over the next week. If they are not then being more companionable, I shall remind Elizabeth she must make more of an effort. After all, Georgiana is young and naturally reserved, and it has been a difficult time for her. Elizabeth will have to be under-standing and be the one to extend a friendly hand.

Chapter 7

The weather remained poor over the next few days. Darcy cursed the rain for keeping him indoors, but he could find diversion enough in the library or billiards room when he was not occupied with business. He received notes from some neighbours proposing they meet to shoot when the weather improved and while the ladies of the neighbourhood began to call upon Mrs Darcy.

He was uncertain what he should do. Could he leave Elizabeth alone to receive callers? Would she embarrass him with her lack of fine manners? If he were present, he could intervene as necessary, but he had no wish to stay home and receive callers, especially when there was so much to disguise. It was exhausting having to pretend to be happy in his marriage.

In his resolve to study Elizabeth's behaviour, Darcy kept an eye on her. His observations soon showed him that she spent considerable time with Mrs Reynolds. He understood that they met before breakfast each day, and he had witnessed them in conversation two other times, once evidently reviewing one of the household ledgers. He was uncertain how to feel about it. Elizabeth had spoken to Mrs Northmore a fair bit in London, but their time there had been brief enough that he had not worried overmuch. Could Elizabeth learn to be a good mistress? Perhaps it would be better if she took little interest in the day-to-day management of his houses. That would be preferable to an active, incompetent mistress who caused disarray and put his dependents at risk. He had told Mrs Northmore to inform him if she had any concerns about her new mistress and now did the same with Mrs Reynolds.

"I shall," Mrs Reynolds assured him.

"What do you and Mrs Darcy discuss?" he asked. "You seem to spend a considerable amount of time together."

Mrs Reynolds rattled off various household matters, adding, "Mrs Darcy asks about all the servants, their families, how long they have been here and the like. She is inquisitive, but eager. If I may be so bold as to speak freely?"

Darcy nodded.

"I would say she is determined to learn. I am confident she will do well."

This assessment was surprising, but Darcy was gratified by Elizabeth's industry.

DARCY WAS CURIOUS WHEN ELIZABETH APPROACHED HIM AFTER dinner a few days later. Georgiana sat in the corner, reading; he was on the point of opening a book, too.

"There is a little matter I would like to discuss, if you are agreeable?"

He decided to pour himself a glass of wine before beginning what might be an unpleasant, if not protracted, conversation. He went to the drinks table, and, once he returned to where she was, retook his seat. He gestured for her to sit across from him before nodding for her to speak.

"Mrs Reynolds informs me there are several changes she would like to make to the staff at the quarter day. She told me the customary practice has been for her to make recommendations, which you then review."

He gave a curt nod.

"I would very much like to be a party to the undertaking, if you would allow it."

"I do not take your meaning." Did she expect to have a say in engaging new servants, she who had not been at Pemberley a week, and who had no experience in such dealings? A slight motion drew his eye, and he found she was, once again, tapping her foot. He repressed a grin of amusement.

"I simply wish to further my understanding of how the house is managed, and I would like to be familiar with the servants, new and old. 'Tis no great mystery." Her cheeks turned a delightful shade of pink.

He took a moment to answer. "Very well."

Elizabeth nodded and went to sit in a different corner of the room without another word.

Darcy watched her for some minutes before he could attend to his book.

ELIZABETH KEPT HERSELF BUSY, BUT FOUND SHE LONGED FOR A caller or two; with them, there would be conversation and distraction, if only for a short while. For the moment, she occupied herself with matters inside the house, including developing a good relationship with the housekeeper. She was pleased with herself for having summoned her courage enough to speak to Darcy about the quarter day. His stern looks and evident distrust were difficult to bear, but she had gotten what she wished for, even if it did take her an hour to regain her equanimity. She had so wanted to argue with him and demand to know what he found so astonishing in her wanting to actually do what the mistress of an estate should do. But challenging him would serve no purpose other than to make him despise her more, so she bit her tongue. She had to undo a great deal of the needlework she did after their conversation. Somehow, she had made what was meant to be a yellow chrysanthemum—inspired by what she had seen in the gardens—look like an unappetizing yellow jelly.

She received her wished-for company at the end of the week when Mrs Horatia Darcy came to call.

Upon being informed she was there, Elizabeth asked Hudson to send refreshments and said, "Please have Miss Darcy informed her aunt is here. She should come down immediately. And see Mr Darcy is told as soon as he returns."

When Elizabeth entered the room, Horatia stood, and, through an eyepiece, undertook a thorough survey of Elizabeth's person.

"Mrs Darcy," Elizabeth said, "how kind of you to call. I am very pleased to make your acquaintance."

She had to wait a moment before the older woman remembered her manners and returned the greeting. They sat across from each other on matching sofas covered in blue and white striped fabric.

"I am afraid Mr Darcy is not here at the moment. Miss Darcy will join us momentarily."

Horatia nodded and continued her examination of Elizabeth for a moment before speaking. "It is very good to finally see you. The weather has been dreadful! I did not wish to intrude upon you immediately, but a new bride must be visited, and we have all been terribly curious about you."

"I am very glad to meet another of my husband's relations, of course." Elizabeth smiled, but knew it was strained. Horatia was the first member of the Darcy family she had met, but Elizabeth had no doubt the Darcys, like the Fitzwilliams, were disgusted their relative had married a penniless, unconnected country lady. Horatia's manner and words confirmed it.

The refreshments arrived and Horatia fussed over her choice of the small cakes until the servants left the room. "You had a small country wedding, I believe. My brother-in-law John—he was the second son, you know, older than my Charles—wrote to say it would be."

Elizabeth found Horatia's manner of staring at her, a glass of orangeade in one hand and a cake in the other, quite amusing. "Yes. It was held in my family's parish. Miss Darcy and Viscount Bramwell attended."

"Oh, Bramwell!" Horatia waved the hand with the cake. "Such a good-looking young man. So sad his wife died, and their babe as well. It was an excellent match, you know, fortune and very high connexions on both sides. Their parents had talked about it for years. And you are from?"

"My father's estate is in Hertfordshire."

"Your father's estate," Horatia repeated, nodding and sighing in visible relief.

After that, Horatia began to question Elizabeth in earnest. It went on long enough that Elizabeth went from amused, to insulted and frustrated. She longed for the distraction Georgiana's presence would offer and wondered why the girl had not appeared.

Finally, they were joined by Darcy, who smiled broadly as he entered the room and cried, "Aunt Horry. How do you do? How kind of you to call. I apologise for not being here when you arrived."

The accusatory look he gave Elizabeth made her cheeks burn. She knew she had done nothing wrong and longed to defend herself.

"No, no, my dear boy, you have your duties to attend to. I came to see…your wife."

Elizabeth met the stares of her husband and his aunt with a small smile.

When Georgiana entered the room a minute later, she looked far more cheerful than Elizabeth had ever seen her. "Aunt Horry! How good to see you."

Elizabeth watched as Georgiana, Darcy, and Horatia spoke easily. None of them attempted to include her in their conversation, but she did not mind. Being overlooked was better than facing disdain.

How is it possible to feel so alone in a room with three other people?

AFTER HORATIA'S DEPARTURE, DARCY TURNED TO HIS SISTER. "WHY were you not here when I arrived?"

Georgiana, her eyes as round as a full moon, replied, "I did not know Aunt Horry was here until you sent word to me. I would have come down earlier had I known."

Darcy looked at Elizabeth, his expression full of censure.

She suspected that Georgiana was dissembling and chose her words carefully. "How odd. I shall have a word with Hudson. I asked him to have you informed as soon as he told me your aunt had arrived."

"I would hardly bother Hudson about something so unimportant," Georgiana said.

"It is not unimportant, Georgiana. If it is true that Elizabeth asked that a message be sent to you and it was not, we must find out why."

If? Elizabeth silently exclaimed.

Darcy was still speaking. "Are you certain you told Hudson to have Georgiana informed?"

"Yes." *Do you think I am too stupid to remember what I did an hour ago?*

"I find it very odd you did not receive the message, Georgiana. Wh—"

Georgiana interrupted. "Brother, I was studying my Italian, but there was a passage I could not quite make out. Can you help me?"

Elizabeth almost laughed at the mask of innocence Georgiana wore.

Darcy said nothing, but looked between his sister and Elizabeth, at length saying, "Of course, Georgiana."

Hearing the door close behind her husband and sister-in-law, Elizabeth let out a sigh of relief.

My dearest Jane,
We have now been in Derbyshire a week and I am—

ELIZABETH LIFTED HER PEN FROM THE PAGE AND STARED AT WHAT she had written. She could not think of what to say next. "And I am what, exactly? Too much alone, still being dismissed by my husband and new sister?" Elizabeth wondered aloud, the soft sound of her voice a welcomed relief from the silence in which she lived. Longbourn was always so lively and loud, and the stillness of Pemberley felt oppressive by comparison. She returned to her letter, writing about the delight she had taken in exploring the grounds, neglecting to mention the rain that had kept her inside more than she liked.

Mrs Reynolds, the housekeeper, and I have come to an understanding. She would be best pleased if I left the household management to her; however, I insist upon being an active mistress.

Elizabeth's cheeks burned and she gripped her pen so tightly she almost broke it as she remembered overhearing Darcy questioning Mrs Reynolds about her. She had just opened the door to the breakfast parlour one morning when her husband asked whether Mrs Darcy was upsetting the servants.

"What is so terrible about wanting to know their names and how long they have been at Pemberley? What must she think!" Elizabeth was both humiliated that Darcy had made it plain to the housekeeper that he did not trust his new wife, and angry that he had put her into such a position.

I met some of my new neighbours. I have been contemplating the acceptability of writing a short list of commonly asked questions and answers for each person to read at their leisure. We could thus dispense with the usual fare of teasing out my life history and the reasons why so eligible a gentleman as Mr Darcy married poor, unaccomplished, and unconnected me and discuss more interesting subjects.

Elizabeth read the last lines, and, after staring at the sheet for a long moment, threw it into the fireplace. She would try again later.

BEFORE DINNER THE NEXT EVENING, GEORGIANA WAS SURPRISED TO see her brother appear in her sitting room. She had hoped that her question about Italian had distracted him from thinking about Elizabeth's message when Aunt Horatia had called, but she had not been successful.

"It was delivered, Georgiana," he said. "Hudson and I both talked to the footman who brought it to you. Why did you ignore it?"

"I do not recall receiving it, truly. It must be a misunderstanding. Perhaps my attention was on my studies." In truth, Georgiana had been reading a novel when the footman had knocked at her door. Knowing Fitzwilliam was away from home, she stayed where she was, happily anticipating Elizabeth making a fool of herself in front of Horatia, who would tell the rest of the family.

Georgiana was confident her brother believed her explanation, but some time later, at dinner, he questioned her further about how she was occupying her time. She spoke assuredly, albeit vaguely, about music and languages and history. "I admit I am finding it difficult to progress with Italian on my own." Since she spent very little time with it, it was not wholly surprising.

"I shall assist you when I can." Fitzwilliam then asked Elizabeth, "Do you speak Italian or French? I know little of your education."

"Both, although my understanding is imperfect. My French is stronger."

"Perhaps you and Elizabeth could work through the Italian together, Georgiana."

Elizabeth said, "I would certainly be willing to try."

Her brother expressed his approval. Georgiana smiled, neither agreeing nor disagreeing.

HUDSON DELIVERED THE MAIL WHILE THEY WERE AT BREAKFAST TWO days later. Most of it was for Elizabeth, which Darcy remarked upon.

Elizabeth shuffled through her letters. "I am afraid I do not recognise the handwriting on many of them."

"I suspect they are from my family. If you read me the names or directions, I shall tell you who they are. You must reply and begin issuing invitations. The Darcys visit in November and the Fitzwilliams in December."

"Thank you. And, yes, I recall." Elizabeth placed the letters beside her plate and returned to her breakfast. Noticing his surprise, Elizabeth asked, "This minute?"

"One's correspondence, especially when it is from people of importance, should be attended to in a timely manner."

Elizabeth blushed. "I am perfectly aware of that, but I did think to finish my breakfast first." Darcy opened his mouth to reply, but Elizabeth went on. "I would also ask that we go through the letters in another room."

"Why?"

"I would like to have a pen and paper with me." *Now that you will finally tell me about your family!*

Darcy cocked an eyebrow. He dropped something and had to bend over to pick it up. It made Elizabeth realise she was once again tapping her foot; she forced it to be still.

He looked amused when he sat up again.

Whatever could that be about? "I wish to make a list," Elizabeth explained.

"A list?"

"To refresh my memory as needed to ensure I do not neglect anyone. I congratulate you on your ability to remember so many people and their relationship to you. I, however, do not have that skill, not at this time. Perhaps we can do it once you are finished eating. If you will excuse me, I need a moment with Mrs Reynolds."

"Come to my study when you are ready," he said as she walked towards the door. "I have many matters to attend to. Do not keep me waiting."

DARCY FOUND HER IMPERTINENCE DISTRESSING, YET ALSO AMUSING. Or perhaps he meant charming. Whatever her impertinence was, her habit of tapping her foot was indeed very amusing. He had caught her at it at least a half-dozen times.

While Elizabeth opened letter after letter, he carefully explained who the author was. Reaching the last one, Elizabeth glanced through the contents before announcing, "Rosings Park."

Darcy could not believe Lady Catherine had had the effrontery to write to his wife. He pulled the letter from Elizabeth's hand and quickly ran his eyes over the page. "No good will come from reading a letter from that quarter," he pronounced, tossing it into the fire. Seeing Elizabeth's shocked expression, he muttered, "My cousin, Anne."

Elizabeth stood, her colour high. She gathered her other letters and held them out to him. "Are there any others you wish to burn before I can even read them?"

"You are being ridiculous."

"Anne is the cousin you were supposed to marry, is she not?"

"I was never going to marry her," Darcy retorted, growing angry.

"Her mother thought you were. I have not forgotten Lady Catherine. Did Anne expect you to marry her?"

"I am not responsible for what she believed, and you have no right to question me about it." Darcy turned his back to her. "We are finished."

Elizabeth laughed. "You have no idea how much I wish that were so."

He was relieved she was gone before he said something he would later regret.

Tom,

We are settling into life at Pemberley. Georgiana is busy with her studies. I am pleased with her enthusiasm for the work. Estate business occupies most of my time at the moment. Haddon and his sister, with whom you were much taken the last time you met, will spend the day at Pemberley soon.

Mrs Darcy is doing as well as can be hoped for. She has an interest in household management, which is promising as long as she does not upset the servants. She has been introduced to some of our neighbours, and I am not displeased with her manner. I trust that whatever damage she does will soon be forgot and that the worst of the talk will be that I have made a remarkably poor marriage.

I have seen little evidence she and Georgiana are spending time together, but then Georgiana has been working very hard. I shall continue to encourage a friendship, but as they are so very different, it might not be possible.

Write when you can.
FD

Chapter 8

*D*arcy and Elizabeth did not see each other again until dinner. Darcy regretted that they had exchanged angry words, but he was the one who knew Anne, and if he believed there was nothing to be gained by reading her letter, then that should have been the end of it. Elizabeth would learn not to question his decisions.

After a largely silent dinner, they went into the withdrawing room. Once they had had tea, Darcy insisted Georgiana play for them. She had hitherto refused to play in front of Elizabeth, but the three of them spent every evening together, and some music would be a pleasant diversion. With the gentle notes of a Haydn concerto in the background, Darcy studied his wife, her head bent low over her needlework. He had never noticed how richly coloured her hair was, or that her features were so delicate. True, she lacked perfect symmetry—her nose bent slightly to the right and there was some small difference between her eyebrows—but, all in all, it was not an unhandsome face.

Before he knew what he was doing, he had changed seats to be beside her.

Elizabeth visibly started as though she had not seen him approaching. She glanced at him but would not meet his eye as he sat beside her. Perhaps she regretted confronting him earlier, as she should.

In a quiet voice, his eyes on Georgiana, Darcy said, "Lady Catherine has said for many years that she and my mother planned my marriage to Anne while we were in our cradles. My father claimed it was simply a daydream on my mother's part. My father was not in favour of the match and told Lady Catherine so long ago. Lord Romsley and I have repeatedly told Lady Catherine that such a marriage would never take place, and that she should not continue to insist to Anne or to others that it would."

"Why does she persist?"

Darcy took a moment to answer. "Anne has never been presented and spends little time in London. She did not have a Season, and, at five-and-twenty, is near an age at which she is unlikely to marry, although her fortune could still attract suitors. They have always supposed her to be of indifferent health."

"Supposed?"

"The Fitzwilliams and I do not believe there was ever anything very wrong with her. Her lifestyle does not invite good health. She does little either to improve her mind or body. You have, unfortunately, encountered Lady Catherine. Her daughter is very much like her in temperament."

Their eyes met, and, after a heartbeat, Elizabeth slowly nodded.

"You believed her letter was not welcoming?"

He was pleased that she so quickly understood. "I am certain it was not. Reading it would only cause pain and aggravation."

"Thank you."

Her sincerity struck an odd note in Darcy's mind. He went back to his original seat and picked up his book. It was some minutes before he could attend to it.

AFTER CHURCH ON SUNDAY, ELIZABETH WAS INTRODUCED TO THE vicar, Mr Llewellyn. He was pleasant, and Elizabeth intended to talk to him soon to learn more about the parish, particularly any families who might require her assistance, or any good work he felt was necessary and appropriate for the mistress of Pemberley to oversee. The thought of being of use in this way lightened her heart and mind; whether or not she should be Mrs Darcy, she was. She would use her position to help those in need, and to improve the well-being of the local population.

She frequently only saw Georgiana and Darcy at meals. As alone and dismissed as she often felt with Darcy's continued absence from her company, she was beginning to prefer it. He had taken to staring at her when they were together.

If he continues this way, I shall grow quite afraid of him, she thought one morning when she was walking through the sculpture garden. She brushed a yellow oak leaf off a bronze statue of a man with ravens. *Yet, I cannot ask him why he does it. That would be too impertinent, and I shall not give him another reason to despise me.*

She regretted her part in their unpleasant exchange over the letter from Anne de Bourgh but felt justified in finding his behaviour officious. Nevertheless, her position was insecure, and she wished she had reacted with less intemperance. A man such as Mr Darcy would not like a wife who argued with him. His explanation had been unexpected and appreciated, yet she knew he still blamed her for how she had acted, and she was resolved not to make the same mistake again.

"No matter how much he provokes me! If I said only half of what I truly thought—but I will not. I cannot," she mumbled while examining the soft, smooth ruby-coloured leaf of a bush she did not recognise.

Her happiness, her respectability, depended upon being accepted by Darcy and his family. Hard work, diligent application to her duties, and a pleasant, inviting demeanour were the only tools at her disposal. Although it had not been very long since her marriage began, she had hoped to have made some progress by now. At times, it was distressing to feel how little had changed. Another letter, full of unnecessary instruction and advice, had just arrived from Lady Romsley.

As though I do not know how to comport myself! Ridiculous!

She huffed and used the stick she was holding to hit a pile a leaves, sending some of them flying.

"Well, I do not need their love. I am quite convinced I could never love any of them, and so I could hardly wish for them to love me. Tolerance and respect are all I seek."

"I BELIEVE I SHALL GO INTO LAMBTON UNLESS THERE ARE ANY objections?" Elizabeth announced midway through breakfast the next day.

"Lambton?" Darcy exclaimed. "Why?"

"I have not been, and I am curious." The town owed much of its prosperity to Pemberley and Elizabeth felt that it would be a nice gesture for the Darcy family to visit. Mr and Miss Darcy would not, and so it would fall to Mrs Darcy. "Georgiana, I do not suppose you would care to join me?"

"No!" Georgiana snapped, and turned her chin so that it was pointed away from Elizabeth.

"Perhaps you should, Georgiana," Darcy said.

His words surprised Elizabeth as much as they did Georgiana, who stared at him.

"B-but...I must finish a piece of French. I promised Tom I would send it to him today."

Colonel Fitzwilliam was helping her with French via their correspondence. Elizabeth thought it sounded like a very inefficient manner by which to improve one's French but accepted that her disdain might in part be because Georgiana continued to reject every one of her overtures.

"Very well. Be sure you take a footman with you, Elizabeth."

Elizabeth enjoyed the outing, which only wanted the company of a friend to make it truly pleasurable. The town was larger than Meryton and had a very neat appearance. Everyone she met was friendly. She wrote about it to Mrs Gardiner.

Your description of the town convinced me that I should like it, and I did. It is charming. I walked along High Street and went into several establishments all the while trailed by one of Pemberley's most severe-looking footmen. I bought some sheets of music, a pair of warm gloves, and a ribbon in a beautiful shade of purple. The proprietors were far more appreciative of my custom than was warranted.

I am determined to improve my horribly weak skills at the pianoforte. A lady in my position should have some accomplishment to display, and, to own the truth, it will be a way to occupy my time. There is a rather lovely room in the east wing, the walls of which are a delicate pink that reminds me of roses. I will practise there, and no one will have to suffer by hearing my pitiful attempts to learn the new music.

UNBEKNOWNST TO ELIZABETH, DARCY DISCOVERED HER SECRET. He happened to be nearby, and, thinking it was a servant shirking their duties by playing in an out-of-the-way part of the house, opened the door prepared to reprimand the player. He was greatly startled to see Elizabeth crouched over the pianoforte, the fingers of one hand on the keys and those of the other on the music sheets she was studying intently. She did not hear his entry, and he watched as she played a section over and over again.

Why has she chosen such an isolated part of the house in which to practise?

He soon knew the answer. She was not very good. Yet, he was entranced by her efforts and watched until, in frustration, she turned the sheet of music over to hide the offensive notation. Before Darcy could speak, she began a new piece, appearing to rely on memory. Despite his earlier conclusion, Darcy enjoyed her performance. It was a cheerful piece, and Darcy could feel the happiness as well as hear it in the notes.

He had a sudden longing to hear her sing. *Ridiculous. I have never heard her sing and have no reason to think she does it well. Most likely she does not, and that is why she is not!*

Uncomfortable with the feelings her playing evoked, he turned on his heel and walked away.

As Darcy continued his examination of Elizabeth, he was glad to discover that she was making an effort. Her manner when they were at church or had callers was perfectly acceptable, and the reports he received from Mrs Reynolds were favourable. There were trials ahead of her, however, and it remained to be seen whether she could withstand them or not.

They had another spell of wet weather, which local wisdom suggested would soon end. As it did, there would be more calls to receive and make and some parties. He did not accept many such invitations, being discerning in the company he kept. But the calls and parties were necessary and could help prepare Elizabeth for the more arduous social life ahead of her in London.

Without volition, Darcy seemed to encounter Elizabeth more frequently around the house. Several days after first seeing her at the pianoforte, they almost collided as he entered, and she left the library.

"Oh!" Elizabeth exclaimed, jumping back. She clutched several books to her chest.

Darcy stood closer to her than was customary. Looking down at her, he saw the rapid rising and falling of her chest and could almost hear her heart beating.

"I-I thought you had gone. To see a tenant."

Her eyes—had he noticed before that they were brown?—began to dart around the room, landing on him only occasionally. A gentle pitter-patter noise arose which he knew must be her slipper rhythmically hitting the floor.

He dragged his eyes from her feet, past the books, and back to her face. "Potter was delayed by some other business. We shall go later. What are those?" With his eyes, he indicated the books in her arms.

The staccato of her foot quickened, and her cheeks turned the slightest shade of pink. *What could she be about for a simple question to make her so nervous?* "Come." He gestured at her to follow him into the room.

She sat primly on the edge of a rosewood armchair; Darcy sat across from her and held out a hand for the books. He did not find what he expected. Instead of novels, or perhaps some poetry, he found a book on botany, one on geology, and a recent tome—in French—

about Alexandre de Humboldt's explorations. "This is...quite serious reading."

"I did not think you would mind if I borrowed them."

"As I have said, you are free to use the library, provided you take care of the books, and return them when you are finished. I am simply surprised. I did not know you read French."

"Whether you knew it or not, I do."

He would excuse the slight insolence in her tone; he did not wish to argue with her again. "The subject matter?"

"It interests me."

They sat in silence for a moment before words tumbled out of Elizabeth's mouth. "On my walks I have noticed that some elements of the vegetation around Pemberley are quite different from those with which I am familiar. As the climate is not so very different, I was curious about what might account for it and...I find geology...diverting."

The colour on her cheeks deepened. It was quite becoming.

"Geology?"

"I do realise it is not a fashionable study for ladies, but I assure you I do not intend to discuss it in company."

"That is for the best." He would not want anyone to think his wife was a bluestocking. Looking at the book in French, he read the title. "*Le Voyage Aux Régions Equinoxiales du Nouveau Continent, Fait en 1799-1804.*" He looked at her, one eyebrow cocked in question.

"I heard about it some time ago but have not had the opportunity to read it."

"Well, you will find them difficult reading, but if it is how you choose to spend your time when it is not otherwise required, I suppose there is little harm that can come of it." Darcy returned the books to her.

"I assure you I am more than capable of understanding what these learned gentlemen have written."

With that she left. Darcy considered the nature of his wife for several minutes before he retrieved the book he had come for and returned to his study.

It was raining again, and Elizabeth sat near the fire in her sitting room, trying to remain busy surveying the post and household ledgers. She acknowledged that Darcy was a very active master, frequently discussing business with his steward or visiting his tenants. It was admirable, but left him with little time for her, even if he wished to be in her company.

Elizabeth had yet to meet any compatible young ladies in the neighbourhood, but still retained a sliver of hope that, among the families she had not yet met, she would find at least one lady who could fill the role of friend, since it clearly was not a position her sister-in-law wished to hold.

Careful, Lizzy. That sounds too much like bitterness. Who can foresee what the future holds? As Jane would say, you must remain open to the possibilities. Perhaps in time...

Her letters were of the usual variety. There were several from members of Darcy's family, two notes from neighbours, and two from Longbourn—one from Jane and one from Mrs Bennet. She had not heard from her father since leaving Longbourn, even after she wrote to tell him she was well and to describe the libraries in her new homes.

She quickly read through her mother's letter, which was full of the usual gossip and complaints. Only one part drew Elizabeth's close attention.

I have been calculating, and the six months your father has insisted must pass before any of us visit you will be over in February. I do not understand why you and your father concocted such a ridiculous scheme. You have no compassion on my nerves; neither of you do! To be separated from my daughter for so long and at a time when I could be of so much use, for what do you know about being a wife or mistress of a great house? And what if you should fall with child? You must write me immediately when you suspect you are! I hope for your sake that you are not cursed with only daughters as I was. If I had a son, your father would have been much kinder to me. Mr Darcy will expect a son, Lizzy. Do not forget!

"Yes, Mama. Although I fear I shall be unable to give him a child until he decides he can bear my company long enough to conceive one." Elizabeth felt dreadfully vulgar for having voiced such a sentiment. "Perhaps as vulgar as Lady Romsley believes me to be!"

She did not want Darcy to demand his rights to her person, and yet the issue of consummation hung over her like an axe. It would happen sooner or later, and until it did, she was forever wary of Darcy's mood, of how he looked at her in the evening, of any suggestion or hint that he intended to choose that night to knock on her door after they retired.

February will surely find you in London. It will be nothing for you to have one or two of your sisters with you. The others can join you later in the spring. Jane must certainly go. She is sure to catch the eye of some very fine gentlemen. Viscount Bramwell was quite taken with her, and you can see that they are often in company. He could do a lot worse than Jane as a wife. By rights Mary should go, and I am doing what I can to prepare her, but you know your sister! She has no interest in improving her looks. She vexes me greatly. Perhaps it would be best to leave her at Longbourn to keep your father company, and I could bring Jane, Lydia, and Kitty with me. Chaperoning them would be too much for you, so I shall come along to do it for you. Besides, you do not have a mother's eye; you do not know how to promote the interests of your child with eligible gentlemen.

Elizabeth knew that her mother's plans would come to naught; Mr Darcy would never agree to have any of the Bennets visit, not for an hour, let alone for weeks.

DARCY ALSO SPENT PART OF THAT MORNING PERUSING LETTERS FROM family. John Darcy reported on Horatia's recent visit to them. His aunt had not been complimentary when describing Elizabeth. With such a beginning, Elizabeth would find it difficult to earn his family's favour. Lord Romsley wrote and demanded a detailed account of how he and Elizabeth were getting on. He complained, yet again, about Sterling's refusal to discuss remarrying. Darcy suspected Sterling wanted some assurance that his second marriage would be happy, since his first one had not been. Lastly, he read Tom's letter.

Georgiana writes to me diligently. Her letters suggest that she is much restored to her former spirits, and that she is keeping up with her studies. I would like to hear your thoughts on this. Ease my mind by writing that she is happier, that she understands her folly at Ramsgate and has put it into the past.

She does not mention Mrs Darcy. Despite their differences in experience and character, I retain hope they will learn to like each other.

Tom's words reminded Darcy that he still did not understand the state of affairs between his sister and wife. He heard no complaints and so assumed all was well, even as his conscience told him he should gather more direct knowledge. He resolved that, as he continued to study Elizabeth's behaviour, he would discover how she was treating his sister.

Chapter 9

More and more, Elizabeth caught Darcy staring at her or demanding to know what she was doing. He watched as she talked to Mrs Reynolds and asked to whom she was writing. He even insisted on reading a letter she addressed to his aunt Susan. After church one Sunday, he stood some ten feet away and watched as she exchanged words with their neighbours. At breakfast just that morning, he had questioned her closely on the books he had recently found her taking from the library. They had had a lengthy conversation—in French—about the de Humboldt tome. Their food had gone cold, and Georgiana had looked ready to fall asleep at the table, before Darcy had said, "Well, I am glad you found it so instructive. Your French is much better than I expected, although your accent could use a little improvement. You and Georgiana should practise speaking together."

Elizabeth had gone for a long walk afterwards. "He is looking to find fault and it is just as well that my courage is strong," she muttered when she was some distance from the house. How she wished she had Jane or Aunt Gardiner to talk to rather than the wind and whatever animals were lurking about. "I would be afraid to say a single word, otherwise. I must disregard his behaviour and continue as I have started. With time, my efforts will be rewarded."

She prayed she would earn his respect—respect for her efforts, her intelligence, and her judgment. Perhaps then Darcy would trust her enough to allow her the freedom to see the Gardiners and maybe even have Jane stay with her for a time.

During her walks, Elizabeth quickly realised that, given the estate's extent, she would need to ride or drive to visit the tenants easily and to explore parts of the park. She would start with riding, although she had done little of it in recent years and lacked proper attire. She might ask to learn to drive a small vehicle in the future.

I wonder if I should tell Lady Romsley that she forgot to ensure my wardrobe included riding clothes? She laughed when she imagined how the countess would react to such impertinence, then sighed. *Oh, for someone I could tease without risking their censure!*

DARCY SAT IN HIS STUDY AND WONDERED WHERE ELIZABETH WAS. Perhaps playing, as she seemed to do daily? Or was she in her sitting room, bent over his mother's rather ghastly maple desk, writing letters? For several minutes, Darcy looked at his book. Then he studied the fawn and white striped walls and glossy mahogany furniture. He stood and walked back and forth, rearranging several items which had caught his attention as they seemed out of place. At last, he admitted he would not be happy until he saw Elizabeth. It was ridiculous, a sentiment he repeated with each step he took towards the seldom used pink music room.

He found her bent over the instrument, her bottom lip between her teeth. Watching from the doorway, he was struck by a new realisation: she was quite pretty. Her dark hair contrasted attractively with her fine, smooth skin, to which the deep rose of her gown added warmth.

After a few minutes, she did something she never had before: she sang. All thought emptied from Darcy's mind. Her voice was lovely —light, clear, inviting.

She truly was very handsome. How had he never noticed? And the way her neck gave way to…

As the sound of the last note faded away, Darcy turned abruptly and quickly returned to his study where several important letters awaited his attention.

ELIZABETH BEGAN HER MORNING OUTING BY CALLING ON MRS AND Miss Simms. The consequence was that she found herself sitting in an extremely uncomfortable room, occasionally sipping a glass of barley water that was too bland to be enjoyable. The Simmses were one of Pemberley's nearest neighbours, although Mr Simms's estate was nothing to Darcy's. Miss Martha Simms was three and twenty, not especially attractive, and inclined to stoutness.

"It is astonishing to me that you and Mr Darcy should have met at all," Mrs Simms said. "He spends so much of his time in London when he is not in Derbyshire, and yet you say you have been there little? And not during the Season?"

Her voice rose at least an octave at the end of each unwelcome question, a habit which Elizabeth found excessively irritating.

"No, not at all," Elizabeth replied.

Miss Simms sniffled.

"He is with his relatives a great deal, but it was not through them that you met?"

Goodness, how do they know so much about how he spends his time? A quick glance at Miss Simms provided the answer. No doubt the Simmses had hoped that such knowledge would somehow increase the likelihood of a match with Miss Simms. *I trust Martha Simms is not the sort of young lady he would have chosen as his wife. It would show remarkably poor taste.* "I did not know any of them before I met Mr Darcy."

"I absolutely adore London!" Miss Simms said. "We go every year. It is so surprising to me that your parents did not take you. You have sisters, I believe?"

Elizabeth had had the same conversation with Mrs and Miss Simms when they called on her previously, and her tolerance for it was waning quickly. "One older and three younger."

"Your elder sister is not married?" Mrs Simms asked.

"No."

Mrs Simms shook her head and pursed her lips.

"I am even more shocked that your family does not try the Season. But, perhaps, they cannot…" Miss Simms said.

Elizabeth finished Miss Simms' sentence for her, silently thinking, *afford it*. "My father does not like London." Elizabeth kept her voice level and polite but did manage to convey her displeasure. She stood, placed her almost full glass upon the side table, and took her leave. "I must return to Pemberley before I am missed too greatly."

Elizabeth hoped that Miss Simms would receive a thorough scolding for her impolite behaviour. There was only so much of her and her mother's scorn that Elizabeth would tolerate. After all, the Simmses were not part of her new family.

ELIZABETH GRATEFULLY STEPPED INTO THE SOLITUDE OF THE FINE coach. Sinking into the grey velvet seat, she threw her reticule to the bench across from her and closed her eyes. She had known the visit would be unpleasant, but politeness dictated that she return the Simmses' call. She appreciated the opportunity to be away from Pemberley for a time, too. Despite her parting words, she knew very well that no one there had missed her. When she had said she would be paying calls that morning, Darcy had only nodded and continued his habit of watching her as she ate. *Perhaps he disapproves of the way I butter my muffins or finds I am overly loud when I sip my coffee.*

She had asked Georgiana if she would join her, but Georgiana replied with a brisk, 'No,' turning her back to Elizabeth. Elizabeth imagined what she would like to say in light of Georgiana's latest dismissiveness but held her tongue. She knew that in any disagreement between them, it would be Georgiana who garnered her brother's sympathy and *she* who received his censure.

Elizabeth's next call was to Mr Llewellyn. She wished to ask his opinion on any people in the neighbourhood who would benefit from her charity, especially as the cold season approached. To her delight, he did not hesitate to reply openly. Elizabeth listened carefully, considering the possibilities of what she could do, if it met with her husband's approval. Mr Llewellyn mentioned one family who required immediate intervention, and Elizabeth would act, willing to accept any chastisement Darcy later imposed. Regarding the grander plans they discussed, such as a children's school, she would tread with more care.

As she returned to Pemberley, Elizabeth reflected on her interview with satisfaction. Mr Llewellyn was a pleasant gentleman, well-spoken and informed. Their conversation had been, despite the sad nature of some of it, a far easier one than any she had had since coming into Derbyshire.

Darcy took advantage of the fair weather and investigated work being done in several parts of his estate. Elizabeth's image danced in his mind and distracted him, occasionally at inopportune moments. Her individual features might not be remarkable, but the way they came together certainly created a lovely, enticing whole.

The feeling she aroused in him was strange. No purpose was served in reminding himself of the many reasons he should dislike Elizabeth. Yet, was it so bad that he did feel an attraction to her person? No. It was good, if for no reason other than the necessity to sire an heir. It might be just a fleeting desire, but it meant he could let nature have its way rather than force himself to tolerate intimacy with her for as long as it took to ensure he had his heir and, if possible, two or three other children.

As Darcy returned home, he saw Elizabeth's carriage approaching. He steered his horse towards it, dismounting as Elizabeth stepped down.

"Mrs Darcy." He handed his horse to one of the grooms.

Elizabeth said his name and gave him a small, quick smile.

They made their way towards the house, but before they could enter, Elizabeth stopped.

"It is such a fine day. I believe I shall take a walk. There is nothing pressing requiring my attention."

"That is a wonderful idea." He gestured for her to lead the way, and they headed towards the lake. "Upon whom did you call?"

"Mrs Simms and her daughter."

Darcy shuddered. He tolerated Mrs and Miss Simms because he had to. The Simmses had been neighbours of Pemberley's for several generations and were of sufficient consequence to warrant his attention.

"After that, I went to the parsonage to see Mr Llewellyn."

"Llewellyn? For what purpose?"

She explained. Her desire to be involved in charitable works, without any prompting from him, was unexpected.

"You must realise there is no need," he said. "Llewellyn knows that he can discuss any concerns he has with me. Or with Potter or Mrs Reynolds."

Elizabeth averted her eyes, the rim of her bonnet hiding her face. Darcy sensed that she was upset by his words.

He surprised himself by explaining, "I...I did not think you would do such a thing. Not without direction."

The earnest, even eager, expression on her face when she looked at him threw his thoughts into confusion.

"Surely you do not disapprove? I must have some occupation! I have always felt that the ladies of the family should take an interest in the neighbourhood. Jane and I have long done what we could for my father's tenants and those who may, through no fault of their own, find themselves in need of assistance. There is much that can be done not only to alleviate immediate suffering, but to improve the lives of those who are less fortunate. I have simply sought information. I would not do more without your permission, of course."

Darcy was not attending to her words. He was rendered speechless by the passion with which she spoke. He had never appreciated how expressive her eyes could be.

Desire. At that moment, looking into her eyes, framed so magnificently by her dark brows and hair, the gentle curve of her cheeks, her lips so pink and soft, the attraction he had occasionally felt for her coalesced into a powerful surge of desire.

It was most disconcerting.

Elizabeth turned on her heel and walked away. He followed a moment later.

She stopped on a bridge set over a stream. Darcy stood several feet from her and observed as she removed her bonnet and tilted her chin up to the sky. A strand of hair which had escaped its bondage captured his attention. It marred the picture she made, her slender

82

figure wrapped in fine blue cloth, the features of her face silhouetted by the greens and browns of the trees. He stepped forward, pulled off a glove, reached out, and brushed the hair aside, his bare fingers skating across her cheek.

Elizabeth turned to face him. Their eyes fixed on each other's, and, for an instant, it was as though the world, his heart—everything—stood still, waiting for something more to happen.

She began to move away from him, slowly taking one step then another; he was powerless to stop her.

Darcy shook his head and struggled to regain his composure. Elizabeth was twenty or thirty feet ahead of him when he began to walk. It was not difficult to catch up to her, and they continued, side-by-side, in silence, back to the house.

THAT NIGHT, ELIZABETH DWELLED ON THE SENSATION OF DARCY'S warm, firm fingers on her cheek. Their entire walk had been surprising and distressing. She had wanted to enjoy the grounds for a time before facing the lonely cavern of the house. When she was inside, she often felt that she could disappear, and no one would notice she was gone. Outside, the beauty of nature surrounding her, her feelings were less oppressive.

She could not be comfortable with Darcy by her side, yet she had vowed to be receptive to his overtures when he made them and so accepted his company with equanimity. When he dismissed her desire to be active in the neighbourhood, it had been a blow. She had walked away from him before she said something she would later regret.

Oh, how she tried not to give in to disagreeable feelings and thoughts! Seeing Mr Llewellyn had been uplifting. She could do so much good as Mrs Darcy, and, in making a difference to the lives of those less fortunate than she was, she would find satisfaction. But if Darcy did not want his wife to be involved in such activities, if he felt he could not trust her to not disgrace him, or that she should use her time otherwise, what could she do? She could not go against his wishes. He was her husband, and if she hoped to ever earn any measure of his respect, she had to abide by his decisions.

When he had touched her on the bridge, it was as though the

world stopped. For that instant, she felt her loneliness lift. It was the first sign of what could pass for affection she had experienced in weeks. It gave her a tiny glimpse of what Mrs Gardiner had told her—that in the marriage act there could be pleasure without love, that despite the awful beginnings of her marriage, there could be some good—more than what a child represented—to be found in intimacy.

She knew that her husband did not harbour tender feelings for her—or even like her—so that had not been why he touched her. Perhaps it had been an unconscious gesture. Or perhaps he was attempting to tell her that she should prepare herself to receive him as a wife must receive her husband. If this were so, then she suspected such gestures would be repeated in the coming days.

The sensation of being cared for, even knowing it was fictitious, was alluring, and given how lonely and distressed Elizabeth had been almost since the night she first met Darcy, she longed to feel it again.

Chapter 10

"r and Miss Haddon will be here in time for breakfast," Darcy said one evening a few days later.

"Yes," Elizabeth replied.

Georgiana sat across the room with her nose in a novel and ignored them. Elizabeth held her needlework while, across from her, Darcy sat with a book in his hand.

Upon questioning, Elizabeth summarised the arrangements for the visit. The Haddons, who lived fifteen miles away, would be with them for the day. "I am looking forward to meeting Miss Haddon. Georgiana, I hope, will join us for part of the day."

Darcy gave a curt nod. Robert Haddon was one of his closest friends. He wanted the visit to go well. "Georgiana, Elizabeth said that she hopes you will join her and Miss Haddon tomorrow. You should. You need not be working all morning, every morning."

Georgiana nodded without lifting her eyes from her book.

Darcy moved to sit beside Elizabeth. "What are you working on?"

Elizabeth placed her needle in a secure location and handed him the square of linen. "New handkerchiefs."

Darcy saw an unfinished cluster of neat leaves and a partially completed copper beech leaf in one corner and the initials ED in another. It was simple and elegant, and he rather liked it. "Very pretty." He returned the square to her. "Have you considered what you might do with Miss Haddon tomorrow?"

As they talked about the next day, Elizabeth returned to her work. Darcy watched her hands and wondered what it would feel like to have those fingers, the ones which could undertake such careful work or play the pianoforte with so much emotion, dance across his skin.

He abruptly stood and went to sit in another corner of the room. As inclined as he was to stoke the fire of his attraction to Elizabeth, it was too much, too quickly. He would not rush into a physical relationship with her. She was likely in daily expectation of receiving his attentions, but this desire was new to him, and he required more time to become comfortable with it.

THE HADDONS ARRIVED IN GOOD TIME, AND THE USUAL GREETINGS and introductions were made.

"Mrs Darcy," Mr Haddon said affably, "it is truly a pleasure to meet you."

"My brother speaks for both of us," Miss Haddon added. "We wish you both every joy."

Georgiana managed to hide her disgust at seeing Elizabeth so warmly welcomed. Fitzwilliam had reminded her that morning that she would have to spend time with Elizabeth and Miss Haddon. It would not be easy to act as though she was pleased with her brother's marriage when she hated Elizabeth. She did not much like Miss Haddon either; her family was not wealthy or connected enough to be a proper companion for Miss Darcy of Pemberley.

Once they had taken breakfast, the gentlemen went off to enjoy the outdoors. Georgiana excused herself, citing a wish to finish 'one or two things,' and promised to join the ladies for a walk in two hours. That would be long enough to finish the novel she was reading. She had read it several times before and had been forced to stop at a most exciting part when Fitzwilliam came to talk to her earlier. If she had time, she supposed she might look into the history book he had given her to read, too.

DARCY WAS HAPPY TO SEE HADDON AGAIN AND QUITE PLEASED WITH how easily Elizabeth had welcomed his friends. She looked particularly well this morning, in a yellow gown that enhanced her loveliness. As they sat together before breakfast, light from the window had created highlights in her hair, adding a shimmer which made it look soft and inviting. The only jewellery she wore was a plain necklace upon which hung a yellow topaz cross. He prayed the day continued to go well and that the Haddons accepted Elizabeth. If it did not, he would have to question his growing regard, and that would be a pity.

"I am not terribly surprised you kept her a secret, but come, Darcy, confess it all without making me beat it out of you!" With these words, Haddon cuffed him on the shoulder.

Darcy knew his friend did not yet know about the gossip that began in Ramsgate; if he did, he would have said something. He would hear it eventually, and Darcy could only hope to make Haddon believe the false story he and the Bennets had concocted about how he and Elizabeth had met.

After Darcy was finished with his tale, Haddon said, "You never can tell who you will love."

"I admit she was...an unconventional choice for me. That it was unexpected, and one or two other circumstances, led to some...talk."

"Gossip?"

"It originated in Ramsgate, and all too quickly made its way to London."

"Was it serious?"

Darcy nodded, and, in as few words as possible, explained.

"Your poor wife! How distressing! And you and Miss Darcy—I can only imagine how well the Romsleys liked it. It will all have faded into memory by now, and, if it has not, it will next winter when you are in London and people see that you are happy, and that Mrs Darcy is an excellent woman."

"I hope so."

"Come. Let us speak of happier matters, such as the fine day and the excellent sport we shall have!"

"THE WEATHER IS SO LOVELY," ELIZABETH SAID. "IT WOULD BE A shame not to take advantage of it. We shall have an excellent walk with Miss Darcy later."

Miss Haddon agreed, and she and Elizabeth made themselves comfortable to talk and get to know each other.

"I am glad to meet you. We would have come sooner, but, as you know, we are only just returned from seeing my mother's people in Scotland."

Elizabeth nodded. What little she had learnt about the Haddons had come from asking her husband about them when he was in a mood to answer her.

"I have been very curious about you. No doubt, you have had it said to you before today!"

"Yes." Elizabeth smiled politely and took a small sip of her juice.

"There has been a great deal of speculation these last years regarding who Mr Darcy would marry. Some even thought that, given the long friendship between our families, he would consider me. I did not expect it. Darcy men have always chosen their brides from wealthy, titled families and there was no reason to suppose your Mr Darcy would do otherwise. I am not rich enough, or titled, as old and respectable as my family is. No doubt you will encounter many ladies or their mothers who believe they had a greater claim to Mr Darcy than you did. Have you met his friend Mr Bingley?"

"Yes."

"And Bingley's sisters?"

"No."

"He has two," Miss Haddon explained. "The younger remains unmarried and wanted, perhaps even expected, to be Mrs Darcy. It is safe to say that everyone other than Miss Bingley knew she was unlikely to receive an offer from him. Her fortune is greater than mine, as she has kindly informed me, but her connexions are not as good. Their father worked—some commercial enterprise I believe—until Mr Bingley was five or six. Your husband may not mind that in a friend, but in a wife…" She shook her head. "She and Miss Darcy are friends."

Elizabeth struggled to maintain her part of the conversation. Miss Haddon did not think Elizabeth worthy of being Darcy's wife and did not mind if Elizabeth knew her opinion. Elizabeth was disappointed and certain that, as much as Mr Haddon and Darcy were intimate friends, she and Miss Haddon could never be.

WHILE THE LADIES TOOK THEIR WALK, MISS HADDON ATTEMPTED TO engage Georgiana in conversation and Elizabeth left them to it. She was content to give her attention to the surroundings and study the progress the beech trees had made in turning their leaves copper in preparation for the winter and the yellow and red leaves the oaks had dropped and which now rested on the still green lawn, awaiting collection by the gardeners. Soon after returning indoors, Georgiana excused herself, citing her studies.

Once they were alone, Miss Haddon turned to Elizabeth and, with some hesitation, said, "It is none of my concern, but…you and Georgiana do not seem—When I was talking with her, she was very…"

Elizabeth felt compelled to offer some explanation. "I am afraid we are not yet good friends. The change in her life—her brother being married and being made to live at Pemberley with us—has not been an easy one for her."

"I have sometimes worried that she is a little too proud of the Darcy name. It could make her less-than-welcoming to—"

"Those she feels are not her equals," Elizabeth said. She averted her eyes, mortified by her impolitic words.

"I am afraid a great many people would fit that description. Including me."

Elizabeth regarded her companion, and they seemed to share a momentary understanding. She introduced a new topic of conversation, which lasted until they separated to prepare for dinner.

IT WAS ONE OF THE LIVELIER MEALS ELIZABETH HAD HAD SINCE HER marriage. The Haddons shared tales of youthful exploits involving

Darcy and the resulting, often very amusing, consequences. Georgiana even added her voice to the conversation. Elizabeth laughed two or three times and thought that it felt remarkably good to do so once again.

The Haddons left directly after dinner. Georgiana received permission to go to her rooms, offering a vague excuse about a letter to Tom.

Elizabeth felt uncommonly nervous being alone with Darcy. It had been like that since their moment on the bridge. "Y-you and Mr Haddon had an enjoyable visit I gather."

"We did. You and Miss Haddon got along, I trust? Your day was pleasant?"

"Quite."

He was sitting across from her and seemed content to stare at her, which only enhanced Elizabeth's discomfort. Was he waiting for a sign from her that she wished for more of his attention? He could not doubt that she would accept him. She had done all she could to show that she wanted to be a good wife and mistress; that necessarily included giving him children. When his eyes drifted to her topaz cross, she wished she had a wrap with her that she could use to cover herself.

"There are one or two matters I wished to discuss with you. Perhaps now is as good a time as any."

"Yes?" He finished his tea, stood, and handed her his cup, which she placed on the tray as he took a seat beside her.

"It has occurred to me that…" *Oh, it would be so much easier to talk to him if he did not stare so severely!* She cleared her throat and began again. "In Hertfordshire, I could walk wherever I needed to go."

"That will not be possible here."

"In my experience, the tenants, especially the women, appreciate the ladies of the estate calling to listen to their concerns and provide what advice and assistance they can. To visit some of your tenants, I must—"

"You will need a horse. Did you ride much in Hertfordshire, or do you need—"

"A little," she admitted, but had no time to explain as he continued.

"A little. Hmm. I will speak to Maudsley, the stable master, tomorrow."

"I have ordered riding clothes from London. I will not be able to do anything until they arrive."

Darcy nodded. "You must always bring a groom with you when you ride. Potter or Mrs Reynolds will know which families would most benefit from your attention."

"I-I-I have spoken to Mrs Reynolds." Her voice faltered as Darcy narrowed the gap between them. "About preparing baskets for Christmas."

Darcy nodded again. "Do as you like." He reached out and, with the tip of one finger, touched the cross. "This is lovely. I have not seen it before."

Elizabeth's breath caught in her throat. She remained as still as possible, wondering if he would touch her. He did, his fingers skating across her cheek, from her ear, along her jaw and down her neck to her shoulder and across to the edge of her gown. He leaned in until his nose was near her ear, and she felt the softest of kisses on her neck. She involuntarily jumped, her body recoiling at such an unfamiliar sensation, and Darcy's much larger body falling towards hers.

"Forgive me, forgive me." She struggled to catch her breath. Her embarrassment drove her to her feet, and she took several steps to put distance between them. "It—I was quite warm so close to the fire."

Darcy stood and turned away from Elizabeth. Out of the corner of her eye, she watched as he sat in another part of the room and opened a book. She thought she saw his jaw tighten, and he turned the page rather violently, but he did not speak to or look at her. After several minutes, Elizabeth returned to the sofa.

Chapter 11

The next day, Elizabeth paid calls, the first of which was to Miss Pratt, a lady who had once had some consequence, but, upon the death of her father, had been reduced to poverty. Miss Pratt was constantly agitated and spoke more than any other person Elizabeth had ever met. Little of what she said was interesting. Elizabeth felt a great deal of sympathy for her circumstances. Miss Pratt's life was an example of what would have befallen her, her mother, and her sisters upon Mr Bennet's death had she not married Mr Darcy.

I suppose even an unhappy marriage is better than no marriage for a lady in my position. But, oh, it is so—No, none of that, Lizzy! You must keep on and trust that in time your efforts will be rewarded.

After seeing Miss Pratt, Elizabeth paid two calls of charity and two calls to estates neighbouring Pemberley. She felt more herself and satisfied during the former; the latter left her playing a part, doing what was necessary without expecting or receiving any pleasure.

Upon returning to Pemberley, she attended to letters, including one from Lady Romsley.

Elizabeth,
I trust this finds you, my nephew, and my niece well.

The visit from my nephew's Darcy relations is <u>very quickly</u> <u>approaching</u> and you must prepare carefully for it. I am not sure you appreciate how <u>very much</u> it would be to your benefit should you acquit yourself well—or how disastrous should you fail. Knowing you are not accustomed to making such arrangements, I have given it some thought. First...

Lady Romsley's advice would have been more appreciated had it been given with less haughtiness.

Elizabeth replied to the letter after dinner, assuring the countess that everything was being attended to and, yes, she had studied the Darcy family so that she could name them all, &c.

"I am looking forward to them arriving, and I suspect I will then immediately be anticipating their departure," she murmured. "I, who have so enjoyed the company of others, am now dreading it. How did my life come to this?"

GEORGIANA WAS SURPRISED WHEN HER BROTHER APPEARED IN HER sitting room one morning. She believed him to be gone from the house until dinner.

He explained, "I was with Mr Llewellyn. He spoke very kindly about Elizabeth. She has been making calls of charity and is interested in our scheme for a school. But enough about that. I was hoping to convince you to set aside your studies for a short while. We have had little time together of late."

"Of course." Georgiana turned her back to her brother, ostensibly to arrange her books. She did not particularly mind that they had had little time together; his lack of oversight meant she could do as she liked rather than as he wished. She sat and smiled prettily. He also sat, and she thought he looked droll in one of the painted-wood and pink velvet chairs she had chosen when the room was refurbished two years earlier.

"What were you reading when I came in?" he asked.

"I-I was… I am working on French today. I owe Tom a letter." It was the easiest explanation and one she used too frequently when she knew she could not admit to reading a novel or looking through her wardrobe. She felt her mouth slipping into a scowl—she resented having to account for her time constantly—and forced her expression into one of pleasure at seeing him. "It is perhaps a little slow, but I find it helpful and enjoyable."

Her brother hesitated before saying, "Very well."

One or two questions about her other studies led to many more when she could not answer the first with any great accuracy. History was such a bore, and she had hardly looked at Italian in days. Try as she might, her brother must see how little she had learnt since their return to Pemberley, and in the end, Fitzwilliam insisted he would take a more active role in overseeing her education.

"My expectations are not unreasonable, Georgiana. I do not wish you to be buried in books all day. You need to take exercise and perhaps…offer your assistance to Elizabeth. She is making an effort to learn her duties as mistress of this estate. You could help her and, in the process, understand more about the duties of a mistress yourself."

"Yes, Brother." Georgiana spoke softly and bowed her head.

He took one of her hands in his. "It is now almost three months since…since we were in Ramsgate. We are all concerned for your happiness. It was deeply distressing and has had… No. There is no need to discuss what has come of it."

Georgiana stiffened at the allusion to his marriage. She pulled her hand from his, stood, and walked away.

"Georgiana." His voice was equal parts firm and sympathetic.

"I do not wish to discuss it. I trusted someone I should not have, and I can assure you that I have learnt my lesson."

"Perhaps you would be more comfortable discussing this with a lady. Lady Romsley—"

Georgiana shuddered; her aunt was excessively severe.

"One of our other aunts?"

Georgiana brushed aside the heavy damask drapes at her window and feigned interest in the view.

"No, perhaps not. You would have to reveal what happened, and it is best that as few people know as possible. Elizabeth. She is here, and she knows and understands as well as anyone can."

Georgiana turned to stare at him. How could he, of all people, think it was possible that she and his wife would ever be on such terms of intimacy?

"She is your sister, Georgiana. I am making an effort to know her, and you must as well."

She schooled her features, which took considerable effort. "Yes, Brother."

She was very pleased and relieved when he kissed the top of her head and left her alone.

IN HIS STUDY, DARCY FOUND IT DIFFICULT TO ATTEND TO HIS correspondence. His thoughts wandered to the other evening, after the Haddons' visit, when he and Elizabeth had been alone. She had looked so lovely and tempting. He had wanted—*needed*—to touch her, to feel her, to confirm that she was as soft and warm as she looked. Her scent was that of vanilla and jasmine and, before he knew it, he went from thinking that it would be nothing to brush his lips against her skin, to actually kissing her neck. He had been driven by desire and being so free of his customary restraint was not to his liking.

It is just as well we have not been alone since.

Hudson had told him that Elizabeth was returned from paying calls. She was not in her sitting room; Darcy had walked past it not half an hour earlier and heard nothing to indicate she was within.

She must be at the pianoforte.

He could go to her. It was his house, and she was his wife. If he wished to seek her out, there was no reason he should not.

It would be better than sitting here unable to work. I could...talk to her, not just listen. Ask what she is learning, why she only plays there.

He was walking towards the east wing before the thought was finished.

Elizabeth was at the instrument. He could not make his feet carry him into the room, and watched from the door, entranced yet again by the sight of her. Lost in thought, he did not notice when the music ended, and she stood and turned towards him.

"Oh!" she exclaimed. One hand flew to her chest. "I did not know you were there."

Darcy nodded and walked away before he even realised what he was doing.

THE NEXT DAY, ELIZABETH AND DARCY DINED AT THE MORRISES'. Recently retired from the navy, Admiral Morris had leased a nearby estate to determine how he and Mrs Morris liked the neighbourhood. Elizabeth found Mrs Morris to be affable. The other guests included Miss Pratt, the Simmses, and Mr Llewellyn, along with two other families with whom Elizabeth was less familiar. The Darcys were the last to arrive, and they soon went through to dinner.

Elizabeth did her utmost to forget that Darcy was watching her so closely. His expression was inscrutable, and it made her nervous. *How I wish he would stop staring at me. Courage, Lizzy, and confidence. You are doing nothing wrong, and he will have to admit it sooner or later. Perhaps not tonight, but by the time you are, oh, forty or fifty!*

She imagined him as an old man—greying and bent with age—grudgingly agreeing that she was not so very terrible and then her hitting him with her walking stick. Lifting her napkin to her mouth, she hid the resulting smile. *A little humour does so restore the spirit! Would that I—No, Lizzy, only happy thoughts when you are in company!*

After the separation of the sexes and tea, the two young single ladies of their party, Miss Hughes and Miss Simms, played for the company. Elizabeth declined to take a turn at the instrument. When they had exhibited sufficiently, conversation began once again. The atmosphere was easy, Darcy looked content, and Elizabeth was satisfied that the evening was a success.

With this thought in mind, she was particularly affected by Miss Simms's next words.

"Mama and I have been speaking about how enjoyable tonight's gathering has been. We have almost decided upon a date for our own party. Mrs Darcy, it is so strange that you have not done any entertaining at Pemberley! Such a grand house, absolutely meant for enter-taining! But perhaps you are not...?" Miss Simms let her words drift off, not brave, or foolish, enough to complete her sentence.

Elizabeth was angered and hurt that the young woman felt free to say such a thing in front of so many people, as though certain they would understand and agree with her sentiments. She was too shocked to know how to respond and was saved the trouble of doing so when Mr Simms cried, "Martha!"

Darcy approached Elizabeth, holding out his hand. "Mrs Morris, you will not object if I take Mrs Darcy on a short turn in your garden?"

Elizabeth allowed her husband to lead her outside. Did he wish to remove her from an uncomfortable situation, sending a message that he understood the insult and would not tolerate it? Or did he expect her to say or do something improper in response? She certainly wanted to give Miss Simms a setdown she would not soon forget.

The night was clear, but cool. Elizabeth shivered and wrapped her arms around her body. In a moment, she felt Darcy drape his coat over her shoulders. It was heavy and comforting. At the same time, having him so close to her, with no one else around and the darkness overtaking the evening, made Elizabeth's heart beat hard and fast, and her hands trembled. She whispered, "Thank you."

"We shall not remain much longer."

Elizabeth nodded and wished he would say something which would tell her that he was disgusted with Miss Simms, not with her. Clutching his coat more tightly to her body, she said, "Perhaps it will be possible to see the stars tonight. With all the rain we have had, I have not seen them since..." *Since having to marry you and leaving what had been my home.*

"Do you like to watch the stars?"

"Yes. My father taught me the constellations. When I was perhaps two or three years younger than Georgiana is, I became quite fasci-nated with the theories of astrology."

"Astrology? Surely you do not believe—"

"No," Elizabeth hastened to add. "I do not believe the position of the stars determines what happens in our lives, but the idea behind it was diverting. I spent the whole winter reading everything I possibly could. The following year I decided I should learn something about astronomy as well, but I did not find it as engaging." She shivered as a light breeze washed over them.

"Come," said Darcy, and led her back to the house.

When they entered the saloon, everyone fell silent, and Elizabeth's cheeks burned. They had been talking about her. She left Darcy to say their farewells; she managed to smile and curtsey as demanded by the dictates of polite behaviour, but she could not speak.

Darcy sat beside Elizabeth in the carriage on the return to Pemberley. As they approached the house, he picked up one of her hands and traced the length of her fingers. His touch was soothing and light through their gloves, almost like a feather sweeping across her skin. It helped to draw Elizabeth away from her cynical reflections on the evening. She would cling to these feelings as necessary, use the moments of his approval to fortify her against the slurs and slights of others. It did not matter that they were based on nothing more than his appreciation for her in a physical sense and had no goal other than behaving as a man does towards his wife.

"I would have liked to hear you play tonight."

Elizabeth shook her head. "Miss Simms and Miss Hughes have attended to their lessons far better than I ever did."

Once inside, Darcy led Elizabeth into the drawing room and offered her a glass of wine. "Have you called on Mrs Simms often?"

"Three or four times, I believe."

"I see them rarely in London. We do not frequent the same society."

Not knowing how else to respond, Elizabeth nodded.

Darcy stood and aimlessly walked around the room, picking up this trinket and that. He stopped at the doors which opened to the gardens, pushed aside the silk curtains and looked out. "Elizabeth, come."

She joined him, and they stepped out onto the terrace. Darcy shrugged out of his coat, once again gently draping it over her shoulders.

"Look." He pointed upward.

The sky was alit with stars. The beauty of it brought a sense of peace to Elizabeth, and she smiled.

Darcy placed his hands on either side of her face, his thumbs, warm against her cool skin, gently caressing. When his lips pressed to hers the next moment, Elizabeth let go of the breath she had been holding. She had sensed his disquiet since they returned to Pemberley, and for it to end this way, with this display of approval or acceptance —or perhaps simply desire—was a profound relief. The tenderness of his touch was a calming balm, erasing, for the moment, her injured feelings and her loneliness.

Chapter 12

The post arrived before breakfast the next morning bringing with it a letter from Jane. Elizabeth read it at once, two or three parts drawing her particular attention.

My father is well in body, but his spirits continue to be low. I believe he misses you more than he will admit. I know you and he were not on the best of terms when you left, but I am convinced that his mood was born of his concern for your well-being.

Elizabeth had no patience for her father's 'mood.' His behaviour since that dreadful night at Ramsgate had caused her too much heartache.

Netherfield Park is let at last to a married couple named Linnington. I like them very much and I am convinced they will be charming neighbours. My mother would have preferred a single man, the reason why you can imagine, although she has great hopes that they will often have houseguests.

Jane had added a passage after her adieu, the words crowded into the little that had been left of the page.

Lizzy, my dearest sister, please write to me without the disguise I know you usually employ. I am terribly worried about you. If you need me, I will come, regardless of my father's wishes. I am not afraid of his anger or of making the journey on my own.

Elizabeth cared nothing for her father's edict that no Bennet visit her for six months. What prevented her from begging Jane to get to Derbyshire by whatever means she could was Darcy. While she longed to see Jane, her situation was tolerable. There were moments when it was very difficult. While she was lonely, she was not desperate; she could manage without Jane. Seeking Darcy's permission for her sister to visit would not end well. Even if he could be prevailed upon to agree, he would be unhappy about it. The relationship between them was improving, and she could not risk damaging the fragile state in which they now lived.

AFTER BREAKFAST, SHE REPLIED TO JANE'S LETTER, WRITING AS cheerful a response as she could. When she was finished, her thoughts wandered to the kiss she and Darcy had shared. It was so tender and yet so undeniably a kiss meant to convey *something*, and she suspected that something was her husband's desire that they be a true man and wife. The thought did not disturb Elizabeth as much as it had even a month earlier. She was becoming used to him and knew that he was not vicious or cruel. The way he kissed and caressed her might be his means of letting her get accustomed to the idea of consummating their marriage.

The kiss. It had lasted for an unknown amount of time before simply ending. They had spoken about the stars for a moment before seeking the warmth of the fire. Although she was tired, she did not attempt to excuse herself, not knowing if he had further expectations of her. He must have noticed her trying to cover a yawn, however, because, after some little time, he sent her off to bed.

She had been relieved. She would have acceded had Darcy so much as hinted that he wished more from her, but she did not feel she could accept him into her bed with equanimity so soon.

"But it need not be…unpleasant. And," Elizabeth said, her breath creating a circle of fog on the window, "he is handsome. That is sure to make the whole business…more acceptable."

She giggled and shook her head, wishing she had someone to tease other than herself. Darcy would not like to be teased, any more than he would like her arguing with him.

"I am certain Lady Romsley would agree that Mrs Darcy ought not to behave in such a manner. Such charming, humourless relatives I now have!"

DARCY STOOD AT THE WINDOW OF HIS STUDY, DISAPPOINTED TO SEE that it was raining yet again. With a sigh, he sat and began a letter to Tom. He wrote of his recent conversation with Georgiana.

I own I was dismayed at how little progress she has made. She could not have been dissembling every time she said she was with her books, yet it is all but impossible to believe she could have learnt so little in all the hours she purported to be working on this or that. I have been too easy on her and will supervise her progress more closely. In December or January, we must decide what to do with her after the winter. Will she return to Pemberley with me, or is she better off in London with a companion?

Elizabeth has become quite an active mistress. She has given no indication that she finds Georgiana's company a displea-sure. I shall continue to encourage Georgiana to befriend her, but I cannot force her compliance.

Darcy tossed his pen aside. His mind would insist on thinking about Elizabeth. He remembered placing his coat on her in Mrs Morris's garden and imagining what it would feel like to replace it with his arms, to allow his hands to trace the line from her shoulders down her arms, encasing her in his grip and trapping her to him. The way she had looked when he took her onto the terrace to see the stars, the tilt of her chin as she looked skyward. It was almost as though she were offering herself to him. He could not resist, not after the way she had tempted him all evening—the way her lips clung to the glass as she drank, the way the fabric of her deep blue gown, which so perfectly complemented the tone of her skin, stretched across her bosom. She was coercing him towards a precipice. When he fell over the edge, what would he find? A place in which his self-control, all his effort to regulate his feelings and actions and maintain himself as an honourable gentleman, failed. Each time she allowed his caress, he wanted more. It felt wrong, yet she was his wife.

It struck him then. He resented it. That was what continued to cloud his thoughts regarding Elizabeth, even after all of these weeks. He was bitter about the fact that necessity had made Elizabeth Bennet into Elizabeth Darcy.

Darcy stood, his chair almost falling backwards. Three or four long strides brought him to the window where he stopped. His teeth ached from the way he was clenching them, and his heart raced. He would never cease to regret that he had been compelled to marry Elizabeth. Why should he? It mattered not that Elizabeth was not as horrible as he had feared she would be, or that he found her so attractive. He knew his situation could be much, much worse. Suppose Elizabeth had been more like Martha Simms!

Resentment was why he had not yet succumbed to his desire. Once he did, it would be the final admission that this was his life. She was his wife, he would have no other, and his children would be hers.

Several slow breaths restored his ease. *Well, old man, you understand yourself at last. I said I would make the best of this situation and now...now it is time to do just that.*

TO THE DELIGHT OF ALL THREE DARCYS, THE NEXT DAY WAS CLEAR. Darcy went shooting and had a satisfying amount of success. At dinner, he learnt that Elizabeth had received her riding clothes from London and had taken a short ride under the guidance of the stable master.

"Good. He is an excellent instructor. Where did you go?"

"Nowhere in particular this first time. I will go see the Jameses and Martins tomorrow," Elizabeth said.

"Very well. Remember to always bring a groom with you. And you, Georgiana? Did you take advantage of the fair weather?"

She had and spoke of walking in the gardens and drawing. She promised to show him the results of her labour another time.

After dinner, Darcy made Georgiana sit with him and discuss what else she had accomplished that day. He had given her a list of questions pertaining to her study of history, telling her that he wanted her to write out the answers for him to review. Now he found that she could produce no such thing.

"I did do the reading, Fitzwilliam. And I thought about the answers, but I am afraid I must have misunderstood. I did not realise you wished for me to *write* the answers. Should I fetch the drawing I made today? Truly, it was such a fine day, and I spent ever so long—"

"Another time. Let us review what I wish to see you do regarding history and Italian so that there are no further misunderstandings."

When he was finished his explanation, Georgiana went to the pianoforte, and he went to talk to Elizabeth, who was busy writing.

"What has captured your attention so completely?" Darcy asked.

"A list of questions and tasks to which I must attend. I am attempting to organise my thoughts."

"Oh?"

"Preparations for your family's visit, which are well underway. I did wish to ask you about one or two things."

"Which are?"

Before she could answer, Darcy suggested they go sit together on one of the sofas. It was uncomfortable standing by the desk where she had placed herself. He sat beside her, almost but not quite as close as he wished to be, but his sister was in the room. Elizabeth tugged at her shawl—an ivory and turquoise knit that looked too thin for the time of year—and addressed his question.

"Whom, if anyone, would you like me to invite while your family is here?"

"The Haddons. Mr Haddon would wish to see John and Frederick. They were boyhood friends. What else? It seems quite a long list."

Elizabeth rattled off a number of items from menus, to gifts for the servants on St Stephen's Day, to making arrangements with Mr Llewellyn for a holiday celebration for the village. Darcy was surprised with her thoroughness. He had never thought about all the preparations that were necessary for a large house party or the holiday season and was gratified that Elizabeth was overseeing it. With Mrs Reynolds's assistance, of course; the housekeeper would have managed it herself in the years since Lady Anne's death, although he seldom entertained as many people as they would see in the coming weeks, and there had been no village celebrations to worry about.

The colour in Elizabeth's cheeks deepened. "I know Mrs Reynolds is capable of undertaking much of this, but I should ensure every detail is attended to and take some of the work upon myself."

There was something in Elizabeth's expression—perhaps the set of her jaw—that made Darcy suspect she would begin tapping her foot. He listened for and was pleased when he heard the dull thudding noise, which showed that he had been right. "As you see fit. It is almost two months until Christmas, however."

"The time will pass quickly with so much to do," she insisted.

Darcy nodded, no longer interested in the subject. He had had an excellent notion. "Do you dance?"

Her eyes fixed on his. "Yes, of course."

He looked over his shoulder and asked Georgiana to play something to which he and Elizabeth could dance.

"You are not serious?" Elizabeth's expression showed surprise and, Darcy thought, a touch of delight.

He held out a hand to her. "It is unlikely we shall make it through the holidays without having to dance at least once. Like all worthwhile, and not so worthwhile, accomplishments, it requires practise."

Georgiana had stopped playing—her fingers poised over the keys —and looked at him, her mouth agape. To be fair, his request was unusual, but he knew she would enjoy playing something different from her usual fare and watching them. Their evenings were often rather slow; this would liven up the atmosphere. Besides, it was a way to have Elizabeth close to him.

They spent a pleasurable thirty minutes thus engaged.

Perversely, tonight of all nights, Georgiana did not retire to her rooms early, as was her custom. Although not precisely wishing his sister away, Darcy had anticipated being alone with Elizabeth. Georgiana read, unaware of his wishes—he could hardly announce them—until Elizabeth, unable to deny her fatigue, excused herself.

Chapter 13

Darcy was anxious about his relations' rapidly approaching visit, and his questions about Elizabeth's preparations followed them into the withdrawing room after dinner the following week. He sent Georgiana to her apartment to complete some work on history that should have been done days earlier, and Elizabeth wondered if he had done so to ensure they would be alone. Georgiana had been retiring later and later recently. She did not know why; it was not as though the girl was acting any friendlier, not even towards Darcy.

"I am confident that everything that can be done, has been done, or will be before anyone arrives. I have discussed menus with Cook, the kitchens are well stocked, Mrs Reynolds and I have drawn up room assignments, and the guest chambers will all be cleaned and aired. Extra help has been hired. I have sent invitations to our neighbours and written to Miss Haddon."

Darcy accepted the tea Elizabeth prepared for him as she spoke and sat down across from her. His anxiety was plain to see and she both wanted to soothe him and throw something at him. This was at least the third time she had told him the same information. She under-stood he was anxious, but enough was enough!

"It is important that it goes well."

Reassuring, calm, and for goodness' sake, think before you speak, Lizzy! "I assure you I am giving it all the attention it deserves, and I shall do everything I possibly can to ensure that it goes well."

The Darcy family was large, above twenty not including young children and more distant cousins, but only eight would visit, to Elizabeth's immense relief. They spoke about the visit for another ten minutes before Darcy was satisfied. While retrieving her sewing, Elizabeth let out a surreptitious sigh of relief and rolled her eyes.

Darcy read for a short while before setting aside his book and staring at her. Elizabeth pretended not to notice. They spent a quarter of an hour this way.

"Elizabeth, come. Play for me." Darcy stood and held out a hand.

Elizabeth secured her needle and folded the cloth she had been working on, gently placing it in the basket. She smoothed the skirt of her gown as she stood. *Courage, Lizzy, courage! You have nothing to fear from him.*

She walked directly to the instrument, forgoing placing her hand in his, and sat. "What would you like to hear?" she asked, despising the tremor in her voice.

Darcy sat next to her, leaving only a sliver of bench between them. "Anything."

Elizabeth nodded and spent a minute or two perusing the available music and trying to stop her hands from shaking. She finally found a piece she thought she could play with some success. If she stumbled over a note here or there, it was just as likely due to Darcy's closeness as it was to a lack of skill.

As she looked for a second piece to play, Darcy whispered, "Sing for me."

His voice was deep and something in it caused Elizabeth's heart to race. She thought it would almost be best if she kissed him rather than continue to wait for him to kiss her. She knew he meant to, and waiting for that moment to come was robbing her of what little equa-nimity she retained.

"I-I-I don't have any music with me." Georgiana's music included no songs, as she did not sing.

"You do not need it."

He sat so close to her that their legs almost touched, and she knew it would not be long before she felt his hands and lips on her. She was nervous, but longed for this night, this…event, to be over. She could make the transition from maiden to wife without engaging her heart. So long as she remembered to guard herself against expectations that could never be fulfilled, did not ever allow herself to dream that he could feel true affection for her, she would be well. She would allow herself to be anxious—it was only natural—but not frightened.

Just as she finished reminding herself of these important matters, she felt his lips brush against her neck. Her voice faltered, and her fingers stilled.

"Sing." His mouth was close to her ear and his breath created a pleasurable tickle on her skin.

She did as he commanded, and he placed slow, soft kisses on her neck, then the part of her shoulder not covered by her gown. His kisses became more intense, yet were still gentle. It felt wonderful. There was no shame in admitting it. He was her husband, and there was no barrier to what they did together, or to her taking what pleasure she could from it.

As soon as her song ended, Darcy pressed his lips against hers and pulled her closer. The kiss deepened and his hands explored her body, touching her in places she had never before been touched by a man. She reminded herself not to shy away from him, to accept his attentions as a good wife should, and, most of all, to breathe. What they did was natural, and with time she would grow accustomed to it.

A noise in the hallway outside the room startled them. She jolted away from Darcy. She listened but heard nothing more. Elizabeth stole a cautious glance at her husband. His eyes were fixed on her, his chest rising and falling rapidly. He did not move away or suggest she resume playing. To Elizabeth, the message was very clear.

"We should…perhaps we should…" She swallowed heavily. "P-perhaps we should retire."

She could not look at him and could only trust that he heard her. Her voice had sounded so far away, almost otherworldly, that a small part of her was not sure she had spoken at all. Elizabeth slowly stood. She kept her eyes lowered, and, when he also stood, she walked out of the room, knowing that he would follow.

When they reached the door to Elizabeth's chambers, she whispered, "I shall need…twenty minutes."

She slipped inside her room, closing the door behind her without again looking into his face.

ELIZABETH HURRIED DREWE THROUGH HER WORK OF PREPARING Elizabeth for bed. She wanted some minutes of solitude before Darcy joined her. Once alone, she changed her nightgown to one she deemed more attractive and removed the tie from her hair. She snuffed the candles, leaving only one lit, and paced.

Soon enough—or perhaps too soon, Elizabeth was not sure—she heard a soft knock on the door which separated their rooms.

"C-come."

She watched as the doorknob slowly turned, and the door creaked open. Darcy took a few steps into the room and stopped. Elizabeth could feel the weight of his eyes on her, and the air seemed heavy with anticipation. When he failed to approach her, Elizabeth, with one last reminder of the many reasons she wanted him here, forced her legs to carry her to him. She slowly looked up, determined to appear accepting and unafraid. She put her hands on his chest, feeling the rapid beating of his heart and the warmth of his body, and said his name.

It was all Elizabeth could do not to give way to shock at his sudden fervency as he kissed and touched her. When he carried her to bed and placed himself atop her, a stab of fear, brought on by the violence of his actions, was banished as she forced herself to remember that, for this moment, he valued and accepted her as his wife.

She allowed him to do what he liked, but she had no idea how to act, what he might want or expect from her. He was, she supposed, as gentle and considerate as a man could be in such a situation, but it hurt, and she had to bite her lip to stop from crying out; she could not prevent the few tears that filled her eyes. She was glad for the darkness and the protection it provided. It would be impossible to carry on if she could see the lack of affection in his eyes.

It did not last long. She felt Darcy's body shudder, and he rested his head on the pillow by hers, his inarticulate grunts transformed into moans, his voice slurring her name over and over.

Gradually, her heart stopped racing. He removed himself from her. She thought he might leave immediately, but instead he rested on his side next to her, his chin on her shoulder and an arm draped across her belly. They did not speak, although he did, three or four times, kiss her shoulder or cheek, which she found comforting.

"Are you well?" he whispered at length.

She nodded.

A short moment later, he spoke again. "Did I hurt you?"

Elizabeth shook her head. "No." Her whisper was even softer than his.

He seemed satisfied with her response, and they continued thus for some time, both of them remaining silent. After Elizabeth attempted to hide a yawn, he chuckled.

"I shall let you sleep." He kissed her, one long, gentle final embrace, before he said good night, slipped out of her bed, found his clothes, and returned to his own room.

Once alone, Elizabeth righted her nightgown, and ran her fingers through her tousled hair. The actions felt unnatural. She made sure the bed curtains were completely closed. She then settled underneath the thick blankets, closed her eyes, and waited for sleep to claim her.

ELIZABETH AND DARCY DID NOT SEE EACH OTHER UNTIL THEY MET outside the breakfast parlour the next day.

"How are you this morning?" Darcy looked at her much as he always did, although he sounded more at ease, pleased even.

"Well." She grimaced, not happy with the way her voice wavered and certain her cheeks were bright pink. "And you?"

"Very well."

They entered the breakfast room and said good morning to Georgiana.

"You had a productive evening, I hope, Georgiana," Darcy said.

Georgiana smiled and nodded when her brother spoke to her, but did not otherwise respond. Elizabeth thought she saw a quick flash of discomfort cross Georgiana's face. She suspected Georgiana was not spending as much time on her studies as she was supposed to, but that was for Darcy to determine.

"What will you be doing this morning?" Darcy asked.

"I-I," Georgiana stammered. "I have letters to write. To Aunt Margaret." She turned to Elizabeth. "Lady Romsley."

"Thank you, Georgiana. I did understand to whom you were referring."

Darcy stared at his sister, his brow furrowed, and Elizabeth briefly wondered if he would say something about Georgiana's rudeness. She was not surprised when he did not. *I will have to be satisfied that he is less dismissive than he used to be.*

"And you, Elizabeth, what do you intend to do this morning?"

"I will call on Mrs Morris and several families Mr Llewellyn mentioned to me."

As they spoke, Elizabeth blushed under his gaze, suspecting that he was remembering what had happened between them the night before. He was in an uncommonly good mood, and for that she was glad. It was her responsibility to make her husband happy, just as it was to make his home comfortable, visit his tenants, and everything else she was trying to do. Nonetheless, what had happened was so new that she could not be entirely at ease.

I suppose with time it will be as usual an occurrence as anything else is in this marriage of ours.

ELIZABETH'S FIRST CALL WAS TO MRS MORRIS. SHE THANKED THE older lady for including her and Darcy at the recent dinner party.

"It was a pleasure to have you, and I hope we might repeat the experience often," Mrs Morris said. "I shall be bold, perhaps too bold for what is considered polite society, and apologise for the awkwardness at the end of the evening. I am afraid a certain young lady of our acquaintance has too high an opinion of herself and too low a one of the understanding of others."

Elizabeth did not wish to pursue the subject of Miss Simms, so simply nodded. "One reason for my visit this morning is to invite you and Admiral Morris to Pemberley. My husband's relations will be staying with us, and we would like to have you to dinner while they are here."

Mrs Morris accepted immediately. Upon questioning, Elizabeth explained that this visit was from the Darcy family, and that the Fitzwilliams would join them at Christmas.

"My goodness," Mrs Morris laughed, "you will be busy! And will any of your family be visiting soon?"

Elizabeth was taken aback. The question was by no means offensive, but the idea of her family being invited to Pemberley was so unlikely that she had not expected anyone to ask. "N-no. I expect to see them when we go to London in the winter." That was not precisely true, but Elizabeth had to offer some explanation.

"I am sure you miss them very much."

Elizabeth smiled and took a sip of her tea. It had seemed warm and comforting earlier, but now was tasteless, as though nothing could be gained by continuing to drink it. She did miss Jane and the Gardiners, and even her mother and younger sisters.

"I would think it very hard to be a new bride and be so far away from a lady who might...be of assistance when it was needed. It is a very great change. We have not known each other long, but if there is any way in which I might be of use, please do not hesitate to ask. I know I am not as good as your own mother might be, but I do like to think I have gained a little bit of sense and knowledge in my years as a wife and mother."

Elizabeth did not know how to feel about this most unexpected speech. It was very kind, and Elizabeth longed to speak openly with someone. But she had too many secrets to keep to make that possible. *If only Georgiana—No, Lizzy. There is no point dwelling on such wishes.* Perhaps one day, she and Georgiana would be like sisters to each other, or at least friends. It would make life at Pemberley happier for both of them. *Maybe when I make her an aunt. A baby would bind all three of us together.* "Thank you, Mrs Morris. It is very kind of you. Now do, please, refresh my memory. I believe you said that your niece was staying with you this winter?"

THE FOLLOWING MORNING, ALMOST BEFORE IT WAS PROPER, MRS Simms, *sans* her daughter, called on Elizabeth. Elizabeth assumed the Simmses had learnt that the Darcys were entertaining soon and wished to secure an invitation. Mrs Simms was left to wait almost twenty minutes before Elizabeth joined her.

"I apologise, Mrs Simms. I was not expecting callers quite so early."

"Not at all. I have a number of calls to make today and wished to begin with you."

Mrs Simms smiled, although the way she tugged at her clothes and played with her reticule said much about her discomfort. Elizabeth thought she richly deserved it and was fortunate Elizabeth had not had Hudson send her away.

"Your family is well, I hope?"

"Quite," Mrs Simms replied. She looked everywhere but at Elizabeth. "My daughter, uh, Miss Simms was…indisposed this morning, else I am certain that she would have, that is to say, been happy to have accompanied me. Pemberley is such a delightful house to…visit."

"Thank you. It is my honour to be its mistress."

Mrs Simms coughed into her handkerchief. "I believe Mr Darcy's family arrive soon?"

"We expect *our* family to being arriving on Wednesday."

Mrs Simms pursed her lips. "I am sure it is keeping Mrs Reynolds very busy."

Elizabeth purposely looked dismissive. "Mrs Reynolds and I have prepared everything to my satisfaction."

Mrs Simms peered at Elizabeth through narrowed eyes. "Mrs Reynolds is an excellent housekeeper. I do not believe anyone can fault her management of Pemberley."

Elizabeth was curious enough about how far Mrs Simms would go to let the woman continue uninterrupted. It was amusing, in an odd sort of way, and she would laugh about it later when she was alone. *If only Fitzwilliam were not so humourless. How I would like to share this with someone!*

"I am sure it has been a great comfort to Mr Darcy to have such an excellent woman in charge of the house."

"I am sure it was." Elizabeth's tone was amiable, with just a touch of heat. "And now, fortunate man that he is, my husband has two very capable women ensuring Pemberley is well-managed. I assure you, Mrs Simms, that I am more than prepared to tend to my guests. No deserving person will find their reception at either of my homes in any way lacking."

Mrs Simms had the grace to look a little contrite, but her chief reaction was one of shock. "Of course, of course." Mrs Simms' soothing tone irritated Elizabeth. "I am sure Mr Darcy has nothing to complain about, nothing at all." She smiled at Elizabeth, no doubt hoping it looked genuine.

It did not, and Elizabeth grew more disgusted. "Nothing whatsoever."

"W-will you do much entertaining while Mr Darcy's family is here?"

"While our family is here? Some." Before Mrs Simms could formulate a response, Elizabeth stood and exclaimed, "Oh my, I had no idea how late it was! Did you not say that you have a number of calls to make this morning? I would not wish to delay you."

As Elizabeth rang the bell to have Mrs Simms escorted out, she chatted about nothing and successfully avoided hearing the lady's voice again that morning.

"ARE YOU LOOKING FORWARD TO SEEING YOUR FAMILY?" ELIZABETH asked Georgiana as they went into the withdrawing room after dinner the next day.

Fitzwilliam said, "The house will be a very different place with them here."

"Y-yes. Of course." Her aunts and uncles were sure to ask her about Elizabeth. Tom, Lady Romsley, and her brother had all lately reminded Georgiana that she would have to act as though she were happy. Since she was horribly afraid that someone would learn about Ramsgate, she would have to find a way to do it.

She had nothing further to say, yet still felt annoyed when her brother engaged Elizabeth in conversation instead of paying attention to her. *As though I am a child to be seen, but not heard, instead of fifteen years old, soon to be sixteen!*

They spoke about boring household matters. The small smile on Fitzwilliam's face told Georgiana that he was impressed by Elizabeth's knowledge although she found nothing to admire about it—it was no more than Elizabeth should know. The blush on Elizabeth's cheeks, which Georgiana did not understand at all, also drew her ire.

"Shall I play?" Georgiana said, her voice slightly louder than usual, effectively ending their conversation.

Elizabeth retrieved her sewing, and Fitzwilliam opened a book. Georgiana was satisfied with this arrangement, but after some while her brother abandoned his book and went to sit beside Elizabeth. They shared a few whispered exchanges, and, without her fingers stopping, Georgiana saw Elizabeth nod and her cheeks turn pink. Georgiana even believed she saw Fitzwilliam touch her cheek.

It was impossible that her brother liked Elizabeth, that he might wish to…do whatever it was married couples did. Her understanding of the intimacies of marriage was vague. Wickham had caressed her, just as her brother caressed Elizabeth, and had kissed her three times, but he had cared for her, had wanted to make her his wife. Or he had pretended that he had. She was not always certain which it was, and it hardly mattered at this moment.

Georgiana closed the pianoforte; only her love for the beautiful walnut instrument kept her from slamming the fallboard. She retrieved a book, not caring what it was, and sat across from them. Fitzwilliam retrieved his book, and Elizabeth resumed sewing. When Elizabeth had finished whatever it was she was working on, she put her things away and announced her intention to go to her rooms.

Fitzwilliam stood. "I believe I shall retire as well."

Georgiana closed her book so quickly that the sound it made startled her. "B-but Fitzwilliam, I wanted to ask about…about something I read. History. It was about…the Battle of Agincourt. There was something I did not fully understand."

"Of course."

Elizabeth said her good nights and at last left brother and sister alone.

Darcy remained with Georgiana as long as she could hold his attention. The sooner he was out of the room, the sooner he would be in Elizabeth's bed. His attraction to her continued to grow, and he enjoyed letting his feelings free. He had been attracted to other women in his life, but what he felt for Elizabeth was somehow different. It was likely just that he had, reasonably and understandably, feared their marriage would be a disaster. As it happened, his wife was very pretty, he had conquered his resentment, and he was a very satisfied man.

What dissatisfied him was how little his sister had learnt about the Hundred Years' War. He left her with a promise to give her a different book to study. The ones he had already told her to read—if she had indeed done so—clearly did not explain the history well enough.

When Darcy went through to Elizabeth's bedchamber, he found her in bed, sitting with her back to the heavy wooden headboard, her knees bent, and covered with blankets. There was a book in her hands. She set it aside as he discarded his robe and climbed in next to her. Elizabeth extinguished the last candle.

"What were you reading?"

"Shakespeare. *Henry V*. Georgiana's question put it in mind, and I happened to have a copy in my sitting room."

Darcy was surprised, although, since her taste in books was quite broad, he should not be. "I should have Georgiana read it. It would add to her education of the era."

Tired of conversation and thinking about what his sister was or was not doing, he kissed his very handsome, very alluring wife.

Chapter 14

Elizabeth and Mrs Reynolds toured the guest apartments. Elizabeth was satisfied with the general condition of each room, but dissatisfied with the decoration.

Mrs Reynolds, as though reading her thoughts, said, "It is a very comfortable room, I dare say, but rather out of fashion."

Elizabeth smiled. "I was just thinking the same. I shall speak to Mr Darcy about renovations."

"You will wish to start with your rooms."

Elizabeth did. Time had not made her like the chartreuse walls and heavy walnut furniture in them any better, but she was uncomfortable approaching Darcy about making changes because the expense would be significant. He had seemed unhappy when she ordered work done to her apartment in town. *But he does seem...less displeased of late. And, truly, the rooms need attention. I am mistress, and it is my duty to keep the house in good order.*

With these thoughts in mind, she spoke to Darcy about it at breakfast, saying, "Mrs Reynolds and I were talking about perhaps refurbishing some of the rooms this winter."

"Oh?"

"Some of the guest chambers. They are rather..."

"It has been years since most of them were done. I expected you would wish to attend to your rooms first."

His eyes met Elizabeth's. Was he censuring her for not attending to it earlier? Did he think she was eager to spend his money? *Will I ever stop trying to read his mind instead of simply asking him what he means?* "I-I—There were other matters demanding my attention, although, I shall admit that I would like to."

Darcy nodded his agreement, and they went on with their meal.

DARCY STRUGGLED TO ATTEND TO HIS BUSINESS. HIS UNCLE JOHN AND cousin Frederick were arriving in a few hours. They would be the harshest critics of Elizabeth and his marriage. The Darcys were a proud family, justifiably so, and all of them were expected to marry well to uphold and improve the family's standing. That pride might keep them from liking Elizabeth, especially since they could not know about the great service she had rendered Georgiana.

He was pleased with how well Elizabeth was doing in her role as mistress, and gratified with the state of their relationship. *It could all be so, so much worse. Soon this visit will be over—and as much as I enjoy seeing my relations, I will be very glad when it is—and we can return to our quiet family party.* He sighed. *I cannot hide her away from the world always; she will have to learn to manage among good society. First the Darcys, then the Fitzwilliams, and then*—again he sighed—*the* ton.

He prayed that Elizabeth withstood the examination of his family with the grace he had seen her display, when, for one, faced with Miss Simms's attempt to insult and discompose her. He could not entirely trust her, however, and must be prepared to offer assistance if it were needed.

Pushing these thoughts aside, he returned to his papers.

DARCY, ELIZABETH, AND GEORGIANA GATHERED IN THE GREEN saloon to greet the Darcys. Elizabeth walked around the room, looking up at the artwork on the walls, examining the pattern on a Chinese vase, adjusting the position of the figurines on the mantle. She knew Darcy watched her and could not face the doubt she expected to find in his expression. She believed that she was as good and worthy as any of his family, but they did not, and her husband and his relations had the power to make her life happy or miserable.

At last, Hudson escorted five people into the room, four of middle-age, and a young lady several years Elizabeth's senior. She smiled at Elizabeth in such a manner that Elizabeth almost had to believe it was a genuine expectation of friendship.

"Welcome to Pemberley," Darcy said. "Elizabeth, let me introduce you to our family."

Darcy named his aunt and uncle John and Susan Darcy, his father's cousin Frederick Darcy, Frederick's wife Julia, and their daughter Rebecca.

"It is a great pleasure to finally meet you, Mrs Darcy," John said. "We have been wishing to do so since we first heard of your betrothal to my nephew."

"Indeed," added Frederick, his voice deep and solemn.

Rebecca rolled her eyes and smiled at Elizabeth again. "I was very glad to hear that my cousin had at last found a lady he wished to marry."

"Rebecca," Frederick said, and Rebecca's eyes fell to the floor.

"Would you care for refreshments? Or perhaps you would like to go to your rooms?" Elizabeth asked. "Dinner will be in an hour and a half."

"Perhaps that would be best," Darcy said. "There will be time to get to know each other at dinner."

Rebecca said, "Travel is so tiring, is it not? But I did so long to come to Pemberley to meet my new cousin. And to see you as well, Fitzwilliam, and you, Georgiana." She laughed a little, nervously glancing at her father.

Elizabeth spoke without thinking. "Travel is tiring, but I am glad you have come. I believe you are from Norfolk?"

"Yes." Frederick peered at Elizabeth through narrowed eyes. "We do live in Norfolk and spend most of our time there."

"Have you been?" Rebecca asked. When Elizabeth shook her

head, she went on, "It is lovely, although with the delights of Derbyshire before you, I am certain you have no desire to—"

"I would like to go to my room now," Susan interjected. "A moment to rest before preparing for dinner would be most agreeable."

"Of course." Elizabeth jumped to her feet and rang the bell.

DINNER WAS UNEVENTFUL, YET UNCOMFORTABLE FOR ELIZABETH. SHE felt under constant observation from the newcomers as well as her husband. The separation of the sexes was prolonged and conversation among the ladies mostly involved Georgiana's aunts fussing over her. After some minutes of this, Elizabeth and Rebecca were able to escape to a separate corner of the room.

"You are very brave to have so many of us visit at once. Not, I suppose, that you had any say in the matter. From what my father has said, I gather he and Uncle John demanded that you and Fitzwilliam have us so that we could meet you. Ever since Uncle George died, they have tried to act in his stead, as though my cousin was still a schoolboy. They believe he should seek their advice on important matters. They were insulted that he did not, although I am very glad that he acted as he did. Darcy or not, he should be allowed to marry where he wished and not adhere to some ridiculous notion of only marrying a lady who had the proper credentials. Oh, not that I mean that you are in any way lacking!" Rebecca cried, pulling at the hem of her wool shawl. "I do beg your pardon. I have a dreadful habit of speaking without thinking, and sometimes it does get me into terrible trouble."

With an effort, Elizabeth managed to give a polite smile. She could not help but think of her own tendency to act without thinking. It appeared that Rebecca, like so many others, found Darcy's choice of wife shocking, and disapproved of it. "No offence was taken, I assure you. You have younger brothers, I believe, one of whom will be joining us?"

Rebecca nodded. "Freddie. He is travelling with Uncle John's two eldest sons, Jack and George. I imagine you will meet the rest of the family in the spring, in London."

Elizabeth kept Rebecca speaking about her brothers and cousins until the gentlemen joined them. Darcy's expression was very dark, and she suspected that John and Frederick had been telling him of their disapproval of his marriage. The two older gentlemen said little to Elizabeth, but she felt their constant scrutiny. Most of the party retired early, claiming fatigue after their long journey. Elizabeth was happy to say good night to them, and to Darcy, who spoke not a word to her after dinner.

GEORGIANA WAS PRESENTED WITH THE TRINKETS HER RELATIVES brought for her after breakfast. Among them was music for a new concerto by Joseph Woelfl Georgiana had been particularly anxious to learn. Susan expressed a wish to hear her play the piece, and Georgiana promised to spend the morning at her instrument practising it.

"If your sister can spare you, that is."

Elizabeth regarded the two ladies, who were looking at her. It was the first time that morning that Georgiana acknowledged her presence. Elizabeth arched her eyebrows, feigning ignorance of the issue under question. When Georgiana explained, Elizabeth had to give her credit; Georgiana sounded as though she did not despise her.

"Of course, Georgiana. I shall have you informed if you are needed."

Thanking her aunt one last time, Georgiana flew from the room.

The men took advantage of the good weather to have some sport, and Elizabeth was left with the ladies, who were happy to talk among themselves or explore favourite rooms. Rebecca looked longingly at Elizabeth as Susan and Julia made her go with them to the conservatory. The older ladies had insisted Elizabeth need not accompany them, and, seeing she was not wanted, Elizabeth had attended to her correspondence.

Shortly after noon, the three gentlemen cousins, Jack, George, and Freddie, arrived. Their party complete, the house was busy. Elizabeth hardly knew how the hours passed and certainly could not explain how it was she found herself alone in a small parlour with John, Susan, Frederick, and Julia. She had no doubt it was by their design.

"How fortunate that we, at last, have a chance to know you, Elizabeth," said John. "You do not mind if I call you Elizabeth, do you, my dear? You are a member of the family now. You must call me Uncle John."

Elizabeth smiled, although it did not reach her eyes. With the way they watched her, she felt as though she was upon a stage with them judging her performance. *Or perhaps a prisoner in the docket.* The thought amused her and gave her a boost of courage.

"You must know how…anxious we have been to meet you," Julia said.

"Fitzwilliam has told us so little about you. Why do you think that is?" Frederick asked.

"I am sure I have no idea." Frederick looked poised to bark out another question, and Elizabeth continued to speak to forestall him. "Perhaps he is simply worried that he would bore you. That once he started talking about me, he would not be able to stop, and you would be desperate for a way to end the conversation." She chuckled, but no one joined her.

"You met him where? How?" the gentleman next demanded.

Elizabeth sighed and straightened her shoulders. She prayed that she could hold her temper long enough to get through the next while. *They might be rude, but you cannot be, Lizzy! Not if you ever expect them to like you.*

After Frederick's question was answered, there were many others about her family, her education, her experiences and accomplishments, their wedding, who she had met, and what she had done since the start of her marriage. The questions came from all quarters and were in no particular order.

As this attempt at 'getting to know her' continued, Elizabeth's patience thinned and she worried she would accidentally say something that would raise their suspicions or that would offend them. She had not expected to be welcomed warmly by the Darcys, but they seemed determined to think the worst of her, perhaps even believed she had somehow trapped Darcy into marriage.

She was on the point of risking their censure by calling an unceremonious end to the interview when the door to the parlour opened, and Hudson entered.

"Viscount Bramwell, Mrs Darcy."

The collective eyes of the room's occupants flew to the doorway, and, sure enough, there stood Sterling Fitzwilliam.

"Good day." His eyes darted around the room as though looking for someone. *Or perhaps he is simply wondering why I am here without Darcy to ensure I do not speak amiss.*

At last, he turned to Elizabeth, a scowl on his face. "So terribly sorry to turn up unexpectedly like this. Thought I would pop by, see how you were getting along and all of that. I am sure you can find a place for me. Anything will do—dusty attic, unused servant's quarters."

The others began to greet him. Frederick's deep voice sounded displeased as he said Sterling's name.

I suppose it is gratifying to know I am not the only one he dislikes! "My husband did not say you would be joining us. Welcome." Elizabeth realised her words made little sense as she said them, but she was so glad for the interruption that she had spoken without thinking.

"Oh, he did not know." Sterling offered her a quick smile.

It was enough to make Elizabeth feel a little kindly towards him, especially as his appearance meant an end to her previous conversation. "I am certain we can do better than an attic. Please, do join us while a room is made ready."

"Why are you here?" Darcy demanded when he and Sterling were alone in the room Elizabeth had had prepared for him. It was a ghastly space, full of large, heavy pine furniture that was more practical than comfortable, with dark green walls, and fabrics faded to a dull brown. His irritation with his cousin was briefly replaced with relief that Elizabeth would soon rid Pemberley of such displeasing décor.

"My parents wondered how you were getting along. And knowing you were facing an invasion of Darcys, it seemed like a kindness to come and lend my support. Rather nice of me, don't you think?"

Darcy scowled in response to his cousin's smile. "How long are you staying?"

"I might impose upon your hospitality until my parents arrive next month. My mother wanders Romsley Hall, muttering about everything that she must, without fail, teach Elizabeth before the Season. I must warn her."

Darcy growled in reply and stalked out of Sterling's bedchamber.

Chapter 15

Elizabeth was preparing for dinner when Darcy entered. Once her maid was gone, he asked about her interview with his family; he had not known about it until it was over.

"What did they want?"

Elizabeth continued to regard herself in the mirror. "An opportunity to know me better. It was nothing really." *They were rude, officious, astonished that you of all men would choose someone like me, arrogant—*

When he nodded and asked nothing further, she was quietly relieved. He touched her, the smooth tips of his fingers running from her temple down to and along the bone of her jaw. She closed her eyes and sighed as the sensation washed away the annoyance and pain that accompanied her memory of the conversation with his relations. The gentleness felt akin to affection and soothed away her unhappiness for the moment. She would use his caress to give her strength for the evening ahead. It reminded her why she would continue to do everything within her power to be the best possible Mrs Darcy. She could withstand, without complaint, the slings and arrows of those around her as long as she had some mark of acceptance from him, and this, she was discovering, was a pleasant way to experience it. In this she would find her contentment, and when, God willing, she had a child, she might even find some happiness.

STERLING SAT BY ELIZABETH AT DINNER. HE RESPONDED HALF-heartedly, if at all, to her questions and repeatedly glanced down the table. It was not Sterling alone who acted oddly. Elizabeth had not known that Rebecca could be so quiet, or that Georgiana could speak so easily.

After dinner, Susan insisted Elizabeth and Georgiana sit with her.

"I did so enjoy our conversation earlier, Elizabeth," Susan said. "Your life as my nephew's wife must be a tremendous change for you. From what I understood of your family, it is quite…different from the Darcys."

Elizabeth saw a smirk on Georgiana's face before the girl could mask it. "I find I am adjusting quite well."

"Oh? I was asking Georgiana at dinner about how you occupy your time, but she had little to say."

Since she ignores me as much as possible, how would she know what I do? Elizabeth did not like the bitter taste of the thoughts which ran through her head. She smiled at Georgiana in a way that she prayed looked fondly. "Georgiana has been very busy with her studies and music. It is a joy to hear her play, is it not?"

Georgiana managed to smile in return. Fortunately for both her and Elizabeth, Susan was happy to speak about music; Elizabeth let her companions do so, adding a few words now and again, while understanding that neither truly wished to hear her opinion.

After the gentlemen joined them, Elizabeth spied Rebecca sitting alone, a look of alarm on her face, and went to join her. Sterling approached at the same time and claimed the seat next to Rebecca, leaving Elizabeth to sit across from them. She considered leaving them to enjoy a private conversation, but Rebecca's blush and imploring look made her remain. Sterling spent the next several minutes trying to ignore Elizabeth and engage Rebecca. Rebecca said as little as possible and kept her eyes lowered, until a stern-faced

Frederick came to tell her that Julia needed her elsewhere. Rebecca stood and walked away with her father.

"Bloody hell," Sterling muttered. After a moment, he looked at Elizabeth. "Georgiana behaving herself?"

Elizabeth nodded.

Sterling looked dubious. "She is spoilt. I hope she will not be so stupid in the future, but I would not wager above fifty pounds on it." With this extraordinary statement, he rose and went to join the other young men.

ELIZABETH ASKED REBECCA TO TAKE A WALK IN THE SCULPTURE garden with her after breakfast the following morning. The day was cool, but not unseasonably so, and those trees that dropped their leaves in the autumn had largely done so. The air was still, and the only sound apart from their voices was that of their boots on the stone pathways.

Rebecca said, "I am so pleased that Fitzwilliam chose to marry for love and not for more material considerations, regardless of what he was taught."

Elizabeth felt her reserve become thicker with every allusion to her marriage and did not speak for fear of not sounding as happy as the other woman assumed she was.

"I was once engaged to be married. He was a good man, very kind, and he cared a great deal for me. I returned his affection although I do not believe I loved him, not in a grand, romantic sense at least."

They arrived at an iron bench and Elizabeth suggested they sit. "What happened?"

"He died. It was a carriage accident." Her tone suggested that although Rebecca was sorry about it, she no longer grieved. "It was almost two years ago, and my mother teases me constantly about finding a husband. Why should I marry? I have enough of my own fortune to be comfortable, and I have a large family, most importantly Freddie, who will always give me a home. I vowed after Mr Cayson died that I would only marry a man I know truly loves me and with whom I shall be happy."

She spoke with a vehemence Elizabeth did not understand, but she suspected it had something to do with Sterling Fitzwilliam. *How very interesting. I wonder—No. It is none of my concern. How ridiculous it would be to interest myself with other people's lives when I so wish people were less interested in mine!*

THE HADDONS ARRIVED TO GENERAL DELIGHT. ELIZABETH FOUND THE senior Mr Haddon as affable as his children. He, John, and Frederick spent their time reminiscing. Georgiana continued to favour spending time with her aunts. Robert Haddon was happy to join the other young men in whatever sporting pursuit was on offer. This left Miss Haddon, Rebecca, and Elizabeth to themselves. It was impossible for Elizabeth to be entirely relaxed, especially when Darcy or their marriage was mentioned, but she was more comfortable with Miss Haddon and Rebecca than she was with the others. Georgiana was with her aunts most of the time, but when all the ladies were together in the afternoon and evening, Elizabeth was surprised by her sister-in-law's behaviour. Georgiana treated her with more openness and politeness than she ever had before.

The change was noticeable enough that Miss Haddon remarked upon it after dinner. "I see that Miss Darcy is happier in her sister. I am glad for her and especially for you. Being among a new society as you are, I am sure it is comforting to have a friend always at your side."

Incapable of doing more, Elizabeth smiled and nodded. She vowed that she would not give in to wishes which had little chance of being fulfilled.

JUST BEFORE BREAKFAST THE FOLLOWING DAY, ELIZABETH HAPPENED to be looking out of the window of her sitting room. She saw Rebecca, Miss Haddon, Mr Robert Haddon, and Sterling taking a turn around the grounds near the house. Rebecca and Mr Haddon walked ahead of the other two, and he spoke animatedly, while Sterling glared at his back and ignored Miss Haddon.

Seeing they were headed inside, Elizabeth went downstairs to greet them. Darcy returned from wherever he had been at the same time.

"Good morning!"

"Good morning, Elizabeth," Rebecca said. "It is such a shame you could not join us for our walk."

"I was busy with Mrs Reynolds, I am afraid." She smiled at Rebecca as her eyes took in Sterling's continued frown, now matched by one on her husband's face. Catching Elizabeth's attention, Miss Haddon rolled her eyes.

"We should join the others for breakfast," Darcy said. "Mrs Darcy." He gestured to Elizabeth to lead the way.

Sterling moved to Elizabeth's side. "Come, come, Darcy. There is no need to be so formal around us. We are all family here. More or less." He sent a pointed look to Robert Haddon.

Elizabeth took Sterling's proffered arm, pulling him away from the other man. "I would thank you to be polite to my guests," she muttered.

"I assure you I am always polite. I had the very best of upbringings and could not fail to be polite. I am even polite in my sleep."

"I do not care what you do in your sleep," Elizabeth retorted. "It is what you do as a guest here, and no, you were not polite to Mr Haddon."

"If I was not it was his own fault."

"The Haddons will be at Pemberley until Monday."

"I promise not to challenge him to a duel."

Darcy overtook them. "A duel?"

"Nothing to concern yourself with, Cousin."

"Excuse me." Elizabeth stopped to await the others, allowing Darcy to pull Sterling into a quiet room. He could deal with his cousin; she had come a little too close to debating with him for her comfort.

"What did Elizabeth say to you?" Darcy asked.

"I believe your wife was not happy with my manner towards Haddon. It was nothing." Sterling waved a hand dismissively.

There was a slight pause during which neither man spoke.

"You did not see him!" Sterling snapped. "His intention is perfectly clear. A marriage alliance with the Darcys would be quite a coup for his family. Rebecca deserves a great deal more than Haddon."

"Rebecca is in the happy position of being able to choose her fate."

This only made Sterling growl in anger, which confirmed Darcy's suspicions regarding Sterling's unannounced arrival. He had never considered the situation before, but he was pleased for Rebecca that she was at liberty to choose her marriage partner. Both he and Sterling had to live with the consequences of not being able to do so. For Sterling, it had meant an unhappy few years, followed by the grief of losing his wife and child. Feeling a sudden sympathy, he said, "Perhaps you should...remove yourself."

"No!" Sterling barked before leaving the room.

THAT DAY'S DINNER PARTY AFFORDED DARCY AN OPPORTUNITY TO observe his family, his sister, the neighbours they had invited for the evening, and Elizabeth. By and large, the company was happy and well-occupied, and Darcy was satisfied. He watched with delight as Elizabeth ensured the comfort of all her guests, and was pleased that Georgiana spoke easily with Elizabeth. He had long thought that it would benefit Elizabeth to be on good terms with Georgiana, who could show her what it meant to be a lady of their social sphere. Now he believed that Georgiana would gain a great deal by having a close relationship with Elizabeth. He and Tom had often lamented the fact that there were no female cousins closer to Georgiana's age with whom she could have formed a natural, intimate friendship. Now she could have something even better—a good-humoured, conscientious lady to call sister.

His wife was the perfect example of loveliness, almost designed to attract him. She wandered gracefully around the room, collecting disquiet or awkwardness and somehow turning it into cheer. Elizabeth had that happy ability to converse with everybody. Some of his family still viewed her with suspicion, but she was able to raise a friendly smile on Uncle John's face and a polite one on Cousin Frederick's, both of which were significant coups.

She smiled and laughed, and he appreciated the way her countenance always displayed her interest in the conversation around her. Indeed, he had witnessed signs of her happiness many times in recent weeks, whether at home, at church, or at one of their neighbours.

She should be pleased with her situation, and she is. He brushed aside such minor irritations as Miss Simms's insult; Elizabeth had too much wit to mind what such a ridiculous lady said. *She gained a great deal by our marriage, and she is the envy of many, to be my wife and mistress of Pemberley. I am glad she can appreciate it.*

At the end of the day, Darcy escorted Elizabeth to her chambers, caressing her cheek lightly before leaving her to walk to his own rooms. When he joined her some little time later, she was in bed. He would have liked more time to enjoy the sight of her in such a state of undress, or with even less covering her body, but she always extinguished the last candle the moment he entered. He could touch and hear, but he would like to see as well, to look upon her form and see her expression, the brightness in her eyes and the blush upon her cheeks, as he kissed and caressed her and joined their bodies.

Although he derived great enjoyment from the act itself, Darcy also very much liked the moments afterwards, before he left her to her sleep. She said little, if anything at all, other than good night as he crawled out of her bed to return to his, but her hands would rest somewhere on him. It was such a peaceful time, a time when the rest of the world and all its cares ceased to exist. So he felt, and so, he supposed, did she.

THE FOLLOWING DAYS PROGRESSED WITHOUT ANY UNDUE DISRUPTIONS or difficulties. Darcy felt more and more at ease. He took pleasure in having about him those whom he considered good company and in whose presence he felt most comfortable. After the first week, John and Frederick ceased their admonishments regarding his marriage. He knew they were not reconciled to his choice of wife, but they at least stopped arguing with him about it.

There was pleasure too, in seeing Elizabeth managing as well as she did among his family and in seeing her and Georgiana on friendly terms. Elizabeth never mentioned the Bennets or her aunt and uncle or any friends she had had before their marriage. She seemed to understand they did not belong in the life of Mrs Darcy. If his family and friends knew the Bennets, he would be ridiculed, if not reviled, for having such in-laws, and Elizabeth would find it very difficult to gain their approval.

Their visitors left with the customary promises of seeing each other again soon. Sterling decided to go stay with friends who lived nearby until his parents and siblings arrived in a few weeks. Darcy, Georgiana, and Elizabeth returned to their quiet occupations. Halfway between the departure of one set of relations and the arrival of the other, Darcy and Elizabeth went to stay with the Haddons at Greenfield for several days, joining a small party of other people whom Darcy knew. When at home, they were in some demand amongst their neighbours, although not nearly as busy as Darcy knew they would be in town.

After returning from a dinner party one night, Darcy found himself impatient to retire. It was a sort of madness, his desire for Elizabeth. There were days during which he could not tear his eyes from her, when he strained his ears to hear every word she spoke, when he longed to have every morsel of her attention turned to him, and when he could hardly keep his hands and lips off her. He could not put a name to his feelings for her. When among their neighbours, and even his family, she shone so brightly compared to the other ladies—in her manner, her address, and her appearance. Apart from desire, there was a sort of pride that she, that vision of loveliness and elegance, was his.

Tonight, he was in no hurry to leave her bed. They had retired earlier than usual, such was his eagerness, and he was not yet tired or desirous of being alone. He felt at peace. Whatever problems remained seemed inconsequential when he was in Elizabeth's bed.

"My family will be here soon," he said.

"Yes. Lord and Lady Romsley and Colonel Fitzwilliam arrive in three days' time."

His hand lazily caressed her body, which was warm and supple. "Sterling will return then as well."

"Have you in mind any particular entertainments? You had not yet decided when last we spoke."

"Mm," Darcy mumbled. "We could invite some people to dinner on Christmas Day. The Morrises. My aunt will not object to Mrs Morris's company. Llewellyn, naturally. Miss Pratt. My uncle was on good terms with her father. I can think of nothing else."

"Very well. I shall make arrangements."

Her voice was a little listless which he took as a mark of tiredness. He spent a moment kissing her good night then left her to her sleep.

Chapter 16

*E*lizabeth was in her sitting room writing letters and organising parcels to be sent to Longbourn and London. They contained Christmas presents for her family, such as ribbons and confections and toys, which she had been collecting during her visits to Lambton. Elizabeth had been relieved to learn that her new family did not exchange gifts. She would have no notion what she could give Darcy and Georgiana that they would appreciate, let alone what the Romsleys would find appropriate.

My time has been much better spent purchasing gifts for the servants, arranging the boxes for Fitzwilliam's tenants and those who require our charity, and organising the celebration for the parish. What a lot of work it is. It is a very good thing that I happen to enjoy it, even if it will be unappreciated by my new family!

She wrote a cheerful letter to Jane and one to Mrs Gardiner, repeating much of what she had said to Jane and adding,

You asked for more particular news of my relationship with my husband and new sister. I am afraid that Miss Darcy and I still

are not friends, though she did seem happier with my company when the Darcys were here. Perhaps that was the beginning we needed.

Of my husband, I have little new to say. The closer to his relations' arrival we get, the more anxious he becomes. I believe he has less doubt of my ability to appear among his distinguished family without embarrassing him than he previously did, but doubt does remain. Do not think that it disturbs me. I will continue on as I have been doing, and I will accept his mistrust, his aunt's instructions, and his uncle's glares with composure. My courage, as you know, always rises when faced with adversity. In ten years, or perhaps two or three beyond that, I feel confident that Mr Darcy will accept that I shall not insult his guests or demand Cook provide nothing but sweets for dinner!

Reviewing what she had written, she frowned. It did not entirely suit her, but she did not have time to re write it. She would trust her aunt to understand and make light of her joke. She did not wish to burden Mrs Gardiner by complaining about a situation neither could change.

"Perhaps, if I am very lucky, Lady Frocester and Mrs Surtees—or Marian and Catherine as I should call them, since we are all one big happy family—will be kind and look past my low origins and lack of suitability. It is unlikely, I suppose, but so is my being Mrs Darcy!" She chuckled, determined to extract every morsel of pleasure possible from the upcoming festive season, even though she could not be with those she loved.

THE ARRIVALS CAME OFF WITHOUT ANY PARTICULAR DELAY, AND Elizabeth met the Fitzwilliams' two daughters and their husbands. She found the ladies to be just as she had supposed they would be—fashionable and very proud. Lord Frocester and Mr Surtees were, she supposed, pleasant enough, although she spent little time in close discussion with them. They were more interested in speaking to their father-in-law about politics, or their brothers-in-law and Darcy about sport and estate management.

Lady Romsley arrived at Pemberley much as an expected summer storm might descend upon one. You might dread it and prepare for it, and, when it struck, it was unpleasant, but a relief to be done with. Lady Romsley closely questioned Elizabeth about the Darcy family's visit, expressing neither approval nor disapproval. Elizabeth longed to ask why everyone was so worried that other members of the family would discover Georgiana's folly, but she did not dare. She could only suppose that they did not trust it would remain secret, and that the aim was to keep Georgiana's reputation as unsullied as possible. Elizabeth hoped that Georgiana would one day prove worthy of the effort they were all taking on her behalf, and, if at all possible, show a little gratitude.

DARCY HAD ANTICIPATED HIS FAMILY'S ARRIVAL WITH A GOOD amount of cheer and confidence. They would be good company, and it would be pleasant to have other gentlemen in the house. Elizabeth had won Rebecca's favour, and he prayed that it would be the same with Marian and Catherine. If the Darcy and Fitzwilliam families stood firm in their acceptance of his marriage to Elizabeth, even if they did not like it, there would be few among the *ton* who would dare to snub her.

He had most anticipated seeing Tom, and they found the opportunity for a private conversation soon after his arrival. Darcy spent a considerable amount of time worrying about his sister. In the years since his father's death, Georgiana had been at school and afterwards with Mrs Younge. She had never lived with him as she was doing now, and the circumstances were by no means easy. Knowing what was right to do with her was difficult. Was he being too demanding or too lax?

"I am not dissatisfied with her progress," Tom said. "Her French has improved, although slower than I would have thought likely. However, the way we have gone about it has not been efficient. Letters take time to write and be delivered."

"And her other studies?"

Tom grimaced. "I am not pleased with her progress, and I know you are not either. She admitted to being slow to attend to her books when you first came to Pemberley. That she attributes to the summer and, as she said, her need to think about it."

"Did she talk to you about Ramsgate?"

"No more than she has you. I can hardly be surprised that a girl of her age should not wish to confide in her two male guardians. It requires a female, someone she trusts. The only two ladies who know about Ramsgate are my mother and your wife. My mother hardly invites confidence. My sisters have never thought so. They are more likely to confide in their maids. Then again, they have spent more time with their maids!" Tom laughed. "I am pleased to see Georgiana is so easy with Elizabeth."

"They were getting along quite well when the Darcys were here."

"Not enough to speak openly about Ramsgate?"

Darcy shook his head and shrugged. "I do not know. I have suggested it to Georgiana, but she says nothing when I do. I have not thought to ask Elizabeth. I shall."

"That would be helpful." Tom smiled slyly, and there was a note of amusement in his voice as he said, "Speaking of Elizabeth, I could not help but notice the change in your relationship. Am I wrong to suppose that you have become…better pleased with your wife?" He laughed heartily. "I tease, but you know that if you can be happy with her, even a little, I am very glad of it."

Darcy rolled his eyes and wished he could control the way his cheeks heated. Tom might be his dearest friend, but he did not like anyone so readily understanding his feelings.

"She is quite pretty, and her manner is not displeasing," Tom said. "But enough about Elizabeth! Let us return to Georgiana."

GEORGIANA HAD RATHER ENJOYED HAVING HER DARCY RELATIONS TO stay, but after three days she greatly anticipated the Fitzwilliams' departure. Lady Romsley and Tom were quite unaccountably severe with her, beginning the very day of their arrival. Her aunt had sought a private interview during which she wanted to discuss Elizabeth and, even worse, Ramsgate.

About Elizabeth, Georgiana said, "We are so different that it is not easy to be friends." She imbued her voice with regret, knowing it was what the countess expected to hear.

"Of course, my dear child," her aunt cooed. "No one, least of all me, believed it would be easy for you and Elizabeth to like each other, but I am very glad to learn that you are making the effort. Now, let us return to last summer."

While Georgiana expected such rough treatment from her aunt, she did not expect it from the once dear Tom. She wanted to scream; it was unpardonable that they continued to treat her like a schoolgirl when really she was quite grown up. Had Wickham not been so horribly deceitful, she would have been a wife of almost five months by now! If she had been prepared for that, she hardly deserved to have her relations lecture her again and again.

Not that I would have liked to have been Mrs Wickham, not if he could lie to me so easily. She silently huffed as she pretended to listen to Tom. *But I would not have been so stupid about being married as Elizabeth is. Always rushing here and there, doing work that is best left to servants. I suppose it is because she was so poor and does not know better. I do not see why Fitzwilliam finds it so admirable.*

Tom said, "I am pleased with the improvement in your French. It is regrettable that Elizabeth is not familiar with the language—or Italian—so that you could practise with her, but we cannot change her deficiencies. Your other studies, however—"

Georgiana leapt into the conversation, her eyes wide and her expression showing innocence and chagrin. "I know I did not do as much as I should have, and I am so terribly sorry."

He patted her hand. "Your brother and I expect you to do better in the coming weeks. Now, about Elizabeth. First, let me say that I am very pleased to see that you and she are getting along so well. She is your sister, and I know you always wished for one. It must be very comforting to have another young lady here. Your brother says that she is doing well with her new duties. Really, it seems that everything is proceeding much, much better than any of us could have supposed it would."

Georgiana lifted her handkerchief to her face and coughed. When she felt equal to responding, she said, "Very true."

Whenever she was not alone, Georgiana said and did what everyone expected to hear and see. It was exhausting having to constantly be on her guard, careful to make everyone believe she accepted Elizabeth. She supposed they were so concerned about people learning the truth—as was she—that they had tricked themselves into forgetting how awful Elizabeth was. Georgiana was too intelligent to do that.

Georgiana told lies about her studies, too. At first, she feared that Tom or her brother would discover them, but they had not. Each time she exaggerated about something or other and no one realised how she had stretched the truth, she felt emboldened, more secure in continuing to go on as she had been doing for months, really since the day she saw Wickham in Ramsgate and he had convinced her not to tell her brother of his presence.

"I AM PLEASED THAT YOU AND MARIAN AND CATHERINE ARE friends," Darcy whispered. He lay beside Elizabeth, his arm across her belly. "The Haddons arrive soon. They will be a welcome addition to our party. You will like to see Miss Haddon."

"Yes." Her life was a deception, and the effort of it was wearing on Elizabeth. She spent the morning either with Lady Romsley reviewing household arrangements, or listening to Marian and Catherine discussing the Season and life among the *ton,* which sounded little better than torture to Elizabeth.

I lie by deed and by word, without any relief from it, separated from those who love me and whom I love, surrounded by people I cannot trust. Elizabeth forced her mind away from these dark thoughts. Indulging in her unhappiness served no purpose. Fitzwilliam would despise her for it, as would his family. There could be no reason for her to bemoan her life as Mrs Darcy, after all.

"Tom was glad to see that you and Georgiana are on good terms. You are doing well, the two of you, are you not?"

It would do no good to be completely open with him. "There is nothing of which I can complain."

"Has she discussed last summer with you?"

Elizabeth shook her head.

"I did not suppose she would. It is too soon, perhaps."

Not knowing what he meant, and not particularly curious, she closed her eyes as Darcy tightened his grip, pulling her closer for a few more minutes before he returned to his bed.

JUST AFTER BREAKFAST THE NEXT DAY, GEORGIANA FOUND HERSELF alone with her aunt and Sterling. "I am looking forward to our outing later this morning," Lady Romsley said. "Are you, Georgiana?"

"Y-yes, Aunt."

The newspaper Sterling held in front of his face muffled, but did not hide, his noise of doubt.

"It should be enlightening," Lady Romsley said. "I had no notion that Surtees had an interest in geology and certainly no expectation that Elizabeth could explain anything about it. It was good of your brother to introduce the scheme. Once he did, Elizabeth could hardly refuse."

Elizabeth entered the room at that moment, adding to Georgiana's misery.

"Elizabeth, we were just discussing this morning's expedition. Are you looking forward to it?"

"Very much," Elizabeth replied as she sat.

The subject of geology had arisen at dinner, and Darcy had told them about Elizabeth's interest in it, particularly as it pertained to the country around Pemberley. At his urging, a plan had been made for them to drive through the neighbourhood, stopping where Elizabeth felt necessary to explain the local land formations as she understood them. They would end with a visit to Lambton where they would partake of refreshments at the inn before returning to Pemberley. Georgiana tried to demur, but her brother and Tom insisted she be part of the excursion.

"It was very right that you arranged it after my son-in-law displayed such an interest. It is a hostess's responsibility to see that her guests are properly occupied and amused."

A snort came from Sterling's direction. Over his newspaper, he said, "I think you can trust Elizabeth to remember what is expected of her and to act accordingly."

He lowered the paper and looked very pointedly at Georgiana. She decided that she truly hated him. Almost as much as she despised Elizabeth, who she was certain wanted to laugh.

As Lady Romsley said, "That is quite enough, Sterling," Georgiana mumbled, "Excuse me," and left the room as quickly as possible.

LADY ROMSLEY FOUND ELIZABETH AND MRS REYNOLDS IN Elizabeth's sitting room the following morning. She insisted they continue their conversation. After the housekeeper left, Lady Romsley waved in a manner Elizabeth found imperious and told Elizabeth to take a seat across from her.

Is this not my room, in my home? She guarded her expression so that her exasperation did not show.

"I have not been in this room in, oh, ten years or more," Lady Romsley remarked. "You have not changed it. I can hardly suppose you like the decoration. Anne always did have ghastly taste, just as her sister does. You must do something with it."

Elizabeth gave her a tight smile. "I have discussed the matter with Fitzwilliam, and plan for the work to be done whilst we are in London. Several of the guest chambers require re-decoration as well. Perhaps your ladyship would be so good as to advise me." Elizabeth did not feel the need for advice, not from the countess or anyone else, but she hoped to disarm Lady Romsley with the request.

Lady Romsley silently scrutinised her for a moment. "I would be happy to guide you. Enough of that for the moment. I wish to speak to you about the Season and a…delicate matter."

Oh joy!

"I have been making plans for the Season. Fitzwilliam and I have spoken about it…"

Without soliciting my opinion, of course. Why would it matter?

"…and we have agreed that the earl and I shall host a ball to introduce you." The countess paused and looked at Elizabeth expectantly.

"That is generous."

Lady Romsley bowed her head to acknowledge Elizabeth's gratitude. "We have not decided on the date, but before Easter. It will be important to see you introduced among our society as soon as we can arrange it. We must make people see that those terrible stories about you and my nephew had no basis in fact."

The countess spoke for some minutes on the subject. Elizabeth listened, but allowed her thoughts to wander to her choice of colour for her rooms—*dusky pink, or perhaps a pale blue?*—as it was nothing she had not already heard many times over.

"The more delicate matter regards your duty to my nephew."

Elizabeth's spine stiffened.

"Pemberley is not encumbered by an entail. My nephew can leave it to any person of his choosing, even if their birth was…questionable. I am certain you understand me."

Elizabeth clenched her teeth and stared at her aunt-in-law, praying she finished her speech before Elizabeth was no longer able to contain her temper. Lady Romsley, as much as she might believe she was being helpful, had no right to speak to her in this way.

"It would be much better if the line were to continue in the proper way. My nephew, to speak plainly, requires a legitimate heir, and it is your duty to give him one." Softening her tone, the countess added, "Your marriage was not contracted in the usual way. Naturally he, and you, needed a period of time to become reconciled to it. It has now been almost four months, and it is time to…well, it is time. You must be welcoming to my nephew, perhaps even encourage his particular attentions. You are not what he expected in a wife, and he may be hesitant, despite the fact that you can be quite pretty."

"How kind." Elizabeth stood. "I assure you that I have every intention of fulfilling all my duties as I see fit. I must go down. It is the breakfast hour."

"Elizabeth—"

Lady Romsley's displeasure was clear, but Elizabeth could no longer listen to such talk. "I thank you, Lady Romsley, but I assure you there is no need for further discussion. Please, I would like to go down now."

The two women looked at each other. Margaret Fitzwilliam was a formidable woman, but Elizabeth found she could be one too.

"News of an impending child would do much to negate the

suggestions that my nephew is unhappy with you. If such proof is not soon offered, we will speak on it again."

She swept out of the room as Elizabeth muttered, "No, we most certainly will not!"

THE HADDONS ARRIVED ON THE TWENTY-THIRD AND WOULD REMAIN until St Stephen's Day. They had not been at Pemberley long before Elizabeth noticed that Tom and Miss Haddon enjoyed each other's company a great deal. The entire party was together, waiting to go through to dinner, and there was something in Tom's manner as they spoke which struck Elizabeth. After a moment's observation, she detected a gentleness in his expression which she was not used to seeing. Tom escorted Miss Haddon in to dinner and seated himself at her side.

After the ladies retired to the withdrawing room, Elizabeth sought Miss Haddon's company.

"It had not occurred to me that you would know the Fitzwilliams quite well. I understood your brother had met the viscount and the colonel, but for some reason, I did not consider that you, too, would be familiar with them. How silly of me!" Elizabeth laughed.

"I have known all the Fitzwilliams for many years. My brother considers Colonel Fitzwilliam a good friend." She blushed a little as she referred to Tom. "Miss Darcy seems happy. I noticed it in November, and it seems her good mood continues."

"She is happy that the colonel is here, I believe. They are very close."

"You met him when you were in London, I think?"

Elizabeth nodded. "He arrived in town the day after I did and stayed almost until we came into Derbyshire. He is a very pleasant gentleman." Elizabeth did not particularly like Tom, but he was not offensive, unlike his mother. Most particularly, she wished to hear Miss Haddon speak of him.

Speaking softly, Miss Haddon said, "Yes, he is."

Elizabeth found the wistful tone of Miss Haddon's voice curious. Used as she was to knowing the details of her family and neighbours' affairs—Mrs Bennet was quite the gossip—she wanted to better understand the lives of those in her new circle.

Catherine Surtees called to Elizabeth to join her and her sister to settle a debate about songbirds. It kept her occupied until the gentlemen came into the room. Tom kept Miss Haddon engaged for the rest of the evening, giving Elizabeth no opportunity to continue their rather interesting conversation.

Chapter 17

When Elizabeth awoke Christmas morning, her first thoughts were of Longbourn and the gaiety of holiday celebrations with her family. The Gardiners would be there, and the house would be alive with noises and preparations for going to church, a special feast, and an exchange of gifts. There would be singing and laughter and, whatever disagreements or frustrations might arise, love and happiness. These thoughts created a sense of nostalgia in her, but also one of good cheer. Regardless of where she was, or who she was with, it was Christmas and the weather was fine. She would have a wonderful day no matter what!

After church, Darcy and Elizabeth, Lord and Lady Romsley, Tom, and Georgiana attended the celebration the Darcys had sponsored. Georgiana wanted to return to Pemberley directly, but a look from Lord Romsley had silenced her. They did not remain for very long but managed to exchange greetings with a number of people.

"That was quite pleasant," Lady Romsley said when they were all settled in the carriage.

"It was," Darcy agreed. "Elizabeth did a commendable job. The children in particular were enjoying themselves."

Elizabeth, sitting across from Darcy, was surprised by his acknowledgment and immediately uncomfortable with the eyes of the Romsleys and Tom upon her. "Mrs Reynolds's assistance was invaluable. I could not have done it without her. Mr Llewellyn and his housekeeper helped, too."

"It would not have gotten done, not to such good effect, without your efforts," Darcy insisted.

Speaking to Elizabeth, Lady Romsley said, "I understand you took a particular interest in the boxes for my nephew's tenants."

"Yes."

Elizabeth got no further as Darcy once again leapt into the conversation. "She spent many evenings sewing for them among her other efforts."

"Oh? Very commendable. And the servants?" Lady Romsley asked. "Have you—?"

"Elizabeth procured gifts and has written notes for all of them."

Tom laughed. "You have been busy."

"There is a great deal a mistress of a fine estate must manage," Lady Romsley said.

"Yes, Mama, I do recall your tireless efforts. Georgiana, it would do you good to assist Elizabeth. In the process, you would learn a great deal."

Georgiana, her face turned to the window, murmured a diffident agreement.

"Elizabeth," the countess said, "you must encourage my niece to join you. She is not out, but it would not be inappropriate for her to make some calls with you, especially those of a charitable nature."

"Georgiana knows that she is welcome to accompany me, or assist me, at any time."

Georgiana glanced at her, and Elizabeth smiled. Their companions were watching, which likely accounted for the brief smile and nod Georgiana gave her before returning to her study of the passing landscape. *But perhaps...*

Lord Romsley, evidently tired of the subject, asked who would be joining them for dinner. Elizabeth was quite pleased to leave her husband to answer.

"Lovely decorations, Mrs Darcy," Admiral Morris said. "Very festive." He gave his hostess a smile as he accepted a glass from his host.

Elizabeth had had the withdrawing room festooned with the traditional greenery and holly. There were other ornaments, too—of ivy, rosemary and bay, spices, apples and oranges, and ribbons—creating not just a feast for the eyes, but a delicious fragrance in the air. The Yule log burned in the fireplace. She had had smaller seasonal decorations distributed throughout the house, too.

The admiral, his wife, and niece had just arrived, bringing with them Miss Pratt and Mr Llewellyn. Introductions were made, and Miss Amy Morris, a pretty young lady of nineteen, was immediately taken under the wings of Marian and Catherine. They were happy to discuss fashion and London and travel with her. Georgiana sat with them and listened.

"The celebration in the village this morning was wonderful," Mrs Morris said. "You are to be congratulated, Mrs Darcy, for I have it from a very good source," she looked at Mr Llewellyn, "that you were its architect."

Elizabeth thanked her and mentioned everyone else involved. She was sitting with Mrs Morris, Miss Pratt, and Lady Romsley. Darcy joined them.

"I am sure they were all very helpful," Mrs Morris said, "but you must not be so hasty to dismiss your efforts. Your new niece, Lady Romsley, has made a very strong, and very favourable, impression on the neighbourhood in her few short months among us."

Lady Romsley smiled, and Darcy said, "Indeed."

The countess seemed satisfied with her company, and Elizabeth was pleased. She had been a little anxious about how Lady Romsley would like meeting the Morrises, but had reassured herself several times that Darcy would not have asked for them to be invited had he been concerned. *No doubt she and the earl condescend to accept the*

Morrises' company only because the admiral is the second son of a baronet!

"Oh, we are very fortunate in Mrs Darcy," Miss Pratt said. "Mr Darcy most of all, of course, and Miss Darcy, but such a dear, sweet lady he brought to Pemberley. She cannot but be an asset to us all. She is so generous and so kind with her time. Not just to me, mind you, although she does come to see me at least once every week, despite having so many demands on her time. Many of our neighbours are so kind as to call, and you may be sure that everyone is full of the warmest praise for Mrs Darcy. Every time she comes, she brings such lovely treats. It is really too much, and yet she will never hear a word of thanks!"

"I am grateful for your kind words. Mrs Darcy is an asset to my family, and no one could be happier than I am that she is doing well in her new role. Except perhaps my nephew!"

There were a few polite laughs at the countess's words. Elizabeth was too surprised by them and the smile Lady Romsley gave her to know how to respond. It looked genuine, but it could not be. Darcy, too, was looking at her with approbation, which was, admittedly, quite nice.

Dinner was remarkably fine, even by Pemberley's high standards, and Elizabeth was happy to see that everyone was talking and laughing and enjoying themselves. The one partial exception was Mr Llewellyn. When Mr Llewellyn had met Miss Haddon in November, it had appeared to Elizabeth that he liked her, and that she had found him agreeable company. Now, Elizabeth saw him looking with some regret at Miss Haddon, who was again seated beside Tom. There was nothing particularly marked in their behaviour, and yet it was obvious that they very much enjoyed each other's company.

Elizabeth was sorry to see Mr Llewellyn's disappointment. She liked him and thought he would make some lady a very good husband. She also believed that Miss Haddon would make some gentleman a very good wife.

Oh my, I must take care not to turn into a matchmaking mama before my time!

During the separation of the sexes, Elizabeth and Miss Haddon had a few minutes of conversation.

"I am very glad that you and your brother and father could be with us."

"Thank you again for inviting us. You have arranged everything so well. The dinner was wonderful, and the company is very agreeable. If I did not know better, I would say that you even had a hand in arranging the weather. It is not unheard of that we would have snow at this time of the year, too much to make such a gathering possible." She nodded towards Mrs Morris, who was speaking with Georgiana. "Will Georgiana play tonight?"

"I hope that she will agree to play Christmas carols." Elizabeth had taken pains to find out which ones Georgiana knew.

"That would be such fun!"

The gentlemen soon joined the ladies, and their merry party continued. As they drank tea, Elizabeth looked around the room; she saw with satisfaction that Georgiana was sitting with her brother. Seizing the opportunity, Elizabeth excused herself from her present company and walked over to them.

"Georgiana, it would be so agreeable if you played. You told me that you know many Christmas carols, and I am sure that our guests would appreciate hearing them today of all days."

"That is a wonderful idea!" Darcy exclaimed, turning to his sister.

Georgiana stammered a reply. "I-I... In front of all these people? Brother, do not make me."

"It is not so many, Georgiana, not when you consider that most of them are family."

"And, other than Miss Morris, you have played before everyone here. You did last month."

Brother and sister stared at her for a long moment.

"Elizabeth will sing while you play, if that makes it easier for you."

I shall? I suppose that was an order, not a request. Elizabeth had envisioned herself and others singing as Georgiana played, but to have her husband say it in such a way, and without at least soliciting her opinion, was too much.

Darcy stood, one hand on Georgiana's elbow forcing her to rise as well. He escorted her to the instrument as he announced, "Georgiana has agreed to play Christmas carols for us, and Elizabeth will accompany her."

Elizabeth smiled pleasantly and walked towards the pianoforte, saying as she did, "I hope that anyone who is so inclined will sing. In my father's house, we often sang carols after dinner on Christmas Day."

"How…quaint," Marian said to her mother who was sitting at her side. Her voice carried well enough for Elizabeth to hear, although she did her best to ignore it and to only pay attention to the voices of those who liked the idea.

Darcy did not sing, but as Georgiana played through six or seven songs, several other people did. Darcy's attention was firmly fixed on Elizabeth while she sang, which she tried not to notice lest his expression discompose her. She did not care to speculate what thoughts lay behind it. After the singing, Georgiana volunteered to play music so those who wished it could dance, as she had for Fitzwilliam and Elizabeth several times.

The festivities continued even after the Morrises, Miss Pratt, and Mr Llewellyn took their leave. Georgiana and Lady Romsley retired early and Lord Romsley soon afterwards, but most of them sat and talked late into the night. It was not until the early hours of the next day when the last of the party went up to bed. To Elizabeth's surprise, she was politely asked about her family and life at Longbourn, and, although Darcy and Sterling looked apprehensive, others seemed almost interested in her stories.

All in all, as Elizabeth prepared for sleep, she was satisfied with the day. It had been enjoyable, and she was sure that the majority, if not all her guests, would agree. Even Georgiana had seemed happier than usual. There were moments that had threatened to dampen her good mood, but she would not dwell on them.

OVER THE NEXT TWO DAYS, FIRST THE HADDONS THEN THE Frocesters and Surteeses departed, leaving a much quieter party at Pemberley. For the most part, Elizabeth could not say that the four days between Christmas and the day last of her guests were to leave Pemberley were unpleasant. Lord Romsley remained gruff in her company, and Tom remained aloof, but polite. Sterling was, in his own way, entertaining when he decided to be. Despite the volume of Lady Romsley's conversation, it was seldom overly offensive. Georgiana became increasingly friendly towards Elizabeth, and Darcy was in good spirits. The sense of easiness, while not complete, was greater than Elizabeth would have anticipated before the Fitzwilliam's arrival.

It created within her a quandary. She had promised herself that she would keep a guard on her heart when entering the married state. She had known that her new family would not like her. Darcy had proven that before they even left Ramsgate, and everything he did from that time until the day of their wedding, and in the weeks after it, showed that she was correct. He despised that she was Mrs Darcy. She had heard him say it, and his actions had shown it again and again.

Georgiana, too, hated her, or at least she had previously. Of late, it was more difficult to understand what her sister-in-law was thinking. She talked more, including to Elizabeth upon occasion, and smiled in an unaffected manner, which, Elizabeth remarked, made her quite pretty and approachable. Was it only because of the presence of other people? A tiny voice inside Elizabeth wanted to believe that it was more than that.

It was against Elizabeth's nature to cling so stubbornly to that which made her unhappy. Even as one part of her urged reserve and low expectations, another part of her could not help but recall the moments which spoke of a better, brighter future. They shone like the most brilliant lights, ones she could see behind the thick walls she had erected around her heart, and she longed to go to them, to embrace the hope and comfort they offered. Lady Romsley, after her disgusting impertinence regarding Elizabeth's need to provide Darcy with an heir, had been much kinder and certainly not as terrible as she had been when they first met. Her incessant chatter about the Season could even be interpreted as wanting to make the experience as pleasant for Elizabeth as possible. Georgiana was being more agreeable. The last months could not have been easy for her; perhaps she had simply needed time to recover from Ramsgate, and to observe Elizabeth before she was comfortable with her.

And Fitzwilliam. He did treat her well, better than many men in a similar situation would. His mood was much improved compared to when they were first married, and on those nights when he came to her, he was so gentle. When he stayed by her side afterwards, softly caressing her and speaking with her, it felt wonderful. She told herself —many, many times she told herself—that what he felt for her was nothing but desire and a wish to create the heir he needed, and that, however much it might seem like approval or even a tiny bit like affection, it was not.

But was it impossible that he could feel something for her? That he might approve of her, might even like her? Perhaps, thanks to her efforts, he accepted that she was capable of being a good wife and mistress, even if he never would have considered marrying a Miss Elizabeth Bennet. Perhaps he accepted that the situation was not as terrible as he had feared it would be, that they might find some happiness together.

Perhaps, Elizabeth thought—hardly daring to believe it, and yet not quite capable of making herself dismiss the thought—the day she had longed for, the day when she earned some measure of acceptance and affection, had come, and much, much sooner than she had ever dreamt it might.

Chapter 18

They breakfasted earlier than usual on the day of the Fitzwilliams' departure. Afterwards, Lady Romsley requested Georgiana's company in her chamber. Tom and Darcy went to Darcy's study, leaving Elizabeth to sit with Lord Romsley and Sterling.

Georgiana suspected that her aunt's purpose was to repeat, yet again, what she had said upon her arrival, and that, in so doing, she would repeat Elizabeth's name a dozen times; with each repetition, Georgiana's disgust and anger would grow.

Her dire predictions came true.

"I have been very pleased with the effort you are making, Georgiana. It is good to see you being on such happy terms with Elizabeth. I know that some of it has been pretence."

Some? thought Georgiana.

Lady Romsley was walking around the room, ensuring her maid had not overlooked some object while packing. Georgiana was glad for her aunt's distraction; it meant that she did not see Georgiana's grimace. It was easier to withstand the conversation if she did not have to guard her expression.

"As you continue to spend more time with her, I trust that you truly will learn to look upon her as a friend and sister."

Georgiana quickly schooled her features when the countess looked at her over her shoulder.

"I must say that Elizabeth exceeds my expectations. The servants like her, as do your neighbours, which is much in her favour. Even your uncle had several nice things to say about her. It remains to be seen how she will be received in town. The terrible stories which circulated about her and your brother will not have been forgotten, and her origins will be enough to ensure that some people will always see her as inferior. We cannot help that."

Georgiana was convinced that her aunt's talk of Darcy's marriage and the speculation was to remind her why her brother had decided to marry Elizabeth. Lady Romsley would never let her forget what she had almost done, and she felt all the injustice of her aunt's good memory. It was all to show that Lady Romsley, just like so many others, blamed her for Elizabeth's presence in their lives, which was so very, very unfair. She never could have foreseen that being friends with George Wickham would end with her brother married to such a woman!

"What I want to impress upon you is to continue the efforts you have started. Elizabeth is your sister. It would be good for you to accompany her, and to aid her as she executes her duties."

The countess went on for some minutes, but Georgiana ceased listening. She went to the window, shifting her position a little this way and that as though seeing something of interest in the view. Were her aunt and uncle actually beginning to like Elizabeth? Georgiana could understand them being relieved that Elizabeth was not as vulgar as her mother was, but relief did not equate with liking.

It was not only Lord and Lady Romsley, either! Tom continued to press her to be friends with Elizabeth, to think of her as an elder sister. Marian and Catherine had said some very kind—and undeserved—things about Elizabeth before they left, as had most of her Darcy cousins when they had been at Pemberley. Her brother was starting to admire her, too—that had been obvious for several weeks. Just thinking about it made Georgiana shake her head; how could they? Elizabeth had no right to be among them, and even if everyone else forgot that, Georgiana would not. She took some comfort in knowing that the last of her family was leaving Pemberley. She could cease to pretend to like Elizabeth—except when Fitzwilliam's presence required it—and would no longer have to listen to person after person speak kindly about her. *Oh, for the day I leave this house for good! I will have my come out in another year, and then I will get married. It cannot happen soon enough!*

TOM AND DARCY WERE STILL IN THE LATTER'S STUDY WHEN Georgiana and Lady Romsley joined the others.

"Ah, good, Margaret, you are here at last," Lord Romsley said. "I want to get started. Elizabeth, go tell my son and nephew that we are ready to depart."

Elizabeth clenched her jaw firmly shut at such an imperious demand. Was she a servant? Sterling said as much, but she dismissed his suggestion that she ring for Hudson or a footman to deliver the message. After sitting with the gentlemen for the last half an hour, and especially after her uncle-in-law's comment, a minute or two alone was an attractive prospect.

TOM AND DARCY AGREED THAT GEORGIANA WAS MORE CHEERFUL, and that time and seeing her relations had been beneficial.

"Georgiana is beginning to like Elizabeth and look upon her as a friend. She told me as much yesterday," Tom said. "The logical outcome is that Georgiana will confide in Elizabeth about Ramsgate. It would do her good to talk about it."

They spoke about Georgiana a little longer before Darcy introduced another subject.

"What are you going to do about Miss Haddon?"

Tom sighed deeply and sunk further into the leather armchair, placing the coffee cup he emptied with one final sip onto a mahogany side table. "There is nothing to do. Believe me, I have thought about it a great deal, and I always reach the same conclusion."

"She is a very kind, sensible lady."

"I know. But she cannot be the one for me. I could marry her, but do you think that my affection would survive the disgust of my parents? They like her—they like all the Haddons—but that does not mean they would welcome her as a daughter-in-law. Do you think that my affection would long survive when the novelty wore off, and I found myself married to a lovely woman, but poor? I do not. There is too much against it. You know my circumstances. I cannot afford to marry a lady with only ten thousand pounds. As a bachelor, my pay and what money I have settled on me are sufficient." He paused. "I could not be happy with the life I would have to lead with Miss Haddon as my wife."

"Tom—"

"Don't. Please, I beg of you. I know what you would say, and I do not want to hear it. It cannot be Miss Haddon. She is neither rich enough nor of high enough consequence. You know what is expected of us when we marry, and I cannot find any fault with it. Neither could you. It is the way our world works."

"My situation is different."

"The principle is the same. You may have had to marry Elizabeth, but you never would have otherwise. What is it you said? You never would have known an Elizabeth Bennet, let alone considered her for your wife. By comparison, Miss Haddon is well placed to be the wife of the master of Pemberley, or the second son of an earl, or even the eldest. Elizabeth had nothing to recommend her."

"True, Tom, but—"

ELIZABETH HEARD NO MORE. SHE HAD BEEN ABOUT TO ENTER THE study when her movements were stilled when she heard Tom say, "It cannot be Miss Haddon." She was not shocked by Tom saying that Darcy would not have married her unless he had to, although she questioned why Tom had found it necessary to voice it. What distressed her was her husband's agreement with Tom's other statement—that Miss Haddon would have been a more appropriate Mrs Darcy, and that Elizabeth had nothing to recommend her.

It was like a slap across the face. For a long moment, all Elizabeth could do was reflect on how terribly foolish she had been to believe that her husband was beginning to truly like her, even approve of her in light of the effort she was putting into being a good wife and mistress. Esther Haddon, who, in terms of fortune and consequence, was better than Elizabeth, was not good enough. If that were true, Elizabeth, who had been thrust upon the Darcy and Fitzwilliam families, could never gain their acceptance. Darcy would never forget how much he hated their marriage.

She could not think about it at the moment. She had a duty to perform, and she would not falter. She was, for better or worse, Mrs Darcy, and she would act the part. Taking a deep breath, she forced her emotions into submission, and opened the door.

ELIZABETH WAS ABLE TO FAREWELL HER GUESTS WITH COMPOSURE. Darcy announced that he would be in his study, attending to business. She nodded and did not notice when Georgiana left her a moment later without saying anything. After speaking with Mrs Reynolds, Elizabeth went to her rooms intending to write letters, but she could not. Again and again she thought about what she had heard and her recent hope that maybe she had earned some respect and regard from Darcy and his family. Not love; she was not so foolish as to think that any of them could love her.

He did not actually say that he still despises being married to you, Lizzy.

She stood, looking out at Pemberley's great park, and questioned every mark of Darcy's kindness. *It was just because there were other people around. It was just to fool people, trick them into thinking that he was happy with you.*

"No," she whispered. It could not be just that. When they were alone in her bed and he was so gentle with her, when he remained by her side, his body draped over hers, or held her in his arms as they spoke before he left her, that could not be to trick anyone. He could not behave as he did then and not feel something for her, some affection even if it was not very much. Could he?

Neither the cold winter air when she was walking outside, nor the company of her husband and sister-in-law at dinner could pull Elizabeth's thoughts away from her sombre inner debate. Rather, sitting with them added to the back and forth of the voices in her mind. Georgiana spoke with relative cheerfulness, as did Darcy. This was proof that they were beginning to accept her. She so wished to feel that she no longer had to suffer from the loneliness that had been with her since the day they drove away from Longbourn, and that she could find some true happiness being Mrs Darcy. But caution had been her guide and solace for so long that it could not be so easily dismissed. If she did, she risked disappointment.

"You are very quiet, Elizabeth. Are you well?" Darcy asked.

Elizabeth stared at him for a moment as her mind repeated his question. She had been too distracted to follow the conversation. "Y-yes. I am tired, I suppose."

She was almost able to convince herself that the expression on his face was one of concern when he said that she looked pale and encouraged her to retire early.

ELIZABETH'S SPIRITS WERE SOMEWHAT RENEWED AFTER A NIGHT'S sleep. She was determined to remain optimistic, yet her heart was heavy as she joined her husband and sister-in-law for breakfast.

"We are fortunate that the weather is fine for our dinner with the Morrises," Darcy said towards the end of the meal.

Elizabeth smiled faintly before taking a sip of her coffee.

"You still look pale, Elizabeth. Are you sure that you are well?"

"Yes, perfectly."

Darcy made a noise as though he remained uncertain. "You would do best to stay indoors. I would not want you to become ill."

His mark of concern lightened Elizabeth's heart, and she agreed without feeling that he was being officious. It made her hopeful about Georgiana. Elizabeth had let her resolution to befriend Georgiana slip away in the face of her many slights, but she would renew her efforts. After all, Georgiana had been kinder of late. It very well could be because of a genuine desire to be closer, to perhaps one day be true sisters and love one another.

"I am off to my study," Darcy announced. "Potter will be here soon, if he is not already."

Alone with her sister-in-law, Elizabeth said, "Pemberley will be so quiet now that it is just the three of us again."

Georgiana nodded and kept eating, her eyes on her plate.

"It will be a month, perhaps six weeks before we go to town. Do you anticipate it?"

Georgiana huffed and briefly looked up from her plate. "Yes."

Elizabeth could not stop. She had to know if Georgiana's recent friendliness had been sincere, even a little. "I have heard quite dreadful tales about the winters in Derbyshire. It has not been so severe recently. Does it truly get so very cold and snowy?"

Georgiana gave an exaggerated sigh, and rolled her eyes.

Elizabeth said a silent prayer, and, with her heart beating unaccountably hard, said, "Georgiana, as you know, I am refurbishing some of the guest rooms. Would you like to help me?"

Georgiana dropped her fork and knife. "Why would I want to do that?"

"Because Pemberley is your home. I would like you to be comfortable here. I would appreciate the company."

Georgiana gave a mirthless bark of laughter, and glared at her. "I meant why would I want to spend one minute with you if I did not have to? I did what I was supposed to do when my family was here. I did what Tom and my brother have been telling me I had to do."

Elizabeth felt sick, and, without meaning to, said, "I had hoped— it seemed you were beginning to—"

"Beginning to what?" Georgiana stood and looked down at Elizabeth. "Like you? Are you really that stupid? I pretended to like you, but that is all it ever was, for me, for *all* of us—a deception. I will never accept you as Mrs Darcy or my sister, and if you think that anyone else will, that my aunt does or that my brother does, then you are even stupider than I thought. We all acted, just as we had to, to trick people into believing that everything was well, but it is not, and it never will be as long as you are here! You will never belong, and I will never like you!"

Georgiana rushed out of the room.

GEORGIANA'S DIATRIBE FELT LIKE A KNIFE RUNNING THROUGH

Elizabeth's belly. Gone were any feelings of hope she had had, all of them replaced with shame at allowing herself to let her guard down. The pain of her unhappiness and loneliness came crashing down on her. This is what her life would always be, living among people who would never think well of her, and who would always believe that she had no right to be there. There was nothing she could do to change their opinion.

Hardly knowing what she was doing, Elizabeth stood and exited the room, calling on all the dignity she could muster lest she encounter one of the servants. She needed to be alone in her rooms; she would tell Drewe that she was tired and was not to be disturbed.

Darcy was near the stairs, although Elizabeth hardly saw him.

"What is wrong with Georgiana?"

Elizabeth laughed bitterly as she walked past him, praying fervently he would leave her alone.

He did not. He followed her up the stairs and into her chambers, closing the door behind him.

"Elizabeth, what is wrong with Georgiana? I saw her running to her rooms. What happened after I left the breakfast parlour?" he demanded.

Elizabeth just shook her head, keeping her back to him. *Leave me be, oh please, just go!* She could not speak, could not open her mouth, or find innocuous words to say to excuse her behaviour or Georgiana's. Pain and rage were welling up within her; if he did not soon leave her, she would be unable to restrain them.

"I demand that you answer me!"

Her self-control at an end, Elizabeth spun around and cried, "What is wrong with Georgiana? The same thing that has been wrong with her for months! Me! She hates that I am her sister. She is disgusted at having to be in my presence. I do not need to explain her feelings any more than that. You know them all too well. You share them. No one wants me here. No one wants me to be your wife, to be Mrs Darcy. She does not, your family does not, you do not. *I* certainly do not."

"What? I do not underst—"

"I have always known that you hated having to marry me. Why should I be surprised that even now, even after everything I have done, you cannot forget your disgust? How could I have been so stupid as to think that you, that *any* of you might have started to accept me?" The last was said to herself.

"I do not understand you."

His tone, full of restrained anger and shock, made her look at him. How dare he act surprised and affronted!

Elizabeth's resulting laugh was bitter. "Do you think so little of my understanding? Do you think I could not see how you and your family, even your friends, *all* of you look upon me with scorn? That none of you believe I deserve to be your wife? Perhaps then it would surprise you to know that I do not want to be Mrs Darcy, I have never wanted to be Mrs Darcy, and I hate every day that I am Mrs Darcy."

"How dare you insult me in such a manner?" he spat. "I gave you my name, you who were nothing more than the daughter of an insignificant country gentleman! Had I not acted as I did, you and your whole family would have been ruined. In becoming my wife, you gained more than you ever could have hoped to find in marriage. All the advantages of this situation are yours. You have nothing of which to complain."

"Of course," she mocked. "What have I to complain about? What is respect or-or affection when there is social position and gowns to be had?"

Before Darcy could reply, she continued, "I do not expect you to understand. You who value money and status above everything else. Believe me, you have made it plain, all of you, that I am not good enough. From the very beginning, again and again I have been confronted with the fact that none of you see any value in me, that you never could because I was no one other than Miss Elizabeth Bennet, with no fortune to offer, no connexions, nothing you care about. Do you think that I could not see how my family disgusted you, even when we were in Ramsgate?"

"Should I have congratulated myself on being forced to marry a woman whose connexions were so decidedly beneath my own?"

"From the very beginning of this farce, you have impressed me with the fullest belief of your arrogance, your conceit, your selfish disdain for the feelings of others, even of *me*, of your *wife*! Regardless of why we married, I *am* your wife, and yet you could not treat me with even the tiniest bit of kindness. Not even then, not even directly after I saved your sister from that blackguard!"

Tears stung her eyes, but she would not let them fall. She continued, not allowing Darcy time to respond. "Do you think I did not know how you watched me, looking to find fault, how everything I did, everything I said was under scrutiny? You told me as much when you returned to Longbourn. That as your wife, everything I did and said was under inspection.

"Every day I have tried to do my best. I tried even before we were married. I wrote to you, asking you to tell me about yourself, hoping that you would see it as I did, as an opportunity to know each other, but you did not. You never wrote anything of substance, or any word of reassurance. You could not be moved to so much as tell me about your family when I asked, to tell me about the life into which I would be thrown, out of no wish or decision of my own.

"And how did you behave after you took me away from my home? Away from people who, whatever their faults, at least cared about me, at least loved me, and treated me with kindness. You behaved with contempt, with complete disregard. That is all I received from you and everyone in your family.

"But did I say anything? Did I cry about my fate? No! I did everything I could to be a good wife, and a good mistress, and even a good sister to the girl whose actions did this to me."

"My concerns were justified!" Darcy barked. "I did not know you. After everything I witnessed in your father, and in your mother and sisters, how could I have any trust in you? You have never been a part of my world. Your family, your upbringing could not prepare you to be my wife. Why should I have trusted that you would not shame me?"

"Oh yes, of course," Elizabeth scoffed. "How could I ever measure up to the vaunted status of the Darcys? Perhaps I would have done better to emulate you. I should think of nothing other than my own feelings, my own wishes and desires, doing what I want, when I want, with no regard whatsoever to anyone else. That is what it means to be a Darcy, is it not?"

"That is going too far!"

She turned away from him, and shook her head. "Nothing I do

will ever be enough. I have learnt my lesson. I should have known it months ago, when you could not be bothered to talk to me during the journey to London. You could not even bear to be in the carriage with me! Or when you said no more than a dozen words to me on our wedding night, or left me to eat alone the following night so that you could talk to your cousin."

She spun around to face him. "Well, I was good enough that night in Ramsgate, good enough to save your sister, Miss Georgiana Darcy, with all her fortune and consequence, all her proper education and good breeding. I was good enough to save her from making a horrible mistake, from doing something so against all propriety, and consequently saving you and your family from the scandal her actions would have wrought, to say nothing of what she would have suffered as George Wickham's wife. I wish to God, oh how I wish I had been anywhere other than at my window that night. At least then I would not be paying for my moment of impetuosity with the rest of my life! At least it would not have cost me my happiness! It is just as well I did not do it for your thanks because I certainly have never been the recipient of your gratitude, let alone Georgiana's."

"No thanks? Did I not marry you? I have given you everything, more than you ever had a right to expect."

"Oh yes, I know that only too well! You would never have humbled yourself so much as to befriend, let alone marry, an Elizabeth Bennet. I have heard you say it often enough, I have heard it again and again from your family. Believe me, I would never have married you if I had had any choice whatsoever. What can you offer me that is of any real value? Nothing! You may think that I gained a great deal, but I have not, not one single thing that is of any importance to me."

"You have said too much."

"Have no fear. I will go on doing as I have done all along. I shall do everything in my power to be the best Mrs Darcy I possibly can be, despite my low origins and the fact that by all rights I never should have been granted such an august position. I will continue to fulfil all my duties, suitably grateful that you have found one use for me at least."

Darcy took a step backwards.

"I will keep a smile on my face, burying my discontent so that you need not witness it and have yet another reason to despise me. There is no one here who would care or who would not do as you did just a moment ago when you laughed at my misery, reminding me that I can have no cause to repine, not when I am so fortunate as to be your wife."

"You have said quite enough, madam."

"Then by all means, go. I never wished you here." She turned away from him, praying again for his departure.

As soon as Elizabeth heard the sound of the door closing behind her husband, she threw herself upon her bed, and, for the second time since becoming Mrs Darcy, wept.

Chapter 19

Never had Elizabeth and Darcy cursed the timing of an event more than they did their dinner engagement that day. The drive to their neighbours' home was silent, and they did not so much as look at each other. Darcy was too full of anger and insult, and Elizabeth of anger and regret.

There was little of note about the party. As much as Darcy tried to avoid seeing Elizabeth, he could not entirely do so. Without volition, his eyes sought his wife. At first glance, Elizabeth seemed to be much as she ever was—at ease, and looking just like Mrs Darcy should. He resented that she could be so comfortable after hurling such disgusting words and accusations at him.

I let the fact that she is not, outwardly, as vulgar and ignorant as the rest of her family blind me. I let the fact that she is pretty lead me into complacency, the fact that I could desire her trick me into believing that she is less objectionable, that somehow she was an acceptable wife, when she never could be.

On second glance, his bitterness decreased marginally because she looked a little pale. His opinion did not alter significantly after a third or fourth look, but somewhere around the fifth or sixth, when his eyes lingered ever so slightly, it occurred to him that Elizabeth, just like he, was only pretending to be easy, and that below the outward veneer of good cheer, she was not at all comfortable.

Darcy was not prepared to think well of her, and violently banished all such thoughts, refusing to allow his attention to wander to her again during the meal.

When the gentlemen joined the ladies in the withdrawing room later, it was only natural that Darcy looked for Elizabeth. When she took a seat by Mrs Morris, Darcy happened to position himself so that he could hear the conversation without them knowing that he was nearby.

Mrs Morris said, "You do not seem quite yourself this evening, Mrs Darcy. You are not ill, I hope?"

"No," Elizabeth replied. "Just a little tired."

Mrs Morris smiled at her kindly. "You have been very busy with your guests and the holidays. Perhaps now you will be able to get the rest you need."

Elizabeth smiled politely and asked about the Morrises' winter plans. Mrs Morris said that Elizabeth could next expect to encounter them in London, if she would allow Mrs Morris to call on her there. It was true that Darcy did not see many of his Derbyshire neighbours socially in town, but he would not object to meeting the Morrises. He approved, therefore, when Elizabeth answered kindly, and said that she would be honoured to see her in town.

Darcy refused to pity Elizabeth no matter how tired she might feel. She should feel ill after abusing him so thoroughly. Nonetheless, he ordered the carriage earlier then he usually would. It was only with his feelings in mind; he had no wish to remain in company longer than was strictly necessary.

Once in the carriage, Elizabeth sighed deeply, rested her head against the back of her seat, closed her eyes, and ran a hand over her forehead. Darcy suspected she had a headache. He would not feel sorry for her.

At Pemberley, Hudson greeted them. "A fire has been lit in the withdrawing room, madam."

Darcy wished he could immediately quit Elizabeth's company, but habit made him disguise his true feelings from the servants. He dismissed the butler, and led Elizabeth into the room.

ELIZABETH WARMED HER HANDS BY THE FIRE, HER THOUGHTS HEAVY. Hearing the door close and Darcy walking about the room, she took a deep, fortifying breath, and turned to face him. She could not meet his eye as she spoke to him for the first time since their angry exchange that morning. She forced herself to sound as contrite as possible. Nevertheless, her voice was tight, controlled, and colder than she intended.

"Fitzwilliam, I apologise for my words earlier today. I should not have spoken to you that way. I know how f-fortunate my situation is, and I...I am sorry."

Elizabeth could not humble herself any further, not this night. She would pay a price for being foolish enough to believe he or Georgiana thought any kindlier of her now than they had the day her unfortunate marriage began. Her penance to her husband would be far larger still, if she hoped to recover the understanding of sorts they had reached. He had treated her well, as careless of her feelings as he had been, and better than many men would a wife they did not want. She could only imagine what he thought of her now, how she must have sunk in his opinion. If she could not repair some of the damage she had done, her life would be far worse than it had been, devoid of what small comforts she had previously enjoyed.

She did not have the heart to do more than offer a simple apology at the moment. She needed sleep and time to consider how she should begin what seemed like a monumental task.

"If you could excuse me for the night. My head aches." The words sounded foreign to her, as though spoken by a stranger. It was ridiculous and unjust to have to ask for his permission to retire when she was not well, but she would have to be very careful and contrite in her behaviour to him in the future.

Without looking directly at him, Elizabeth saw his curt nod. She dropped a shallow curtsey, and left him.

DARCY DISMISSED HIS VALET, CHANGED INTO NIGHTCLOTHES, POURED a healthy measure of brandy, and fell into a soft wing chair by the fireplace. He let his resentment flow over him like a tidal wave. How had this day happened? After breakfast, when he had gone to his study, he had learnt Potter would be delayed by at least an hour. He had decided to find Georgiana to ensure they were in agreement about what she needed to accomplish that day.

Such an innocent wish had been met by horror. He saw Georgiana reach the top of the stairs and run towards her rooms. Before he could follow her to ask what was wrong, Elizabeth had appeared looking... he had no words to describe it. He accompanied her to her rooms to ask for an explanation. Her initial silence had made him angry and anxious, but oh how much he preferred those feelings to what had resulted when she spoke so unjustly, so bitterly, and cruelly. The utter rejection of her words had crashed through him, ripping him into pieces.

He stood and began to pace, his agitation too great for him to remain still. How dare she speak to him as she had? Had he not treated her with kindness and consideration ever since that awful day in Ramsgate? He could have packed Georgiana into a carriage and fled Ramsgate the next morning, leaving Elizabeth and her wretched family to whatever fate awaited them. Sterling had said it long ago— he would have recovered from any scandal which arose. His name and fortune assured him of that. Georgiana's reputation had been utmost in his thoughts, along with his own, but that was nothing of which to be ashamed; those feelings were natural and just, and he would not apologise for them. The fact of the matter was that he had acted to Elizabeth's benefit, as well as his and Georgiana's.

What thanks did he get for being an honourable gentleman? None whatsoever. He had a wife who despised him and thought nothing of throwing the most hateful, baseless accusations at him, and in-laws who were an embarrassment to even think about, let alone see. He had a wife who—

He stopped abruptly, and almost tumbled over his feet as he stepped towards the window. He pressed his forehead against the cold glass, hoping it would cool his temper and help to banish her image and the sound of her voice from his thoughts. They created in him too strong, too violent a feeling. It would take a great deal more than her few words of apology to assuage his contempt.

Am I supposed to sit across from her at breakfast and pretend nothing has happened? Am I to ask her what she will do with the day, or listen to her prattle on about some insignificant matter in the same voice that just this morning painted me as the most unfeeling of men? "It cannot be borne."

He looked out into the night. The world seemed like an empty void outside of the shell of Pemberley. At the moment he hated Pemberley, hated the place he had always called his home, the place where he had been happiest, because she was here. He had to be away from her. Distance might allow him to discover a way to tolerate her presence again.

I shall go to London.

He would tell Quinn at first light and they could be off before breakfast. He would use the excuse of business, claim a sudden need to look into some problem that could not wait until February.

He would go to London. There, at least, there was no Elizabeth.

"Why?" Georgiana cried when Darcy informed her of his imminent departure.

"Business. A matter I thought—"

"Take me with you! I can be ready to leave in a trice."

"No."

"Oh, please," she said. "There is nothing to keep me here, and I could be company for you on the journey, and in the evenings."

"No." He struggled to think of an excuse to soften the blow of an outright rejection. "I travel as quickly as I can, and I shall be very busy in town. I would be no company for you."

Before she could say more, he stood. "I shall send word of my return." Spying a novel lying beside her on the settee, he added, "Attend to your studies. You know what you should be doing, and we shall review your progress when I return."

He placed a quick, soft kiss on her forehead and started towards the door. With his hand on the doorknob, he paused, and, over his shoulder, said, "Be kind to Elizabeth. She deserves your goodwill."

He left the room, and returned to his, shaking his head as he walked. He did not know what had made him say what he had about Elizabeth. She had said something about Georgiana at the start of her hateful speech, had she not? What was it? He dismissed the question as soon as it entered his thoughts. Trying to recall what it was meant he had to think about her, and he would not. He went to hurry Quinn's preparations, longing to be gone.

ELIZABETH REMAINED IN HER SITTING ROOM, CONTEMPLATING breakfast and wondering how she could possibly face her husband. She would have to be very careful and offer him another apology when she felt capable of saying more than she had the night before.

As discontented and lonely as Elizabeth had been, she feared the outcome of her angry words would make her situation far worse. She had injured her husband's pride and challenged his character. She expected he would revert to treating her at least as poorly as he had when they were in London. Darcy would never admit there was truth in what she had said. She would be fortunate if he accepted her apologies, and agreed to put the argument behind them. If he began to treat her in as hurtful a manner as Georgiana routinely did, she could not bear it.

But she would have to find a way if it came to that. She would try to make amends. Was she not the one who always made the effort to befriend her husband and sister-in-law, to be a good wife, a good mistress, and a good sister? Now she would have to be the one to accept responsibility for the argument, to be contrite, and do everything she could to make their situation as easy as possible.

Elizabeth felt the sting of tears forming—not tears of sadness, but ones of unmitigated resentment. It was at this moment that her maid delivered a note. Elizabeth thanked her and sent her away before Drewe could notice her distress.

Business calls me to London. I shall be away several weeks.

FD

She gazed at the words, written in Darcy's fine script, for several long moments before folding the sheet neatly, walking to the fireplace, and dropping it into the flames. It was soon no more. Elizabeth returned to the sofa, and sat down again.

"I suppose I no longer have to worry about how to act towards him at breakfast."

What did she feel? Relieved he was gone? She could use these weeks to determine her best course of action, what manner she should adopt when they were next together, what she should say or do to repair the damage she had caused.

Or was she upset he left without doing her the courtesy of telling her himself, angry that, instead of contending with the difficulty she represented, instead of making the effort, he was again ignoring her? *Just as he did before the wedding when he could not write more than a line or two in a letter to me. Just as he did after the wedding when he would not even sit in the same room with me, or when we came into Derbyshire, and he avoided my company for as many hours of each day as he possibly could.*

It seemed, on balance, anger would win out. "He is insufferable."

Muttering invectives of his selfishness and the arrogance which allowed him to think so cruelly of her, even though she was his wife and had never, until yesterday's regrettable interlude, given him any reason to think ill of her, Elizabeth gathered her wrap and her book, and went downstairs in search of breakfast. She would not let his behaviour rob her of her appetite.

MEMORIES OF ELIZABETH AND HER UNFORGIVABLE WORDS HAUNTED Darcy during the journey to London. He would never act in the callous manner she had described. He had been plunged, most unexpectedly, into a terrible situation when he went to Ramsgate, and he had, from that day forward, acted with the best of intentions and to the best of his ability.

What particularly provoked him was Elizabeth's suggestion that she had never wished to be intimate with him. This implied he had somehow forced or coerced her, and he would never, never have done so. The mere thought of it made him feel ill. He had seen evidence she was willing to become a true wife to him. The evening he had inadvertently kissed her neck and she had recoiled from the shock of his touch, had he not refrained from anything further? When he had kissed her that night on the terrace, she had returned his embrace. Then, on the night when they consummated their marriage, she had been the one to suggest they retire; she had invited him into her room. He would never have demanded she give him her body.

He could not abide the memories of their nights together, the times he had held her in his arms and felt more peaceful than he ever remembered feeling. Those memories left him angry and resentful. And they hurt. He had thought better of Elizabeth than she deserved. He had looked for the good in her and thought he found it, but he had been wrong. He was disappointed in her, but also in himself.

Darcy arrived in town to find everything prepared for his stay despite the short notice. The housekeeper informed him Elizabeth's rooms were still being worked upon, but he was assured there would be no disruption to him. Darcy accepted this and everything else Mrs Northmore said, hardly hearing her. His only order was that he was, without exception, not at home to visitors.

Darcy spent the next week ignoring the outside world, immersing himself in work, and, in so doing, keeping reminders of Elizabeth under some control. He still spent more time than he liked reiterating again and again what he had been telling himself since their exchange of angry words. He read treatises on new agricultural and animal husbandry techniques, sending Quinn to the booksellers in pursuit of various works. He reviewed his portfolio of investments, searching for ways to improve his fortune. It was one of his duties as master of Pemberley, and he had to make up for Elizabeth's lack of dowry.

I am sure she never thought of that! he silently grumbled. *Marrying her brought with it many evils, and this is but one.*

He perused the shelves in his library for books to distract his mind. The morning he inadvertently pulled a tome on botany off a shelf, and was almost overwhelmed by the memory of Elizabeth speaking animatedly about the subject, her eyes shining with curiosity, he finally left the house. He took a brisk walk, his hat pulled down over his brow and his head lowered, hoping to avoid recognition should he happen across any of his acquaintance. He prayed the cold would soothe his passions, and, finding the exercise slightly helpful, he began to walk or ride daily, doing his best to avoid people he knew.

Mrs Northmore suggested two or three times that he look into Elizabeth's rooms to see the changes she had ordered, but he would not. He wanted no reminder of Elizabeth, not for as long as he could avoid it.

At the end of his first week in London, a note arrived from Lady Romsley.

Fitzwilliam,
I would reprimand you for being in town and failing to inform me of it, but I have no interest in spending my time in such an endeavour. Your uncle remains at Romsley, but Sterling is here with me. Come to dinner tomorrow. It will be just the three of us.

Darcy wanted to refuse. How could he explain his presence in London and failure to inform her of it? He could not admit he and Elizabeth had argued. His aunt would give him unwanted advice, and Sterling would laugh at him. He preferred to be alone and at home, where he could nurse his grievances in private.

Knowing he could not avoid it, he accepted the invitation.

Chapter 20

or the early part of the meal, Lady Romsley kept them busy demanding to know what had precipitated his unexpected journey to town and sharing the recent news about family members and mutual acquaintances. She told Darcy some of his father's relatives were in London, and, as he would be in town for another week and a half, she would arrange a dinner party.

Part way through the meal, the conversation turned to the subject Darcy most wish to avoid—Elizabeth.

"Aside from improving her wardrobe, I am concerned about preparing her for the scrutiny she will confront. I did try to discuss the matter with her while I was at Pemberley, but she does not seem to understand that her behaviour, how she speaks, what she says, how she comports herself, all of it will be closely watched. There is no hiding her origins, and her manners are not those of someone familiar with good society."

Sterling interrupted her. "For goodness' sake, when are you going to admit there is nothing wrong with Elizabeth's behaviour?"

As mother and son went back and forth for a moment, Darcy

ignored them, and allowed his thoughts to say what he could not utter out loud. *Ha! If you knew the terrible way in which she spoke to me, her unjust attack—She is worse than her mother.*

No, his better sense cried, *you cannot compare her to Mrs Bennet. Elizabeth has never been vulgar or less than proper. Sterling is correct; until the morning of our argument, there was never anything wrong with her behaviour.*

Darcy heard Sterling say, "You forget that I have been in Elizabeth's company more frequently than you have. I am the one who has been to that village, whatever it is called, where her father has his estate. I was at Pemberley in November, as well as with all of you in London after the wedding."

"That is immaterial," Lady Romsley replied. "Elizabeth is incapable of knowing how to behave in society because she has not been properly prepared for it. Her father and, more importantly, her mother have never been among good society."

"I don't give a bloody—"

"Sterling!"

"I do not care," Sterling said slowly, "who her father is, or how the rest of her family acts. There is nothing wrong with Elizabeth's manner, and, lest anyone has forgotten, let me remind you that she is Mrs Darcy because of something *Georgiana* did. Elizabeth prevented Georgiana from ruining her reputation, if not her life, and dragging us all into scandal."

Lady Romsley and Sterling continued to exchange words while Darcy's mind once again wandered.

Georgiana, there is something about Georgiana. He remembered asking Elizabeth why Georgiana was running to her rooms. It was then that Elizabeth had lashed out at him. *Could Georgiana have done —? No. Georgiana is not responsible for what Elizabeth said; Elizabeth is.*

"Enough!"

The strident tone of his aunt's voice again recalled Darcy's attention.

"Elizabeth did quite well when we were in Derbyshire," Lady Romsley conceded. "She is not without intelligence, which certainly helps. Fitzwilliam, you should encourage Georgiana to spend more time with her. Elizabeth is not what we would have wanted for your wife, but she is exerting herself. I am by no means saying that I like her, but, if she continues to impress me with her willingness to become a proper wife to you, then, in time, I might change my opinion."

A fortnight earlier Darcy would have been grateful for his aunt's words. Now he knew Elizabeth did not deserve his aunt's acceptance. He would have to impress upon Elizabeth the absolute necessity of behaving properly when they went into society, no matter how difficult or disagreeable she found it. He had not thought it would be necessary after seeing her with his Derbyshire neighbours, but after *that* morning... He could not abide anyone saying his wife was vulgar or did not know how to comport herself among the *ton*.

When dinner was finished, Lady Romsley stood. "I shall leave you. I have letters to write, so do not think to join me. Enjoy your conversation." She gave her son a pointed look before sweeping out of the dining room.

Sterling groaned, and accepted a glass of port before waving the butler, who had entered as the countess exited, out of the room. The two men sat in silence for a few minutes before Sterling spoke.

"You look like a man who has had one hell of a row with his wife."

Darcy startled and spilled a small amount of his drink on his coat.

"You need not deny it."

"I am not discussing this with you."

"I recognise the look," Sterling went on blithely. "God knows Cassandra and I had more than our share of arguments. You may recall she was not my choice of wife any more than Elizabeth was yours."

Darcy made a noise of exasperation hoping it would discourage his cousin from saying more. He began a study of the room, looking anywhere other than at Sterling. He was certain that his cousin would find a confirmation of his suppositions in his eyes, although the way he was acting probably told Sterling everything he needed to know.

"Cassandra and I were always too much alike to deal peacefully with each other. Our families wanted us to marry, and so we did. But neither of us ever truly accepted the situation. A shame, really. I do not think we accepted the possibility of being happy together."

Sterling stood, genuinely lost in a rare moment of gravity. He poured himself another measure of port, and held up the carafe. Darcy shook his head, and watched as Sterling returned to his seat.

"Perhaps if she and the child had lived, and if...well, perhaps things would have been different." After another solemn silence, Sterling laughed, his expression brightening. "If only Tom were here. We would make quite a merry party. Three men brooding over women, none of whom likely deserve it."

Darcy saw a flash of pain in Sterling's expression. He did not know if his cousin was thinking about Cassandra, Rebecca, or both ladies.

"Seriously, Darcy, I have had more than sufficient time to think about my ill-fated marriage. I know Cassandra and I could have done better. You know what our lives are like. The need to do the family proud, and fulfil your duty by marrying the right person is ingrained from childhood. In retrospect, I never stopped resenting that I had to marry Cassandra rather than someone of my own choosing. I believe she felt the same way. It prevented us from being happier than we were, and even from treating each other with more kindness."

Sterling stared at the liquid in his glass for a long moment before drinking it in one mouthful. "Enough of that. I only say so because it might benefit you. I like Elizabeth—and you know how few people I deign to like. Given the circumstances of your marriage, I would expect you and she to be at odds. At least until you learnt to know each other."

"You are correct. That is enough." Darcy had no more intention of discussing his argument with Elizabeth now that Sterling had shared his experiences than he had had at the start of their conversation. He was on the point of taking his leave, when Sterling laughed.

"Well, if you think that was disagreeable, be glad I spared us the talk my mother wanted me to have with you." There was a look of amused expectation on Sterling's face.

"Out with it. If you do not tell me now, you will only intrude upon my privacy to tell me tomorrow."

"Only because it is so bloody awful it must be shared. Not many women would dare to travel the paths that Lady Romsley does." After a dramatic pause, he continued. "My esteemed mother wanted me to remind you that you require an heir, preferably a legitimate one, and to encourage you to, as she said, get on with it."

Darcy groaned in disgust.

"Oh yes, she really did." Sterling was almost gleeful at the utter impertinence of Margaret Fitzwilliam's interference. "She then said a lot of words about it doing you and Elizabeth good if she is—Oh, you know what I mean, or rather what my mother does. If people see that she is going to provide you with this heir, then they will believe that you are happy and in love and all of that."

Darcy groaned again, and slide down the chair, resting his chin on his chest.

"I told you it was too ridiculous not to mention. I doubt you needed my mother's advice in any case." He guffawed.

"I am not talking about Elizabeth with you," Darcy snapped.

"I am not asking that you do."

They were silent for a minute.

"I really do rather like her. She has more sense and intelligence than most of the ladies I know. Most of the men, too, for that matter."

"Bramwell!"

Sterling made a face of mock contriteness. He then insisted on sharing some gossip about Lady Catherine and Anne de Bourgh, who was, it seemed, on the point of marriage to an impoverished minor peer with a rather questionable reputation. Darcy had little interest in hearing it, and was able to escape the house some quarter of an hour later, fortunately without seeing Lady Romsley again.

ELIZABETH WAS CORRECT THAT GEORGIANA WOULD NOT JOIN HER FOR breakfast after Darcy's departure. As the day wore on, she accepted that their separation should not continue, as much as she enjoyed it. She found Georgiana in her sitting room with Miss Amey, her maid, whom Elizabeth dismissed. When they were alone, Elizabeth turned to face her sister-in-law.

"You have no right to send Amey away!"

Georgiana's petulance was not a surprise, thus it failed to discompose her. With as neutral an expression as she could maintain, she allowed a long moment to pass before speaking. "Yes, I do. Your brother is gone, likely for several weeks—"

"You are to blame, I know it!"

Elizabeth carried on calmly, as though Georgiana had not spoken. "Although I fully appreciate the temptation to see each other as little as possible, it will not do. I do not care whether or not you speak to me, but you will present yourself for breakfast and dinner every day, and you will remain with me until at least eight o'clock."

Georgiana glared at her in a way that spoke both of disbelief and disgust.

"I shall not have the servants saying that we cannot get along even enough to sit through meals together. I shall dismiss Hudson and whatever footmen are present, and we need not speak. After dinner, you will play or read, whichever you like, as long as it is in the withdrawing room. What you do outside of the times I require your presence is your own affair. Whether you attend to your studies or not is none of my concern. You answer to your brother or cousin in that regard."

"And if I refuse?"

"When your brother returns, I will tell him that your behaviour has caused talk among the servants. I will ensure that none of them are reprimanded. Dinner is in one hour." Elizabeth spun on her heel, and left the room.

Elizabeth next sought out the housekeeper. "Mrs Reynolds," she paused to emphasise the importance of her next words, "if Miss Darcy requests any meal—breakfast or dinner—in her rooms, check with me first."

Mrs Reynolds locked eyes with her mistress. "Yes, Mrs Darcy."

Elizabeth was confident that the housekeeper understood her. It was rather gratifying.

THE DAYS PASSED SLOWLY FOR ELIZABETH. GEORGIANA GAVE HER sour looks and angry silences, but she followed Elizabeth's orders. Elizabeth made calls and discussed household affairs with Mrs Reynolds. She toured the rooms which required re-decoration, and made decisions about wall colour and furniture, trusting that despite his anger, Darcy would not forbid the expense just to injure her. She read, sewed, practised the pianoforte, and walked and rode when the weather was agreeable.

Most of all, Elizabeth contemplated the argument and what it would mean for her marriage. She sought to determine how to repair the damage created by her rash—but true—words. She was angry with Darcy for running off to London, and the longer his absence wore on, the more vexed she became. At times, Elizabeth almost longed for him to return. In a month, they would be in London together, among people they wanted to convince of their supposed love and happiness. They would never be able to do that if they remained so at odds. More often, she dreaded his return, afraid their time apart was being used to nurse his anger and feed his contempt. She worried about how he would treat her when he returned.

Elizabeth considered writing to Mrs Gardiner, laying the whole of the matter before her, and begging for advice. But she was too ashamed of her behaviour to do so.

Stupid, stupid girl, she reprimanded herself as she paced around her sitting room. *What have I done? A few minutes of relief telling Fitzwilliam just what I think and feel is not worth the price I will pay.*

She dropped onto a sofa, picked up a cushion, and used it to muffle first a scream, and then her tears.

SEVERAL DAYS AFTER DINING AT FITZWILLIAM HOUSE, DARCY encountered Charles Bingley while walking in the Park. Darcy knew he was not fit company, but endeavoured to be polite.

"I am glad to see you!" Bingley smiled brightly. "What brings you to town? Do you remain for long?"

"No. I had business. Mrs and Miss Darcy remain at Pemberley. You must excuse me, Bingley. I have an appointment."

"Of course. You must dine with me. The day after tomorrow? Yes?"

Darcy could think of no ready excuse and agreed. The distraction might do him good. He presumed they would meet at one of their clubs, or at Bingley's rooms. But on the day of the dinner, Bingley sent word that Darcy should join him at the Hursts' townhouse. Bingley's sisters had learnt of the engagement and insisted upon seeing him.

Darcy groaned. He did not hold Bingley's sisters and brother-in-law in much esteem, and he knew they would ask about Elizabeth, but it was too late to avoid the meeting.

"We were so surprised, Mr Darcy, when Charles told us he had seen you," Caroline Bingley said at dinner. "Whatever could have brought you to London at such a time?"

"Business."

"You are always rushing here and there on business," Mrs Hurst said. "I cannot contrive how you keep so busy. Neither Charles nor Mr Hurst have so many demands on their time."

"Yes, but Louisa, they do not have the management of an estate to occupy them. I have never seen a finer estate than Pemberley."

Miss Bingley sighed wistfully and looked at Darcy, who ignored her hints for an invitation.

"Pemberley is a marvellous place," Bingley exclaimed. "Mrs Darcy must delight in it."

"Ah, yes, Mrs Darcy," Miss Bingley said.

Darcy regarded her with suspicion. Miss Bingley had a biting wit and seldom showed restraint when using it upon her acquaintance, or even people she did not personally know.

"How is Mrs Darcy faring in her new position? I understood that she is unaccustomed to estates as grand as yours, Mr Darcy." The look she gave him was full of false sincerity.

"Mrs Darcy is doing well."

Mrs Hurst asked, "Is she? I am glad to hear it. Caroline and I were so worried that she might find the transition from being a Miss Bennet rather challenging."

"Why would it concern you?" Bingley asked. "She struck me as an intelligent, capable lady. I told you that after I met her. I have no doubt that she greatly enjoys her new position and does it great credit."

How like Bingley to see so much good in someone he met for just a minute or two.

"One would have to be truly insensible to not enjoy being mistress of Pemberley and member of such an illustrious family," Miss Bingley simpered.

"I am sure that she gets as much enjoyment from it as is appropriate. Being the mistress of Pemberley requires a great deal of effort, not all of which can be classified as pleasant." Darcy spared a glance for his host who was, as always, more interested in his plate and glass than the people around him.

"Mr Darcy, whatever can you mean?" Miss Bingley asked.

"Being Mrs Darcy," he replied with gravity, "requires visiting my tenants and seeing to their needs, many charitable calls to the poor and unfortunate in the neighbourhood, as well as managing a large household of servants, ensuring their well-being, settling disputes, and so forth. I say nothing of overseeing household management, the decisions that must be taken, and the accounts to keep in order, and the social visits. Mrs Darcy is also involved in bettering the community."

As Bingley remarked on how diligent a lady would have to be to undertake so much, Darcy saw the sisters exchange a look of slight revulsion. They would never willingly spend their time visiting tenants and discussing their worries, or bringing pots of stew to the poor or sick. *Unlike Elizabeth,* he thought before he could prevent it from happening.

"Surely an estate such as Pemberley has other people to do such... chores!" Miss Bingley cried.

Bingley said, "Darcy has already said that he wishes his wife to do it, and I think that he is right." He had to speak over his sisters' exclamations of surprise.

"Hear, hear," Hurst cried before signalling to the footman to refill his glass.

"I trust you do not send your sister with Mrs Darcy," Miss Bingley said. "Such a dear, sweet girl. Her disposition could not bear to witness the conditions the lower classes have to endure, or her health withstand the exposure."

Over Bingley's expression of shock that his sister would say such a thing, Darcy spoke.

"I would hope that no one over whom I have a duty—be they one of my tenants or a family in my parish—would live in such mean conditions that I would hesitate to have my sister witness them. And why, Miss Bingley, would you think that I would allow my wife to visit where I would not allow my sister to go?"

Miss Bingley quickly retreated from her statement, claiming she was misunderstood. Mrs Hurst directed the conversation to other subjects, chiefly gossip about their friends and acquaintances.

Dinner took excessively long, and as the conversation could not hold his attention, it gave Darcy time to observe. Mrs Hurst and Miss Bingley exhibited a pettiness he had not appreciated before. Had he failed to recognise it, or was it simply more obvious now? It was so unlike Elizabeth. Other than Wickham, he could not recall ever hearing her say an unkind word about anyone, even those who deserved her censure, such as Mrs and Miss Simms.

She said a great many unkind things about me. It was perplexing. If Elizabeth were so unlikely to condemn those whose behaviour warranted it, how could she have spoken so harshly to him?

Miss Bingley and Mrs Hurst had the appearance and manner of ladies of fashion; the look and behaviour, then, of the sort of lady he had always imagined he would make his wife. It seemed so superficial, so shallow, when compared to Elizabeth. They were not sincere in their expressions of friendship and esteem. They were not kind.

Neither of them would have gone to the aid of an unknown young lady. The thought came unbidden, unwelcome. He would not think well of Elizabeth, not yet. There would come a time when he would have to dwell on her finer qualities so that he could bear to be in her company, but tonight was too soon.

The more he observed the ladies, the less he liked what he saw. He concluded that neither of them would make a good Mrs Darcy. Neither of them would tolerate poor, unfortunate Miss Pratt, let alone look upon her with kindness and sympathy. Neither of them would call again and again on a family such as the Smiths, who lived near Lambton and seemed mired in misfortune.

Darcy took his leave soon after dinner, giving them no hope of seeing him again before he returned to Pemberley.

As he sat by the fire in his bedchamber, he remembered being at Mrs Morris's dinner party, and thinking that he was glad not to have ended up with someone like Martha Simms. To this, he now added,

"Or Miss Bingley." It would be a terrible chore to take a Martha Simms or Caroline Bingley and turn her into a good wife and mistress, if it were even possible.

It struck him then, quite forcibly, that of all the times he had studied Elizabeth, ready to correct her, to manage her, and help her become a good Mrs Darcy, he had never had to do so. She used her good sense, intelligence, and compassion—the same characteristics which made her fly to Georgiana's assistance—as a guide, and they had not failed her. She, of whom he had expected so little, had excelled in her new position. *Without any help from me.*

It was the kindest thought he had had regarding Elizabeth since their horrid argument, and he felt his anger lift just the littlest amount. But it was not nearly enough to erase the fact that she had so unjustly condemned his character.

Chapter 21

A fortnight after leaving Pemberley, Darcy again presented himself at the Fitzwilliams' townhouse to meet John and Susan Darcy and several of his cousins for dinner. It was not an enjoyable evening, but it was not as terrible as he had expected it to be. Elizabeth was complimented, which, until his better-self prevailed, he could little credit. He had to agree that she had done well during their house parties. She had exerted herself to prepare for them. He remembered her long list of tasks, and her insistence that she would not leave the arrangements to Mrs Reynolds.

It was not very much, but, combined with the kind thoughts he had experienced after dining with the Hursts, it softened Darcy's heart enough to allow other pleasant sensations to enter. Of most significance was that Elizabeth had apologised, which was in her favour. He could not know what had led her to say such hurtful things, but he acknowledged that perhaps some extraordinary circumstance had left her in a quarrelsome mood.

When he arrived home, he passed by the door to Elizabeth's apartment. He took two or three steps, stopped, and, a moment later, walked back to the door. After a pause of several seconds, he reached out, opened it, and stepped inside before he could think of a reason not to. The lateness of the day made it difficult to take in all the details, but he saw enough for now. His survey was indifferent and brief. He returned downstairs to while away the time until he was tired enough to end his day.

RETURNING TO ELIZABETH'S ROOMS THE NEXT MORNING, DARCY decided they were very pleasant. The colour—the walls covered in a light green paper with an ivory design of vines and small flowers— was soothing, and the rooms seemed lighter, fresher, and more comfortable than he remembered them being. He walked around the spaces, his fingers brushing a painted wood table. They showed taste and were elegant without being ostentatious.

A good reflection of Elizabeth's character.

He ran a hand over his mouth. Elizabeth could be graceful, it was true. She dressed well, and looked very much like Mrs Darcy should. She was not inclined to be showy, and she had displayed good sense and understanding, except on that morning.

Suddenly weary, he fell into one of the new chairs.

He should return to Pemberley. Soon. He had one or two items of business to complete, since he began them as a way to justify his trip to London.

He would have to find a way to forget how she had spoken to him. He would remember her good qualities, some of which were reflected in the choices she had made in decorating her rooms. Yes, he was resolved. He would soon return to Pemberley. When Elizabeth offered another apology, as he expected she would, he would graciously accept and agree to overlook her attack on his character. After demanding an explanation for her behaviour.

THE NEXT MORNING, DARCY SOUGHT SOME PAPERS HE REQUIRED IN order to review the terms of an investment he had made the previous summer. He found them in a strongbox, and, in removing them, uncovered a small case which came from the jewellery shop he favoured. The hair clip it contained was a pretty little thing, but he did not know where it came from, or why it was in his box.

Then he remembered. He stared at it sitting in his palm, his lips parting and brow furrowing. He bought it in August, when he was in London before marrying Elizabeth. Sterling had come to see him, insisting that he had to stop hiding away.

"You might pay a visit to a jeweller as well. Select a trinket—something a man would give to the woman he loves enough to marry."

Darcy accepted the soundness of his cousin's advice and together they had gone to the shop. After looking around for a minute, Sterling fixed on a display of hair ornaments.

"A hair clip. Just the thing!" Sterling declared. "What colour is her hair?"

"What?" Darcy asked, hating every minute of their outing. He had much rather be at home, using business affairs to distract his mind, instead of being out and pretending to be a happy man.

"Her hair, what colour is it?"

Darcy had to think about it for a moment. "Brown. I believe it is brown."

"Oh my God," Darcy mumbled, "I did not even give it to her. A damn bauble I bought to fool whatever unimportant, gossiping people happened to be studying my behaviour. It has been sitting here since I returned home from the club Sterling dragged me to afterwards and I tossed it in here with my papers. I played the part of a man happy to be engaged, but I resented every minute of it. I could not even give this stupid clip to her. I hid it away. Why?"

He desperately tried to remember what he had been thinking at the time. *I was worried about my sister. I dreaded marrying Elizabeth, hated the speculation and knowing that people were talking about me and Georgiana.*

Again, he examined the hair clip, turning it over. He laughed, although there was no humour in it. *I picked it at random, without any thought of giving it to her or knowing—or caring—what she would like. I did not think of her at all, did I?*

He tossed the clip onto his desk and pressed his eyes closed. He tried to recollect any gift or token he had given Elizabeth. After searching his memory almost frantically, he finally admitted that, in the almost five months of their marriage, he had never given her anything, not a single gift to mark his esteem or approval for her efforts. He had not even thought to do so.

Would she even like it? It was pretty and decorated with coloured gems of some sort. *Perhaps, but you cannot get around the point that it was not chosen with her approval in mind. That would have required thinking about her, and I did not. I thought of Georgiana, and I thought of how much I despised having gossip linked to my name. I did not want my honour questioned by the hint that I had behaved in a dissolute manner, that I had seduced a gentleman's daughter, or refused to live up to my obligations to a mistress. I thought about what it could mean for Georgiana's future should the truth be discovered. I did not think about Elizabeth.*

Georgiana. Elizabeth had said something about her at the start of their row. What was it? He knew it was important, but again, try as he might, he could not remember.

He attempted to convince himself that he had done nothing wrong regarding Elizabeth, and that he had always acted with honour. *I could hardly help doing so. Such behaviour is ingrained in me.*

Yet the hair clip sitting on his desk, mocking him, was proof that he had not. He had not even remembered it when they were in London after the wedding, when it would have been nothing to retrieve it and give it to her.

He shuddered thinking about his wedding day. Mrs Bennet rejoicing in her good fortune, her vulgar manners making him feel physically ill.

Not Elizabeth. She had not behaved so coarsely—not that day or any other day. Darcy tried to remember what Elizabeth had looked like when she joined him at the church, forever resigning the name Bennet in favour of his, or later when they boarded the coach for the journey to London.

He could not. No matter how hard he tried, he could not summon any image of the woman he had just married and taken from her home. Had she not said something about that during their argument? Longbourn was her home and the Bennets were her family, whatever their faults, in the same way the Darcys and Fitzwilliams, whatever their faults, were his. Elizabeth had been removed from her family, forced to marry someone not of her choosing, just as he had been.

One could argue that she had made a splendid match of it, far beyond what a lady in her circumstances would usually expect to make, but that was not the material point. Although he had convinced himself it was. He had told her it was, too, had he not? During their argument, he had said something about it, said that she had no cause to repine.

No. He could not have said it. Surely not. He sighed, knowing he had, and that it was wrong to do so. He dropped the hair clip onto his desk, the sound it made muffled by the papers he had been reviewing. In a strictly practical sense, it was true that Elizabeth had made a very beneficial, even extraordinary match, but, nevertheless, she had been forced to marry a man she hardly knew, just as he had had to marry a lady who was a stranger to him. If he had hated the necessity, she, who had so much sense, must have as well. She must have seen the evil in it rather than delight in the riches which would be hers as Mrs Darcy.

The day was almost done when he at last accepted that Elizabeth would feel as he did. He had never considered her sentiments on the matter—not in Ramsgate and not in all the months of their marriage —but she, who was so sensible and intelligent, would hate being forced to marry against her will. His wealth and name would do nothing to erase that fact. It was too much to bear or contemplate so late in the day, so he dragged himself upstairs, and allowed sleep to claim him.

UPON RETURNING TO THE HOUSE AFTER A RIDE THE NEXT MORNING, Quinn reminded Darcy that he had still to respond to a note from his solicitor. It had been that need which had sent him to his strongbox the day before. He quickly ate breakfast and penned the reply before locking himself in his study, saying that he was not to be disturbed. He intended to force himself to recall the argument with Elizabeth. He had to make sense of what had happened that day. He could feel himself on the cusp of some great, vitally important awareness. Elizabeth had been so angry and had behaved so unlike herself. He had to know if he bore any responsibility for it.

It had started when he saw Georgiana rushing towards her rooms soon after he left her and Elizabeth in the breakfast parlour. Something had transpired in those few short minutes to upset both ladies. What had Elizabeth said to him when he asked? She had laughed, a bitter, perhaps even anguished laugh and...

"She said that Georgiana hated her and hated that she was there," he murmured.

But that was impossible. Georgiana had longed for a sister. Elizabeth would be an excellent sister and wonderful friend for Georgiana. They appeared to get along well when his relations were at Pemberley. Why would Elizabeth believe that Georgiana hated her? *Elizabeth must be exaggerating or-or she misunderstood.*

He needed more information and that only Elizabeth and Georgiana could supply. He would seek it when he returned to Pemberley.

What else did Elizabeth say? Think!

She had said something about him disliking her, just as Georgiana did. Elizabeth could not have meant it. His behaviour showed that he liked her a great deal. True, he had not wanted to marry her, but he had, and he did not exactly regret it now that he knew her, and understood what an estimable woman she was. Few ladies would have fared as well as Elizabeth had since last summer. Few would have put as much effort into learning and executing their new duties as she had.

Again, he decided that she must have been embellishing. She had been fiercely angry, so it was understandable. She must accept that he and his family were all naturally hesitant about her when she first became Mrs Darcy. They had not known her, or anything about her, except that she was not from their station in life. Their concerns had been justified. But she had earned their approval, particularly his. He had expressed it time and again. It was downright obstinacy to deny it.

"No, damn it!" *There is more to this than exaggeration or a deliberate attempt to wound my feelings.* He sighed and moved from the armchair behind his desk to the flaxen-coloured sofa where he could be more comfortable in body, if not in mind. *Elizabeth does not act in that manner. She would not say something simply to injure another person. Do justice to her. She is all that is good.*

One phrase ran through his head again and again. *I do not want to be Mrs Darcy, I have never wanted to be Mrs Darcy, and I hate every day that I am Mrs Darcy.*

She had truly meant it, and it left a deep ache in his heart. Could she have been so miserable without him seeing it? What did that say about him? "Nothing good or honourable. And what did I say to her? That she had nothing of which to complain."

But she did, at least to her way of thinking. She had dismissed his wealth and social position, wanting instead—what? Respect and affection. Surely, he must have shown her both. Surely, at the very least, he had shown her that he valued her. It was true that at first, knowing what her family was, he had been wary. But Elizabeth was nothing like her parents or younger sisters. It seemed almost ludicrous to him, now that he knew Elizabeth, that a woman such as Mrs Bennet was her mother.

Now that he knew Elizabeth. That was an important point. Now he valued and respected her, and liked her, but he had not when they were first married, had he? How could he have done so? He had not known her.

And she did not know you or Georgiana. Did you think that she would like you and respect you simply because of who you are, because you are rich, and the grandson of an earl? Did you think she would be eager to be your wife, or befriend your sister, a girl she had to save from doing something so incredibly stupid?

Darcy was not sure that he wanted to answer those questions just yet. He returned to his memory of what she had said to him that morning.

She had seen him watching her and believed he had been looking to find fault. And he had been. He might say that he wanted to understand how to assist her with her new duties, but he had expected her to be lacking, because, despite being a gentleman's daughter, despite her intelligence, she was not his equal. He had dismissed her, treated her as a necessary evil, and, there was no way around it, seldom thought about her wishes or feelings. She had said that he had failed to provide her with any sort of reassurance before the wedding, that he had refused to tell her about his family, or what her life would be like once they were married, and it was all so very true.

"I did absolutely nothing to help her or reassure her before I took her away from her home and her family," he whispered.

If he could not be bothered to give her a silly trinket, he certainly could not be bothered to write her a proper letter. And after the wedding, those weeks in London and when they first went into Derbyshire, he had been no better. She had said that he and his family had treated her with contempt and disregard. Contempt was too strong —he absolutely believed that—but disregard? That, he had to accept. He had not thought about her except as an unwanted problem, something to be dealt with later, always later, and only when it was no longer possible to avoid. And she had not complained. She had simply carried on with what she saw as her duty, without any guidance or assistance from him. As she said, she did everything she could to be a good wife and mistress and—he had to believe this was also true—sister.

Darcy thought about everything she had done in the months of their marriage, really since the very beginning, when she immediately began to study the management of the townhouse. And what had he done? Refused to show her the house, said almost nothing to her, and, as she had said to him—and now he could hear the pain in her voice —left her to dine alone because Tom was there.

Contempt was, it appeared, not too strong a word to describe his behaviour towards her after all, at least when they were betrothed and first married.

He groaned, covering his face with his hands, and resting his elbows on his knees. He had acted as though she were not more important than...than what? Whom would he treat with so little regard? There were few, and all of them were very much of the same sort as George Wickham. *And I would have taken more notice of him, knowing it was at my own peril that I ignored him.*

That was how he treated the woman who had saved Georgiana from a miserable fate. Had he not told Elizabeth how grateful he was? Georgiana must know that she was extremely fortunate that Elizabeth had had the courage to interfere and stand firm against a man such as Wickham. Darcy had thanked God again and again—*but apparently not Elizabeth*, he thought—that she had been watching the street that night, and had been willing to go to his beloved sister's rescue. And in return, he had completely and utterly failed her.

DARCY WENT FOR A LONG WALK, TRUSTING THAT THE COLD JANUARY air and the dampness which seemed to seep into his bones would calm his agitation. When he returned to his townhouse, he requested a light meal and a hot drink, and shut himself in his rooms.

Elizabeth felt she had paid with her happiness for helping Georgiana at her darkest moment. He had thought a great deal about his own happiness and bleak future. He had despised having to marry a woman he saw as his inferior, and she had known it. Darcy concluded that she had overheard him conversing with Tom or some other person. It did not matter that he had not said it directly to her. He had felt it, talked about it in a careless fashion, and likely expressed it to Elizabeth in many indirect ways.

As much as he did not want to, he owed it to Elizabeth to confront the most disturbing of her allegations. Knowing how he had failed her, he had to acknowledge it was possible that she had accepted him into her bed only out of duty, and that he had failed to think about or consider her feelings on the matter.

Overcome, he slipped from his chair to the floor. He pulled his knees up to his chest, and buried his face in his arms. Had she truly believed that she had to give herself to him against her inclination? *Why would she not? What did I ever say or do to assure her that I would make no such demands of her, not unless she too wanted*—He felt as though someone had kicked him in the stomach.

He could so clearly hear her bitter words. "I will continue to fulfil all my duties, suitably grateful that you have found one use for me at least."

She believed that despite his contempt he had 'found a use' for her, that she was just an object to satisfy his baser needs. He had never viewed any woman in such a way. He had found great comfort and peace and satisfaction—emotional as well as physical—in being with Elizabeth, and he had assumed she had as well.

Standing, he went to the window, which overlooked the busy street, and watched as people, horses and carriages went by, the rhythm of their movements bringing some calm to his agitated nerves. *I assumed. I never asked, I just assumed. I am selfish and arrogant, just as she said. I thought only of myself, never of her. Oh God, how I congratulated myself on finally being willing to bed Elizabeth, to accept her as my wife! When did I ever think about her, about what it was like to be taken from everything she had known and thrust into my life and my protection? I did not take very good care of her, did I?* As a particularly large coach lumbered past his door, he mumbled, "I could not have done worse had I deliberately set out to abuse her."

Tears stung in his eyes. He would hate himself had he treated anyone so poorly. That it had been Elizabeth, who was so lovely and warm and good, so truly good, was disgusting to him. Had she not flown to Georgiana's aid? Had she not done everything she could to be a wonderful mistress to his servants and tenants, attending to their needs, and those of the poor and unfortunate of their community?

Not even Elizabeth could despise him as much as he despised himself at this moment.

Chapter 22

$\mathcal{D}$ arcy struggled with his new understanding of himself and Elizabeth. Her impulsive action had saved Georgiana from a life of misery only to, Elizabeth felt, condemn *herself* to one instead.

"That need not be. That will not be," he vowed.

Somehow, he would find a way to alleviate Elizabeth's unhappiness. He owed her that much at least. Regardless of any other reason he might have to make Elizabeth happy, he was forever in her debt for saving Georgiana from a life of regret and sorrow. He had been so caught up in his own misery that he had overlooked this simple, vital truth.

Elizabeth thought he would scorn her for being unhappy. How meanly she thought of him. *What have I done to make her think otherwise?* he silently wondered. *What have I done to show a woman like Elizabeth, one who cared so much about an unknown girl and her safety, or who would demand, as she did, the right to be of use to one's tenants and the Miss Pratts of the world, what have I done to show such a woman that she should think well of me? My money will not buy her favour. The right to call an earl uncle will not matter to her.*

As he continued to force himself to remember the months of their marriage, he found more and more reason to be mortified by his behaviour. He had not been intentionally cruel to Elizabeth, but that was no comfort when measured against how little he had considered her feelings.

How little wealth and connexions mattered to him now! He had bemoaned her lack of dowry and the position of her family, but they meant nothing compared to her character. He could find hundreds of reasons to esteem Elizabeth. He could see it all so effortlessly now. She had applied herself from the very beginning in order to make their marriage as easy as possible. With no guidance from him, she had taken her place as his wife, fulfilling all her new duties, doing even more than he had hoped his wife would. Time and again it had been the same.

She knew that she should be able to ride because it would allow her to more easily visit his tenants. He had ensured there was a suitable horse in his stables for her, but had he gone with her? Had he offered to assist her, even after she admitted that she was no horsewoman? No.

Had he introduced her to his tenants, accompanying her when she started visiting them, giving her what information he could to ease her way? No.

Had he gone on calls with her, or sat with her when their neighbours began to visit? No, other than when Horatia came to see them, and only because he owed his aunt the deference paid to an older relative, and because he knew she would delight in gossiping about Elizabeth with his other relations.

He could go on and on with such ruminations. Had he taken the time to know Elizabeth? No, not until they had been married a month at least, and by then his paltry efforts could not make up for how little consideration he had shown her before. Had he told her about the people she would meet, sharing his opinions, his knowledge of their characters? No, but he should have. Would it have been so onerous a task to tell her, for instance, that Mrs and Miss Simms were petty, ignorant women? Had he even, after Miss Simms's insult the night of the Morrises' dinner party, talked to Elizabeth about what had happened? Had he assured her that he found nothing lacking in her abilities, that whatever the Martha Simmses of the world said, he knew that she was more than capable of being Mrs Darcy?

No, of course he had not, because he was, just as she had told him, a selfish being, never thinking of others, or at least not of her, the person whose feelings and well-being should be of utmost concern to him.

He was truly contemptible.

It was the next day before Darcy could convince himself to consider what he should do rather than continue to dwell on his past mistakes. Elizabeth had apologised to him. She must know that he did not deserve it, and yet she was willing to humble herself to him for the greater good. Believing he would not accept the truth of her words during their argument, she had provided him with a way to reconcile. In return, he had run away to London without even doing her the courtesy of telling her in person. He had written her a curt note, congratulating himself for doing that much.

He liked her. There was no denying the point and he did not wish to. There was no shame in liking your wife. He had always hoped to do so, and, if he were fortunate, to feel a greater affection than that for her, whoever she would be. He rather suspected he liked Elizabeth a great deal, more than he had acknowledged. He respected her, too, because of everything she had shown him about her character.

He laughed. She had not done any of it to demonstrate the sound-ness of her character to him. She had acted as she had, from the night they met in Ramsgate until the time she said her words of apology, because it was the proper, honourable way to behave, and she, who was so naturally good, could do no different.

And now he must face the painful truth that he liked and respected her, and she did not feel the same way towards him.

Elizabeth was unhappy, and he owed it to her—as his wife, as a person he thought well of, as someone he had wronged—to make amends, and to do everything in his power to make her happy. She was lonely, too. He was not certain how he knew, but something in the tenor of her voice, or how she had acted that awful day, told him with complete confidence that she felt alone.

Why would she not? I removed her from her family. What was it she said? That whatever their faults, they at least loved her.

He had seen little to like in the Bennets, except perhaps for Jane. But it was not his opinion of her family that mattered, not absolutely at least, which is how he had behaved. He had condescended to allow Elizabeth to correspond with them, although he intended that they would never meet. He told himself that her failure to talk about the Bennets or her aunt and uncle was an acknowledgement that they had no place in the life of his wife. How morbidly droll it all seemed. Elizabeth did not talk about them because he had never done anything to hide his disdain for them. She may even have worried that if she reminded him of her relatives, he would tell her that she had more important things to do than spend her time writing to them. The worst of it was that he very well might have. Perhaps when they had a child he would have demanded she sever the connexion completely, as though a half an hour spent writing to her sister or mother or aunt would take away time she should spend with his son or daughter.

Elizabeth, kind-hearted, sensible, caring Elizabeth, would be an exceptional mother. Although, unless she was already increasing, there was a very real possibility they would never have a child. He could not insist that she welcome him into her bed, and it seemed impossible that she would ever ask him to share her bed again, not unless she desperately wanted a baby, and that desire grew stronger than her hatred of him. He would have to refuse an invitation issued under such conditions; how could he do otherwise?

What should he do? Perhaps he could make some gesture regarding her family. It would show her that he did not mean for her to remain cut off from them, and that, as they were her relations, they were also his, and whatever his feelings, he would accept them and tolerate their company. If she knew this, and if he placed no barrier to Jane visiting her, it would do a great deal to address Elizabeth's loneliness and unhappiness.

Should he go to Longbourn on his way north? He did not want to. Try as he might, he could not summon a wish to see the Bennets, or a way to look forward to such an occasion with anything resembling equanimity. It would put him out of his way to stop at Longbourn, too. The journey to Pemberley was already prolonged by at least a day in the winter, and Meryton was not on a direct route. It would not be possible to stop at Longbourn without staying the night before continuing northwards.

In thinking of the impracticality of the scheme, Darcy accepted that he was suiting his own feelings. He did not wish to see the Bennets, at least not without Elizabeth to act as an intermediary.

There was the aunt and uncle. The one who was in trade.

Could he?

He did not know where they lived or what their name was. Calling on them, like stopping at Longbourn, was impractical.

Darcy sat at his desk, rested his head in one hand, closed his eyes, and sighed. They were excuses. It was true that going to Longbourn was impractical and would likely be unpleasant, but it was not impossible. As for the aunt and uncle, discovering their name and direction was a very easy matter. Lord Romsley had commissioned a report on them before the wedding, and Darcy had the written account. He sought it out, quickly finding it in the same strongbox the hair ornament had been in, and read the opening lines.

Gardiner; the uncle was called Gardiner, and he lived in Gracechurch Street.

But how could he go to see them? Mr Gardiner was in trade, and Fitzwilliam Darcy of Pemberley did not visit tradespeople except on matters of business. Elizabeth could not expect it of him.

Of course, Elizabeth's expectations of him were very low.

That combined with the memory of the night he met her, of his frantic walk to locate the place named in the note he found in Georgiana's room, penned by Wickham, showed him what he must do. He had never been more near panic than he was that night in Ramsgate. He did not know the town well and had had to find strangers to ask for directions. The relief he had felt on turning the final corner and seeing Georgiana standing under a streetlight with Wickham and an unknown lady was indescribable.

Elizabeth. Lovely, courageous, fierce Elizabeth, who had flown from her house to help his sister, and who had then found herself forced to marry a man who had never deigned to show her how grateful he was for her intervention. For her he could, and he *would* call on the Gardiners of Gracechurch Street. Elizabeth would know then that whatever his objections to her connexions had been, he was willing to do better. It was a gesture, and he prayed it would mean more to Elizabeth than if he simply returned to Pemberley with pretty words of apology at the ready.

THE NEXT MORNING FOUND DARCY STANDING OUTSIDE OF AN attractive, well-kept house in Gracechurch Street. He knew it was the house he sought, but hesitated before approaching the door. He could not imagine finding it easy to converse with the Gardiners. What could he say to them? What could they have in common? Knowing that Mr Gardiner was Mrs Bennet's brother made the whole thing seem more doomed to failure. However, he had promised himself that he would call on them and spend a quarter of an hour in their company. Mrs Gardiner would write to Elizabeth, Elizabeth would know that he had done it, and, he trusted, think at least a little better of him. It would demonstrate that he acknowledged that he must amend his conduct.

Before his behaviour could be noticed and remarked upon, he knocked at the door, waited until it was answered—by a manservant, which surprised him—and handed over his card. The man returned in a minute, and asked him to come through to the morning room.

Darcy stepped into the room to find a woman, younger than he had expected, who was in a great state of agitation. She had been pacing before he was announced, his card in one hand, the other upon her chest. She was pretty and fashionably dressed.

"Elizabeth?" she cried, her eyes imploring him to speak.

"No, no." He shook his head. "She is well. She was perfectly well when I left Pemberley."

"Oh, thank God!" The lady sat, covered her face with her hands, and took several deep breaths.

"I—"

"Forgive—"

They both stopped. She smiled politely and stood again.

"Please forgive me, Mr Darcy. When I saw your card, I am afraid my mind flew to the worst possible reason for your call. I am Mrs Gardiner, as I suppose you have realised." She curtseyed.

He bowed. "Mrs Gardiner, I-I... No forgiveness is needed. I..." He had not expected such a beginning and did not know what to say. "I can only apologise for causing you distress and for not...being able to make your acquaintance before now."

Mrs Gardiner smiled at him again in a polite, reassuring manner. "Please, Mr Darcy, be seated. I am afraid that Mr Gardiner is not here else I am certain he would be happy to meet you as well. Elizabeth is well, you said?"

"Yes." He imbued the single word with resolution. "She was in the best of health when I left Pemberley a fortnight ago. Business called me to town, and I decided that before I returned to Derbyshire, I would pay my respects."

"That was very kind of you. Will you not sit?"

He nodded and this time did take a seat. As he did, he noticed that the room was well-kept and modern in appearance. The mahogany furniture gleamed, and the yellow walls and ivory fabrics made for a very comfortable, inviting atmosphere. "Not at all. I had hoped to see your husband, although I did not think I would, not as I came so unexpectedly. Elizabeth has spoken of you often. I believe she said that you lived for a time in Derbyshire, in Lambton?" He had slept very poorly the night before and had used the time to remember anything Elizabeth had ever said about the Gardiners.

"Oh, yes, they were happy days, and I shall always believe that Derbyshire is the very best of counties."

Mrs Gardiner asked if he would take refreshments; he did not feel he should refuse. She spoke easily, which encouraged him to do likewise, first about Lambton, then about Elizabeth. He discovered that Mrs Gardiner's father had been the proprietor of The George, the largest and finest inn in Lambton, until ill health had required him sell it to the current landlord. She did not say much about her family, however, and instead they talked about their common knowledge of the town and neighbourhood. The usual quarter of an hour for a proper first call had gone by twice before Mrs Gardiner asked him how much longer he would be in London.

"But two or three days," Darcy replied. "I do not know what Elizabeth has told you of our plans to return for the Season?"

"The last she wrote was that she believed you would be in London by the middle or end of February. My niece Jane will be coming to stay with us then. I do not know if Elizabeth had heard yet before you came to town."

Elizabeth might have, but she would not have told him. His discomfort must have been obvious, because Mrs Gardiner spoke on, smoothing over the awkward silence of his failure to reply.

A short time later, Darcy took his leave. The visit had gone much, much better than he ever would have believed possible, but he had been there long enough for one morning. He had business to attend to if he wished to depart London on time, and he suspected that Mrs Gardiner did, too. It was the impulse of the moment, but he decided he could do better than leave it to Mrs Gardiner to write to Elizabeth of his visit. He could bring proof of it with him.

"I would be happy to carry a letter to Elizabeth, if you like," he offered.

"That is very kind of you, Mr Darcy."

Her tone of voice suggested she was going to demur, and he did not want her to, not unless she had no need to write, or would not have the time to do so before his departure. He wished to do this favour for Elizabeth, and for Mrs Gardiner. She had been incredibly welcoming, although she must have known that he had looked upon her and her husband with disapproval. His failure to recognise them before now said as much.

"It is not kindness, Mrs Gardiner. I would be happy to do so. Perhaps if I were to call the day after tomorrow, you would have time to write to Elizabeth, and I might be so fortunate as to meet Mr Gardiner?"

There was a slight pause while Mrs Gardiner considered him carefully. He felt as though she understood more about his situation than she possibly could; Elizabeth had promised to tell no one what had really happened in Ramsgate. It was disconcerting, and yet he sensed he could trust her.

"I would be very grateful if you would. I am certain that Mr

Gardiner would be pleased to make your acquaintance, and he will endeavour to be at home that morning."

TWO DAYS HENCE, DARCY RETURNED TO GRACECHURCH STREET AS arranged. He approached the house with more confidence than he had at his first visit, although he was apprehensive about meeting Mr Gardiner. He was, after all, brother to Mrs Bennet, and it was possible that he had married exceedingly well.

But, like his wife, Mr Gardiner had the manner and air of an intelligent person. The Gardiners' home denoted people of some affluence, and Mr Gardiner's current prosperity was no doubt due to his hard work, quick wit, and sound judgment—traits his niece shared. They spoke easily on several subjects, such as travel in the winter and Mr Gardiner's love of fishing. Darcy was still undecided as to whether or not he should go to Longbourn, and he sought the Gardiners' opinion. They had been to see the Bennets at Christmas; one or two remarks they made suggested to Darcy that they did not find such visits entirely agreeable.

Darcy said, "We did not stop in Hertfordshire when we left London in September. I have not been in town since then, but now that I am, I wondered if perhaps I ought to take the time."

The Gardiners were quick with their assurances that it was not necessary. "You must wish to return to Elizabeth and your sister," Mrs Gardiner said. "Going to Longbourn would extend your journey by at least a day."

"And I suspect," Mr Gardiner added, a bit of wry humour appearing in his eyes, "that the company of those in Derbyshire is preferable to you."

His wife hushed him. "Of course, Mr Darcy finds his sister and Elizabeth better company. If for no other reason than the fact that he does not know the Bennets very well. Mr Darcy," she turned her attention to him, "do not feel that you must go to Longbourn. Even were they to know that you considered it and decided against it, no one there would blame you, given the circumstances. Another time would do as well."

Darcy did not know what circumstances Mrs Gardiner was referring to, but he decided she meant the inconvenience to him. He had started a little when she said it, but remembered that the Gardiners did not know about Ramsgate. Darcy thanked them for their advice, and, after collecting a small parcel for Elizabeth—containing a letter from Mrs Gardiner as well as notes and drawings from her children—he took his leave.

Darcy was glad that he had sought the Gardiners' acquaintance. He enjoyed their company, and seeing them when he and Elizabeth were in London would not be the onerous task he had expected he would have to learn to tolerate for his wife's sake. Elizabeth would be pleased that he had gone to Gracechurch Street. *Perhaps not pleased. But she will at least understand the meaning behind it. I will not be ashamed to know the Gardiners, regardless of what anyone else thinks.*

When the carriage approached Mayfair, Darcy decided not to immediately return home, and directed his driver to let him off at Piccadilly. He had an errand or two to attend to first.

DARCY LEFT LONDON THE NEXT MORNING. HIS TIME THERE HAD BEEN instructive, and he felt that he knew himself better than he ever had before. Although he did not know exactly how he would go about it, he vowed that he would show Elizabeth that he could be a better man. If he were fortunate, he would be able to make her life one with which she could be content. He prayed that it was not too late, that he had not done so much damage that she could never regard him with anything other than dislike. If she were generous enough to, in time, forgive him, they could be friends. If he were very fortunate, their marriage would be one in which they could both find satisfaction. He wanted yet more for her. He wanted her to be happy.

Chapter 23

Darcy was four days on the road, but found that the time passed quickly. The books he brought to occupy him during the long hours in the carriage remained largely unread. He could not stop reflecting on everything he had discovered about himself and Elizabeth in the last week. She had become so very important to him, not only because she was his wife, and thus entitled to his consideration, or because she was the lady who had saved his sister, but because of who she was, and because of that indescribable something that made one person like another.

On the last day of his travels, the weather deteriorated. It was ludicrous that after a journey of over one hundred miles, the last fifteen might make the difference between whether he slept in his own bed or at an inn that night, but so it was. Given the uncertainty, he did not alert Elizabeth to his impending arrival until he was certain he would reach home, giving her only an hour or so notice.

Upon reaching Pemberley, Darcy's feelings were a mixture of apprehension and eagerness. He had a monumental task ahead of him

—that of gaining Elizabeth's forgiveness—but he was longing to get on with it. Hudson welcomed him and told him where he would find Elizabeth and his sister.

Seeing Elizabeth again compounded Darcy's sense of shame many times over. She looked pale and thinner than he remembered. Although she stood at his entrance and mumbled words of greeting, she would not look at him, and she was unusually reserved, cold even. He could not have expected more, but it was nevertheless distressing. Georgiana said something about going to dress for dinner. Darcy believed he responded, but he could not be certain. However it happened, he was alone with Elizabeth. She watched the door close behind Georgiana, and when she stole a glance at him, he saw wariness in her eyes.

Dear God, is she afraid of me? How can I ever make this right? An apology, even throwing himself at her feet and begging for mercy, would not be enough. He could only show her, through his improved manner, that he would do better by her, that he had learnt to behave as a gentleman should.

"How-how have you been?" he asked.

Elizabeth gave an indifferent shrug, but did not answer. "It is only a half an hour until dinner. I can ask to have it delayed. I-I was not sure exactly when you would arrive."

"No, I would not have it delayed for me. I shall go and prepare. Excuse me."

He left the room as quickly as he could, suddenly overcome by a need to be away from her and the guilt and shame her presence aroused.

GEORGIANA HAD FELT HER BROTHER'S ABSENCE MORE THAN SHE HAD supposed she would. At first, she treated it as a holiday, doing very little of the work he had assigned her. She read what she pleased, played when she felt like it, and, when her legs required exercise, visited the galleries or conservatory or went onto the terrace if it were not very cold outside—always careful to avoid Elizabeth.

After the first week of Fitzwilliam's absence, she began to feel that the days were very long. Conversations with her maid quickly became boring as Amey had little to say, and Georgiana would never be so lonely that she would seek Elizabeth's company. She wanted to speak to someone more sensible than her maid, and she wanted some diversion. When she learnt that her brother would be home that very day, she had been pleased. She had so many questions to ask him about what he had done and whom he had seen and if he had brought her anything from London. How she wished he had taken her with him!

Unfortunately, he was distracted and unhappy at dinner. "There is nothing more I can say, Georgiana. I did little you would find amusing, and saw almost no one outside of our family. Tell me, what did you do while I was away?"

"Oh, I, uh…" She took a mouthful of ragout and was very grateful when her brother, after a quizzical look at her, turned his attention to Elizabeth.

"And you, Elizabeth? How have you managed to stay occupied while I was away?"

He spoke more gently to Elizabeth than he had to her, his own sister, which annoyed Georgiana to no end. He sat forward, leaning over the table, his eyes fixed on Elizabeth.

"Nothing of particular note," Elizabeth said at length.

"Did you see anyone?"

"No, not…that is, a few people. Most have left the neighbourhood. I did see Mr Llewellyn."

"Oh?"

"To talk about the school."

"School?" Georgiana exclaimed. Was Elizabeth hoping to make Fitzwilliam send her to school? She had been to school—unlike Elizabeth—and could not be sent back, as though she was twelve, not almost sixteen. It would be humiliating.

"The school we wish to establish in Lambton for the local children, those whose families cannot otherwise afford to educate them."

"Oh." Georgiana sighed with relief.

Fitzwilliam turned back to Elizabeth. "What did he have to say?"

"He wanted to inform us that he has received pledges of support from several families. Mrs Morris, he said, was very enthusiastic about it."

"Excellent. I look forward to hearing what else Llewellyn had to report."

Fitzwilliam smiled. Georgiana noticed, but did not think Elizabeth would, since her eyes were on her plate. What little she had put on it remained uneaten. She never did seem to eat very much—not that it mattered to Georgiana. Both Fitzwilliam and his wife were behaving very oddly, and it was tortuous to have to witness it. She really hoped the meal would soon end and she could escape their company for the evening.

"I saw Lady Romsley and Sterling when I was in London, as I said. We met again when my aunt had some of my father's family to dine. They all asked after you and said how much they enjoyed being here."

His words made Elizabeth look at him, and, in response to his smile, she nodded.

That, fortunately, marked the end of the conversation, and the meal progressed at a pace more to Georgiana's liking.

DINNER WAS UNCOMFORTABLE FOR ELIZABETH. SHE HAD BEEN agitated from the moment they received word that Darcy would be home that day, and seeing him had made it worse. She felt so many different emotions upon his arrival and had no notion how to make sense of them. She picked at the little food she had bothered to put on her plate, and could not say what she was eating when she did introduce some of it to her mouth. The way her hand shook when she tried to drink the wine had alarmed her. She studied Darcy, wary of his mood. His manner confused her. She saw nothing of the disgust she had expected and could not discern what he was thinking or feeling.

She spoke as little as possible, certain he would find fault with whatever she said. Georgiana wanted his conversation; he had much better give it to her. Elizabeth knew she had been wrong to try to befriend either of them. She ought to have seen, right from the start, that they would be happier if she said as little as possible and made herself as invisible as she could so that they could pretend she did not exist.

But Elizabeth knew that was impossible. She was Darcy's wife and would have to find a way to go on as she had before their argument, despite knowing that they saw her presence as an evil. If she had managed to do it before their argument, she could do it again. But at the moment, she could not find the strength to exert herself. If he looked angry and contemptuous, as she had expected him to, she might have done better.

After dinner, Darcy excused himself, saying that he would meet Georgiana and Elizabeth in the withdrawing room. When he joined them, he held several parcels. Darcy approached Elizabeth and placed a small stack of books on the table next to her. When she looked at it and then at him, he spoke.

"I thought you might be interested in these. I also…this is for you."

The package was wrapped in paper, and although she took it when he held it out to her, she made no move to open it. Her brow furrowed, and she again looked between it and her husband before her eyes settled on the package.

"Open it," he urged.

Confused and wary, she slowly undid the string and peeled back the paper to find a thick wrap of fine wool. It was very soft, and a rather lovely shade of coral.

"I-I did not know if you had such a thing," Darcy explained. "Even in a house such as Pemberley, it can be chilly at this time of year."

Elizabeth stared at the garment in her lap. Before she could do more than murmur her thanks, he thrust a much smaller parcel at her.

"And I brought this. For you. From London."

Elizabeth reached out to take the package. Because it was so unexpected that her husband would have anything for her upon his return, and because she would never have thought to find her aunt's writing on one of the parcels he brought her, she did not immediately recognise what she was seeing.

Darcy spoke again. "From—I went to call on…your aunt. And uncle. I met him, too. The Gardiners."

"The Gardiners?" she exclaimed, her eyes flying to his, certain she had misunderstood. "You went to see the Gardiners?"

Darcy nodded.

"My aunt and uncle?"

Darcy nodded again. "I thought I sh—They were very…nice. I liked them both. Very much. Excellent people. Uh, Mrs Gardiner said that Miss Bennet will be with them at the end of February. Did you know?"

Elizabeth slowly nodded.

"Ah, yes. Good. You will like to see her again, will you not?"

Elizabeth still did not speak; it was difficult to breathe, let alone think of words to say. He pointed at the small parcel in her hands.

"A letter from Mrs Gardiner. And she said that her children wrote you. Or drew pictures. Or both."

Elizabeth looked at the parcel, then again at him, not certain she understood what he was saying.

"You will wish to read them." Darcy's words came quicker now. "Please do. I shall speak to my sister and not disturb you further."

ELIZABETH WAS NOT THE ONLY PERSON IN THE ROOM WHO WAS stunned by his confession that he had gone to see the Gardiners. Georgiana had watched as her brother approached Elizabeth and gave her the parcels he held. She cared nothing for the books because it was exceedingly unlikely that he had brought any that she would like, but he had no other parcels, and it was inconceivable that Fitzwilliam should return with gifts for Elizabeth and not for her. When he talked about seeing Elizabeth's family, Georgiana was even more shocked, and she decided that she must have misunderstood. She was convinced that her brother had left Pemberley because he was upset with Elizabeth, and, if that were so, he could not have done her family the courtesy of calling on them. It would be a mark of great condescension for Fitzwilliam Darcy to recognise Elizabeth's aunt and uncle, but to do so after Elizabeth did whatever it was she had done to drive him away from his home was impossible.

When he began to walk towards her, she hardly had time to compose herself before he was there, sitting next to her. At dinner, when he asked how she had occupied herself during his absence, it occurred to Georgiana that she should be nervous. She had done very little of the studying she was supposed to do. Now it seemed silly that she had spent so much time reading novels and looking through her wardrobe, imagining what new clothes she would get when they went to London. She would need new things, especially if she could convince Fitzwilliam and Tom that she was old enough to start attending some social functions. She had supposed his return would be heralded by a letter, giving her two or three days at least to do enough to satisfy him that she was diligent about improving her mind. She was afraid that he would now ask her more about her studies.

"Oh Fitzwilliam!" she squeaked.

"Georgiana."

"I was going to ask to be excused. I know that you and Elizabeth will have much to talk about—"

"No," Darcy interjected. "Elizabeth has letters to read, and I would speak with you. Tell me how you have occupied your days while I was away."

There followed ten exceedingly uncomfortable minutes for Georgiana. Her brother did not think much about the letters she had written to Tom and was not so easily put off questioning her about Italian and history despite the number of pieces she mentioned practising on the pianoforte. Not even her promise to show him the drawings she had lately done helped.

His expression and tone were stern. "I thought I had made my expectations clear. We obviously need to have a serious conversation. Tomorrow, after breakfast."

"Yes, Brother." While she knew she ought to have done more studying, she felt that he was being very hard on her. *Probably because he is unhappy with Elizabeth, but he does not want to argue with her!* "P-perhaps I could go to my apartment now?"

"You should be with us, not alone in your rooms. I have just returned after several weeks away, and I would like to spend the evening with you and Elizabeth. If you like, you could play. I have been looking forward to hearing some music."

Playing being preferable to talking, Georgiana walked to the instrument and opened it.

ELIZABETH WATCHED AS DARCY WALKED ACROSS THE ROOM TO Georgiana, bewildered by his manner and actions. He had brought her a gift. He had never done such a thing before, although her wardrobe had been a great expense—and she was convinced he resented every farthing. It seemed so improbable that she had to assure herself it was true several times before she began to believe it. She took the wrap into her hands, unfolding and refolding it. She ran her hands across its soft surface and played with the fringe. It was a very thoughtful gesture, as was bringing her books to peruse. He had managed to select ones that were exactly what she would have chosen. The wrap and books were astonishing enough. That she held in her hands a parcel which came from her aunt, and which he had collected himself was... Elizabeth did not have a word strong enough.

Praying that her aunt's letter contained an explanation, she turned her attention away from watching him to read it.

My dearest Lizzy,

You may imagine with what surprise and trepidation I received word that Mr Darcy was at my door yesterday morning. My surprise I am sure you can easily understand. My trepidation, my dear niece, was on your part. No sooner did I have Mr Darcy's card in my hand than I was convinced something evil had befallen you. I do not believe I gave him any sort of greeting before imploring him to tell me that you were safe. I quite frightened him, and, despite his assurances, I shall not be entirely easy until I hear from you that you are well.

What can I say? He was all politeness, despite being uncomfortable. He stayed more than half an hour. He remembered that I had lived in Lambton, and we talked about our shared recollections and about you in a very friendly manner. He volunteered to return so that I might send a letter by him, and when I naturally hesitated—it was a very great courtesy for a man such as him to do for me, even if I am your aunt—he insisted, and even said that he hoped he might find Mr Gardiner at home! I shall tell you about that visit in my next.

I do not know what to say about him, Lizzy. I am still so shocked by his appearance that I cannot find the words. He was very kind. I do not know what provoked such a civility on his part, and I look to you for explanation. I do not believe he will forget that he offered to carry a letter to you, and so I shall make so bold as to have the children, who have been wanting my attention this hour or more, write to you as well and include some of their art work. You need not praise their efforts to me, my dear—save that for the children's ears. They do long to see you, as do your uncle and I. We have even allowed ourselves to hope that Mr Darcy's coming to us as he did means that we might be able to meet when you are in town in a few weeks' time.

Do let me hear from you soon. I will not rest until I have it from your hand that you are well. I remain your most loving aunt, &c.

M. Gardiner

Elizabeth read the letter several times before she could make sense of it. She looked at the pictures from her cousins, a sad smile on her face as her fingers traced the lines they had drawn. The eldest two wrote and told her about their busy lives and expressed the wish that they would soon see Elizabeth.

How I would like that! Elizabeth had believed that it was less and less likely that Darcy would ever allow her to be with her family. After the dreadful things she had said to him, she had convinced herself that she would have to act very, very contrite and re-double her efforts to show Darcy that she would do everything in her power to be what he thought his wife should be. But in the short time since his return, he had defied her expectations. She did not know what to make of his behaviour. He was not angry, or even indifferent.

I am too tired to think on it more this day. I cannot believe it is anything other than an attempt on his part to show me that he is better than I said he was. He cannot bear the affront to his character and seeks to demonstrate that I was wrong so that he can despise me with impunity.

She sighed and surreptitiously ran a hand across her forehead. She felt the incipient throbbing of a headache. She had had them all too frequently of late, no doubt a product of her anxiety and inability to eat more than a little at mealtimes.

In the coming days, he will show his true nature. Such an act cannot last. Tomorrow, I shall apologise again. Then perhaps I can repair enough of the damage I did so that we can...be comfortable again. Or he can be comfortable again. Happiness is not to be mine while I bear the name Mrs Darcy.

Elizabeth was not as careful as she hoped. After she tried to hide several yawns, Darcy came to her.

"I am afraid you are not feeling well."

"I am a little tired."

"You are not ill?"

Elizabeth shook her head.

"I am glad to hear it. You should retire. Do not deny your inclinations on my account. I do not suppose I shall remain downstairs for long today, in any case."

No, not after your journey, but if you were intending to do so, my tiredness would not matter, would it? You would either require me to bear you company, or rejoice in being free of that which you do not enjoy, Elizabeth thought bitterly, not caring about the contradiction in her words.

"I believe I shall." She stood, bowed her head by way of saying good night and left the room, not even thinking to take her leave of Georgiana.

There was no point in doing so. Georgiana never said anything to her on the evenings they spent together during Darcy's absence. As soon as eight o'clock came, Georgiana would depart without so much as a glance in Elizabeth's direction. Earlier in her marriage, it might have caused at least a little pang to be treated so dismissively by Georgiana or Darcy, but no longer. Despite her promise to herself that she would not feel any affection for the people in her new life, she had let a little hope remain in her heart, and the result had been her terrible confrontation with her husband—one which would have serious repercussions for her happiness and possibly her well-being. Whatever was causing his changed behaviour, it was not because he had accepted that any part of her feelings, expressed so unintentionally and disastrously during their argument, was just.

She had learnt her lesson.

Chapter 24

It snowed during the night, but not so much that Darcy could not enjoy fresh air and exercise before breakfast. Seeing Elizabeth again was more difficult than he had imagined it would be. While she claimed not to be ill, he wondered if that were true. Certainly, she had had the headache; he had seen her running a hand over her forehead and trying to disguise at least four yawns before he had encouraged her to go to bed. Perhaps her loss of appetite at dinner only demonstrated how uncomfortable she was in his company. She had hardly looked at him during the meal, and, at one time, he had heard a dull thudding noise that he recognised as her foot tapping the floor. Hearing it then, in combination with her air of disquiet, pale visage, and lack of appetite, made him understand that she did it when she was agitated.

How he hated himself for not understanding that sooner and, worse, for finding it amusing.

At least she appeared to like his gift. He had returned the hair ornament to his strongbox. He despised the sight of it and all that it represented; he could not imagine ever giving it to her. The shawl had been selected with her in mind, as had the books. Giving your wife of five months a gift when you never had before was an awkward business, but if it brought her even a little pleasure, it was worth every moment of his discomfort and more.

He did not know what to say to her. How he wished she had told him weeks ago that she was unhappy! He should have known, but he did not, either because he did not know her well enough to understand her feelings, or because he had not wanted to know. He did not blame her for not confiding in him. But he sensed that there was still more for him to learn, and it greatly worried him.

The other problem weighing on his mind was Georgiana. Once again, she had neglected her studies, and he would not be the least bit surprised to find that she had done nothing at all of a serious nature while he was away. He decided not to wait until after breakfast to talk to her. Once he returned to the house, he would seek her out.

GEORGIANA WAS OUT OF BED VERY EARLY THAT MORNING. SHE WAS furiously reading one of the history books. Weeks earlier, Fitzwilliam had given her a list of questions she was expected to write answers to, but there was no time for that before the after-breakfast inquisition. She might be able to talk around it if only she could absorb enough information to make it sound like she knew more than she actually did.

She was chagrined when her brother entered her room well before breakfast. She attempted to hide the book.

"What were you reading?"

"Uh…" Georgiana could not decide what she ought to say.

Fitzwilliam arched his eyebrows and held out a hand. Grimacing, Georgiana gave him the book. He sighed and sat.

"You should have finished this weeks ago, Georgiana."

Georgiana was well aware of that, and at the moment she heartily wished she had. But it was so dry and dull, and really, who cared if her knowledge of the Hundred Years' War was imperfect? It had no relevance to her life. "Yes, Brother."

"Then why are you only reading it now?"

"I-I-I am not. I have read it. I was…only reminding myself of something."

Georgiana did not know if Fitzwilliam believed her exaggeration, but she rather suspected not. After a long moment of silence, he began to ask about the war, and, after several very weak responses, he asked to see what she had written in accordance with his instructions. As she had written nothing, it was not a request she could fulfil.

Fitzwilliam sighed again. "Georgiana…"

"It is just that I do find history very…difficult." She stole a glance at her brother and saw that his countenance was rigid. She desperately sought a way to escape further questioning, but nothing came to mind.

After a very long minute, he spoke, his voice firm and displeased. "Let us leave aside the question of history for the moment, then. What about Italian?"

Therein followed a difficult few minutes during which Georgiana attempted to use her knowledge of French to answer his questions about Italian. She mentioned her letters to Tom, but that did nothing to assuage him.

Fitzwilliam shook his head, and scowled. He drummed his fingers on the dreadful history book. "What, exactly, did you do while I was away? Other than write to Tom and practise at the pianoforte, that is."

Georgiana kept her eyes lowered and tried to look contrite. She truly did wish she had spent at least a little time doing what he had asked.

Darcy grunted. "What, if anything, did you do with Elizabeth while I was in London?"

She lifted her head and sounded as cheerful as she could manage. "Oh, I ate every meal with her—breakfast and dinner—every day, and we stayed together in the evenings, too."

Her brother looked no more satisfied with this answer than he had been with her earlier ones. She did not understand it. In a moment, he said that they should go down to breakfast; he did not want to keep Elizabeth waiting.

Georgiana just managed not to roll her eyes at his mention of Elizabeth. She stood, anxious to end the interview.

"Not just yet. I am not happy with the progress you have made. You are not a child who can spend her day in play. Because you cannot seem to progress without greater supervision, this is what we shall do. Each morning, after breakfast, or perhaps later depending on what my other duties entail, you will come to my study with your books, and while I work, so will you."

It sounded dreadful to Georgiana, but she acquiesced as prettily as she could. She hoped that he would soon become too busy with other matters and would relent. If it did not happen before they left for London, it would once they were in town.

"Tom and I were mistaken to believe that you would be able to attend to your studies with the diligence he and I showed at your age. I shall discuss it with him when we are in London, but for now we shall try this new arrangement." He stood. "Come. That is enough for the moment."

GEORGIANA PRESENTED HERSELF AND THE HORRIBLE TOME ON THE Hundred Years' War to her brother's study shortly after breakfast. She discovered that he had drafted a revised work calendar for her. What followed was a very long ninety minutes during which Georgiana diligently read. She did not feel that her mind was in any way improved by the exercise.

At the end of it, he came and sat beside her. "Georgiana, I wish to ask you about the day before I left for London."

Her brow furrowed as she tried to remember.

"It was the day after our aunt and uncle departed," Fitzwilliam reminded her. "I am particularly interested in what happened at breakfast."

He paused and Georgiana looked at him, her eyes round with anticipation.

"I left you and Elizabeth."

Must everything be about Elizabeth? I would wager that she told him I was not doing enough studying, and that is why he is being so hard on me. So intent was Georgiana upon these thoughts that she almost missed the remainder of her brother's question.

"I was only gone for a few minutes, not more than five, and when I returned, you were running to your rooms. Elizabeth was...in a very strange mood afterwards. I know that something transpired between the two of you. What was it?"

It took a moment, but then she remembered. Elizabeth had asked her to do something or other; it did not signify what. She had told Elizabeth plainly that she had no interest in spending time with her, which Elizabeth ought to have known, and, if she had not, then it only showed her stupidity. Was that when Elizabeth did whatever it was she had done to drive Fitzwilliam away from Pemberley? "Nothing that I can recall. Why?"

"I hoped nothing upsetting had happened." Her brother regarded her for a long moment. "Well, you have earned a rest. I have usually found interspersing my work with exercise helps to refresh my mind. You might wish to work on Italian later this morning, or continue with the history if you prefer."

He expected her to do more studying that day? Somehow, she managed to say a demure, "Yes, Brother."

BREAKFAST, LIKE DINNER THE DAY BEFORE, HAD BEEN DIFFICULT FOR Elizabeth. She supposed she could have found a way to avoid her husband's company, but there was nothing to gain by it. Sooner or later, she would have to spend time with him.

At the end of the meal, Darcy had said, "I hope we shall have time later this morning to talk."

What could she say? They did have to talk, although Elizabeth dreaded the upcoming interview. She would have to offer him another apology, and, with the time of it soon upon her, she had to decide what to say.

Her husband had gone to Gracechurch Street. Fitzwilliam had gone twice to Gracechurch Street, seeking out the acquaintance of her aunt and uncle. Six months ago, when he had learnt of the Gardiners' existence, even one month earlier, he had been disgusted by the mere thought of them. She had feared he would refuse to allow her to continue her correspondence with them, yet now he had sought out their acquaintance. He had a purpose in doing so, but, try as she might, she could not determine what it was.

A walk did little to settle her thoughts or help her prepare for the apology she would offer when they were alone. She prayed that whatever she managed to say when the moment came would appease his wounded self-esteem sufficiently that, over time, they could regain some of the ease they had developed during the months of their marriage. He was a good man, and the fear she had felt upon first seeing him again was unjust. He might despise her, but he would not abuse her.

Elizabeth was writing to Mrs Gardiner, assuring her aunt that she was well and explaining the argument she had had with her husband, when the gentleman himself found her. They sat across from each other, she perched on the edge of a heavy William and Mary styled walnut chair and he on a matching sofa. He looked around the room. Neither spoke for a minute, then both did at the same time.

"To whom were you—?"

"I wanted to—"

"Please, go on," Darcy said.

Elizabeth cleared her throat and kept her eyes lowered. "I wanted to apologise for—"

"No!"

The harshness of his tone made her recoil, but she straightened her spine and refused to show her anxiety.

He stammered, "I-I, it is best not to dwell on it. We must... I hope that we can put it behind us and—"

"Learn to deal together harmoniously," Elizabeth said without forethought.

Darcy nodded. "There is no need to think that we need to sort it all out... Not in a month, or even...We have time. To learn how to, I mean. To make everything...better."

Elizabeth slowly nodded two or three times. His manner continued to confuse her, and she did not like it.

"To whom were you writing when I came in?" he asked. "If you do not mind telling me."

"My aunt."

"Ah. Georg—How was it while I was away? I mean, how was Georgiana while I was away? Did you and she get along well?"

She gave a quick nod.

"You have to tell me how she acts when I am not with you.

Perhaps I should know, but I do not. I assumed that you liked each other, that you were growing closer, but now…I do not know what to think."

What should she say? Being open was impossible, yet he would not accept silence. "It was as I had thought it would be. We were together at breakfast and dinner and in the evening. We did what we would always do. She played or read, and I read or sewed or wrote letters."

They sat in silence for a very long moment until he said that he would let her return to her letters and left the room.

Elizabeth burned the letter she had started. She could not account for Darcy's behaviour, but she had seen enough to make her decide to wait before telling Mrs Gardiner about their argument. She wrote a very different letter, assuring her aunt that all was well and making light of Darcy's visit to Gracechurch Street, saying that he had expressed pleasure at having met her and Mr Gardiner.

IN THE FOLLOWING DAYS, DARCY WAS PLEASED THAT GEORGIANA began to make progress with her studies, but he could not banish a sense of unease about her. When he had asked about Elizabeth and that dreadful morning, he was almost certain that she had lied. And when the three of them were together, there was more than a lack of friendliness between his sister and wife, and he found it troubling. He greatly anticipated having a long conversation with Tom when they were all in London.

He wished that he saw even a little proof that his efforts with Elizabeth were having an effect. She still looked tired and unwell.

With Georgiana, all I have to do is make sure that she is actually spending time at her books. I have no idea what to do with Elizabeth and no one with whom I can discuss it.

Darcy tried again and again to talk to her, but Elizabeth's manner was not inviting or encouraging. He had taken to reading aloud in the evenings as a way for the three of them to interact more. Elizabeth appeared to enjoy the pastime, which was more than he could say for Georgiana. Elizabeth would discuss the books with him, but otherwise said little when they were together. It was painfully evident that she was uncomfortable around him and that her spirits were depressed, which only made it more difficult for him to say or do anything to improve their situation. It would take time before she would confide in him about Georgiana or her feelings, but she was reluctant to even tell him what she would do that day.

Whenever they were together, he longed to reach out and caress her cheek, to know that, despite her outward coldness, she was still warm. He wanted to hold her and tell her how truly sorry he was, but he knew he had no right to do so and that, if he attempted any such thing, she would only pull away, or, perhaps worse, allow his embrace despite hating it.

No, that was not *perhaps* worse, he decided; it would be *infinitely* worse.

After several days of frustration, he realised that, howsoever it transpired, he spent little time with Elizabeth, other than at meals and in the evenings. He would not be able to show her that he was changed and intended to do better for her unless they were together more often, and he resolved to seize upon every possible opportunity.

One occasion arose a week after Darcy's return. He came across Elizabeth and Mrs Reynolds while on his way to his rooms in search of a letter. The housekeeper took her leave.

"What were you and Mrs Reynolds discussing?"

"We were reviewing the plans for renovating the guest rooms. You will remember, I trust, that we discussed it before your family visited."

"Will you show me?"

Elizabeth's eyes flew to Darcy's, demonstrating her surprise at his question. Had he truly given her reason to believe he took so little interest in what she was doing? He supposed he had. When they were first married, he had been concerned about her creating discord, and he had talked to their housekeepers about Elizabeth's conduct several times to assure himself that she was not causing problems, or acting in a manner of which he would not approve. *What an impression of their new mistress I must have given Mrs Reynolds and Mrs North-more. Suggesting that Elizabeth, capable, intelligent, sensible Elizabeth, would not be a good mistress. I pray Elizabeth never learns of my interference.*

He stifled a sigh. Once it was evident that Elizabeth was not embarrassing him, he truly had ceased to pay attention to her household management, except when he asked about her preparations to receive his family.

"Now?" she asked.

"Unless you have something else you must do."

She agreed, and showed him the spaces she had decided most needed attention. Elizabeth told him about colours and themes, and he nodded and asked several questions. Once they were finished, he escorted her to her chambers.

"I was on my way to collect a letter when I saw you and Mrs Reynolds," he explained as they went into her sitting room. "The rooms will be much improved. What have you decided you would like to do in here?"

"I-I-I have not thought as much about it."

"Oh?" Her rooms were bordering on ghastly. As dearly as he had loved his mother, her taste in decoration had never been to his liking. Something he ought to have told Elizabeth, perhaps. "You should, and soon if the work is to be done while we are away. The renovations must start here. The guest chambers are not as important."

"I...had not..."

"I suppose it was being in town that made me think of it. Your rooms there are almost complete."

"I see."

"You will like what was done. I hope. It is very...pretty. You will be pleased. I hope."

Elizabeth nodded and even managed a faint smile. "I am glad you approve."

"Please say that you will plan your rooms before you and Mrs Reynolds continue with the guest chambers?"

Elizabeth nodded yet again. "If you like."

"I insist. Please."

Elizabeth nodded once more.

He could think of nothing else to say and she remained silent.

"Well, I shall return to my work and let you get on with what you were doing."

Darcy left, reasonably pleased with the interlude. At the very least, Elizabeth must understand that he wanted her to see to her own comfort—as improving her chambers would do—before concerning herself with the appearance of guest rooms that were only occasionally used. *And I showed that I am interested in what she is doing, and, I pray, that I am confident in her abilities as mistress. It is a beginning.*

Chapter 25

*A*t breakfast two days later, they spoke about their return to London.

"We should leave in a week, depending on the weather," Fitzwilliam announced. "If that is agreeable to you."

He spoke to Elizabeth, not Georgiana. The former may not have noticed, but the latter most certainly did. After more than a week of her brother's close supervision, Georgiana was beginning to question her desire to return to London. If it were to be more of the same when they were there, she might prefer to stay at Pemberley. At least then she could do what she liked, and she would not have to see Elizabeth. But if she were in London, she could witness Elizabeth's inevitable failure among the *ton*. There were also the pleasures of London to consider—shopping, excursions, perhaps a concert or two, and dinners if she could convince Fitzwilliam and Tom she was old enough.

"It will take us four or five days at least, longer if we are so unfortunate as to encounter poor weather."

Elizabeth made a small noise of agreement.

"What will you do this morning?"

"Nothing of particular significance."

"No? Will you be making any calls? Perhaps going into Lambton, or…?"

Georgiana could not understand her brother. It was almost disgusting the way he was soliciting Elizabeth's attention. But if he spent more time with Elizabeth, then he might cease to make so many demands of *her*. She was tired of studying and being serious. She wished to amuse herself. Was that so wrong?

Elizabeth admitted that she had several calls to make.

"I shall go with you, if you do not mind," Fitzwilliam said.

"The only calls I intend to make today are of a charitable nature."

Fitzwilliam insisted he would go with her, no doubt to make sure she did nothing embarrassing, and Georgiana was glad to hear that her brother would be out of the house. She would be free of his watchfulness for a few hours.

Her happiness was short-lived.

"Georgiana, you and I should meet directly after breakfast so that we are in agreement about what you will do during my absence."

DARCY WAS VERY GLAD THAT HE HAD TAKEN THE OPPORTUNITY TO accompany Elizabeth. He was beginning to realise how much he missed her. He missed the ease with which they had interacted, he missed feeling that he could go to her side and speak to her whenever he liked, and he missed the sound of her voice.

As he watched her while on their calls, he was struck anew by how well she comported herself. She went about being Mrs Darcy with quiet dignity. She had responded to their unfortunate situation with a remarkable show of strength from the very beginning, always doing everything she could to make the best of it. It was the mark of an exceptional person, and one he liked very, very much—more than he had hitherto realised. He vowed again that he would do better. He would be the best Mr Darcy he could be, the best husband and protector because Elizabeth deserved nothing less.

ON THE THIRD MORNING OF THEIR JOURNEY TO LONDON, DARCY found Elizabeth in her room at the inn.

"I am afraid we are not going anywhere today. The snow that fell overnight has made the roads impassable."

Elizabeth went to look out of the window. "I had expected as much. It looks pretty, but it is not travelling weather."

The fresh snow might make a pretty scene, but he had eyes only for her. Two days in the carriage had done a little to ease relations between them. He had learnt that Elizabeth could not read in the carriage as it made her ill. Perhaps it was only boredom that left her more willing to speak with him, or perhaps it was a genuine improvement in her mood. Her spirits had been very low since his return from town. He did not blame her, but if he had managed to coax her into a little more cheerfulness, he would be very glad. To keep her occupied, he had also read aloud now and again, and he recalled games that he and Georgiana had played on other occasions. He was pleased that Elizabeth seemed to enjoy the activity. When Darcy asked, she readily shared some of the ways she and her sisters had amused themselves during long carriage rides.

The time spent together had confirmed to him that his sister and wife were not on good terms. He had suspected as much, but when he had raised the subject with them, Georgiana would do no more than admit that it was true, and Elizabeth said even less. Darcy felt that both ladies could say a great deal more, particularly Elizabeth.

He remained anxious about Elizabeth's health. She seemed unwell and her appetite remained poor. He suspected it was due to melancholy, and he prayed that she would be happier once she saw Jane and Mrs Gardiner. How horribly arrogant he had been to dismiss Elizabeth's family, not caring about her feelings at being separated from them, to say nothing of theirs at being separated from her. He would have refused to allow his wife the comfort of seeing the people she loved best in the world because he believed them beneath his notice. As Elizabeth would say, their position in life mattered less than their character, and having met the Gardiners, he could never be ashamed to know them. As for the Bennets, they were his parents- and sisters-in-law, and nothing else should matter. He did not have to like them, and perhaps he never would, but he was determined to meet them with equanimity for Elizabeth's sake, and because it was the right thing to do.

"The innkeeper believes that the roads should be passable by tomorrow."

Elizabeth nodded.

"He told me that our breakfast will be ready whenever we like."

Elizabeth nodded again.

"I should tell Georgiana about the change in our plans, and then perhaps we should eat if that suits you?"

"Very well."

"I shall return for you in a moment."

Elizabeth continued to look out of the window. She pulled the woollen shawl she wore more tightly about her arms. He recognised it as the garment he had brought with him from London, and it made him smile.

IT WAS A DULL DAY. THE DARCYS REMAINED TOGETHER IN THE parlour which had been set aside for their use. Several hours after breakfast, Elizabeth was writing letters, while Georgiana and Darcy read.

"Elizabeth," Darcy said, "would you care to go for a walk? I imagine you would. The cold and snow will not deter you from taking the fresh air, at least for a short while."

Elizabeth agreed to the excursion.

"Georgiana? The fresh air and exercise would do you good."

"Pray do excuse me, Brother. I am afraid that I feel a little soreness in my throat. I did not want to mention it, and I am hopeful that it will not progress, but..."

Darcy looked dubious, but turned and said to Elizabeth, "Shall we meet here in a quarter of an hour? Will that give you enough time to prepare?"

Elizabeth agreed though she was not certain how she felt about the prospect of walking alone with her husband. He had been always close by of late, almost since he had returned from town; she could not understand or like it. The way he had insisted on reviewing the renovations to the guest rooms—no doubt to assure himself that she was not doing anything dreadful when, truly, it would be difficult to make some of them uglier than they were.

Although he did insist that I change my rooms. That was...unexpected. After their argument, she had convinced herself that he would not agree to the expense. Not only had he insisted, he had asked her about it again, and said her plans sounded lovely.

And making calls with me! When I first went into Derbyshire, how I would have welcomed his company and assistance in knowing the people around me. I do not need it now.

Observing him while on their calls had been interesting. Elizabeth supposed that she should have known that Darcy understood the circumstances of the families they visited. He attended to his duty as the master of Pemberley and the principal landowner in the neighbourhood with diligence. Elizabeth would not say that he was happy visiting the cottage of this family or that, but he hid whatever distaste he felt.

That is not fair, Lizzy. He was perfectly polite and attentive, and it was plain that he has been to see each of those families before. It costs you nothing to give him the credit he is due.

She sighed. She felt rather mulish about harbouring unpleasant thoughts about her husband, but she had tried to think the best of him for weeks, only to be disappointed. She would not put herself in a similar position again. If she felt her resolution weakening, she only had to remember Georgiana.

How droll it was when she talked about feeling poorly! The look on Fitzwilliam's face! I am convinced he no more believed her than I did. Well, she is his to manage. It has nothing to do with me.

Elizabeth was ready before Darcy and was present to witness him returning to the parlour with a book, which he immediately placed in his sister's lap.

"If you are not going to exercise your body, you might as well exercise your mind."

It was Shakespeare's *Henry V.*

"You can read your novel later. We shall discuss the Shakespeare at dinner."

With clear reluctance, Georgiana set aside her novel. "Yes, Brother."

Despite knowing it was wrong, Elizabeth found Georgiana's discomfort highly amusing.

Darcy took care that Elizabeth should have the clearest paths through the downy snow and insisted she take his arm lest there be icy patches. The day was clear, the sky a beautiful azure, and sunlight made the snow sparkle.

"Has a date been fixed for your sister's arrival in London?"

"The most she can say is that it will be at the end of February."

"You will be happy to see her again."

"Yes." Elizabeth drew out the word ever so slightly. His statement made it sound as though she could see Jane. He had alluded to it before, but she would not take it as a certainty until she and Jane actually met.

"She will stay with the Gardiners?"

"Yes."

Darcy nodded. For a moment, the only sound was the ice cracking beneath his boots as they continued to walk. "I know that you will be much occupied with Lady Romsley. There is little we can do about that. There is the ball next month and any number of other events she wishes us to attend, as well as what she tells me will be a prodigious amount of shopping. When you do have a free morning, send the carriage to Gracechurch Street if you think it is needed. You will know better than I whether it is necessary."

Elizabeth found this a most extraordinary speech, and she took a deep lungful of the cool, crisp air in an attempt to dampen the sudden surge of hope she felt. She longed to believe he truly meant for her to see Jane, and perhaps even the Gardiners. It seemed so outrageous, and she was afraid of suffering disappointment if it did not come to pass.

"I do not mean to imply," Darcy hastened to add, "that your sister or the Gardiners would find it a hardship to come to Curzon Street without you sending a carriage. I simply do not know... It might be easiest to send the carriage. That is all that I meant."

Elizabeth could not help but notice the agitation with which he spoke, and it was against her nature, regardless of her feelings, to ignore it. She lightly pressed his arm. "I will remember."

Elizabeth was surprised that she could be as easy with him as she was. She did not understand what had brought about the change she saw in him, but she welcomed it. *Perhaps he feels that there is no point dwelling on the argument. We cannot and must not air our strained relationship for the entire world to see. We do not want anyone speculating on the state of our marriage. He is willing to act as friends, and I will endeavour to do the same.*

She would keep her expectations in check. He would not like her or feel any affection for her, and she would do him the favour of not liking him or feeling any affection for him in return. It was best for both of them if she remembered that. It might spare them another scene such as the one she had created that dreadful, unforgettable morning.

MUCH TO THEIR MUTUAL RELIEF, THEY WERE ABLE TO RESUME THEIR journey to London the next morning. Georgiana largely ignored her companions. They chatted, and Fitzwilliam would sometimes read aloud, but always some dreadfully boring book. Elizabeth appeared to enjoy whatever it was; Georgiana could not determine whether she truly did or not, and decided it did not signify. It was more amusing to think about everything she would do in London, beginning with shopping and ending with attending a small, private ball if she were fortunate. Surely someone in their family or among their intimate acquaintances would give one, and if she asked her brother and Tom nicely, they would agree that she could go even if she could not dance. After more than four long, dull months at Pemberley, she longed to enjoy the diversions town had to offer.

Georgiana broached the subject, saying, "Fitzwilliam, I have been thinking. In April, I am sixteen. I had hoped you and Tom would agree that I am old enough to start attending some social functions. Smaller events—plays or concerts or-or if someone in the family were having a dinner party, or a small ball. I would not dance, of course."

"I shall have to think about it."

"If I am to do so, then I shall need new things. I shall anyway, because it will soon be spring, but—"

Her brother interjected, "Georgiana, the question of whether you will be permitted to attend anything other than small family dinners is not one which will be settled today, or by me alone. Tom's opinion must be sought. In any event, nothing of the sort will be possible until at least after Lady Romsley's ball for Elizabeth."

"I could go shopping with our aunt."

"No. As I said, I shall talk to Tom about it, but do not expect us to make a hasty decision."

It took Georgiana more than half an hour of reflection to decide that her initial attempt had not been completely without success. He had not said that she was too young or that it was too soon or anything like that. She would talk to Tom as soon as she could and convince him.

When they reached London, Darcy escorted Elizabeth to her chambers, which were now fully renovated. "I hardly recognise the rooms, they are so changed. I hope you are pleased."

Elizabeth smiled faintly in reply as she walked around the space, examining each alteration. Gone were all traces of Lady Anne's ornamented style, all of it replaced by fresh, light decorations. She had chosen well, she thought. The light green wallpaper with its pattern of vines and flowers reminded her of the country, which is what she had wanted when in town. The painted wood furniture added brightness to the room—a contrast to a city that often seemed dark to her—and was much less-embellished than that which it replaced.

"I shall see you downstairs for dinner."

Elizabeth nodded and watched as her husband left. After days of being so much with Fitzwilliam and Georgiana in the small space of the carriage, it was comforting to be alone, at least for the moment. She thought back to her walk in the snow with him. He had implied that she should invite Jane to call at Curzon Street. Darcy's words could also have meant that he expected the Gardiners to visit, but upon this Elizabeth had no reliance. It was still incredible to her that he had gone to Gracechurch Street, and she had no confidence that he truly meant to recognise them.

She sighed. She did not understand what Darcy wanted her to do, and asking him was out of the question. She was unwilling to risk the comparative ease they had by speaking to him openly. She berated herself for lack of courage, especially since she usually thought of herself as having a great deal of courage, but she could not bear it if she were to confront him and her worst fears came true, and she had to again witness his contempt.

With effort, she pushed aside these morbid thoughts. *Much better to spend these minutes appreciating the changes in my rooms.* She truly felt that they were *her* rooms now, and she was proud that her efforts had created such pleasant, comfortable spaces.

It was a hollow feeling. Beautiful rooms did not erase her unhappiness. She remembered what it was like to enter them for the first time. As impossible as it seemed, she felt that the breach between her and Darcy was now even greater than it had been on that day. In some ways, she felt even more alone and more hopeless than she had then.

THEY WERE INVITED TO DINNER AT FITZWILLIAM HOUSE THE NEXT day and presented themselves at the appointed time.

"There you are," Lord Romsley said. "I had begun to think you would be late."

Sterling rolled his eyes behind his father's back. "Do not mind my father, Elizabeth. He is a stickler for punctuality, which means that everyone must be early if they wish to avoid his disapprobation."

"Really, Sterling," said his mother.

"Oh, leave the boy alone, Margaret. He is just having a laugh at my expense. I hope I am not so humourless that I would take offense that easily."

Lady Romsley examined Elizabeth's outfit closely. She was quick about it, but Elizabeth noticed. Rather than irritate her, however, it induced fatigue. The coming weeks would be very trying, and Elizabeth wondered how she would find the heart to withstand it.

"Catherine and Surtees arrived yesterday," Lord Romsley said at the start of dinner.

"They brought the children, of course," Lady Romsley added. "Marian and Frocester will be here in a day or two."

Lady Romsley looked expectantly at Elizabeth who said, "I am sure your ladyship will be pleased to have her children and grandchildren nearby again."

"Several of the Darcys are here already," Darcy announced. "The rest will arrive next month."

Elizabeth heard a low noise of displeasure from Sterling. She supposed it would be agreeable to see Rebecca again—she had been pleasant company—but she could not anticipate seeing the other Darcys.

"We must talk about arrangements," Lady Romsley began, then fell silent until the servants left the room. "Elizabeth, we must begin shopping. Tomorrow if you will. You will need a great deal before you are prepared to face the *ton*."

And I cannot possibly go shopping on my own. I would, naturally, make the most vulgar and inappropriate of choices. I could not help myself, given my lowly origins.

"I need new things, too!" Georgiana exclaimed.

"Elizabeth will begin attending social events almost immediately," Lady Romsley said, "and you, Georgiana, are not yet out."

Georgiana could not hide her look of disappointment quickly enough.

"I understand that a girl of your age likes to go shopping and have pretty things, but you must not think only of your own pleasure. You cannot need very much." There was enough irritation in Lady Romsley's voice to chastise the most stubborn of girls. "You have hardly grown since last year. There will be time enough to shop for you once Elizabeth has everything she requires."

Darcy spoke before his sister could. "Georgiana, I told you on the way to London that we would not discuss it at this time. I shall raise the matter with Tom, but not until after the ball."

Sterling laughed. "Oh, do tell, Darcy. You cannot speak so mysteriously and not expect someone to demand an explanation."

Darcy explained Georgiana's wish for the Season.

"Good God, no!" exclaimed Lord Romsley.

Elizabeth lifted her napkin to her mouth, hiding the laugh the earl's outburst occasioned. Sterling did not bother to mask his amusement.

Georgiana's face became bright pink, and she lowered her head.

Lady Romsley soothed, "Really, Georgiana, your brother is right. There can be no question of it for now, not until after Easter, I would say. In May, I shall present Elizabeth to Queen Charlotte, and there will be many other obligations. I leave it to your guardians to decide, but my opinion is that I do not see how or why it should be done this year. You are not yet sixteen. You will have your turn."

Lord Romsley decided that this was an opportune moment to remind Elizabeth that she would have to take care during the Season. His voice was brusque. "You must appear happy. You and my nephew must look like a couple married only six months who threw aside convention to marry. You will be moving in very different company than that which you are accustomed to…" He continued on this theme for a minute.

"We understand, Uncle," Darcy said. "You can rely on Elizabeth's good sense, as I hope you know you can rely on mine."

After Sterling muttered his agreement, the room fell silent. Elizabeth could only look at her husband in surprise that he had spoken in her defence to his family. Darcy glanced at her and gave her a quick smile before returning his attention to his dinner.

Chapter 26

$\mathcal{D}$ inner with his family provided Darcy with more to contemplate. Elizabeth sat impassively and ate little, which concerned him. As his aunt spoke about the Season and shopping and everything she intended to accomplish in the coming days, he recalled Elizabeth saying that she would do whatever was expected of her. He wondered just how large a gap there was between what she was expected to do and what she would *like* to do.

Given the speculation regarding their marriage, they were right to dread this Season, but there was more to the Season than gossip. Would Elizabeth enjoy the balls and concerts and parties? Darcy knew Georgiana loved shopping, but did Elizabeth? And what was her rapport like with Lady Romsley? His aunt lacked delicacy, and, while he was grateful that she was willing to help Elizabeth become established as his wife, he wondered whether Lady Romsley's advice and assistance might be officious.

When the earl spoke, it was easy to see the tightening of Elizabeth's jaw, and he could hear a gentle tap-tap noise which could only be her foot hitting the floor. He wished he had told her that his uncle frequently spoke to all of them in such harsh, demanding tones. It would not belie her feelings, but it might have helped. Darcy spoke, hoping to distract Lord Romsley. Elizabeth's surprise was expected, but still disappointing. That did not signify. What was important was that her foot stopped tapping at the floor, and her jaw relaxed enough to allow her to eat her dinner.

It was a small victory, but he was glad of it.

ELIZABETH WAS SURPRISED AND SUSPICIOUS WHEN LADY ROMSLEY deferred to her choices and desires regarding colours and styles for her new garments without argument. As Elizabeth had another matter worrying her, she chose not to think about it. They were in the carriage, on the way to yet a different warehouse—this time in search of bonnets—when Elizabeth took advantage of a private moment.

"Lady Romsley, it is Fitzwilliam's birthday next week, and I would like your assistance finding an appropriate gift for him. I have turned my mind to it," *not for very long, admittedly,* "but I am afraid I have been unable to settle upon anything."

"I am so pleased that you are making the effort to be a good wife to my nephew. Of course, I would be very happy to help you select something."

After they purchased two bonnets for Elizabeth—one a deep red that Lady Romsley said went very well with her complexion, the other a blue creation adorned with flowers and ribbons that made Elizabeth think of the spring—they went to a jewellery shop. Elizabeth overlooked the snuff boxes the countess suggested since Fitzwilliam rarely took snuff, and purchased a fob watch. Having accomplished this task, she asked Lady Romsley's advice regarding how to mark the occasion.

"I thought perhaps a dinner for some of the family would be best. We have just arrived in town, and there is not much time to make arrangements," Elizabeth said.

Her ladyship agreed. "The earl and I shall attend, as will Sterling. Some of the Darcys, too. You can manage such a dinner well enough on your own, although I am glad to offer assistance if you find the exercise too hard on your nerves."

Nerves? For one dinner? Has she forgotten everything I did at Pemberley?

"When it comes time to invite people outside of the family, I shall naturally oversee your efforts."

Elizabeth suppressed a sigh. *Naturally! I suppose that if I err horribly and it is just the family, they will forgive me even as they despise me. Someone from outside of the family, however, would be sure to let everyone among the* ton *know that I am little better than a barbarian.*

ELIZABETH DID NOT WANT TO TALK TO GEORGIANA. SHE DESPISED THE part of her that made her do what she felt was right, knowing that her sister-in-law was likely to be disrespectful. Georgiana was in her small private parlour reading a novel.

"Georgiana," Elizabeth said from the doorway.

Georgiana glanced in Elizabeth's direction, but did not otherwise acknowledge her.

"Georgiana," Elizabeth repeated, keeping her voice firm. She would give the girl one more chance to acknowledge her properly. If she did not, Elizabeth would leave.

Georgiana sighed loudly, and, with a heavy scowl on her face and eyebrows arched, looked up at Elizabeth.

"I have purchased a gift to mark your brother's birthday next week. Lady Romsley and I shall be shopping again the day after tomorrow. If you would like to accompany us so that you might find something for Fitzwilliam, and assuming your brother does not object, you may."

The girl did not speak.

"Yes or no, Georgiana? Would you like to go with us?"

Georgiana nodded once.

"Pardon? Yes or no? I am afraid you *will* have to speak. I would not wish to misunderstand you."

Georgiana glared at her.

Elizabeth felt perfectly justified in turning around and starting to walk away. "No it is then."

"Yes!" Georgiana cried.

Elizabeth kept walking, her back to her sister-in-law, but did acknowledge Georgiana's response with a shallow nod. If the girl saw it or not, Elizabeth did not know and did not care. *Let her suffer some moments of discomfort not knowing if she will be allowed to go shopping, an activity I know she enjoys. Perhaps next time, she will treat me with a little more respect. My attempts to befriend her did me no good; this change in attitude might yield surprising results. Or not. It hardly matters.*

AT DINNER, DARCY ASKED ELIZABETH ABOUT HER TIME WITH LADY Romsley, but she would say no more than that it had been uneventful. He spoke a little about his day before falling silent. He was learning that it was very difficult to have a conversation with people who will not respond. He was thus pleasantly surprised when Elizabeth spoke towards the end of the meal, even though her demeanour was formal.

"I shall be shopping with Lady Romsley again the day after tomorrow. We thought that Georgiana might accompany us, if you have no objection."

"I do not object as long as you and my aunt are content to have her with you."

"I also wished to ask for your thoughts on holding a dinner next week for some of your family. To mark your birthday."

"My birthday?" Darcy had not realised that Elizabeth knew when his birthday was, but decided that he had underestimated her again. Elizabeth had, in all likelihood, learnt the date of his and Georgiana's births soon after they were married so that she could be prepared to celebrate the occasions. To his shame, he did not know when Elizabeth's birthday was. He did know she had not been one and twenty when they married. It was possible that, since then, she had a birthday that was unacknowledged by her husband.

"It is next week, is it not?" she asked.

Darcy nodded. "I did not realise you knew. Though I should not be surprised that you do."

"Would it be agreeable? I spoke to Lady Romsley, and she thought that it would be...appropriate."

"It-it is not necessary." Elizabeth's last words then entered his consciousness. "Appropriate? Did she tell you that you must? Do not feel that you have to attend to everything she says. My aunt can be—"

"No," Elizabeth interjected. "I simply thought… It would just be some of your family. I could send invitations tomorrow. If you are agreeable, that is."

Darcy was not certain what he wanted to say. He wanted to thank her and assure her that he did not expect her to go through any bother for him. He wanted to discover if his aunt had been too demanding, or if the countess, intentionally or not, was unkind.

He looked at Elizabeth as he tried to find the words to say. She held herself so rigidly and her expression seemed so cold, just as it had for days and days. She could not want to celebrate his birthday out of any affection for him. It was simply what she felt a proper wife would do.

You gave up any right to her affection long ago. When, I wonder? The first time I refused to answer one of her questions? When I would not even look at her after I promised myself to her at the Longbourn church?

It was almost impossible to keep from abusing himself when he considered her. It grew worse with each mark of her goodness. But this was no time for such dark reflections, and he attempted to force them away. They would, no doubt, return as he lay in bed that night praying that sleep would find him.

"Yes. That would be…agreeable. Thank you." He was unable to find any other words.

Elizabeth nodded and returned to picking at her food.

Did she cry? he wondered. *On our wedding night, perhaps, when I did not say more than was strictly necessary to her. When else might she have given in to her unhappiness? The first night that we…* This line of thought was even more inappropriate for the dining parlour, and, to prevent a recurrence, he spoke as much as he could for the remainder of dinner—anything to avoid thinking of how very much he had hurt Elizabeth, and how unlikely it was that she would ever forgive him.

GEORGIANA WAS HAPPY TO HAVE THE DIVERSION OF A SHOPPING TRIP with her aunt. Much to her chagrin, her time in London so far resembled the last weeks in Derbyshire. After the dull months at Pemberley, she had anticipated amusing herself, yet Fitzwilliam required her to bring her books to his study after breakfast every morning so that he could supervise her efforts to, as he said repeatedly, 'improve her mind.' He was treating her as though she were a schoolgirl, even all of these months after—well, after *that*. When Elizabeth had mentioned the excursion, Georgiana had been torn. She did not wish to be with Elizabeth, especially not in public where she would have to pretend to like her, but she did want to go shopping. It would not take long to find a gift for her brother, and there would then be time to find one or two things for herself.

Two failures on her part caused her some vexation. First, that despite putting on her most pleasant face and not complaining at all as Elizabeth chose so many lovely new things, she could not convince her aunt to spend any time on her needs. It was not so outrageous that Georgiana would want new gowns or so impossible to find time that morning to order them. At the very least, she had thought that she would return to Curzon Street with a new bonnet or two, but it was not to be.

Her second failure was not finding out what Elizabeth had bought for Fitzwilliam. Her brother should like her gift more than he did Elizabeth's, but without knowing what Elizabeth bought him, how could she make the best choice?

In the end, Georgiana bought him a book. She was not happy with her purchase, especially since the volume she initially selected had to be replaced by one of Elizabeth's choosing. When Elizabeth saw what Georgiana was going to buy—some dull looking book of poetry—Elizabeth said, within the hearing of Lady Romsley, that Fitzwilliam had recently read it. Lady Romsley then asked Elizabeth what she thought he would like! Elizabeth, attempting to demonstrate some sort of superiority, spent a few minutes looking around the booksellers before offering Georgiana the choice of two books. Listening to her aunt thanking Elizabeth and commending her for her attention to Fitzwilliam's tastes was going too far. Georgiana really, really did not like having a sister.

ELIZABETH COULD NOT ACCOUNT FOR HER LOW SPIRITS. SHE HATED feeling unhappy and tired all the time, but she could not shake off the cloak of discontent. She sat alone in her bedroom preparing for the dinner party and forced herself to consider her blessings.

Within a week, I shall see Jane and I will find the courage to ask Darcy if I might go to Gracechurch Street. The worst that can happen is that he will refuse. He has been kind since he returned to Pemberley and has not made any demands of me. For this I am very grateful. He is willing to put our argument behind us. I am thankful for that, too. I was convinced that his resentment would be great. Perhaps it is, but he is taking the trouble to not let it rule his behaviour. I must acknowledge that is a mark of his goodness. We shall soon be much in company and he will be able to mask his true feelings for me. I must do the same regarding my feelings for him.

She sighed and stared at her image in the mirror, not pleased with what she saw. What remained of Lizzy Bennet was rapidly fading away. In her new, very expensive pomona silk gown, her hair dressed in the latest fashion and wearing gold and peridot jewels that had been among the Darcy family collection which her husband had given to her two days earlier—she looked...*foreign.* No, she looked like Mrs Darcy. *And Mrs Darcy and Lizzy Bennet are two entirely different people.* She sighed again.

Tomorrow, Mr Bingley calls with his sisters. He was agreeable when we met, and I hope his sisters are the same. I am in town now, and perhaps I shall meet some ladies my age who could be...friends. Friendly acquaintances at the very least. I should like that.

All in all, her situation was not so very bad. She thought it was possible that she and Darcy could learn to be comfortable together; she would be content with that. There was a great chasm between them that precluded more, and it would take something extraordinary, and thus very unlikely, to bridge it.

THEY WERE FOURTEEN AT DINNER, AND THE PARTY WAS A SUCCESS. Conversation was lively, and everyone present seemed to wish to be pleased, even his uncles John and Lord Romsley.

I pray that will make it easier for Elizabeth, Darcy thought.

Perhaps when the ladies are alone, Aunt Susan will occupy Lady Romsley, and Elizabeth will be at liberty to enjoy the company of the younger ladies. His cousin Jack's betrothed, Miss Trivett, was among the party; she seemed agreeable, and Darcy hoped that Elizabeth would like her.

Darcy spent as much time watching Elizabeth as he could. Once again, despite whatever she might be feeling, she was acting just as a caring, attentive wife should. But as much as Elizabeth played the part of Mrs Darcy excellently, he knew there was a great deal missing. They might be seeing Mrs Darcy, but they were not seeing Elizabeth. Darcy was not sure that even he knew who that was. He wondered if Elizabeth knew, or if she had lost sight of herself during the months she spent, in her words, doing everything she could to be a good wife and mistress.

And sister, he thought, as his eyes wandered to Georgiana. He would be glad when Tom was in London. They had a great deal to talk about, and he hoped that Georgiana would confide in Tom about her relationship—or lack of one—with Elizabeth.

Darcy believed that he had had glimpses of the real Elizabeth. She was the person who delighted in the outdoors and had learnt the ins and outs of Pemberley and its servants in very little time. She was the Elizabeth who made calls of charity with as much enthusiasm, if not more, as she did social calls. She was the Elizabeth whose curiosity and quick mind led her to read about geology, and which had allowed her to become so knowledgeable despite a very indifferent education. She was the Elizabeth who would fly to the aid of Georgiana and who valued respect above his wealth and name. She was the Elizabeth who presented to him a very thoughtful birthday gift, one that suited him perfectly, although he knew he could not do the same in return. He had, at least, learnt when her birthday was. Elizabeth would be one and twenty at the end of June.

Six months married, and only now do I know when her birthday is, and I had to use subterfuge to hide my ignorance from her. Selfish and arrogant she called me, and selfish and arrogant I have been. Well, today I am eight and twenty and not, I trust, too old to reform my character.

Mr Bingley called as arranged the next morning, bringing with him not only his sisters, but Mr Hurst as well. Mrs Hurst and Miss Bingley were very fashionably dressed—a touch over-dressed for a morning visit, in Elizabeth's opinion.

No sooner were they in the room and introductions completed, than Mr Bingley exclaimed, "Mrs Darcy, I am delighted to see you again!"

His joviality brought a smile to Elizabeth's face. "And I you, Mr Bingley." Turning to the ladies, she said, "Please do take a seat."

Georgiana linked her arm with Miss Bingley's and led her to a sofa. Mrs Hurst joined them. Georgiana's evident delight put Elizabeth on her guard.

"Mrs Darcy," Miss Bingley said, "it is so good to finally meet you. Mr Darcy has been very secretive about you. I hardly knew what to expect when we entered the room." She tittered.

Elizabeth did not know what to make of her comment, or the fact that Mrs Hurst joined her sister in laughing.

"I am afraid I do not understand what you mean, Miss Bingley," Darcy said.

Elizabeth turned her head to stare at him. The coincidence of his voicing what she had been thinking was striking.

"I have hardly had occasion to talk to you about my wife. I believe I have only seen you and Mrs Hurst once since I married."

Mr Bingley said, "You must know, Mrs Darcy, that there are many among our acquaintance who are anxious to meet you. You will be the talk of the *ton* this Season! And there could be no worthier object, I am sure."

"Really, Charles, what a thing to say! Mrs Darcy does not want to be the talk of the *ton*," Miss Bingley cried.

"As I am confident that what people would say about my wife, at least those with any sense, and therefore the only ones whose opinions could possibly matter, would be pleasing, I see no reason why Mrs Darcy would mind being the talk of the *ton*, as you say. Or did you have some other sort of talk in mind, Miss Bingley?"

"Why, Mr Darcy, whatever could you mean? I know that you do not like to be the object of gossip—"

"Why would anyone?" Darcy interjected. "We all know that what passes as gossip is mostly fictitious and rarely well-intentioned. I did not believe we were speaking of gossip, however. Your brother, I thought, was referring to kindly meant comments about my wife and interest in making her acquaintance."

"Of course, I was!" cried Mr Bingley.

Elizabeth took a quick study of their guests. Darcy knew them well, and she got the distinct impression that he was not overly fond of the ladies. His expression did not show it, but he was drumming his fingers on the arm of his chair, and she saw a muscle near his eye spasm. Of Mr Hurst one could hardly think. He sat upon his chair ignoring them, and they seemed content to ignore him in return. Mr Bingley still impressed Elizabeth with his easy manners, but Miss Bingley and Mrs Hurst were not going to be her friends.

Why did I think otherwise? Look at them chatting so easily with Georgiana. Surely that, if nothing else, proves that I could not like them, and they could not like me.

The Bingleys and Hursts departed after an appropriate time with many promises of seeing each other in the near future. Elizabeth hoped it would not be very soon.

Chapter 27

ews soon reached Darcy House that Tom Fitzwilliam and Jane Bennet had arrived in town, creating much excitement. Tom would call the next morning, and Elizabeth immediately made arrangements for Jane to visit the day after.

Tom and Elizabeth had only enough time to greet each other before Elizabeth took the place he had recently vacated next to his mother in her fine town coach, the Romsley crest sparkling in the morning sunshine. While Elizabeth and Lady Romsley attended to their business, Tom, Darcy, and Georgiana ate a late breakfast. Tom and Darcy then retired to the latter's study.

Before she left them, Georgiana asked, "Brother, you will talk to Tom about my idea?"

"Yes, Georgiana," Darcy replied. She had reminded him of it the previous day, and he was tired of hearing about it. Her smile, and overly opened eyes also vexed him for some reason.

"Georgiana's idea?" Tom asked once they were alone and comfortably seated.

Darcy rolled his eyes. "Georgiana hopes that we shall agree that she is old enough to attend a few select social events this Season."

Tom laughed. "You are not serious."

"She is in earnest. She has talked about concerts and plays and perhaps small dinners, and even a private ball or two, at which she knows she would not be allowed to dance."

"She is not yet sixteen! I had not envisioned her coming out for another two years. It is too soon. Even what she suggests is too much. Do you not agree?"

Darcy nodded. "I do, but you know Georgiana will not like that decision."

"Yes, well, she cannot have everything she wants. We can tell her we shall revisit the matter in September. There is always the Little Season. It might keep her from complaining so very much."

"Tell me, how has everything been since I was at Pemberley? You said little in your last letter, other than that she did not do as much with her studies as you had hoped she would when you came to town. Why did you come to London, anyway?"

"Business."

"It was unfortunate that you could not delay it until the three of you returned together. At least Georgiana had Elizabeth for company. They were getting along quite well when I was there."

Darcy exhaled sharply. "I know that we thought it was getting better, but it has not. I have had to conclude that what we took for friendship was only Georgiana pretending for the benefit of others. When it is just the three of us, they barely speak."

Tom regarded his cousin for a long moment before saying, "Really? I seem to recall her telling me that the situation had improved. Not long after you went into Derbyshire, she wrote that it was very difficult with Elizabeth. She felt that they were so different, that Elizabeth's background was so far removed from hers that it was not easy for them to find common ground, but I was under the impression that Georgiana was growing more comfortable with her. At least as much as possible."

"Georgiana never said anything like that to me."

Tom shrugged. "I gather Elizabeth's family is not as well-mannered as Georgiana is accustomed to. Sterling said as much, too. That would add to Georgiana's discomfort."

"Whatever the behaviour of Elizabeth's family, no one can find fault with her conduct. In any case, it is not only Georgiana's manner towards Elizabeth that has me worried."

Tom raised his eyebrows. "Have you considered that what you have witnessed is Georgiana responding to something Elizabeth has done? Are you so sure that it is Georgiana's behaviour towards Elizabeth? Why might it not be the other way around?"

"What do you mean?"

Tom lifted his hands in supplication.

"No," Darcy insisted. "Trust me. There is a problem between them, and I truly believe it is because Georgiana has not been welcoming to Elizabeth's overtures. Get Georgiana to be open with you. She will not be so with me. I have tried, but she will not acknowledge that there is a problem. Perhaps she is afraid that I shall take Elizabeth's part against her."

Tom nodded. "I shall. I suspect we will find there is a simple explanation for what you have witnessed."

"I hope so, but, as I wrote, it is not only the situation with Elizabeth. It is, again, the matter of her studies. I returned to Pemberley after being in town, and she had done nothing. It was not a matter of being unsure about what I wanted her to do. She simply did not do it."

"What did she say?"

"A lot of things that added up to very little."

The two men looked at each other and were silent for a long moment.

Tom said, "I admit we might have expected too much of her when you first went into Derbyshire, but she should have accomplished something of significance by now, even if she has had to work on her own."

"I have suggested to her many times that she and Elizabeth could work on some of it together—French, Italian, history. It would have given them a way to know one another, and to keep each other company while I am occupied. It would have helped Georgiana. Elizabeth was willing."

"Helped Georgiana?" Tom laughed and scratched his temple.

"Really Darcy, I am glad you are finding merit in your wife, but..." He shook his head. "I made the same suggestion to Georgiana. I thought if she enlisted Elizabeth's assistance, she might progress with French more quickly than we were by exchanging letters. But, as Elizabeth is not familiar with the language, it seems rather that working with Elizabeth would slow her progress."

Darcy stared at him. "Elizabeth not familiar with French?"

"There is no shame in it. Given Elizabeth's family, I should not have expected more."

"Did Georgiana tell you that Elizabeth does not know French?" Darcy felt almost lightheaded as a disturbing realisation struck him.

"Yes. What is the matter with you?"

Darcy's heart started to race, and heat rose inside of him. His head spun with a feeling of anger he did not like. "What exactly did Georgiana tell you about Elizabeth, and when?"

"When?" Tom repeated, his brow furrowed. "Many times since September. The last must have been in November, or early December —one of the last letters I received from her before I travelled to Pemberley. She told me, with regret, that Elizabeth could not possibly be of assistance with her studies, because Elizabeth had no education of which to speak and knows no French or Italian."

There was no mistake. Georgiana had repeatedly lied. Darcy's heart pounded so hard, he thought he might have a fit of apoplexy. In a low, trembling voice, he said, "She lied."

"What?"

Darcy locked eyes with his cousin, who seemed more confused than troubled. "Georgiana *lied* to you. Elizabeth has a very good command of both French and Italian—far better than Georgiana's—as well as history and much more beyond that. Geology, for one, or were you too preoccupied with Miss Haddon to notice?"

Tom sat back in his chair, his lips parted. It was a moment before he spoke. "Perhaps Georgiana misunderstood?"

"She did not. She knows, and she lied," Darcy whispered. "She lied about Elizabeth."

He stood and went to ring the bell. When a footman came to the room, Darcy ordered him to tell Miss Darcy to come to the study immediately. "Is Mrs Darcy returned?"

"Not yet, sir."

"As soon as she is, direct her here."

While they waited, Tom sat, his face impassive, and Darcy paced. He had the sense of something breaking inside of him, a restraint on his feelings that was shattered by the certain knowledge that Georgiana had gone far beyond not attending to her studies or befriending Elizabeth.

GEORGIANA WALKED TOWARDS THE STUDY, BELIEVING THAT HER guardians wanted to talk to her about her desires for the Season. They might require a bit of convincing, but she felt certain that she would be able to bring them around. She was not asking for so very much.

As soon as Georgiana entered the room, she knew that whatever her brother and Tom wanted to talk about, it was not concerts or dinner parties. Fitzwilliam looked at her and immediately barked, "Sit."

Georgiana dropped into the chair across from Tom. She glanced at him, but his expression seemed as menacing as her brother's, if not more so, and she lowered her eyes to her lap, frantically trying to guess what had happened and how she should present herself.

"Did you tell Tom that Elizabeth could not help you with your studies because she lacks the necessary knowledge?"

Georgiana had a brief, momentary hope that she had misheard him. "F-fitzwilliam?"

He spoke slowly, enunciating each word carefully although his voice shook. "Did you tell Tom—"

"More than once," Tom interrupted, his tone firm and cold. It made Georgiana tremble a little; she clasped her hands together to still them.

"—that Elizabeth knows neither French nor Italian and has a poor understanding of history, and therefore could not, in any way, help you with your studies?"

Tom said, "She also told me that when the three of you were alone, Elizabeth was prone to exhibiting her mother's vulgarity."

"What?" Darcy cried.

Georgiana's eyes flew to Tom. *No! No, no, no! Please say no more!*

Tom gave a solemn nod. "She said as much once or twice in letters to me. She also begged me not to say anything to you, because you seemed to be more comfortable with your wife, and she did not wish to cause you distress by making an issue of it. Somehow, I no longer believe any of it."

Both men turned to Georgiana. She felt as though she could not breathe. Her eyes darted around the room, looking everywhere but at the two men who were her protectors, and who, she knew, loved her better than anyone else did. She truly had not believed they would ever discover her exaggerations and equivocations.

WHEN ELIZABETH ENTERED THE ROOM, DARCY GLANCED AT HER AS Tom stood and waved her over to one of the moss green wing chairs. She did not understand what was transpiring, but clearly it was something of significance. Across from her was Georgiana, who shot her an angry look.

In a tone which almost masked his fury, Darcy ordered, "I want you to apologise to Elizabeth for lying about her."

Elizabeth gasped. Seeing she would get no explanation from Darcy at the moment, she looked to Tom. He gave one quick nod. His jaw was tightly clenched, his arms crossed over his chest, and she was very glad that his anger was not directed at her.

Georgiana sat with her head held high, but her eyes lowered.

Darcy spoke again, this time more severely. "Georgiana, I demand that you do it this instant."

Georgiana remained silent, but tilted her chin upwards.

"Georgiana!" Darcy barked, the volume of his voice rising precipitously.

Georgiana's chin quivered, but she otherwise did not move.

"Georgiana Catherine Darcy, I expect you to admit what you have done, and apologise!"

Darcy's restrained rage made Elizabeth understand how wrong she had been to fear him in January. As he stood over his sister, who had told some sort of lie about her, Elizabeth now knew what a fearsome Fitzwilliam Darcy looked like. Yet, she also knew that, as enraged as he was, he posed no physical danger to Georgiana. When she had worried about her treatment at his hands after speaking so candidly to him at the end of December, she had done him an injustice. He was not a violent man.

Despite everything Georgiana had done to her, Elizabeth did not feel even the slightest bit of pleasure to witness Darcy demanding Georgiana account for her behaviour, something that ought to have happened long ago, in her opinion.

Georgiana spoke, her voice tremulous. "I have nothing to admit. There is nothing that she can help me to learn, and it is not fair to expect me to like her, let alone be her friend!"

Elizabeth felt Tom's eyes on her and shrugged. After everything that had passed between her and the girl, she could not be surprised.

"Why did you lie to Tom about Elizabeth? Why?" Darcy demanded.

After biting her lips together for a moment, her hands clenched so tightly that her knuckles were as white as her gown, Georgiana cried, "So that I would not have to spend one minute longer than necessary with her! I want her to go away. She should not be Mrs Darcy. She does not deserve it. Everyone knows that!"

Elizabeth heard Tom gasp. It appeared that Darcy also had not expected Georgiana to say something so frank and spiteful as he stared at her, his lips parted, unmoving. There was silence in the room for the better part of a minute.

"What?" Darcy took a deep breath, slowly releasing it. He resumed speaking in a more moderate tone, although the calmness of it was deceptive. "I cannot believe you just said that. Why is Elizabeth my wife?"

Georgiana did not answer.

His voice grew louder. "Why, Georgiana? Why did Elizabeth and I marry?"

Georgiana remained silent.

"Must I remind you?" Darcy hissed. "Elizabeth is my wife because of *you*. Have you forgotten what you did? How can you of all people denigrate Elizabeth after what she did for you? Have you never considered what she saved you from, what your life would be now if she had not gone to your aid? *Have you?*"

Georgiana recoiled, but still did not speak.

When Darcy made his next demand of her, it was at little less than a roar. "Have you forgotten? Should I remind you?"

Georgiana's body gave one large shudder, then stilled. Elizabeth could see the tautness in her shoulders and arms.

"You were going to elope. You are fifteen and you were going to elope with a man more than ten years your senior, a man with whom you knew I no longer associated. Did you not wonder why? What were you thinking when you became entangled with him? Did you ever stop and consider what kind of man he had to be to convince a girl so much younger than he is to elope? Do you have any idea what an elopement would have meant for you and for your family?

"You must understand that what he wanted was your fortune. That, and the ability to revenge himself on me. Do you need me to tell you what your life would have been like as Mrs Wickham? How long do you think he would have valued you, or professed his love for you? No longer than it took to sanctify the marriage. He would have squandered your fortune and left you broken and miserable, with a ruined reputation, a ruined life, because he knew that that would be his best revenge on me—and all because I would not support his dissolute habits with Darcy money. Do you understand that?"

Darcy was far from finished. "And what about the rest of us? How do you think we would have felt had you thrown away your life on a man like Wickham? I do not speak of the scandal, of our name and our reputation being dragged through the mud because of your stupidity. How do you think those of us who love you, who have cared for you, and done our best for you would have felt, knowing that you betrayed us by doing something you knew was so very wrong? What were you thinking when you agreed to let him make love to you, to convince you that you loved him in return—enough to—"

His anguished tone pierced through Elizabeth, but she refused to act. It was difficult not to, seeing how pale he was and the utter sorrow of his expression. It was a forceful reminder that, as angry as he was, he loved his sister, even though Elizabeth could not.

"What did we do?" He took two or three deep breaths before continuing. "How did we fail you so much that you would consent to something so certain to end in misery for us all? Was it some grand romantic adventure? Was Wickham the hero who would save you from—from what?"

He paused to laugh, but the sound of it was so morose that it caused a sharp pang of sympathy in Elizabeth's belly.

"From a life of luxury and a family who loved you. Is that what Wickham the romantic hero was to save you from?"

Georgiana remained silent, but her lower lip was quivering alarmingly. Elizabeth, observing her, could tell that at any minute tears would fall down her cheeks. She had seen the look before on that night at Ramsgate, when this whole, miserable charade began. Elizabeth did not wish to feel pity for Georgiana, but a small part of her saw in Georgiana a young girl who, for whatever reason, made very bad, very selfish decisions.

There was a note of pleading in Darcy's voice when he next spoke. "What do you think would have happened had Elizabeth not gone to your aid that night? Do you think Wickham would have let you return to me to tell me about your plans to marry? He would not because he knew I would never agree."

The entreaty in Darcy's voice began to fade. "Elizabeth, who did not know you, who knew none of us, acted from the very best of instincts to help a foolish young girl who had put herself into a dangerous situation. What was her reward for it? She was made to marry a man she did not know or risk her reputation and that of her beloved sisters and family. And you, what have you done to thank her? You have lied about her, and you can sit here and speak so dismissively of her, of she who has been your truest friend!"

His voice rose to a roar again. "You owe her your gratitude and your allegiance, and you owe her an apology for lying about her to Tom and who knows who else and for thinking so meanly of her!"

Georgiana's fists tightened into balls, and she lowered her chin to her chest.

"Are you so selfish that it does not matter to you what your actions have cost others? Not only Elizabeth—I, too, am paying the price for your folly. I had to marry a woman I did not know in order to protect your reputation, that of our family, and that of the woman who saved you from ruining your life. Do you care? Clearly, I have made many, many mistakes where you are concerned—"

"As have I," Tom interjected.

"But were any of them so awful that it could justify what you did? I thank God that Elizabeth is the wonderful person she is. If she were anyone else, I cannot even imagine what misery could have been mine."

There was a long moment of silence. Georgiana's shoulders shook. Darcy remained standing over her, his chest rising and falling rapidly. Elizabeth stared at her husband, wary and curious about what he would do next.

His voice sounded gravelly. "I should not be surprised that you lied about Elizabeth, that you could be so deceptive and manipulative and hide your disdain so well. You lied about Wickham. He was in Ramsgate for weeks, and you never once mentioned him in your letters to me or to Tom or to anyone else, did you? What else have you lied about? How far back do we have to go to find out where it started? Have you deceived us all for years? Was that sweet, loving girl I always believed you to be nothing but a façade? Did your lying begin in Ramsgate? We know it did not end there. What else has there been since?"

He looked up, away from Georgiana for the moment, as though trying to remember.

"Aunt Horry's visit. I remember that. I returned to the house to find Elizabeth alone with my aunt, and you said that you did not receive a message to join them, but the message was sent. You simply ignored it. Why? To make it more difficult for Elizabeth? When I found out that Elizabeth's message had been delivered, you said that you must have misunderstood, and I gave you the benefit of the doubt.

"It was the same thing with your studies, and I cannot even imagine how many lies you told about that. And I made excuses when you failed to progress. You needed more guidance than I initially gave you, I thought. I suggested that you have Elizabeth help you, but did I question whether you did or not? No, of course not. I blame myself for being too blind to see what is now becoming so obvious."

Tom interjected again, "We both have made many mistakes with her. Do not take this all on yourself, Darcy."

"How much you could have learnt from her, and I do not just mean about French or Italian or history or botany or any other subject. She, who never had your advantages, has learnt, through her own initiative, her own curiosity. She was not content to be an ignorant woman who can only talk about fashion and novels. *That* is what I would have you learn from her. How to be a woman worthy of respect and regard."

Georgiana scoffed. Tom made an angry growl.

"How dare you?" Darcy hissed, his face blotched. "After everything I just said, after everything you should know, you can still dismiss Elizabeth in such a way? Your name and fortune mean nothing of importance. Your character is what we are discussing, and it is seriously lacking. Your youth cannot excuse the flaws I see, and neither can any failure on my part or on Tom's. I may not have done everything perfectly, but that does not excuse you. You told Tom that Elizabeth did not receive a proper education, and it is true that her education cannot compare to what you were fortunate enough to have. But that has not stopped Elizabeth from improving her mind, from gaining knowledge, from becoming a respectable woman. Something you currently are not."

Georgiana began to cry; she covered her face with her hands.

"I compare you to Elizabeth and I know who is the better person, whose character is more worthy of praise. That you can think so little of her, given everything she has done for you and everything she has done to make the best of a situation you created, is disgusting to me."

Georgiana's sobs became louder.

"How much you have betrayed us all, Georgiana. I can hardly conceive that it is possible, and yet I know it is. Where is your remorse about what you did last summer? Where is your remorse for what it has meant for me and for Elizabeth? We come back now to how this started. Elizabeth and your lies about her—the blatant ones about her knowledge and manner and the ones you have been telling yourself about her worth and about what you owe her."

The sounds of Georgiana's misery filled the room when Darcy fell silent for a moment. He looked down at his sister, his expression stern, nostrils flaring as his chest rose and fell heavily.

"I have learnt my lesson, even if you have not yet learnt yours, and I promise you—and Elizabeth—that I will do whatever it takes to make you understand and to help you to become a better person, as I know you can be. We have been too easy on you. Good God! Did we not learn after Ramsgate that we could not trust you? Stop this nonsense, Georgiana, and do as I asked. You are acting like a child. Although that does seem a fitting description of your behaviour these many months. Now, Georgiana!"

Georgiana jumped at the volume and rage of her brother's voice as he said those last two words. The only effect they had, however, was to increase the volume and strength of her tears.

Without volition, Elizabeth stood and in two or three long strides was beside Darcy and lightly placing a hand on his arm.

"Fitzwilliam." The calmness of her voice surprised her. "I do not think Georgiana is capable of doing so at the moment."

Darcy closed his eyes and hung his head. He covered Elizabeth's hand with his and raised it to his mouth, pressing his lips against her fingers.

He spoke again to Georgiana. "Do you see? Even after everything you have done to her, she still thinks of you. Even after what you have taken from her, she still offered you friendship, and even at a moment such as this, she thinks not of herself and what she is owed, but of your feelings." He closed his eyes again, lowering his head, but he did not release Elizabeth's hand.

Elizabeth was uncomfortable with Darcy's praise and confused by the scene which she had just witnessed. The sentiments her husband had expressed regarding her were surprising, and she wished for a long period of solitude in which to consider them. When she went to him, she had not acted out of any particular regard for Georgiana's well-being. It had been an instinctive action, not unlike that which had her fly to Georgiana's assistance that night at Ramsgate.

Elizabeth did not believe she could remove her hand from Darcy's had she tried, such was his grip on it. She did not know what to say to ease his distress, and, as Tom escorted Georgiana out of the room, stood silent by his side, her eyes fixed on him.

Chapter 28

Tom took Georgiana to her bedchamber. She threw herself onto a divan and sobbed, an activity she maintained until forced to admit that Tom had no intention of speaking. Any hope she had of sympathy from him was gone. Just as, months earlier, she had been angry when her brother stood aside as Tom chastised her, now she was livid that Tom had stood by while Fitzwilliam said such hateful things to her. She would never apologise to Elizabeth and was furious that Elizabeth had borne witness to her humiliation.

Picking up a book she had left beside her bed, Tom looked at it with disgust. It was a much-loved novel.

"Is this what you have spent your time on? Novels? Fairy tales, perhaps, with Elizabeth cast in the role of evil stepsister? Something is damaging your character. I doubt we can blame novels alone, but they cannot be helping, filling your head with romantic drivel. How can you fail to know that they are meant for amusement, not as a guide to life?"

Georgiana gasped as he started to collect all her novels, and as he explained, "There will be no more novels until we see improvement in your manner. No novels, no pianoforte."

"You cannot do that!" she cried. Her heart raced and she began to stand, only to fall back onto the settee when she saw his forbidding expression.

"I most certainly can! No novels, no pianoforte until you convince us that you take your studies as seriously as you do your music. You will apologise to Elizabeth, and you will mean it. You will henceforth treat her with the consideration she is due. These are initial prohibitions until your brother and I decide what we need to do to fix the problem you have become."

Georgiana glared at him. She felt lightheaded and knew she was breathing too rapidly, but could not stop. How could he be so cruel?

"Do not look at me like that. Not after what you have done to your brother and Elizabeth, two people who have sacrificed because of your choices. It is badly done, Georgiana. More than badly, it is hateful."

Georgiana's face burned with indignation.

"We will discuss all of this again and again and again until we are convinced that you understand your errors. For now, spend your time thinking about what we have said to you."

He rang the bell, and, when Georgiana's maid answered, issued his orders. "Miss Darcy is not permitted to leave her room for the remainder of the day unless Mr Darcy or I say otherwise. Please see that all the books in her possession are collected immediately. I shall have a footman come to take them from you."

After Tom was gone, Georgiana buried her face in a pillow and screamed.

ELIZABETH LED DARCY TO A SOFA AND MADE HIM SIT. HE COVERED his face with his hands and spent several minutes struggling to regain his composure.

"That morning, after my family left Pemberley and we... exchanged words, what happened with Georgiana? She will not admit to anything, and I have not had the heart to press you. Please, I need to know."

Elizabeth returned his gaze for a moment before looking away. How could she ignore his pleading tone? She chose her words carefully. "I asked if she would join me while I decided how to re-decorate the guest chambers. She let me know that she had no intention of spending more time with me than was absolutely necessary."

"Why did you never—No, I need not ask. You never said anything because you had no reason to suppose that I would have believed you or done anything about it even if I had."

He stood and walked to the window. Elizabeth followed his movement with her eyes, shocked at his words. Even after hearing him chastise Georgiana, and even knowing he had said one or two very complimentary things about her, Elizabeth could not believe he had admitted that her silence was understandable. His next words, and his sorrowful tone, surprised her even more.

"I am sorry, Elizabeth. I have tried to show you, but...I do not know if I ever... I am truly sorry."

It was too much for her to take in all at once, and she did not respond. They remained as they were until Tom returned some minutes later.

"I shall leave you." Elizabeth stood.

"No, stay," Darcy cried, adding to Tom, "She is my wife, and let us not forget that she has more understanding of young ladies of Georgiana's age than we do. Please, stay, Elizabeth."

Not feeling that she could disoblige him, Elizabeth returned to her seat; the gentlemen joined her.

"I suppose we do not have to discuss the matter of Georgiana participating in the Season any further." Tom gave a short, humourless laugh.

Darcy asked, "Did she say anything?"

Tom shook his head. He recounted the measures he had put into place. "It was a decision of the moment. I saw one of the da—forgive me, Elizabeth. I saw one of her novels, and the next thing I knew, I was telling her she was not permitted to read them any longer."

Elizabeth listened, but she had no intention of participating in their discussion. The gentlemen reviewed what they knew about Georgiana's behaviour during and since her time at Ramsgate. Elizabeth was asked about her relationship with Georgiana. She would say no more than that Georgiana only behaved in a friendly manner when they were in company with others.

"What do we do now?" Tom asked.

Darcy sighed and shook his head, rubbing a hand across his forehead. "I have no notion. I am too exhausted to think."

Elizabeth thought that he did sound and look drained. His voice had never sounded so thin, and his face was pale. The temptation to open her heart to him, to pity and comfort him, and do whatever she could to ease his distress, was strong, but far too dangerous. She longed to flee the room. So much had happened, and she very much wished for a period of solitary reflection.

"Elizabeth, do you have any suggestions?" Darcy asked.

Elizabeth was almost incredulous that he had asked for her opinion on such a matter. Tom, who had seldom talked to her or paid her any heed, was also waiting for her to respond. She looked between the two men, her mouth opened to speak, but she struggled for something to say. She did not want to be a party to this conversation, and most certainly did not want to be responsible for making any decisions where Georgiana was concerned.

At length, she offered, "Howsoever it is that you choose to address this situation, I do know that if Georgiana believes I am involved, she will hate it even more." *Hate me even more.*

Tom said, "Elizabeth says something very wise. It will not help to give Georgiana another reason to be unhappy with her sister-in-law."

Darcy looked at Elizabeth. "I may deserve to suffer for my failures—"

"And me for mine," Tom interjected. "I will have my share of blame."

Darcy continued, acting as though he had not heard his cousin. "Of all of us, you least of all deserve to suffer for what happened last summer, and I will not allow anyone to treat you with disrespect. Never again."

Elizabeth nodded and stood. The gentlemen followed suit. "I shall leave you. I have things to attend to before dinner. Am I right to suppose that Georgiana will not be coming down?"

"I do not trust myself to speak to her again today," Tom said, and Darcy nodded his agreement.

"You will remain?" Elizabeth asked Tom. "You and Fitzwilliam will wish to speak further."

Darcy was quick to answer. "We can talk before dinner, and after, if necessary. We shall meet you in the drawing room shortly."

Elizabeth wondered if his thoughts had travelled to the same place hers had—to the day after their wedding when he and Tom had left her to dine alone. Today she thought she might prefer it. She nodded and left them to their discussion.

ELIZABETH FOUND IT IMPOSSIBLE TO ATTEND TO HER DUTIES. EVERY word that Darcy said that morning, every aspect of his manner, had to be remembered and considered. She did not know exactly what Georgiana had lied about, but it was immaterial. Elizabeth's conscience had prickled more than once when she thought about the deception she was called upon to live, but she could not see how that and what Georgiana had done were the same.

She was no less than astonished by Fitzwilliam's anger that Georgiana had treated her with scorn. He had sounded disbelieving and disturbed that Georgiana could harbour such hateful sentiments towards her; Elizabeth would have expected him to understand Georgiana's feelings. And he had suggested that she had given up a great deal by being forced to marry him!

He heard some of what I said, she reflected with a mix of pleasure and astonishment.

As for Darcy's insistence that Georgiana apologise…

I suppose I am grateful. She laughed. *I do not expect Georgiana to actually apologise, not insofar as a genuine expression of contrition, and as I do not expect it of her, it is a very good thing that I no longer care what she thinks of me.*

Fitzwilliam had also said one or two things that could be considered praise, as though he saw in her something of value, despite her lack of fortune or connexions. And he had apologised—although he had not said for what—and claimed that he would not allow anyone to treat her with disrespect.

Elizabeth's heart raced. She covered her cheeks, which were suddenly quite warm, with her hands, hoping to cool them. It could mean so much. "No, it does not change anything," she told herself two or three times. "I pray we can find a way to-to be comfortable, but that is as far as I can go."

She rested her head against the back of the sofa and closed her eyes. It seemed to her that since the night she met Georgiana and Fitzwilliam Darcy, her life had become a never-ending series of calamities which left her constantly on guard, ever-watchful of her words and actions, ever-questioning what she must do. Somehow, she would find her way through it. Georgiana could no longer hiss spiteful words at her, which would be a relief. If she did, Elizabeth would tell her husband, and he would act in her favour. She prayed that that was the result of the morning's dramatic disclosures, but she knew that she would not really believe it until there was a reason to test Fitzwilliam's resolve.

BEFORE PARTING TO PREPARE FOR DINNER, DARCY AND TOM AGREED that there would be no separation of the sexes since they would be only three. Thus, when they finished eating and Elizabeth stood and announced her intention to leave them, Darcy and Tom followed her into the withdrawing room. Elizabeth asked that tea be served immediately.

No sooner were they settled then Tom spoke to Elizabeth. During their earlier conversation, Tom had asked Darcy to tell him about Elizabeth and the months of their marriage and said that he felt he owed it to her to acknowledge his own lack of consideration.

Tom said, "Elizabeth, I apologise. I did not give you the credit you deserve, never in all the months that you have been part of this family. I believed what Georgiana told me, never thinking whether I should or not. When I was lately at Pemberley, I allowed…personal concerns to consume my attention, and I did not think to question what she wrote or said to me, even when what I saw contradicted what she had said."

Elizabeth murmured a thank you.

The gentlemen sat close by Elizabeth. "My cousin and I are horrified by Georgiana's lies and her defiance."

"Absolutely," Darcy agreed. There was so much that he felt he should say and that he wanted to say to Elizabeth, but her continued stoicism made it difficult for him to form sentences. Had he allowed too much to escape his notice, treated her with indifference for too long for her to ever do more than hate him? Did he now, after so much had happened, have the right to ask for her forgiveness? He was afraid that the answer was no. The day had started out so well; he was happy to see Tom again. Now, he wanted nothing more than to crawl into his bed and let sleep claim him. Or go for a long solitary ride across the grounds he loved so much at Pemberley. *Or do anything that will let me pretend this has all been a nightmare from which I will soon awake.* He drained his cup and forced himself to attend to the conversation.

"I never would have supposed it possible for her act like this." Tom shook his head.

"Before last summer, as far as we can recall at least, there was never anything like this. She was spoilt by the family—by all of us. I cannot deny that. She was young when my father died." He sighed and shook his head. "Even after what she did in Ramsgate, it was stupid of me of us—but it never occurred to me that she would tell such lies or..." He exhaled a breath full of frustration. Elizabeth deserved so much from him, and he felt completely incapable of giving it to her. She was so reserved, only showing signs of liveliness if they were in company.

Other than that moment. The moment she had come to him when he was lost in berating Georgiana and put her hand on his arm. The gentleness of her touch had washed over him, taking with it the worst of his anger, and leaving only deep sadness. She had that power over him. *More power than anyone has ever had.* One touch, and he felt soothed, felt that somehow everything would be well. What he had felt at that moment was—

He watched his cousin talk to Elizabeth. *It does not matter what I felt. Elizabeth hardly wants to be in my company unless she must. I cannot blame her, especially now that I know how Georgiana has behaved towards her. How could I have been so stupid, so blind? I shall pay the price for that.*

He took a deep breath and looked more carefully at Elizabeth. She was so lovely. How he yearned to caress her and whisper into her ear that he would make everything better, that she need not feel so alone or unhappy or unappreciated. How he would love to feel her arms about his waist, her body pressed to his. There he would find repose from his burdens and anxieties. There, somehow, he could tell her that he regretted so much and would spend the rest of his life proving to her how much he esteemed and respected her if she would only let him.

Elizabeth finished her tea, stood, and put the cup onto the tray.

"I shall leave you," she announced. "You have much to discuss, and I would not wish to keep you from it."

Darcy was on his feet before she finished speaking. "That is not necess—"

Elizabeth shook her head. "I have letters to write. I shall be in my sitting room."

She wished them good night and left the room.

As expected, Elizabeth did not see Georgiana at breakfast. Being alone with Darcy was not an enviable position, but it was better than being in company with him and Georgiana. Her mood was further elevated by the knowledge that Jane was expected to call that morning.

Unfortunately, this was also a source of anxiety. She had thought about it a great deal after rising, and knew that she could not be easy until she spoke to Darcy.

"I am surprised that your cousin is not here. Mrs Northmore mentioned he was with you earlier," she said, pushing a small piece of ham around her plate.

"He was, but he could not remain for breakfast. He was required elsewhere, but intends to return later this morning."

Elizabeth nodded.

"I am afraid we did not get very far yesterday. Discussing Georgiana, I mean. Perhaps it was too soon to expect more. The shock was still too great."

Elizabeth smiled faintly. "Perhaps."

They were silent for a minute as Elizabeth gathered her courage enough to ask the question that was pressing on her mind.

"Fitzwilliam, it occurred to me that perhaps today is not the best day for me to entertain my sister."

"No."

Elizabeth felt a sharp stab of disappointment. *I should be used to the feeling by now.*

Darcy quickly continued, "I mean to say that I do not agree. You have missed your family, and I would not have you postpone the visit because of what has happened. I must run an errand after breakfast. Georgiana will remain in her room. Do not feel that you should change your plans. Do *not* change your plans, not because of…what happened."

Elizabeth was perhaps more grateful for these words than she had been for anything he had said to her since the day they met. She wanted to thank him, but suspected it would sound odd.

It was some minutes before either spoke. Awkwardness made Elizabeth ask if Tom would join them for dinner. Darcy said he could not and only hoped they made more progress in their discussions before Tom had to attend his evening engagement.

"The difficulty we face is not speaking again and again of the past, but of deciding what to do now. We are at a loss."

Elizabeth could sense his despondency. "As you said, it is perhaps too soon to expect more of yourselves." They were the most comforting words she could devise.

"The restrictions Tom instituted on the spur of the moment will remain. She was not pleased when we told her earlier."

"No, I imagine she was not." The words were out of Elizabeth's mouth before she had time to think about them, and she instantly regretted her tone, believing it had been sarcastic. Fortunately, her husband seemed not to notice, or, if he had, he did not fault her for speaking so.

"I remember what you said yesterday about it being better if you were not involved in deciding Georgiana's fate, but if you have any advice, I would like to hear it."

The earnestness in his voice impressed Elizabeth with the truth of his words. She did not have anything which she felt she could suggest to him, however, and shook her head.

As she was preparing to leave his company a short while later, she did have one thought which on impulse she shared with him. "If Georgiana is not used to accepting such decrees from you and your cousin, it might take her time to trust your sincerity, to trust that you will not...forget. That you will be...consistent."

She inclined her head in lieu of saying anything further and left him standing, staring after her, in the corridor outside of the breakfast parlour.

Chapter 29

Despite knowing it was not dignified, Elizabeth paced restlessly in the morning room as she waited for Jane. So many carriages went by without stopping it was near to driving her mad. It had been six very long, very lonely, very trying months. Finally, after living among those who did not like her, and who were constantly judging her, she would be with one who simply loved her.

At last Elizabeth heard the sound of the front door opening and the butler, Mr Mallon, greeting someone.

She stopped her restless walking when the door opened. Mallon announced, "Miss Bennet," and Jane stepped into the room. Elizabeth felt tears begin to pool in her eyes. She smiled, and so did Jane. As soon as the butler closed the door, she and Jane discarded all decorum and flew into each other's arms.

"Oh Lizzy! How good it is to see you!"

Elizabeth just managed to refrain from sobbing. The sisters held each other for a long moment. When Elizabeth felt capable of controlling the most violent of her emotions, she spoke. "Jane, it is so, so wonderful to see you."

They made themselves comfortable on one of the room's elegant sofas, hands clasped, and simply looked at each other.

"How I have missed you!" Elizabeth exclaimed.

Jane smiled. "And I you. Are you well? You look pale. I am under very strict orders to report on your looks, in detail, to my aunt."

"I am perfectly well," she said out of habit. "If I am pale, it is only because I have seen the sun so infrequently of late. The weather was dreadful in Derbyshire, and I could not get outside as much as I would like. But you! You are as beautiful as ever and a very, very welcome sight!"

"And Mr Darcy and Miss Darcy? They are well, I hope?"

Elizabeth nodded. "I do not believe we shall see them this morning. Mr Darcy is out on some matter of business which could not be delayed, and Miss Darcy is indisposed. 'Tis nothing, I assure you, but I believe she will keep to her room." Thinking as well of everyone as she did, it was unlikely Jane would feel slighted by Darcy and Georgiana not greeting her. Elizabeth felt it, although she had no wish to expose Jane to Georgiana if it could be avoided. "Tell me, how is everyone at Longbourn?"

Jane was happy to answer, and, until refreshments were served an hour later, they spoke about Longbourn and Meryton. Elizabeth smiled and laughed and felt more light-hearted than she had for months. It was delightful to see and hear and touch one of the people she loved best in the world.

Jane asked about Pemberley and Elizabeth's new neighbourhood.

"What can I say that I have not already? Pemberley is beautiful, and Lambton is much the same as Meryton, although larger and more prosperous. Of the people I regularly see, I have written much." She mentioned Mr Llewellyn, Mrs Morris, and Miss Pratt, along with a few others.

"I am so relieved to know that you are making new friends, Lizzy. I have been very worried about you. But you and Mr Darcy are… happy? Miss Darcy is recovered after her disappointment?"

Elizabeth had known that Jane would ask. "I own it has been difficult at times, but yes, we have…come to understand each other better. It was never going to be easy. It could not be, under the circumstances. But pray, Jane, do not spend a moment worrying about me."

"Aunt Gardiner has acquaintances in Lambton who all say that Mr Darcy is a good man."

"He is. He attends to his duty as master without fail and is very generous in supporting local charities, in giving assistance to the poor, and in improving the welfare of the local populace. It is a great comfort to me to know that he does all this, not because it is his duty, but because he could do nothing less."

It was a great surprise to Elizabeth that this praise so easily flowed from her mouth, but she knew it was true. She just wished he attended to his duty as a husband with the same diligence. *But that has changed. He has been so much more attentive and kind.* She shook the thought away, and said, "I believe my situation is at least as comfortable as I have a right to expect, given the circumstances of my marriage."

Jane looked uncertain.

Elizabeth laughed at Jane's gently furrowed brow. "Truly, I have nothing of which I shall complain, and now that you are here with me, I am as happy as I can possibly be. I have missed you so! Tell me how long you will be in London."

"I am not certain. Perhaps until after Easter."

"We shall meet as often as possible while you are here, and I hope you will be able to come to Pemberley in the summer." It was a wish dear to Elizabeth's heart, and she vowed to find the courage to ask Darcy if she could have Jane to stay. Seeing Jane emphasised how much she missed having a friend with her, and she promised herself that she would do whatever she had to in order to show Darcy that she deserved to have her sister with her for two or three weeks. "Tell me about the family who have leased Netherfield. Are you and Mrs Linnington still friends?"

"We are. She and Mr Linnington are a welcome addition to the neighbourhood."

"And have my mother's prayers been answered? Does Mr Linnington have a brother in want of a wife? Or perhaps Mrs Linnington does?"

Jane blushed, and she no longer met Elizabeth's eye.

"Jane! What have you not told me?"

"Lizzy, do not tease me," she begged. "Mrs Linnington does have a brother. Mr Hawarden. He is a very amiable gentleman."

"And when did the very amiable Mr Hawarden come to Netherfield? I must conclude it was not long ago else I am sure my excellent sister would have told me about him. Or my mother would have!"

Jane laughed. "I shall never be able to continue if you tease me!"

Elizabeth promised to remain quiet, and Jane explained that Mr Hawarden had come to Hertfordshire in December. "He lives in Cheshire at his father's estate which will one day be his. Oh!—He is all that a gentleman should be, and I believe you will like him."

"Am I to meet him?"

Jane looked at her, uncertain. "I hope that you may, if Mr Darcy does not object. The Linningtons and Mr Hawarden are to come to town soon."

"Is there a particular reason I should like Mr Hawarden?"

Acutely embarrassed, Jane shook her head. "No, there is nothing like that. But...I do like him very much. More than any other man I have met before."

Elizabeth clasped her sister's hand. "Does he return your regard?"

Jane smiled shyly, and her voice softened. "I believe he does. They go to Cheshire for Easter, and I believe I shall accompany them."

Elizabeth's eyebrows arched high on her forehead and she demanded that Jane tell her everything there was to know about the Hawardens. She kept Jane speaking for a very long time and concluded that Jane not only liked Mr Hawarden, she very probably loved him.

DARCY WAS RETURNING TO THE HOUSE LATER THAT MORNING AND MET Tom just about to knock at the door. He explained that Jane Bennet was visiting with Elizabeth, and Tom agreed to greet the ladies before the two of them went into his study to continue debating the matter of their ward. Opening the parlour door, Darcy stopped at the threshold and stared at Elizabeth. He rarely saw her laugh and had not heard the sound of it, other than in the form of a polite titter, for weeks. She was laughing freely and looked so genuinely happy that it both gladdened and saddened him.

He was determined not to despair. Elizabeth's parting words at breakfast, about the need to be consistent with Georgiana, meant more to him than that he should remain firm with his sister. He thought it possible that Elizabeth referred to his behaviour towards her, too. Perhaps she could not trust his changed manner until he had proved himself by remaining thus for some time. He vowed to himself that he would not falter. He would demand Georgiana reform, and he would continue to do everything possible to show Elizabeth that he was, thanks to her, a better man. It might not win him Elizabeth's regard, but if it could lessen her unhappiness, that would be reward enough.

"Oh." Elizabeth stood. "I did not know you were returned."

"We have only just come in," Darcy explained. He smiled, but although Elizabeth returned the gesture, the carefree attitude she had exhibited a moment earlier was gone, and he regretted it. She immediately looked away and ran her hands down her skirt. He turned to Jane. "Miss Bennet, welcome. I am very glad to see you again."

He introduced her to Tom, and they said all that was proper.

"Mrs Gardiner did not come with you?" Darcy asked.

Darcy saw Jane's confusion and the surprise on Elizabeth's face. He had thought Elizabeth understood his intentions, but apparently, she had not. Or she had not trusted he was sincere. He swallowed his dismay, knowing this was not the time to dwell on his failings.

"I am sure she has many demands on her time. I do hope she will be able to join you next time you call. Mr Gardiner as well." He became bolder, determined for Elizabeth's sake that there would be no further misunderstanding. "I imagine Elizabeth has explained how busy my aunt is keeping her at the moment, but I hope we shall both be able to call at Gracechurch Street soon."

"My aunt and uncle would be happy to see you again, Mr Darcy," Jane said.

Darcy heard her, but could not say if or how he responded. His eyes were fixed on Elizabeth's, willing her to believe what he said. After a short moment, Elizabeth averted her gaze.

"We should leave you to your visit. After so long, I am sure there is much you have to share. Miss Bennet, please do give my regards to the Gardiners. I hope to see all of you soon."

He again glanced at Elizabeth to see how she took his words while Tom and Jane said the customary words of farewell. There was confusion and hope in Elizabeth's dark eyes, and, as much as he wanted to see more, he was satisfied.

"GRACECHURCH STREET, DARCY?" TOM ASKED WHEN THEY WERE safely ensconced in his study. He accepted a glass of wine.

Darcy did not answer. How could he possibly explain what had happened to send him to Gracechurch Street, even to Tom?

Tom laughed. "You know very well that I shall keep asking until you tell me. You have met them?"

"Yes."

"When and why?"

As the silence between them lengthened, Darcy finally admitted, "In January, and because it was the right thing to do."

"Did Elizabeth ask it of you? That would be quite—"

"No," Darcy insisted. "The Gardiners, who happen to be estimable people, are among those my wife thinks of most highly, along with Miss Bennet. Elizabeth and Mrs Gardiner keep up a regular correspondence, and I decided that, as Elizabeth values them so greatly, I owed it to her to recognise them."

Tom gave a low whistle. "You have not told my mother and father, I take it. If they knew, I would have heard about it."

"I did not ask their opinion, and neither do I require their approval."

"They will, nevertheless, have a great many opinions to share with you when they learn of it."

Darcy shrugged. He would not attempt to argue the earl and countess into liking the Gardiners or even meeting them. "I will do what I feel is best. It is right, and it is necessary."

It took a moment, but Tom nodded.

"The Gardiners are not as you would expect. They are not what I expected, not after meeting Mrs Bennet. I truly do like them both very much."

"You think the horror stories my brother and parents have told me about her family have soured my opinion?" Tom shrugged. "I trust your judgment. If you like them, I am certain they are worthy of it. Come. Georgiana. What shall we do with her?"

DARCY DID NOT SEE ELIZABETH AGAIN UNTIL DINNER. ONCE THEY were settled at the table, he asked about her visit with Jane and the news she had had to impart about their family and Elizabeth's friends in Hertfordshire. Elizabeth said a little about the well-being of the Bennets and Gardiners, then seemed content to remain silent. He felt a now-familiar stab of pain, but he could not blame her for her reserve.

"I do hope you will soon have the pleasure of seeing Mr and Mrs Gardiner here."

Elizabeth nodded and thanked him.

"I do think that for now it is best if they visit you." Darcy felt awkward saying this. He knew his words could be easily miscon-strucd, but Tom's astonishment upon learning that he had been to see the Gardiners reminded him that it would do Elizabeth no good among the *ton* to be known to visit relations in so unfashionable a place as Gracechurch Street. It would be another matter once Elizabeth was known to his society. They would recognise Elizabeth's excellent character, and that would allow her more freedom. Her visiting relations whose condition in life was so much beneath that of the Darcys might be remarked upon, but people would overlook it, or even think it a fine thing that she still acknowledged her family.

He was relieved when Elizabeth nodded and looked as though she were not angry or hurt, but she said nothing and so he remained in some doubt.

She mentioned the Linningtons and Mr Hawarden, explaining, "Mr Linnington has leased Netherfield, which is not three miles from Longbourn. It is larger than my father's estate. Mr Hawarden is Mrs Linnington's brother. Their family's estate is in Cheshire. Jane hopes to introduce them to me when they come to London, if you have no objection."

Darcy was gratified to know that the people Elizabeth wished to meet were well-placed in society. As much as he vowed to know the Gardiners, he was not about to lead a rebellion to demolish the class structure of society. "I do not imagine there could be any objection. Your sister is friends with Mrs Linnington?"

"I believe they have become quite good friends."

"All the more reason to anticipate meeting them." Darcy smiled at Elizabeth, but she only inclined her head in acceptance of his words.

Darcy hated to see that Elizabeth doubted him, but he had to admit that if she had difficulty believing he would welcome people who were so much beneath him in terms of fortune and consequence, it was his own doing. From what she said of the Linningtons, they must be comfortably situated, yet she did not think he would wish to meet them or have his wife do so. What had she said during their quarrel—that he only valued wealth and connexions? He did not wish to believe it was true, but he had shown her that they were, at the very least, of utmost importance to him. Had he not, after all, condemned her, the Bennets, and the Gardiners because they lacked these qualities?

Georgiana has done so. And there are those among the ton *who will never like Elizabeth for those very reasons.*

The question that must follow was whether or not he would care. The answer was easy. No. It might have worried him before, but afterwards it did not, except in that Elizabeth might be hurt by the dismissiveness some would exhibit. He laughed to himself and wondered when exactly he had begun to think of his life as before and after, the divide being the morning when she had exposed the flaws in his character. He owed her so much for helping him to become a better man, one of whom he could justifiably be proud.

As much as he did not like to depress her good mood, he wanted to talk to Elizabeth about Georgiana. She should know what he and Tom had discussed. Tom and Darcy had again told Georgiana that she would have to acknowledge the harm she had done and apologise to Elizabeth. Georgiana had refused to talk to them, refused even to look at them once she understood they had not come to make amends to her, and both men had told her, again, how utterly disappointed they were in her.

"She shows no understanding of what she has done amiss. She

would not even talk to us when we went to see her today. She requires a companion, someone who can give her the attention she needs. It must be someone who is able to govern her, someone we can entrust with the truth, from Ramsgate to her lies about you. We both liked Mrs Younge, and I need not tell you how greatly we erred. It will take time and effort to find the right lady.

"I have to believe that with the right guidance, Georgiana will accept responsibility and will try to make amends. She is my sister. If she will not, she is still my responsibility, at least until she becomes of age. If you had known her when she was younger, she was so sweet, so loving, and I must believe that that person is still part of her. But you have never seen it, and I will not attempt to convince you. Georgiana will have to undertake that task if—when—this...whatever *this* is has passed."

After another moment during which neither of them spoke, he said, "Tom and I have decided to enlist my aunt's assistance. Lady Romsley shall be of great help in finding a proper companion for Georgiana, and we hope she shall have some suggestion regarding what to do with her in the meanwhile."

"Lady Romsley does like to be helpful. I am sure she shall have a great deal of advice to give."

"Elizabeth, if my aunt is being officious, please, you must tell me."

Elizabeth nodded, and an awkward silence fell between them as they both attended to their meals. Darcy did not know what to say. He longed for Elizabeth and not just in a physical sense. He knew he would feel so much better if he could touch her and hold her in his arms, but his real need was for her regard. The more he understood the depth of his feelings for her, the farther away she felt. He had stood aside insensibly while she had suffered, and now, he was suffering in return.

At length, Elizabeth said, "I do appreciate her attempts to be of assistance. There is nothing of which I can complain."

His rejoinder was swift. "Nothing you *can* complain about or nothing you *shall* complain about?" He had not missed the nuance in her speech.

Elizabeth's cheeks coloured, and he heard her foot begin to strike the floor.

"I—" she said just as he said, "I apologise."

When he opened his mouth to say more, she shook her head. "I...I shall admit there have been times in the past when your aunt has, perhaps, said something which was not to my liking, but we are... managing well enough."

Darcy sighed and sought words to convince her to be open with him.

"Will it do if I promise that should she do something which I find...upsetting, I shall tell you?" she asked.

His eyes met hers and he felt, for the moment, hope.

ELIZABETH WAS BY NO MEANS AT PEACE WITH THE WORLD, BUT JANE'S visit had done much to soothe her spirits. She had been surprised when Darcy not only came to greet Jane, but brought Tom with him. When she heard that he meant to welcome the Gardiners, the very people he had so disparaged, into his home, she had been stunned. The promise of soon seeing her beloved aunt and uncle was overwhelming. It would be much easier to bear the realities of her situation if she could see those she loved best at regular intervals.

Her cheerier mood was dampened by her dinner-time conversation with Darcy. She did not blame him for being angry and disappointed in his sister. It was to his credit that Georgiana's behaviour discomposed him so. What she was not prepared for were the many emotions she experienced. The sorrow in his voice pained her. His regret when he spoke about Georgiana and not excusing her behaviour to Elizabeth made it next to impossible to remain aloof.

After dinner, Elizabeth found Darcy's company even more uncomfortable. Although he picked up a book, he did not look at it. Rather, he stared at her in a way that hinted at longing. She would not try to understand what he wanted from her; to do otherwise was beyond her ability at the moment. Yet, he had been so changed since his time in town after their argument. Was she wrong to be a little optimistic when he was treating her with more consideration, to believe his changed manner meant more than that he was determined to hide the truth of their situation from the keen eyes of the *ton* who still speculated about their marriage? Had he, perhaps, understood and accepted that some of what she said to him that dreadful morning in December was true? If he had, the changes she had witnessed in him would begin to make sense. His willingness to allow Jane and the Gardiners to call might simply be because he realised she would be happier if she could see them. If that were his motive, it spoke highly of him.

Being sure to mask it as best she could, Elizabeth sighed. If she allowed herself to think well of him, to imbue his actions with the best of motives, she would once again make herself vulnerable to him. She *had* to guard her heart. She could not bear another disappointment, especially with the Season in front of her.

The silence became too much for Elizabeth. She wanted to redirect her thoughts away from Fitzwilliam and his distress, and she wanted him to stop staring at her. At the very least, she could make it less obvious that he was. She set aside her book and asked, "Would you care for some music? Shall I play?"

Without waiting for a response, she stood and went to the instrument, determined to play until it was late enough to excuse herself for the night.

Chapter 30

The next morning, Lady Romsley came to collect Elizabeth so they could make calls. Darcy awaited the countess with Elizabeth, and they were both surprised when Lady Romsley emerged from her carriage after it stopped in front of the house.

"Fitzwilliam, Elizabeth. Let us go inside."

The countess sailed into the house and into the morning room. Elizabeth and Darcy exchanged a look and followed her.

Lady Romsley announced, "I would speak with Georgiana." She sat, her back rigid and her countenance imperious.

"Of course," Darcy said. He rang the bell and sent for his sister.

They waited in silence. When Georgiana appeared, she looked wary, but remarkably defiant. Other than one very unpleasant glare at Elizabeth, she acted as though her sister-in-law was not there.

"Come here," Lady Romsley ordered her niece. "Sit." She used her walking stick to indicate the sofa across from her.

Georgiana hesitated.

After pressing his teeth together for a short moment, Darcy said,

"Georgiana, do as your aunt says." He did not regret that some of the annoyance he felt remained in his tone.

Georgiana sat.

"Tom told me the most extraordinary tale this morning. Perhaps I should not be so very astonished by it, not after the events of last summer. Is it true, Georgiana, that you told outrageous lies to Tom about your sister-in-law and implied more untruths than I can imagine to all of us when we—when I myself—told you how pleased I was that you and Elizabeth were on friendly terms? Have you been avoiding your duties while lying about it to your brother and my son? Have you truly, as Tom said, treated your brother's wife unkindly, cruelly even? Do you deny any of it?" Lady Romsley was visibly seething with anger. Tom had informed Darcy that he would tell his mother about Georgiana immediately and, clearly, he had.

"None of you like her either!" Georgiana cried. "You hate that she is part of our family. I at least am not a hypocrite about it."

"That is quite enough," Lady Romsley said. "If *that* is what will come out of your mouth, then I had much rather you did not speak at all!"

Darcy was watching Elizabeth and saw that at Georgiana's outburst, Elizabeth's face lost its cool politeness and became an image of hurt and anger for an instant before she regained her composure. He wished he had the right to comfort her. Lady Romsley went on to chastise Georgiana for some minutes, while Darcy continued to keep his eyes on his wife, longing to understand how his aunt's words—or those of Georgiana, should she be foolish enough to speak again—affected her.

Lady Romsley said, "Elizabeth may not have had your advantages, but she is a gentlewoman. Do you think we would have recognised you had you eloped, that we would have accepted Wickham the way we have Elizabeth? I assure you that neither I nor your uncle would have known you again."

Georgiana gasped and turned to him, her mouth hanging open and red spots appearing on her face.

Stupid, foolish girl, Darcy thought, unable to understand how she did not grasp the seriousness of what she had almost done to herself and all of them. Out loud, Darcy said, "Do you think I would have drained Pemberley's coffers in the hope that he would treat you with some degree of kindness? I tell you now, I would not. So long as you remained with him…" He shrugged, letting the implication that he, too, would have abandoned her stand. He could not truly say what he would have done, but he would never admit as much to her.

A soft sob—of astonishment or sorrow—escaped Georgiana's lips. Darcy prayed it was the latter and that it meant the countess's and his words had gone some way to making Georgiana understand why they were all so angry.

"You betrayed us," Lady Romsley said. "We may have treated you kindly, but that was because we believed you regretted what happened in Ramsgate and what it meant for Elizabeth and your brother. After such a shocking display! I am ashamed of you." She shook her head before abruptly twisting her chin so that she would no longer see her niece, but instead looked towards where Darcy and Elizabeth sat. "Fitzwilliam, Tom has said the two of you would like my advice. I shall have to give it more thought, but I shall do what I can. Elizabeth, we should get on with our morning."

She stood, Elizabeth and Darcy doing so as well.

"Georgiana, return to your room. I will review the history work with you in an hour or two." To his aunt and wife, Darcy said, "I shall see you out, and then I must be off as well, lest I be late for my appointment."

As they walked to Lady Romsley's carriage, Darcy asked for particulars about their morning—upon whom they would call and if they had any other obligations—infusing his voice with more tranquility than he felt. Elizabeth might dread such a morning, and, if she did, he hoped his speaking agreeably about the day, rather than succumbing to his feelings about Georgiana, would bring her at least a little bit of comfort.

THERE WAS LITTLE FOR ELIZABETH TO DO WHILE THEY MADE THEIR calls; Lady Romsley decided who they would see, in what order, how long they would stay, and what they would talk about. She had yet to meet many young ladies she thought might become her friends, but she did not think overlong on it. After all, she had Jane nearby for the next few weeks. She would see Esther Haddon and Rebecca Darcy soon. Of the people she had met since the previous summer, they were among the more pleasant, as was Mrs Morris.

They could never be as Jane is to me, or even as Charlotte Lucas was. It is not possible, not when I must always exercise so much caution.

The effort involved in protecting their secrets and guarding her heart was draining her energies, and it worried her greatly. How could she maintain such rigid resistance to the part of her nature which wanted to ease Darcy's suffering? Georgiana's actions and manner affected him deeply, and a little part of her heart ached for him. But he had hurt her too much to trust that she could safely offer him her sympathy.

"I must say, I am very pleased with your gown for the ball."

Elizabeth shook off her private reflections and hoped that she had not missed much of the countess's conversation. They were in the carriage, slowly making their way to a warehouse Lady Romsley wished to visit as they were supposed to have particularly fine silk stockings available.

"I am glad to hear it."

Lady Romsley spoke for a minute or two about the arrangements for the ball; Elizabeth added a few appropriate words now and again. She was very much surprised when her aunt-in-law said, "It is not yet too late to make additions to the guest list. If there is anyone in particular you would like to invite?"

Elizabeth thought quickly, pushing aside for the minute how gratifying it was to have been asked. There would be no point, other than to cause awkwardness, to suggest Jane, let alone the Gardiners. The countess had no wish to remind her society of the deficiencies of Elizabeth's family. "Perhaps the Morrises. You may remember meeting them in December. Mrs Morris has been very kind to me. Their niece will be with them."

Lady Romsley agreed, and Elizabeth promised to send the Morrises' direction to Fitzwilliam House before the day was done.

ELIZABETH AND DARCY DINED WITH JOHN AND SUSAN DARCY THAT

day. Their eldest son Jack, his betrothed, and her parents were also in attendance. Elizabeth found Miss Trivett to be a pleasant, if not particularly witty, young lady. It would be no difficulty to be in her company, even if Elizabeth might not particularly anticipate it.

Back at Curzon Street, Elizabeth and Darcy spent a quarter of an hour together in the withdrawing room. Elizabeth wondered, as she had on other nights, if he would hint that he wished to visit her bedchamber. After fifteen minutes without any such sign, she felt she could safely excuse herself, knowing she had given him ample opportunity to make one and relieved that he had not.

As Elizabeth stood to leave the room, he asked if she would like to take a walk in the morning before breakfast. "I believe it will be fair tomorrow. You must miss your walks around Pemberley."

Elizabeth did. While the Park could not compare to the countryside, there were trees and she might see early signs of spring emerging. She accepted gracefully and said good night.

TRUE TO DARCY'S PREDICTION, THE WEATHER WAS PLEASANT THE next morning, and he escorted Elizabeth to the Park as planned. Darcy appreciated being able to spend time alone with Elizabeth. With each passing day, they grew busier, and he knew he would seldom have her to himself in the coming weeks. He offered her his arm; when she took it, he rejoiced to have her so close to him. The past few days had been exceedingly difficult, and Elizabeth had a unique ability to ease his worries. He wished he could do the same for her.

They walked in, to him, companionable silence, for five or ten minutes. He watched her take in their surroundings, her eyes studying the trees—still bare of leaves—particularly when there was any movement that suggested a bird or other wildlife might be present, and smiled with her when she saw two grey squirrels chasing each other. Because the sky was mostly blue and it was reasonably warm for the time of year, many other people were enjoying an early morning excursion, too, and the sounds of carriages, horses, and voices filled the air.

"Thank you for suggesting this," she said as they walked by the Serpentine.

"I should have thought of it sooner, but the weather has been indifferent."

Elizabeth nodded.

"We did not have much occasion to talk yesterday. Did your calls with my aunt go well?"

"Yes. Thank you for enquiring."

"Not at all. I would wish to know if you were treated as you should be, if you were welcomed properly."

"Everyone was very kind."

Darcy suppressed a sigh. Her answers were polite, but not necessarily honest. "And my aunt? She was quite upset when the two of you left." He directed her off the gravel path so that she would have a better view of two ducks which were floating in the water.

"She did not speak of Georgiana again."

"Of what did you speak?"

Elizabeth glanced at him, her expression one of suspicion. They walked away from the Serpentine, the ducks having floated out of sight, and towards the exit. A brief gust of wind made Elizabeth check the position of her bonnet.

"I am just curious. She cannot always want to talk about the Season or advise you on this or that. I hope that you have some other conversation."

Elizabeth's face was hidden, and he decided he disliked the style of hat she was wearing. With one slight turn of the head, it was impossible to see a lady's expression.

There was a short pause before she answered. "We spoke about the ball. Your aunt very kindly asked if I wished anyone in particular invited. I suggested Admiral and Mrs Morris."

"It would be agreeable to see them. You are on good terms with Mrs Morris?"

Elizabeth nodded, and they walked for a moment or two in silence.

"I do not expect to see much of our other Derbyshire neighbours while we are in town. I rarely see the Simmses, for instance, unless we happen to be at the same party or concert."

Again, Elizabeth nodded.

They saw several acquaintances and spent a few minutes in

conversation with them before saying goodbye and resuming their walk.

"After dinner last night, at my uncle's, was it—?"

A little smile appeared on Elizabeth's face. It just as quickly disappeared. "It was pleasant. There was much talk about the ball and your cousin's wedding. We spoke a great deal about gowns, none of which I believe you would find very interesting."

"No, I do not imagine I would," he agreed. "I do not imagine my uncle spoke of gowns. When you sat beside him at dinner, I mean." From Darcy's place at the table, he had not been able to detect anything amiss in their conversation.

"No, he did not." Her voice sounded strained.

He stood still, and after one or two false starts, said, "My uncle and Frederick believe that they have the right to act almost as parents to me, in place of my father, as I was but three and twenty when he died. Their advice is…not always gently given."

Elizabeth tugged at his arm so that he would walk again, "Your uncle and I spoke about very commonplace subjects."

"I am glad nothing untoward occurred." Deciding nothing would be accomplished by continuing that line of question, he asked, "Have you arranged a day for your sister and Mrs Gardiner to call?"

"Yes."

"When, if I may ask?"

Elizabeth named a day as they turned towards Curzon Street. At Darcy's instigation, they spoke further about the coming days and the activities which would occupy their time. Elizabeth spoke easily about luncheons and calls and even asked him, albeit with some hesitation, what he would do.

"Nothing so very different than you. Meeting friends at my clubs, attending to matters of business."

They said nothing more until they entered the house. Before Elizabeth went to her rooms, there was another matter Darcy had to discuss with her, and he led her into the morning room. "Tom and I think it would be best to return Georgiana to Pemberley. We cannot give her the supervision she needs here. There would be fewer diversions there and thus fewer opportunities for mischief."

"It sounds sensible as long as there is someone to…" She lifted her hand, hesitant to say what they both knew. Georgiana could not remain alone at Pemberley with no one to ensure she behaved as they would like.

He nodded. "We may not find a companion we trust before then, but that is not what I wanted to say. If we do decide in favour of the scheme, the Easter holiday would be our best opportunity to travel to Pemberley. However, I thought we might go to Longbourn then."

"Longbourn! Oh! I had not—that is, I did not—"

"If we, or at least I, were to go into Derbyshire with Georgiana, I do not see how we could go to Longbourn. We certainly could not do so on the way north."

Elizabeth laughed, but immediately covered her mouth with a hand and looked away from him for a moment. "No, that would not be advisable."

"We could go on the way back to London, but there may not be much time."

Elizabeth stopped him. "I really do not need to go to Longbourn, not…at this time."

"You do not need to return to Derbyshire with Georgiana and me, I suppose, if you wished to…"

"It would appear rather odd if I did not travel with you, would it not?"

Her voice was ever so slightly too high. He shrugged, not knowing what to say since he did not understand her discomfort.

"I have seen Jane and I shall see my aunt and uncle. Truly, I have no need to go to Longbourn."

"Elizab—"

"If you will excuse me. I should prepare for breakfast. It is getting quite late."

She was already at the door when he said, "Of course."

He sighed and stared after her. *Was that because she does not trust me to be with her family, or…?* After a minute, he abandoned his attempt to explain her manner; he would have to wait until she was prepared to confide in him.

A WEEK AFTER GEORGIANA'S DISGRACE, CAROLINE BINGLEY CALLED.

It was early, but, after she assured the butler that Miss Darcy expected her, Mallon showed her into the parlour and notified Elizabeth.

Elizabeth entered the room several minutes later. "Miss Bingley, I am sorry you have been kept waiting. I was not aware that you were expected this morning."

"Mrs Darcy," Miss Bingley simpered, "I am so sorry to have caused any inconvenience. I promised your dear sister that I would take her shopping. I am sure, as busy as you are, you simply forgot. I do not blame you. Becoming accustomed to all that is expected of one during the Season can be very trying."

For a brief moment, Elizabeth almost imagined she heard Miss Martha Simms's voice speaking. Both ladies appeared to believe she was too stupid to understand their implied insults. *Perhaps they equate fortune with intelligence, and since I am lacking the first, I cannot possess the second!* She forced a polite smile onto her face. "No, I am quite certain Miss Darcy did not remember to inform me or her brother about her engagement with you."

"That cannot be!" Miss Bingley cried. "I insisted that she invite you to come with us. She *must* have mentioned it."

"In any case, I am sorry to disappoint you, Miss Bingley, but my sister-in-law is not able to keep your appointment. I regret that we did not know to tell you in advance and save you a trip to Curzon Street."

"I am very sorry to hear dear Georgiana is indisposed. Perhaps I might have a few minutes to talk to her? We are such good friends. And I would be very happy to escort you to some of my favourite shops. My brother and Mr Darcy are such good friends, you know, and I am convinced we shall be as well."

Elizabeth looked all that was apologetic, but remained firm. "I am afraid Miss Darcy is not available—"

"Not even to so good a friend as me?" Miss Bingley interjected. "Impossible!"

Darcy entered the room in time to hear her last statement.

"Miss Bingley, good morning." He bowed and went to Elizabeth's side.

"Oh Mr Darcy, I am very glad to see you! There has been a slight muddle. I was to take your dear sister shopping this morning. She invited Mrs Darcy to join us, but I am afraid that, with so many demands on her time, Mrs Darcy has forgotten."

Elizabeth covered her mouth with a hand and lightly coughed to disguise a laugh. "As I said, I did not forget about your excursion with Miss Darcy. I was never told of it." She turned to Darcy. "I informed Miss Bingley that your sister is not able to join her this morning."

He nodded.

"I am sure she can spare me a few minutes. We are such friends, just as you and Charles are, Mr Darcy." Miss Bingley smiled at him.

He did not return the gesture. "I assure you that Mrs Darcy has a very good understanding. You need not doubt it in the future. My sister is not available and did not tell us you were expected. I am sorry for your trouble."

Miss Bingley pursed her lips into a gentle moue. "Perhaps Mrs Darcy...?"

"I am afraid I am otherwise engaged this morning." Elizabeth spoke with more haste than was necessary.

"I believe you will be late if you do not prepare," Darcy said.

He smiled at Elizabeth, and she quirked an eyebrow in reply. She thought it was possible that he understood that Miss Bingley was not to her liking and was attempting to extricate her from the call.

"Again, our apologies, Miss Bingley. I shall remind my sister that she must tell us when she is expecting callers," Darcy said.

In a minute, Darcy had Miss Bingley out of the room and being escorted to the front door by the butler. To Elizabeth, he said, "I shall talk to Georgiana and determine if she made any other appointments that need to be cancelled."

"It was no trouble." She gave him a quick nod, said that she would go finish preparing for her morning engagement, and walked towards the door. Before she could exit the room, Darcy's voice halted her steps.

"Elizabeth, Miss Bingley... Although I value Bingley as a friend, I cannot think highly of his sisters."

"I see."

"They will attend my aunt and uncle's ball. Bingley was invited as my friend, and Mr Hurst is some sort of distant connexion. My aunt felt it necessary to include him and Mrs Hurst. Miss Bingley could not be overlooked under the circumstances.

"I do not intend to allow Georgiana to continue her friendship with Bingley's sisters. It was ill-advised to allow it at all."

Elizabeth nodded again, this time adding a small smile. "I must go, or I shall be late."

"Of course. I shall see you at four o'clock?" They were meeting friends of his to promenade in the Park.

"You will."

Chapter 31

By far, the highpoint of the next week was the morning Mrs Gardiner and Jane called.

It was wonderful for Elizabeth to be able to embrace her beloved aunt, so much so that Elizabeth came very near to crying—not tears of happiness as she had shed when Jane first visited, but tears of relief and sorrow. She had spent months not knowing if she would ever be able to see her aunt again, and, after the argument with Darcy, she had been very much afraid that he would demand she cut all ties with the Gardiners simply to prove he could.

"I am so happy to see you," Elizabeth whispered while still enfolded in her aunt's arms.

"Oh my dear Lizzy," Mrs Gardiner cried. "Oh my dear girl."

It was some minutes before the three ladies were seated and able to talk. Elizabeth listened eagerly as Mrs Gardiner told her all there was to tell about Mr Gardiner and the Gardiner children. It was such a pleasure to hear the voice of one she loved so much and to see her face that Elizabeth felt she could continue to look at her and listen to her talk—with the added delight of Jane occasionally adding to the conversation—for hours and be quite happy. They laughed over the antics of the children and sighed together when talking about Christmas at Longbourn.

"Your mother will not rest until you and Mr Darcy visit so that she can show you off to the neighbourhood. I am afraid she imagines you draped in the finest lace and covered in jewels every day," Mrs Gardiner said.

Elizabeth groaned. "How far from the truth that is! My mother would be very disappointed with my gowns, even the one I shall wear to the Romsleys' ball, for although there is some very beautiful lace on it, it is not enough to appease my mother's nerves. A little later, I shall take you to see it if you like."

"If we like?" Mrs Gardiner laughed. "I would love to see your gown, and more of the house, if you think Mr Darcy would not object."

Jane agreed. "You must promise to tell us all about the ball afterwards."

"I wish the two of you and my uncle could be there!" Elizabeth cried. "I admit, I am anxious about it. I shall be happy once it is behind me."

"I have no doubt you will hold your head high and charm every person in attendance," Mrs Gardiner said.

Elizabeth rolled her eyes and shook her head at the teasing. "There are moments when I am convinced that my courage will see me through, but at others I imagine I am standing in the centre of the room yelling as loudly as I can that I do not want to be there."

She regretted saying so much the moment the words were out of her mouth and quickly added, "I am exaggerating, of course. Lady Romsley told me just this morning about the guest list, and there are so many people I do not yet know, but who must be properly introduced to Mrs Darcy. I find myself growing quite tired of feeling like one of the exotic beasts at the Tower with everyone walking by to examine me."

"Lizzy, you are making fun, are you not?" Jane asked anxiously.

"Of course! I have met many very polite, perfectly well-behaved ladies and gentlemen. The few who see me as some sort of wild beast are easily out-numbered by those who are kind."

Elizabeth smiled at her sister then turned to her aunt. Mrs Gardiner's eyebrows were arched in question, but she remained quiet as Jane and Elizabeth chatted about the arrangements for the ball.

"I do hope that you are able to come to Longbourn soon, Lizzy. My father misses you dearly."

Elizabeth's expression hardened at the mention of Mr Bennet. "If my father misses my company so very much, he might exert himself and write to me. Until he does, I shall continue to believe that he is very happy to forget that such a person as Elizabeth Darcy exists."

"I cannot explain your father's behaviour," Mrs Gardiner said. "Your uncle spoke to him a great deal when we were at Longbourn for Christmas."

"And I would wager a £100 he said very little about me!"

"I am afraid to say that is true."

"If you could but come to Longbourn, even for a day or two," Jane begged.

Elizabeth shook her head. "I do not know when it will be possible, but not for some time." When Darcy had mentioned going to Longbourn, Elizabeth was surprised by how repulsed she was at the thought of seeing her father again. Neither could she endure her mother's prattle about Mr Darcy's wealth and her endless attempts to convince Elizabeth to take her sisters to London and introduce them to her husband's rich friends. She was just starting to feel confident in Darcy's manner towards her and would not risk the progress they had made by exposing him to her family.

"Perhaps later in the spring," she said, giving Jane her most reassuring smile before introducing a new topic.

IN DARCY'S STUDY, HE ATTENDED TO LETTERS WHILE GEORGIANA sullenly worked through a piece of Italian. After an hour or so, he sat and contemplated his sister for a while, wondering how Elizabeth's visit with her aunt and Jane was progressing. He knew how much she had been anticipating it. She had not told him, but she had been distracted when they went for a walk before breakfast and then as they ate. He had had to repeat himself several times, had noticed a small smile on her face—never directed at him, to his regret—and she had been visibly impatient for time to pass.

Darcy's thoughts wandered to the question of Longbourn and why she did not wish to visit her other relations when she was so pleased to see Jane and the Gardiners. The only answer he had was that she did not trust how he would act when confronted by the Bennets. Yet, he had suggested she could go into Hertfordshire while he escorted Georgiana to Derbyshire, and she had not shown any interest in the scheme. *I cannot know why until she confides in me. I suppose I should be pleased that the thought of being apart from me for a time was not a strong enough inducement that it overcame her reluctance.*

He called for Georgiana's attention. "Elizabeth's sister and her aunt are here, as you know. I wish to pay my respects, and you will come with me."

Georgiana looked incredulous and shook her head.

"Oh yes, you will. This is Elizabeth's family, two of the people she loves best, and we owe them the courtesy."

"B-b-but her aunt! I cannot!"

"Yes, you can, and you will!" Darcy took a deep breath and strained to sound reasonable. It was a struggle not to be perpetually angry with his sister, but he knew expressing it again and again would not help. "Mrs Gardiner is a respectable, intelligent woman. In addition, she is your sister's dearest aunt. For these reasons alone she deserves our attention. It is wrong, very wrong, to judge people solely by their birth. A highly-born person may be vulgar and lacking in morality, while one who is humbler in origins may be well-mannered and everything that is estimable."

Georgiana rolled her eyes. Darcy sighed and prayed that he would soon see progress in reforming his sister's arrogance and disdain. If he could understand why she felt so strongly about Elizabeth, he felt certain that he would find the right words to say to her.

"It is a lesson I needed to learn, and you do as well. If you wish to be a good person, you cannot look meanly upon others. You do not have to love Elizabeth, but you do have to behave towards her in a respectful manner. Part of this is showing kindness to her family. And, Georgiana, I will tell you this—I would be very happy if, as you mature, you took Elizabeth as your role model. You could do no better."

Georgiana stood from the small desk he had placed in his study for her to use and went to look out of the window. He had no doubt that it was to hide her feelings, and he sighed again. Georgiana was not yet willing to understand.

"I require this of you. We will go downstairs and greet Miss Bennet and Mrs Gardiner. You will exchange the usual pleasantries, and you will behave properly. You will remain until I dismiss you. Is that clear?"

She nodded.

"I will be very displeased if you snub Mrs Gardiner, Miss Bennet, or Elizabeth in any way. We go down in ten minutes."

"Mrs Gardiner, it is very good to see you again," Darcy said. "Miss Bennet."

He made his bow and the ladies curtseyed.

"May I present my sister?" He tugged Georgiana forwards. "Mrs Gardiner, my sister, Miss Georgiana Darcy. Georgiana, I am sure you remember Miss Bennet."

"It is very good to make your acquaintance," Mrs Gardiner said.

"I am glad to see you again, Miss Darcy. And you as well, Mr Darcy," Jane said.

Georgiana mumbled a greeting and bowed her head. Elizabeth saw her husband grimace, which did much to allay her irritation. Her first thought upon seeing Georgiana enter the room with Darcy had been one of anger and dread. She knew he would come to pay his respects, but why had he brought Georgiana? If it was because he wanted Georgiana to do Mrs Gardiner and Jane the courtesy of acknowledging them, it was kind. As long as he ensured Georgiana behaved as she should.

They sat, and Jane tried to engage Georgiana in conversation. Elizabeth was relieved that although Georgiana did not speak, she kept her head lowered and managed to look painfully shy rather than indescribably rude. When Elizabeth saw that Darcy kept an eye on Georgiana even as he and Mrs Gardiner chatted, she felt a little easier.

Refreshments arrived, and it was agreed that Darcy and Georgiana would share the light repast with the ladies. Elizabeth was not disappointed to have the opportunity to study her husband's manner towards her sister and aunt. It would tell her much about the changes she had seen in him. It was one thing to allow Elizabeth to see Mrs Gardiner and another entirely to befriend her himself. He showed them every courtesy and appeared pleased with his company.

Once Georgiana had eaten a little and had a glass of lemonade, Darcy sent her back to her books.

"I shall join you shortly, but not for long." He reminded Elizabeth, "I am meeting Bingley at our club, as I believe I mentioned earlier."

Elizabeth nodded and relaxed considerably once Georgiana was gone from the room.

"I understand we shall soon have the pleasure of meeting your new neighbours, Miss Bennet," Darcy said.

"Yes," Jane replied. She blushed.

Darcy then turned to Mrs Gardiner. "I do not know if Elizabeth has yet told you, but we shall go to Pemberley next month for several weeks."

"She did, Mr Darcy."

"When we return, we hope we shall see you and Mr Gardiner here for dinner. I regret that it will have to be after Easter, but we are very much occupied before then."

Mrs Gardiner laughed. "Yes, Elizabeth has told us your plans for the next few weeks. I must say it all sounds quite exhausting."

Darcy chuckled. "It is not to my liking, but it is necessary. I can only be gratified that so many people are anxious to meet Elizabeth. Although the Season has hardly begun, she is already quite the success."

Elizabeth looked at him with some wonder. *Does he truly feel that way? He looks sincere, and when he must hide his true feelings, his expression usually is stoic, not so open and easy.*

Returning Elizabeth's gaze, he said, "I am certain it is no surprise to either you or Miss Bennet that wherever Elizabeth is known, she is very much liked."

Jane smiled and agreed with him.

Mrs Gardiner did the same, but with a pointed, questioning look at Elizabeth, who could not meet her eye.

Darcy stood. "I should leave you. Please give my regards to Mr Gardiner."

WHEN ELIZABETH AND HER AUNT WERE ALONE FOR A FEW MINUTES soon afterwards, Mrs Gardiner said, "Tell me truly, Lizzy, are you well?"

"I am." Elizabeth had a sudden need to smooth a tiny crease in her skirt.

Mrs Gardiner sighed. "I do not believe you are, dear girl. You are too thin and—Oh Lizzy, Jane may not want to see it, but you are unhappy and anxious. I am convinced you and Miss Darcy are more than simply not as close as you had hoped you would be, as you wrote to me, and I believe there is a great deal you have not told me about your relationship with your husband. You are not obliged to confide in me, but you are troubled, I know you are, and if I can help, you know I shall."

Elizabeth felt her composure slipping and struggled to reclaim it, swallowing heavily and taking a fortifying breath before speaking. "It is not so bad as that. Truly, Aunt. These last months have been…very difficult, I shall not say otherwise, but it is improving. I hear Jane returning. Please do not worry her about this."

Mrs Gardiner said nothing more and they turned their attention to enjoying the rest of their visit. Elizabeth found it was not terribly difficult to say goodbye to her aunt and sister when they took their departure. Darcy had been welcoming and all that was polite, and Elizabeth was able to believe she would be allowed to see them again soon.

Chapter 32

*E*lizabeth was glad to be busy the remaining few days before the ball. She was growing anxious about it as it was the first event of its kind which she and Darcy were attending, and it was important that it go well. Lady Romsley continued to remind her that their behaviour would be watched carefully. Everyone should see that Elizabeth and Darcy were happy and that his family, notably Lord and Lady Romsley, supported the marriage. Elizabeth knew her actions would be judged harshly by prominent members of society who, thanks to their own standing, could do great harm to her reputation, which could have lasting consequences for her, her husband, and any children she might have.

"Why I should be held to a higher standard than a woman of more acceptable birth is beyond me," she was wont to mutter at her reflection.

Yet, she would invariably tell herself, *here I am and here I shall remain. Think, Lizzy, of what gives you pleasure. Fitzwilliam. His manner is so different to what you supposed it would be two months ago when he was in London doing you knew not what, and you were at Pemberley with a sister-in-law who would not so much as wish you good morning. He is being very kind, genuinely kind.*

It helped. Elizabeth could not say how or when it had begun, but she found that she was starting to have more confidence in Darcy, and in herself. Certainly, it was because of the changes in her husband, but there was more to it than that. Perhaps it was being able to see Jane and Mrs Gardiner again. Perhaps it was because Lady Romsley, while still demanding, was now hardly ever condescending, or because Elizabeth was finding greater kindness among those she met and even among those who had been happy to dismiss her in the past, such as Tom. Whatever the reasons, she felt more secure.

At least enough to not absolutely dread the ball!

DARCY DECLINED THE OFFER TO DINE AT FITZWILLIAM HOUSE BEFORE the ball. Elizabeth had been diffident about accepting, so he had stated a preference not to. He sensed she was nervous about the evening, but he lacked the confidence to speak to her about it. They would dine at home with Tom to keep them company.

Darcy, Tom, and Georgiana were in the withdrawing room awaiting Elizabeth's arrival so they could go through to dinner. The gentlemen used the time to tell Georgiana that she would be returning to Pemberley, which made her very happy at first.

Darcy and Tom knew they could not leave Georgiana at Pemberley without someone who could command her respect and obedience, and, after receiving a letter from Horatia Darcy informing him that she would return to Derbyshire in time for Easter, Darcy proposed her as a temporary guardian.

He had talked to Elizabeth about it. "Aunt Horry does like to gossip, and sometimes she lets her enjoyment of a good tale overrule her sense. But she is devoted to preserving the family name and would not speak ill of any of us except to another member of the family. We could entrust her with the truth."

Georgiana's mood changed the moment Tom told her of their plan. "Why?" she cried, angry red spots appearing on her cheeks.

"Because, Georgiana," Tom snapped, "we cannot trust you. We trust Aunt Horry to watch you until we can find a companion for you, or until either your brother or I can see to you ourselves. We intend to confide in her so she understands why she must watch your behaviour so closely."

Georgiana exclaimed, "It is too cruel!"

Tom replied, "It is absolutely necessary that whoever has charge of you understands what you are capable of doing—the lies you are willing to tell—so they comprehend the necessity of keeping a strict watch over you."

When she was about to interrupt, Tom added, "There will be no argument or discussion about our decision. Your sister will be down soon. Be kind."

"If you cannot say anything pleasant to her, hold your tongue." Darcy fixed his sister with a stern glare. "I will not have you do or say anything that will diminish Elizabeth's enjoyment of this evening."

Georgiana gave a single, curt nod.

Darcy and Tom stood when Elizabeth entered the room. Darcy knew she and Tom exchanged words, but he could not hear what was said because of the roaring of his heart.

Elizabeth was lovely. Of course, Elizabeth was always lovely, but this evening she was spectacularly lovely. He had known she would be, but actually seeing her was enough to render him momentarily mute. It was not that she looked the part of Mrs Darcy, although she very much did, with her beautiful gold gown and the diamond jewellery he had given her with the ball in mind. It was something in her air, the way she held herself, which spoke of grace and sophistication. Perhaps it was simply that he knew her well enough to understand her worth, perhaps it was that he, at last, had his eyes opened enough to fully appreciate Elizabeth Darcy, or perhaps it was that his deep, appreciative affection for her made him see what he wanted to see—she was a beautiful woman who must be valued and respected wherever she was known. In all likelihood it was a combination of all these that made him wish he had the right to kiss her and whisper his feelings into her ear.

She was looking at him. He had to speak. He stepped towards her and allowed himself the pleasure of taking her hand and drawing it to his mouth for a kiss. "You look absolutely enchanting."

Elizabeth lowered her eyes from his and smiled. A light blush rose on her cheeks. Darcy prayed that her reaction meant she believed him.

UPON ARRIVAL AT FITZWILLIAM HOUSE, THEY WERE TOLD LADY Romsley was still at her toilette and wished for Mrs Darcy to join her.

"Ah, Elizabeth, there you are!" Lady Romsley cried. She stood and waved her maid away. "Let me see you."

Elizabeth stood, seemingly docile, while she was examined.

Margaret Fitzwilliam let out a sigh of satisfaction. "Very pretty."

Elizabeth was agreeably surprised. She had expected no more compliment than that Elizabeth's looks were adequate for the occasion.

The ladies sat, and for the next quarter of an hour, Lady Romsley spoke about the arrangements she had made for the evening. Much of it Elizabeth had heard before, but some of it was useful—the names and relationships of people Elizabeth would meet, this duke who was a cousin to Lord Romsley's father, or that lady who held a great deal of influence amongst the *ton*.

At last, Lady Romsley stood and smoothed her skirts, and Elizabeth did the same.

"We should go down and join the gentlemen. My daughters and their husbands will arrive soon, and our guests will begin doing so as well."

Just as Elizabeth was congratulating herself on surviving the interview, Lady Romsley spoke again.

"There is one last thing I would say to you, Elizabeth."

The tone of her voice had altered. It was not precisely one of warning, although it was serious and put Elizabeth on her guard.

Lady Romsley continued. "Remember that you are one of us now."

Elizabeth suppressed the desire to groan. *So do not behave like a vulgar barbarian!*

"There are those you will meet who will not accept you because of your family, and those who will seek your friendship in order to benefit from being on good terms with Mrs Darcy. There will even be those who offer you friendship simply because they like you. Naturally, you will wish to avoid those who belong to the first two group-ings if at all possible. My best advice is to use your good sense, be yourself, and remember that anyone who is not your friend is not *our* friend."

Elizabeth was too shocked by this sentiment to respond before Lady Romsley, elegant and expensively adorned and fully prepared to demand that the highest circle of London society embrace her new niece, swept past her.

ELIZABETH FOLLOWED LADY ROMSLEY TO A SMALL MORNING ROOM where they found Fitzwilliam, Tom, Sterling, and Lord Romsley, who was scowling.

"Sterling, show Elizabeth around. I am not certain she knows where the card room is, or where we shall have supper. I wish to talk to your brother and Fitzwilliam for a moment."

Sterling stood. "Do we get to greet her first?" He turned to face Elizabeth. "Good evening, Elizabeth. I trust you are well."

"Really, Sterling." Lady Romsley sighed.

"Good evening," Lord Romsley murmured at Elizabeth, nodding his head.

Elizabeth greeted the earl and smiled reassuringly at Darcy before allowing Sterling to lead her out of the room.

"Do not mind my father. He hates having a crowd of people in the house, and he is in a particularly foul mood because of some political something or other. My mother has been buzzing about for days, so she has not been available to coax him into a better humour."

When they returned to the others, Darcy immediately escorted Elizabeth to a sofa.

"Is everything...?" he whispered.

Elizabeth nodded, pleased by his concern.

"My aunt?"

"She was very kind." She gave him a reassuring smile, but he still looked uncertain. *Because he knows you often are not open with him,* she realised.

Tom joined them, bearing a glass of wine for Elizabeth.

"To prevent your voice from becoming hoarse in the coming

hours. You will be saying so many 'how do you dos' and 'so nice to meet yous' that you really are in most terrible danger."

Elizabeth laughed politely and took the glass.

Soon afterwards, the Frocesters and Surteeses arrived, and that signalled the need to prepare for the onslaught of the invited guests. Sterling spoke to no one unless he absolutely had to and grew increasingly restless. Elizabeth saw and knew that Fitzwilliam and Tom did as well since she witnessed them exchanging a pointed look. She suspected it had something to do with Rebecca Darcy, but had little time to think about it. Marian and Catherine demanded her attention, and, although she did not imagine she would become intimate friends with them, she was glad they could be on good terms.

ELIZABETH AND DARCY JOINED LORD AND LADY ROMSLEY IN greeting the guests, and a dizzying number of people seemed to fly past Elizabeth in the coming hour. She knew a few of them and was even glad to see some of those with whom she had a previous acquaintance. Admiral and Mrs Morris, and their niece Miss Morris arrived early in the evening. The weeks since Elizabeth had last seen Mrs Morris had made her appreciate the older woman's offers of friendship more than she had when they were in Derbyshire. Elizabeth was not yet convinced that she could place complete trust in Mrs Morris, but she was nevertheless confident that they could have a good, comfortable relationship.

Mrs Morris said to Elizabeth, "I know that we have you to thank for the invitation, and so I shall say thank you very much. It is quite exciting to be here, especially for my niece."

Miss Morris blushed prettily and nodded.

"I am very glad you could attend."

They exchanged what news they had of their friends in Derbyshire until Tom joined them, and Elizabeth gave the Morrises into her cousin-in-law's care.

The Darcy clan were all invited, and, except for those few who were not in London or were too young to attend, they all presented themselves in appropriate finery. It was no hardship to greet them. Elizabeth had seen many of the Darcys since coming to London, and they all treated her with civility, even John Darcy who she knew still viewed her with suspicion.

Soon after the first party of Darcys arrived, Elizabeth heard her husband sigh deeply. "Fitzwilliam?" she asked softly so that they would not be overheard.

He shook his head and greeted a new arrival.

During the brief moment between receiving guests, Elizabeth looked around her, seeking a reason for her husband's disquiet. She discovered that Sterling had joined them at the entryway and guessed his purpose.

She said, "Oh."

Out of the corner of her eye, she could see Darcy glance at her, his expression questioning.

Elizabeth nodded towards Sterling and whispered, "He is waiting for Rebecca to arrive."

When he appeared taken aback by her words, she explained, "I am not blind, Fitzwilliam. When they were at Pemberley together, it was plain to me that they are more than simply acquaintances. I believe they have not seen each other since November. I am not surprised by your cousin's anxiety, but I am not certain that your other cousin equally anticipates the meeting." She turned back to the guests, a welcoming smile on her face as she said, "Mr Bingley, Miss Bingley how good to see you again."

Miss Bingley soon over-spoke her brother's protestations of delight. "How is your dear sister?"

"Miss Darcy is very well, thank you." Seeing that Darcy had turned his attention to her conversation, Elizabeth explained, "Miss Bingley was so kind as to ask after our sister.'

"Ah."

"Oh Mr Darcy," Miss Bingley crooned, "you know how very fond I am of dear Georgiana. I was so desolate the other morning when our shopping excursion was cancelled!"

"Caroline," Mr Bingley murmured.

Miss Bingley ignored him. "I do hope that I can entice your charming wife and Miss Darcy to spend a morning with me. We would have such fun."

Elizabeth did not trust her sincerity in the least. Her ingratiating, almost flirtatious manner to Darcy was particularly insulting.

"I am sure that my charming wife can answer for herself," Darcy replied.

"I am afraid that will not be possible, Miss Bingley." She was firm, confident that she would not have to tolerate Miss Bingley or Mrs Hurst to please her husband.

Miss Bingley let her say no more before expressing her conviction that Mrs Darcy could not mean it and assuring her that she would be happy to show Mrs Darcy the most fashionable shops at which to spend her money.

"Caroline," Mr Bingley muttered sharply.

"I thank you for the offer. My aunt, Lady Romsley, has been most helpful in acquainting me with her favourite modistes, and I am afraid Miss Darcy is not at leisure to accept your offer." It was humorous that the other lady thought Elizabeth would need her help in any way.

"Mr Darcy, I am sure that Mrs Darcy does not understand that your sister and I have been such friends—"

"Miss Bingley, you astonish me," Darcy exclaimed at the same time that Mr Bingley again attempted to gently tell his sister that she was in danger of going too far. "Do you genuinely believe that my wife would be so ill-acquainted with our sister's ability to accept invitations? I assure you, she is not."

"Come, Caroline," Mr Bingley muttered, taking his sister's arm and pulling her away.

"Let us hope that is the end of that," Darcy whispered.

Elizabeth smiled and nodded and greeted the next guest. If Mr Bingley had hoped to stop his sister from making a fool of herself, and by extension him and the Hursts, he ought to have acted sooner. The woman was intolerable. *She and Miss Simms would get along famously,* Elizabeth thought. *I pray it is something I never have to witness.*

Frederick and Julia Darcy, along with Rebecca and Freddie, arrived soon. "Fitzwilliam." Julia allowed him to kiss her cheek. "Elizabeth, you look lovely."

"Thank you," Elizabeth said. "As do you. Your journey from

Norfolk was uneventful, I trust? I believe you have only just arrived in town."

"Yes. Oh, pray, excuse me, I see my sister."

"Elizabeth." Rebecca held out a hand which Elizabeth took. "You remember my brother, Freddie, do you not? Do not mind my mother."

"Of course," Elizabeth said at the same time that Freddie bowed and spoke.

"I am not so forgettable, am I?" He grinned while Rebecca shrugged, and looked both amused and embarrassed. "Our mother never talks much to family, other than her sister, at crushes. I think she knows that she will have enough opportunity to talk to us when there are not other people around, so she can ignore us for the length of the party."

Rebecca and Elizabeth were laughing at this when Frederick's voice stopped them. "Freddie, do not speak so lightly of your mother."

"Yes, sir." It was quite plain to Elizabeth that he felt not in the least bit discomposed by his father's reprimand although something, and she could guess what, was making Rebecca uncomfortable.

"Bramwell," Frederick muttered.

Elizabeth was not ignorant of Frederick Darcy's dislike of Sterling. She did not know if it was because of Sterling's interest in his daughter or if there were some other reason, and she did not expect to find out any time soon.

"Oh, you have arrived, have you?" Sterling acted as though it mattered not in the least to him. "Good evening." He gave a perfunctory bow, and, although he pretended to take in everyone with his greeting, his eyes were on Rebecca.

"Into the breach, do you think?" Freddie took Rebecca's arm, smiled at Elizabeth and dove into the growing throng.

"Let me show you the way," Sterling said, rushing to Rebecca's other side.

Rebecca sent an imploring look to Elizabeth, who gave her an encouraging smile before greeting another guest.

Chapter 33

*O*nce the flow of arrivals had turned from a flood to a trickle, Elizabeth and Darcy walked around the room. Darcy led them towards people with whom he felt they should spend time conversing beyond the usual greetings. Elizabeth believed she held her own, but, to herself alone, she would admit to a little anxiety. There were an almost overwhelming number of guests from the very highest circle of society. She had never supposed that she would marry someone who called an earl uncle. Darcy was also familiar with dukes, marquises, members of the government, and others whose names she had heard or read about in the newspapers her father ordered. It was humbling and emphasised the great gulf between Miss Elizabeth Bennet and Mr Fitzwilliam Darcy. But, after a while, her nerves receded, her confidence returned, and she knew she owed a part of it to her husband's presence by her side.

Elizabeth and Darcy opened the ball. They were both shocked that the couple standing next to them was Tom and Rebecca; they had expected her to be partnered by Sterling. Rebecca gave Elizabeth a rather weak smile, and Elizabeth gave her hand a gentle squeeze of support as the dance started. She searched the room for Sterling and soon spotted him chatting with Rebecca's mother.

Seeing that Darcy was likewise looking around the room, Elizabeth said, "Sterling is with Mrs Julia Darcy, near the doorway at the back of the room."

"Why is he not dancing with Rebecca?"

Elizabeth shrugged, and when Darcy rolled his eyes, she had to suppress a giggle. It was a silly moment, but one she rather enjoyed.

Between the opening of the ball and supper, they stayed together for the most part, circulating around the room, stopping now and again to speak to one person or another. Elizabeth had no complaints. Everyone was at least civil, and some were very pleasant. The couple received a number of congratulations on their marriage, and, to their great relief, only two or three people hinted about the rumours which had surrounded their betrothal and wedding. If that was partly due to the care Darcy took in who they stopped to speak to and who they avoided, Elizabeth was none the wiser.

Several gentlemen asked Elizabeth to dance over the course of the evening. Before the supper dance, which she reserved for her husband, she danced with Tom and Mr Bingley.

Not long before the supper dance, Elizabeth and Darcy spent five or ten minutes speaking to another young couple, Mr and Mrs Needham. Elizabeth's impression of the Needhams was that they were remarkably well-matched in that they were both excessively silly and inclined to think well of themselves. Mrs Needham spoke so confidently of them meeting often that Elizabeth imagined she would have little choice in the matter. She could only hope that the lady improved upon further acquaintance.

"How do you know the Needhams?" Elizabeth asked Darcy as they waited for the supper dance to commence.

"Needham and I were at school together."

"Have they been married long?"

"A year, I believe. Not more than two, certainly."

"I see. Did you know Mrs Needham before she married your friend?"

"You are very curious about them."

The dance commenced. At her earliest opportunity, Elizabeth said,

"Perhaps I should just ask what I am particularly curious to know." Her heart raced just a little as she awaited his response.

"By all means."

"Do you like them?"

Darcy snorted.

Elizabeth felt her cheeks heat. "It is very difficult to tell from your demeanour, which is just as well, I suppose. It would be horribly rude to display dislike if that is what you felt. I need to know how much attention I should pay to establishing a rapport with them and everyone else to whom you introduce me. I have no way of knowing except from what you tell me or what I can discern from your manner."

It was a minute before they could speak again.

"No, I do not like them, and Needham and I have never been more than acquaintances. I do not see how anyone could like two such popinjays." He smiled at Elizabeth as they were, once again, separated by the dance.

When it was finished, Darcy led her into supper. "I shall endeavour to remember to be more open, but should I forget or not be clear enough, please, Elizabeth, do ask." He stopped by a table, and before she was seated, leaned over and whispered into her ear, "I want you to be happy, to be comfortable, and I would not ask you to befriend anyone you could not like."

Elizabeth stared at him for a long moment as the table around them filled with people made hungry by their exertions of the evening. Reason returned, and she set aside his words, determined to think about them later, when she was alone.

She looked around to see who was nearby. Across from them were Sterling and Rebecca. Rebecca's cheeks were flushed, and she steadfastly refused to look at her companion. Sterling several times said something to Rebecca, but she would do no more than nod or shake her head.

Elizabeth knew that she ate, but she was too enthralled by everything around her to be able to say what. She laughed and talked and listened and, to her great surprise, realised that she was having a remarkably agreeable evening.

THE BALL CONTINUED INTO THE EARLY HOURS OF THE NEW DAY. Throughout it all, Darcy remained by Elizabeth's side, ever attentive to her comfort. Whenever they approached someone new, he told her something about them, such as if Miss So-and-so's many questions became bothersome, she should ask her about Brighton, a topic upon which the lady would speak endlessly, or that this baronet always peered at people through his quizzing glass as though he were examining an insect so, when he did it to her, she should think nothing of it. Darcy even told her, once or twice, that he quite liked the person they were approaching. It was all excellent and much appreciated advice, and she was very glad that she had found the courage to ask him about the Needhams earlier.

It would be too much to suggest that Elizabeth was met with universal warmth. Some of the gathered guests were civil to the barest degree acceptable, staring at her as though she were a foreign object that sparked a feeling of slight revulsion. When Darcy and Elizabeth encountered these people, Elizabeth remembered why she so disliked being Mrs Darcy.

But her propensity to decide that no one would like or accept her was kept in check by her husband's statements in her defence. They were all politely given, even delicately so. No one could take offence at his manner when he said, to Lord—, who made an allusion to hearing that Elizabeth had compromised Darcy to force him into marriage, "I am very fortunate in my wife," or to Mrs— who huffed about unknown country chits marrying above their station, "No one could better suit the role of Mrs Darcy, and, I dare say, no other lady could tolerate me as well as she does."

They were all very pretty sentiments. Elizabeth reminded herself at least three times over the course of the ball that he was just doing what he was supposed to do to convince the *ton* that they had married for love and were very happy together. She would not take his words too much to heart. He could have done far less, it was true, so she allowed herself to appreciate that he exerted himself.

While she was not called upon to praise Darcy, Elizabeth heard kind things about him from many of the guests. Those who had known him since childhood talked about what a good boy he had been —getting into mischief as all boys are wont to do, but always so kind and even-tempered. Others spoke about his loyalty to his friends and his willingness to be of assistance to any who needed it. She was, they wished to say, very fortunate in her husband.

It was some time after supper when Darcy was occupied with several gentlemen that Lady Romsley asked Elizabeth how she was faring. Elizabeth said that the ball was wonderful, she was enjoying it immensely, and had met with many friendly people.

"I have kept your earlier words in mind, and they have served me well." Elizabeth attributed Lady Romsley saying that she was 'one of them' to the effort she had made to be a good wife and mistress. It was heartening to know that something positive had come from it.

A moment later, Lady Romsley made a delicate sniff. When Elizabeth turned to her, she saw that the countess's lips were pressed together, and she was shaking her head. Trying to determine what Lady Romsley saw to cause such dislike, Elizabeth looked into the part of the room the countess was facing and almost laughed when she saw Caroline Bingley attempting to engage Sterling in conversation, no doubt hoping the viscount would ask her to dance. Sterling ignored her until he bowed, a slight smirk on his face, and walked away while the lady was still talking.

"My nephew considers Mr Bingley a good friend, and he seems harmless enough. His sisters, however." She shook her head. "There is some distant connexion between Mr Hurst and my husband's family. One of his relatives did something for one of Philip's fifty or sixty years ago, and between that and Fitzwilliam's friendship with Mr Bingley, we had to invite them. I cannot but feel that Hurst made a very poor choice of wife in Miss Louisa Bingley, although he did desperately need her dowry. And her sister! Dreadful, scheming woman. Do not be fooled by her offers of friendship."

"I am not."

Lady Romsley smiled kindly at her. "Good girl. Come, I see someone with whom you must be better acquainted." With that, Lady Romsley directed her to another corner of the room where two of the matrons of Almacks were standing.

"SHALL I CALL FOR THE CARRIAGE OR WOULD YOU PREFER TO WALK?"

Darcy asked when the ball was coming to an end. It would be unfashionable to do so, despite the short distance, but he suspected Elizabeth would elect to go on foot unless she was very fatigued.

She looked at him, their eyes fixed on each other's. He had learnt that when she did this, she was trying to decide what he wished for her to do or say. "I have no objection to walking if you like," he added.

There was a brief pause before she nodded. "I would prefer it. It is no great distance, and the air would be delightful."

Once outside, Darcy offered Elizabeth his arm, which she readily took, and they set off for home in silence. Darcy found it very peaceful to be walking thus with Elizabeth. He was reflecting that the ball had been a great success, and that Elizabeth had been at ease, when he remembered that he was not the best judge of her feelings. *The only thing to do is ask!*

"The evening seemed to go well," he said. "I did not hate it as much as I expected to, but I am never fond of such large parties. It is a relief to have it done, and without the unpleasantness I knew was possible. I do not believe anything untoward occurred, beyond what one would expect at such a large gathering. Do please tell me if I am mistaken. Did you enjoy the ball?"

Elizabeth nodded, but did not immediately speak.

"Elizabeth?" His voice was soft. He did not want to frighten her, but he so wanted her to trust him at least enough to tell him if anyone did anything to upset her. He felt a gentle pressure on his arm where her hand rested.

"I found it quite pleasurable. More enjoyable than I expected it to be, truth be told. Nothing disagreeable happened, nothing I can recollect at the moment, save that which you witnessed, and even those moments were nothing compared to what I anticipated."

"Lady Fry?" The baron's wife had come close to snubbing Elizabeth, although she had remembered proper manners as soon as Darcy had made it clear that to snub Elizabeth would be to snub him and his aunt and uncle.

Elizabeth gave a light laugh. "She was quite ridiculous, was she not?"

They laughed over several other guests until they arrived at Darcy

House and went into the parlour. She stood by the fire, enjoying the heat and warming her hands.

"You must be very tired," Darcy said after watching Elizabeth for a moment.

Elizabeth turned around to face him. "I suppose I am. I ought to be."

He smiled. "You will feel it once you are in bed."

He stepped closer and took one of her hands in his, happy when she did not withdraw it. "You were a great success tonight, which did not surprise me."

She shook her head but smiled, and he was pleased to think that she trusted his sincerity.

"You were," he insisted. "You are very good with people. You have a way of…charming them. Everyone with any sense whatsoever likes you. Everyone around Pemberley likes you very much. Tonight was the same. Whatever people expected to find in you, you showed them that you are a woman worth knowing."

"Not all of them." Elizabeth said softly.

"There are some people who will not be pleased by anyone who does not meet their standards of birth and fortune." He stopped and waited until she looked him in the eye. "They do not matter—not to me and not, I hope, to you. I am content to treat them with politeness, so long as they do the same for us."

Elizabeth nodded. "Your aunt said something similar before the ball began."

Darcy raised her hand to his mouth and kissed it. He longed to pull her into his arms and kiss her properly. "You should go to bed. I shall see you in the morning."

Elizabeth smiled and looked at him for a long moment before doing as he suggested.

ONCE ELIZABETH WAS IN BED, SHE FOUND THAT SLEEP WOULD NOT immediately come. Her mind was too occupied with the ball, but especially with Darcy. When they had stood by the fire, her hand in his, his compliments dancing in her head, she had felt her heart beating heavily in her chest, anticipating something, but she knew not what. She was almost surprised that he had not hinted that he wished to join her in her bed.

It was a relief. She could not yet imagine accepting his attentions with equanimity although she could now foresee a day when she would be able to. The situation between them was improving. Everything was changed these last few weeks. He was so kind and solicitous of her. It seemed impossible that anything she could have said would have such a profound impact on him and yet—

No. She simply could not allow herself to trust him completely. They were getting along well enough at the moment, and she would do whatever she could to make sure that continued. That was the wisest approach. She would not, could not allow herself to care about him and certainly not Georgiana. She might not find happiness this way, but not being happy was a far cry from being miserable, which is what she would be if she had to suffer another blow such as the one she had in December.

Her eyes grew heavy and she drifted off to sleep.

DARCY, TOO, NEEDED TIME BEFORE HE COULD SETTLE INTO SLEEP. He sat before the fire in his bedchamber, thinking about Elizabeth. What he had said downstairs was true. She had been a great success that night. Her manner was unaffected, and it would be next to impossible for her to be anything other than gracious and courteous, even when faced with a less-than-warm reception. She was remarkable, and he was very, very fortunate that she was his wife. He had been so proud standing by her side throughout the ball and introducing her time and again as his wife. He did not know the word that was strong enough to represent all that he felt about her.

He sighed and closed his eyes, sliding further into his chair. He knew what was in his heart when he thought about Elizabeth, and the pain that accompanied it was his punishment for treating her so carelessly from the time they were in Ramsgate up until his return to Pemberley in January. Even then he had not done enough to tell her that he understood that he had failed her.

Perhaps I should have thrown myself at her feet and begged for forgiveness. If for no other reason, it would have given her a chance to reject me as I so richly deserved.

It was difficult to resist his urge to touch her, hold her, whisper in her ear all that was in his heart, show her all that he felt, but he could not. It was not what she wanted, and he was haunted by the thought that she had only ever accepted him into her bed because she felt it was her duty to do so. As much as he wanted her, he would not so much as hint to her that he wished them to be intimate. He would not burden her with his feelings or desires. She was growing more comfortable with him, and the sadness she had shown earlier in the year was lessened, which was something to celebrate. She had done so much for him and for his family, and he had no right to ask more from her.

Chapter 34

The days and nights that followed the ball were busier than ever, so much so that both Elizabeth and Darcy looked forward to a peaceful sojourn at Pemberley. They would leave in little more than a fortnight. Elizabeth had the pleasure of seeing her uncle when the Gardiners both called one morning, accompanied by Jane. The Darcys also hosted their first dinner party a week after the Romsleys' ball. The Haddons and Mr Llewellyn were in town and would be among the party, along with the Morrises, Mr Bingley, Rebecca, Freddie, Jack Darcy and his betrothed Miss Trivett, and her sister Harriet, and several other couples. Tom and Sterling had been invited as well, but Lord and Lady Romsley demanded that Sterling accompany them elsewhere, and, the morning of the party Tom sent a note declining. He had been unwilling to commit himself one way or the other for days, so much so that Darcy had, the prior evening, expressed his annoyance about it when they met at a concert.

"If you have absolutely decided against Miss Haddon, then do not come," Darcy had told Tom. "If you have changed your mind, or are not yet decided, come."

As Elizabeth and Darcy waited for their guests to arrive, he sat lost in thought, remembering his most recent encounter with his sister.

"Is something troubling you, Fitzwilliam?"

"What? Pardon?" Darcy was startled out of his reflections.

"You are distracted. I hope that nothing is amiss."

Darcy sighed heavily. "Nothing new."

He lapsed into silence for several minutes and did not notice Elizabeth's reaction until the movement that accompanied her standing and going to fuss with an arrangement of flowers on a side table caused him to look up. Her expression was impassive, but he was able to discern the subtle hints of her irritation.

You bloody, selfish idiot! Can you not stop to think about your behaviour and what it means to her, not even for a minute? He forced himself to speak. "It was Georgiana."

She turned around and looked at him. The expression on her face did not change, but she was listening, which was something. Darcy decided that it was better to explain than to leave her to wonder why he was distracted.

"When I spoke to her before going to dress, she was…just as she has been every day of late. She must know that she is greatly at fault about many things, yet she will not say more than is strictly necessary to me or to Tom or even to Lady Romsley."

Elizabeth took a seat across from him. "She must have said *something* to you or Tom about everything that has happened since last summer."

"Remarkably little," he said. "The most she is willing to concede is that she never thought that what she did in Ramsgate would result in my having to marry you. She could not have foreseen such an outcome, no one could reasonably have done so, and thus it really is not fair of anyone to be angry with her about it. She accepts no responsibility for what has passed."

There was no point in saying that Georgiana had spoken resentfully of Elizabeth, going so far as to say that it made her sick to hear Elizabeth's name. She had said that 'everyone' would be happy if Georgiana were not there so that they could give all their attention to Elizabeth, and that that was why Darcy and Tom had decided to 'lock her away' at Pemberley. Darcy had not fully understood that his sister was jealous of Elizabeth, although the knowledge did little to tell him how he should act.

Darcy went on, "She has made it plain that she is very unhappy about our decision to have Aunt Horry act as a temporary guardian. I suspect that she will be even more vocal in her disgust when Tom and I tell her that she will be getting a new maid. But," he sat up straighter in his chair, forced a lighter tone into his voice and a brighter expression onto his face, "I will not let my sister ruin my enjoyment of the evening ahead of us. I apologise for letting my thoughts of her rob me of my civility."

Elizabeth stared at him for brief moment before nodding.

"Tom thinks that we should stop demanding that Georgiana feel or say that which we think she should. Perhaps some weeks apart, when she is at Pemberley and we are here, will afford her the time to understand our objections to her behaviour."

"Perhaps," Elizabeth agreed.

Darcy leaned forward and said her name. He hardly knew what he was going to say, but the idea that had occurred to him some days earlier—that once he did not have the situation with Georgiana so much on his mind, he and Elizabeth might bridge the gap between them—was upon his tongue. He had no opportunity to speak of it however, for no sooner had the sound of her name left his mouth than she was on her feet, walking this time to another arrangement of flowers which seemed to require her attention.

Elizabeth said, "Our guests should be arriving any minute. I am very much anticipating the theatre. I understand it is a remarkably amusing performance. Are you?"

Darcy suppressed a sigh and sat back. He followed his wife's lead and spoke about that evening's entertainments while they awaited their friends.

ELIZABETH LOOKED AROUND THE DINNER TABLE WITH SATISFACTION. Everyone seemed pleased with the food and the lively conversation, although Miss Haddon was a little quiet. Across the table, Darcy sat with Mrs Morris and the elder Mr Haddon. The sombre mood Darcy had had earlier was gone or hidden, and for that Elizabeth was thankful. It was difficult for her to be at ease when she knew he was not. Even if she believed that she understood why he was unhappy, even if she told herself that it had little to do with her, she nonetheless felt anxious and as though she had to carefully consider each of her actions or words lest she incur his disapprobation. It was not right, and she tried to talk herself out of it, but she had not yet found a way to do so.

Every now and then she would catch his eye, and he would smile at her. It was all part of his recent odd behaviour. She returned the gesture as best she could, trying to believe that it was just him acting the part of a happy husband.

In the withdrawing room during the separation of the sexes, Elizabeth did her part to keep the ladies happy. Miss Harriett asked to play while the ladies talked, and Miss Morris kept her company and turned the pages for her.

In doing her duty as hostess, Elizabeth had a few minutes of conversation with Rebecca.

"It is so good to see you again." Rebecca spoke in her customary quick pattern. "I have been so busy since we arrived in town, not nearly as busy as I imagine you have been, but my mother has demanded a great deal of my time, or my aunt has. I do not believe you have ever met the one I mean—my mother's sister. She has no children and feels that she can borrow one of us when she requires a child for some reason. She is not so bad, although she is quite fussy. Everything must be just so, and if you wish to do something in a different way, she is likely to look at you as though you have great big spots on your face, or, if you insist, she calls for her salts. I do not mean to go on and on. You must stop me if I do."

Elizabeth smiled and said that she would not dream of doing so, adding, "It has been very busy. We had hardly a moment to talk when you and your mother called earlier this week—I cannot believe so many people happened to call at the very same time. I might as well call it an unintentional party. I do not believe we had more than five minutes to speak at the Fitzwilliams' ball." There was something charming in Rebecca's demeanour, and Elizabeth had not forgotten that her husband had encouraged her to make a friend of this particular cousin. Elizabeth was by no means decided that she and Rebecca could be good friends, but Rebecca was one of the most agreeable ladies near her own age she had met since marrying.

Rebecca's expression darkened at the reminder of the ball.

"You did not enjoy it? I am sorry." Elizabeth suspected Rebecca's lack of enjoyment was due to a certain viscount, but she had been too busy, and the rooms too full, to follow everything that had transpired between the couple.

"Oh," Rebecca moaned apologetically, blushing deeply, "it was a lovely evening. Lady Romsley is an exceptional hostess. But, it was quite a crush."

"Well, let us speak of it no further."

A little later, Elizabeth sat with Miss Haddon, who asked after Georgiana. Elizabeth knew that her smile was not sincere as she replied, "She is well." Elizabeth never liked talking about Georgiana, and witnessing Darcy's depressed mood earlier further provoked Elizabeth's dislike.

"She is happy, I suppose, to be in London and so close to her cousin, Colonel Fitzwilliam."

"Yes, I suppose she is. He is a great favourite with her."

There was a momentary pause before Miss Haddon spoke again, her eyes averted. "I own I am a little surprised he is not here tonight."

Elizabeth had wondered if Miss Haddon would ask after Tom. She was not sure how much she should say. Like Rebecca, Miss Haddon was among the kinder, more genuine ladies she had met since getting married, and Elizabeth believed that she wanted, and perhaps needed, a better understanding. Elizabeth looked around the room and saw that the other ladies were all well-occupied.

"He was not certain whether or not he would join us, but decided that he...should not." She spoke gently.

It was evident Miss Haddon understood. She kept her head turned to hide her expression, but Elizabeth could see that she bit her lip.

"I am sorry—"

"No." Miss Haddon shook her head decisively. "Do not be. It is better to be certain." She gave a short, rueful laugh. "It was never anything other than a fanciful dream, and it is past time that I give it up. Not all men would do what your husband did."

Not all men, in other words, would marry a woman so much his inferior in fortune and consequence. Elizabeth wondered what Miss Haddon would think if she knew the truth.

"Thank you for telling me. It was truly very kind of you. If you will excuse me for a moment."

Miss Haddon stood and walked across the room to pretend to examine a display of Chinese porcelain figurines. Elizabeth would not have prevented her from finding a few minutes of privacy in which to compose herself, and the allusion to the surprise many felt regarding Darcy's choice of her to be his wife did nothing to make Elizabeth long to remain in her company.

AFTER THE LADIES LEFT THE ROOM, THE GENTLEMEN SPOKE ABOUT politics and the Season, and, as some of the party were new to each other, there was talk about estates and families. Bingley confessed to not yet having decided on so much as a county in which to settle.

"My sisters are wild for me to come to some sort of decision, but every time I mention a possible estate, they find something to complain about before they have even seen it. I had thought about leasing one in Hertfordshire last summer, but that idea went off. Caroline has always wanted a more northern county. She visited Pemberley once and decided that only Derbyshire would do. Now she is suggesting Norfolk, although I have no idea why."

Beside Darcy, Freddie cringed and made a face. "Dear God," he whispered. "That was me. We met at a party, and she was, oh, it was revolting. She flirted with me, and went on and on about our mutual connexions, which really only exist in her mind."

Darcy tried not to laugh at his cousin. It was not truly amusing, but he knew Freddie would not be caught by Caroline Bingley's growing desperation.

"Your sister is not married I take it, Mr Bingley?" Admiral Morris asked.

Bingley laughed. "No, not my younger sister. My older sister is married to Mr Hurst."

"Miss Bingley might be less concerned about your having an estate, or where it is located, if she were settled," Mr Haddon said.

Bingley laughed again. "That is very true, sir, and if anyone here knows of a gentleman looking for a wife, I would be happy to discuss terms with him at his earliest convenience."

Several of the young gentlemen exchanged knowing glances. Miss Bingley was now embarking on her third or fourth Season and likely felt the passing of time. It was no secret that she had harboured hopes that her brother's good friend—Mr Darcy— would offer for her. With that prize no longer an option, she would be anxious to catch another eligible suitor before May when the Season began in earnest. Although her twenty thousand pounds was a very handsome inducement to matrimony, it would not be enough to entice any of the single gentlemen in the room.

The conversation drifted away from Caroline Bingley and on to sport and politics. It was interesting enough, but Darcy hoped to end it soon so that he could return to Elizabeth's side.

As soon as he entered the room, Darcy sought Elizabeth. "Everything is well?"

Elizabeth wanted very much to ask him what exactly he thought might have happened during the three-quarters of an hour they had been apart. It was hardly enough time for the ladies to become so bored of their own company that they argued. Catching sight of Miss Haddon, Elizabeth was tempted to say that no, not everything was well. A perfectly nice young woman was unhappy because his cousin put matters of money and birth above those of affection.

At that moment, Elizabeth realised Miss Haddon truly was 'perfectly nice.' She was not without fault, but it was too much to expect any person to be. It was even possible that when she said that not every man would do what Darcy had, she meant it as a compliment. Miss Haddon might have meant that he had enough sense to choose a woman he (she supposed) loved rather than one with a sufficiently large dowry or a father who was titled. Elizabeth's heart went out to the other woman.

At length, she said, "We managed well enough amongst ourselves."

Darcy smiled at her. "I am sure you did. You are very capable of managing just about any situation, I believe. Nothing…untoward occurred?"

Elizabeth was puzzled by his question. "What do you imagine could have happened?" she asked, speaking, as she did more frequently than she liked, without forethought.

Mallon and one of the footmen entered with the tea trays. Darcy, after naturally looking towards the door when it opened, turned his attention back to Elizabeth. "I wished to ensure that you were comfortable."

Elizabeth nodded and smiled politely. "You may be easy then. Shall we sit?"

Without waiting for an answer, Elizabeth walked towards a grouping of chairs and sofas, leaving Darcy to follow. They sat among the assembled party, and she accepted a cup of tea from the butler, glad to be away from the awkward conversation with her husband.

THE THEATRE WAS A GREAT DIVERSION. DURING THE FINAL PART OF the evening—a comical farce—Elizabeth laughed merrily, to Darcy's delight. It heartened him a great deal to know that she could feel such moments of happiness. She seemed more and more at ease, and her mood was better than it had been when they arrived in London. That he attributed in part to being able to see Jane and the Gardiners, but he hoped that some of it was due to him, that she had seen that he was changed and approved of the man he was becoming. If that were so, it boded well for their future happiness.

After the theatre, they went on to an assembly. Darcy found the number of people at such parties overwhelming, and he disapproved of the behaviour that was often exhibited, but he accepted the necessity of sometimes attending them. At the theatre, he had the security of being in a box. There he could guard Elizabeth from the throng of merry-makers. At a ball such as this, the best he could hope for was to keep her close at hand, and, if he had to turn her over to another gentleman to dance, ensure that that gentleman was one he knew and trusted. His greatest fear was that someone would say or hint at something to make Elizabeth unhappy when he was not nearby. She was his to protect—her body and her feelings—and, as badly as he had failed to do so earlier in their marriage, he was determined not to fail again.

E LIZABETH WAS HAVING A GRANDER EVENING THAN SHE HAD anticipated. The theatre had been diverting, and the assembly was enjoyable, if a bit too crowded for her liking. She knew Miss Haddon was not as gay as she was attempting to appear, and there was another in their party, Mr Llewellyn, who could be happier than he was.

Elizabeth fervently vowed that she would not become a matchmaker, but she rather liked Mr Llewellyn and Miss Haddon. She did not know whether they could like each other enough to consider becoming husband and wife, and when she suggested to Mr Llewellyn that he ask the lady to stand up with him, Elizabeth had no such question in mind. What she hoped to accomplish was that their opinion of the evening would be improved by a little pleasant conversation. If they could be friends, then perhaps in time, they might find they could be happy married to each other. That would be entirely up to them.

Mr Llewellyn demurred.

"If you would rather not dance, then that is the end of it, of course, but I do believe she could use a friend." There was a slight pause. "Her spirits are a little low, but I am sure they will recover in time."

It was with satisfaction that Elizabeth saw Mr Llewellyn and Miss Haddon among the dancers a short while later.

The only other noteworthy event of the evening was Sterling Fitzwilliam's unexpected arrival. Elizabeth happened to be with Darcy at the time. He was always there, by her side, standing guard. It was comforting in a way, but at times irritating, as though he did not trust her to talk to other people on her own. Darcy groaned softly, but clearly enough for Elizabeth to hear. Sterling came to greet them.

"Rather a lot of people here."

"Sterling," Darcy said.

Elizabeth smiled and curtseyed. She immediately began doing

exactly what the viscount was—searching the room for a sign of Rebecca.

"Enjoyable performance?" Sterling asked. "The theatre, I mean. I have heard good things."

"It was." Elizabeth considered saying one or two other polite nothings, but decided there was no purpose. Sterling was hardly attending to the conversation.

The three of them spotted Rebecca at nearly the same time.

"Bramwell."

Elizabeth heard a hint of warning in Darcy's voice.

"No time to hear your advice, Cousin. If you will excuse me." He was walking away before his words ended, and he threw the last of them over his shoulder.

Darcy scowled. Elizabeth suspected he did not favour a union between his cousins. She did not know the reason and was not inclined to ask. She had been about to suggest that they find some of the other members of their party, but one glimpse of his countenance informed her that he would not move. He would remain where he was, his eyes fixed on Rebecca, until he was satisfied she did not require his assistance. It spoke rather well of him. Rebecca was by no means friendless in the room, but Darcy felt he should keep watch over her, and Elizabeth approved of the part of his character which had him do so without thought.

They watched as Sterling pulled Rebecca away from Mr Bingley and some of his friends and into the line of dancers. Soon after the dance ended, Rebecca and Freddie came to take their leave.

"I am feeling a little tired," Rebecca explained. "I have asked my brother to see me home. I am sorry we have not had more time to talk. Perhaps one morning, when you are not occupied, we could visit?"

Elizabeth agreed, and, after thanking Elizabeth and Darcy for the evening's amusements, the siblings departed.

Sterling left not five minutes later without talking to Elizabeth and Darcy again. To dispel Darcy's continuing sombre mood, Elizabeth asked what spring was like in Derbyshire, and what she could expect the weather to be when they were at Pemberley for Easter.

Chapter 35

Rebecca came to see Elizabeth a few days later. The ladies sat in Elizabeth's sitting room, which Rebecca greatly admired.

"It is lovely! I do much prefer your style. My aunt, Lady Anne, did have more decorative tastes than I ever really liked. My mother used to—Well, I should not say that. Lady Anne was really very pleasant, but she was proud. I suppose all the Darcys are, to a certain extent. Some of us can be quite ridiculous about having a name and family history we can trace back so far. The Fitzwilliams, too, can be rather proud, and Lady Anne certainly was. Her father was an earl, and my mother's father was a country gentleman. The difference, despite them being connected by marriage, was not forgotten."

They spent some little while discussing the changes Elizabeth was making at Pemberley, and Elizabeth asked Rebecca to tell her more about Norfolk. She liked Rebecca and had a natural curiosity about a place she had not been to, but it went no further than that. She was distracted, her thoughts on the next day when Jane would bring the Linningtons and Mr Hawarden to call.

Rebecca went on speaking for a while, but her voice became slower and quieter until she stopped entirely. After a moment, and with disappointment in her tone, she said, "I know I do rattle on, forgetting to stop or consider whether or not what I say is of any interest." Her laugh was derisive, but only of herself.

Elizabeth felt dreadful the moment it struck her that she had inadvertently injured Rebecca. It took no longer than an instant for her to recognise that Rebecca genuinely wished them to be friends. Whatever her opinion about Elizabeth's family background or lack of fortune, Rebecca did not mean for it to be an impediment. *And perhaps it does not matter to her; perhaps she meant it when she said she was happy her cousin had made a disinterested choice.*

"No, Rebecca, I am not uninterested." Elizabeth sighed, reprimanding herself. "My mind is much occupied today, and I am very sorry."

Seeing the colour in Rebecca's cheeks, Elizabeth felt ashamed. She had been distant, and although her reticence was necessary when dealing with many of the people she met in her new life, perhaps it was not needed all the time.

Without considering if what she did was right or not, Elizabeth offered an excuse. "I have a very particular reason for being so inattentive. My sister Jane is in London, staying with…some other relatives. I am to see her tomorrow."

"You are very much looking forward to that, I am sure."

"I am." Elizabeth warmed to the idea of confiding her hopes in Rebecca, both because Elizabeth longed to tell someone, and because she thought that it would reduce the injury Rebecca felt. "It is not just seeing Jane which has my mind so much occupied, however."

There was a spark of curiosity in Rebecca's eyes.

"You see—and I know nothing for certain—my sister is bringing several new friends with her."

"Oh." Rebecca's brow furrowed.

"Two of them are neighbours who have leased an estate near my father's. Jane has become good friends with Mrs Linnington, and so I am naturally curious to meet her. It is the third person she brings who really has my mind in a whirl today. Mrs Linnington has a brother who stayed with them for some time, and I believe he and my sister are very fond of each other."

"Oh!" Rebecca cried. "And you think they might make a match of it." She leaned slightly towards Elizabeth, her eyes growing wide with eagerness.

Seeing Rebecca's unaffected interest made Elizabeth smile. "I truly do not know, but my sister is not one to fall in and out of love with just any gentleman. I believe she admires him, and I am anxious to meet him. She might go with the Linningtons and Mr Hawarden to his family's estate in Cheshire for Easter. I shall learn tomorrow what has been decided, and I think that if she does, and if his family approves of her, they will."

When Rebecca smiled it extended into her eyes. She clasped one of Elizabeth's hands. "That is the most excellent news! I understand why you are not interested in hearing about Norfolk today. Meeting the man your sister might marry is far more exciting." She laughed.

Elizabeth laughed as well. "Yes, but I still should not have—"

Rebecca shook her head, stopping Elizabeth's apology. She announced that she would leave Elizabeth to her anticipation, and they could perhaps visit again another day. Elizabeth insisted they make an absolute plan to do so before allowing Rebecca to depart.

THE DARCYS HAD TAKEN TO WALKING BEFORE BREAKFAST EVERY possible morning. As long as Elizabeth and Darcy had no other obligations and the weather was fair, the three of them would go to the Park. Darcy enjoyed being alone with Elizabeth—as they had been on the first pre-breakfast excursion—but he knew that his sister required exercise and insisted that she accompany them. He had been relieved and grateful when Elizabeth continued to go out with them, knowing how little she liked being in Georgiana's company.

This morning was no different than any other. Georgiana, a sullen expression on her face, chose to walk alone, several steps behind him and Elizabeth. He did not like it, and it was not necessary, as he had told her. She could walk beside him—or join them in conversation when they sat down to eat, which she never did—as long as she was polite to Elizabeth. Darcy and Tom had ceased reminding Georgiana that she must apologise. She would have to in time, but, Darcy told Georgiana, she might find it easier if she first started by saying one or two pleasant nothings to Elizabeth each day and if she allowed herself to see what was good and admirable in Elizabeth. Georgiana was stubbornly clinging to her dislike, and none of them knew how to convince her to let it go.

Darcy had asked Elizabeth if such an approach was agreeable to her. "It will require time for her to understand the error of her ways. Perhaps the company of someone new or being apart from us will help. I think that here, knowing she is not allowed any of the diversions London has to offer, and, I am ashamed to say, seeing you do everything I believe she wishes to do, it is…"

Elizabeth had laughed. "Are you saying that—? Do you think that Georgiana is…envious of me?"

They had been in Elizabeth's sitting room at the time, and Darcy went from pacing near the window to taking a seat across from her. He was relieved that her disbelief was not that he was asking her to postpone hearing, let alone seeing, contrition from his sister. He had hated to ask, but he desperately wanted to see some alleviation of the heavy atmosphere under which they were living. It was painful and taxing to go on as they were.

"In some ways. I do not know because she says so little about anything. I hope, I suppose, that if she starts talking and trying to be more at ease with you, it will help."

Elizabeth had agreed, although he suspected it was with reluctance. He was in a difficult position, attempting as he was to find a way to correct his sister, while showing Elizabeth the respect and care she deserved.

Darcy turned their steps towards the house. He glanced over his shoulder to make sure that Georgiana was still nearby and well.

"Your sister and her friends will arrive after breakfast?"

"They will."

"I look forward to meeting them. Is it certain your aunt and uncle do not come?"

Elizabeth nodded. "My uncle cannot spare the time this morning, and my aunt has another obligation."

"I do hope you will meet again before we go into Derbyshire. Our absence will not be long, nevertheless I know seeing them has brought you pleasure."

Elizabeth smiled for a moment and remained silent for several more. They were at the steps of the house before she spoke. "It has. Thank you for...for allowing it."

She gave him a quick smile, but left him no time to respond. Darcy would have appreciated the opportunity to tell her that he was happy to know the Gardiners, that he liked them, and that because they were important to her, they were likewise important to him.

AT BREAKFAST, DARCY SPOKE TO HIS SISTER. "GEORGIANA, AS I trust you know, Miss Bennet is calling this morning. I have explained to Elizabeth that I shall not ask you to meet Miss Bennet's friends— they are not family, and you are not out."

He suspected Elizabeth was glad she would not have to worry about Georgiana's manner to Jane or the Linningtons and Mr Hawarden. It would make the call more pleasant for Elizabeth. It would be easier for him, too; it was difficult to always be watchful lest his sister do or say something insulting or rude. There were moments Darcy worried the strain of these past months would result in him either developing a habit of drinking to excess or succumbing to nerves.

Georgiana nodded.

"What had you planned to work on this morning?"

Georgiana shrugged. "I had not yet considered."

"You have enough to occupy yourself. You may decide."

Georgiana nodded again.

"We leave for Derbyshire in a week, as long as the weather is agreeable," Darcy continued. He knew Elizabeth was listening but would not speak. Georgiana was barely civil to Elizabeth, and Elizabeth felt it was for the best if she refrained from saying more than was necessary to his sister for the moment.

"Tom's duties will keep him in town. He hopes to go into Derbyshire in a month so that he can spend time with you after Elizabeth and I return to London. You will see him as much as possible before we depart. I believe Lady Romsley wishes to speak to you further, as well."

Georgiana's face drained of colour. Darcy suspected it was because his aunt lectured her. Lady Romsley claimed to be severe in what she said to Georgiana, and he believed her.

To Elizabeth, he said, "Were you planning to use the blue morning room? I believe you favour it." It was not commonly used except for family and very close friends, but Jane was not just any caller, and Elizabeth might have decided that Jane's friends did not need to be treated as formally as other callers.

"I...I suppose I shall. I do. Favour the blue room, I mean. It is very pleasant."

Darcy smiled. He often felt like smiling when he looked at her. "I look forward to meeting Mr and Mrs Linnington and Mr Hawarden. I mentioned their names to Tom, and he believes he remembers a Linnington from school. He thought that he was from Kent or Essex."

"Mr Linnington's family is from Essex."

"Perhaps they are the same men then, although Mr Linnington has an elder brother?"

Elizabeth nodded.

"The other gentleman—Hawarden—do you know where he resides? If you told me, I am afraid I forgot."

"Cheshire."

"Cheshire," Darcy repeated. He kept an eye on Georgiana as he engaged Elizabeth in conversation. He wanted to show Elizabeth that he was interested in the people who were important to her sister, but could not relax with Georgiana there. "I wonder what part. There are some very nice places in Cheshire which are not more than sixty miles from Pemberley."

Darcy saw that his words added a gleam to Elizabeth's expressive eyes, which was curious. As the meal was ending, he said, "I should see that my sister is properly occupied, but I shall join you after I do."

Elizabeth stood. "I must speak to Mrs Northmore for a few minutes, if you will excuse me."

Darcy stood as Elizabeth did. She smiled at him before she left the room, and he was happy to smile in return.

ELIZABETH TOOK AN IMMEDIATE LIKING TO HER GUESTS BECAUSE JANE looked so happy in their presence. The Linningtons were well-informed and affable. Of Mr Hawarden, Elizabeth was willing to think especially well, and she found that it took very little effort to do so. His greeting of her and Darcy, while maintaining the strictest civility, showed his wish that they would all be friends.

It was natural that after introductions, the party divided into two—the ladies in one part of the room and the gentlemen in another. Elizabeth, Jane, and Mrs Linnington spoke with ease. Elizabeth saw in Mrs Linnington something she did not at first believe she had seen in any other lady she had met since her marriage began—an artless expectation of friendship.

As the ladies continued to speak, a small understanding formed in Elizabeth's mind. It would continue to grow throughout the visit and was destined to fully blossom over the coming days. The desire to be friends that she saw in Mrs Linnington was not unknown to Elizabeth. Since getting married, she had been fortunate enough to be the recipient of such genuine offers from other ladies. However awkward their early meetings had been, Mrs Morris, Miss Haddon and Rebecca Darcy had shown a similar desire.

Elizabeth's interlude with Rebecca the day before had introduced the notion to Elizabeth, although she had not thought much on it in her anticipation of meeting the Linningtons and Mr Hawarden. The difference lay in Elizabeth herself. She had met Mrs Linnington with the expectation of liking her and being liked in return. When she had met Miss Haddon or Rebecca or Mrs Morris, Elizabeth had been guarded, expecting to see suspicion and disapproval rather than acceptance. *And that is exactly what you saw. You did not look to see friendliness, and so you did not find it.*

This by no means meant that Elizabeth believed she was mistaken to be careful when making acquaintances. Her position as Mrs Darcy was new and precarious, although perhaps not as much as it had been, and she was likely to meet with many disingenuous people, some of whom would still be interested in the previous summer's speculation and learning whether any of it was true. But not everyone would be false. She must remember and believe that.

When refreshments were brought in and the two threesomes joined forces, the six of them spoke with reasonable comfort for people so lately known to each other. They deduced Pemberley and the Hawardens' estate were perhaps fifty-five miles apart. Elizabeth was very happy to hear it. She noticed Darcy looking curiously at Jane, who glanced at Mr Hawarden and blushed.

"I would call that an easy distance," Darcy said.

"Yes, indeed," Mr Linnington chuckled as he grinned at his brother-in-law. "You agree, Hawarden?"

"Oh hush," Mrs Linnington said.

Elizabeth quickly looked away when Darcy caught her eye.

"Mr Linnington," Darcy said, "I mentioned your name to my cousin. He knew a Linnington at school, and I wondered if you were he, or perhaps it was a brother or a cousin of yours. His name is Fitzwilliam, Thomas Fitzwilliam."

Mr Linnington was nodding before Darcy had finished speaking. "I remember him, although I am surprised that he remembered my name. I was a year behind him."

"Perhaps you will have a chance to renew the acquaintance. Are you in London for the duration of the Season, Mrs Linnington?"

"We go to Cheshire for Easter, and Jane has agreed to travel with us. We leave in a few days."

Elizabeth watched as her husband's eye travelled from Mr Hawarden to Jane and back again.

"We go to Derbyshire in a week, as you may know. Do you return to London?"

Mr Linnington nodded. "In early May."

Darcy smiled politely. "I am pleased to know that our plans align so well. I hope that we shall all meet again then."

Elizabeth was cautiously delighted. Everything Darcy had said, his affability and openness, could only gratify her. If Jane and Mr Hawarden did make a match of it, surely her husband would place no restriction on them meeting often, in town or in the country. To have her dearest sister settled so near to Pemberley would mean so much to her.

Elizabeth and Jane found only a moment to speak privately, but it was long enough to say what was essential.

"I am so happy for you!" Elizabeth whispered as they embraced. "He is wonderful."

"Oh Lizzy," Jane cried. "Nothing is settled, nothing can be until… Think of me when I am in Cheshire. I do so hope that his family likes me."

"Of course, they will! No sensible person could do otherwise."

ALONE AFTER THEIR GUESTS HAD DEPARTED, DARCY SENSED Elizabeth was sad. She sighed and slowly walked around the room, her fingers trailing across the painted wood furniture she passed.

"It will not be very long before you see her again. Perhaps five weeks."

Elizabeth offered him a weak smile and nodded.

"We shall inform the Gardiners when we are returned. You will see Jane and your aunt and uncle as soon as may be."

Although she did not look in his direction, she did smile—more genuinely this time.

"Perhaps Miss Bennet will be able to stay with us for a time. With Georgiana in Derbyshire, we shall not have to worry. About her behaviour. Georgiana's, that is. I do not know the best way to express what I mean."

Elizabeth sat at the opposite end of the sofa upon which he was resting, her body turned towards him, and said, "I understand what you meant, and I thank you. Once we are in London again and Jane is as well, then we can decide if it is…appropriate."

"It will *always* be appropriate for your sister to be our guest." His words were quick and firm.

Elizabeth averted her eyes for a moment, before looking up once again and saying a quiet thank you. "We shall be very busy once we return. It may not be…reasonable for Jane to stay. I am happy to see what May brings, truly I am, before we make any decisions."

"Of course." He struggled to find the right way to ask about the state of affairs between Jane and Mr Hawarden. "It is possible that your sister will be otherwise…engaged? She and Mr Hawarden looked at each other a great deal."

Elizabeth grinned, but quickly pulled her lips into her mouth and held them between her teeth, shaking her head. "There is no understanding. I did not even know of Mr Hawarden's existence until I saw Jane earlier this month." She explained that her sister was going with them to Cheshire so that Mr Hawarden's parents could meet her, and, if they approved of Jane, she believed a betrothal would soon follow.

"It will be an easy matter, then."

Elizabeth stared at him for a long moment before she spoke, her tone serious. "You know as well as I do that Jane has nothing but her charms to recommend her."

Darcy took a moment to form his reply, fearing to misspeak at what must be an important moment for them. "There are few, if any, more important considerations."

Elizabeth stood and adjusted her shawl. "I have some letters I must attend to before we leave." She walked towards the door.

Darcy leapt out of his seat. "Elizabeth."

She stopped and, in two or three steps, Darcy had closed the distance between them.

"I am in earnest. I do not know your sister well, not as well as I ought or as well as I would like to, but I do know how much you esteem her. On that alone I know he will be a very fortunate man if she accepts him."

Elizabeth did as he had hoped she would; she met his eye. However, she turned away almost immediately, which made it difficult to know what she was thinking. Did she disbelieve him? Was she suspicious of his motives in speaking thus?

"Her…kindness, her goodness, her character are more valuable than any fortune she could bring to him. I *do* believe that. I wish…I wish I had understood it sooner."

Again, Elizabeth's eyes darted to his, and her cheeks flushed. A pause which seemed to last for minutes passed before she gave a shaky nod.

"I must see to some letters," she whispered, and without again looking in his direction, left the room.

Darcy groaned and ran his hands over his face and through his hair. In the next quarter of an hour, he managed to regain the shards of optimism he would allow himself. After they went to Pemberley and saw Georgiana settled there, he would have the time he needed to convince Elizabeth he truly had changed. He had given her more than enough reason to believe that he had placed very little value on her character early in their marriage, and he could not blame her if she needed time to believe he had so radically altered his opinions.

Chapter 36

A few days later, the Gardiners called. Mr Gardiner did not stay very long, but he wanted to see his niece again before she left London. Mrs Gardiner and Elizabeth shared a longer visit. They had a great deal to say about Jane and Mr Hawarden, going so far as to speculate on their wedding.

"It shall be a far happier occasion than mine was!" Elizabeth said. She attempted to lighten the seriousness of the words—which she had not intended to say—with a grin, roll of her eyes, and chuckle.

Mrs Gardiner took one of Elizabeth's hands in hers. "I am so sorry you had to start married life with such a cloud over your head. You and Mr Darcy." She opened her mouth to say more, but Darcy entered the room at that moment.

Elizabeth, in light of her aunt's seriousness, could not regret it.

"Mrs Gardiner, I am happy to see you again. I had hoped to be in time to see Mr Gardiner, but my appointment lasted longer than I anticipated. Did Miss Bennet and her friends leave without incident yesterday?"

"They did."

"Good. I understand there might soon be reason to celebrate."

Mrs Gardiner looked to Elizabeth for explanation.

"Mr Darcy noticed Mr Hawarden and Jane were...particularly friendly. We spoke of it after they had gone."

"But, of course, we do not know anything." The corners of Mrs Gardiner's mouth twitched upward.

"As you say, Mrs Gardiner. I believe you met Mr and Mrs Linnington and Mr Hawarden when you were at Longbourn for Christmas?"

Mrs Gardiner said she had, and the two, with Elizabeth contributing now and again, spoke about the new tenants of Netherfield and their families for some minutes. Elizabeth was content to observe. It was astonishing, and gratifying, to see how easily her husband spoke with her aunt.

Mrs Gardiner asked after Georgiana, saying, "Elizabeth tells me that your sister has been feeling poorly. I do hope she will improve once she has returned to Pemberley."

Darcy thanked her. "We trust the air in Derbyshire will be more agreeable for her. That reminds me, I had meant to ask if you and Mr Gardiner have thought about visiting Derbyshire. I understand you have not been in some years. We would be very happy to have you and your children at Pemberley. Would we not?"

Elizabeth could not speak, even if she had known what words to say. Her husband, who just a few short months earlier would not have considered meeting the Gardiners, had now invited them to stay at his home. He had sought their acquaintance and had been very welcoming to them over the last weeks, but still, it was astonishing to her. She could not account for so marked a change or truly trust it. The thought of doing so terrified her.

"We have considered it now and again these last few years, but we have no fixed plans."

"We can talk about it further when Elizabeth and I are in London again, and when Mr Gardiner is with us. I shall leave you to enjoy the remainder of your visit."

He and Mrs Gardiner exchanged a very friendly adieu before he left the room.

ELIZABETH WAS LOST IN THOUGHT AND DID NOT PROPERLY RESPOND TO two or three little comments Mrs Gardiner made although she heard that her aunt spoke.

"My darling girl, what is it?"

The question startled Elizabeth out of her reverie. "A-aunt?"

Mrs Gardiner sighed. "Lizzy, my love, something is not right. I have thought it since the first day I was here, but I think I must truly date my suspicions to the morning Mr Darcy appeared in my sitting room so unexpectedly."

Elizabeth looked at her hands, which were folded on her lap, and forced herself not to cry. There was so much she did not understand, and she did not know how she could possibly explain everything that had happened. She was not even certain she should, yet part of her longed to confide in her aunt.

"I know you have not been on good terms with your sister-in-law, and her indisposition makes me wonder if there is not some difficulty with her. It is also very obvious that you are not entirely easy with Mr Darcy. Your letters suggested to me that you and he were getting along quite well, but there is something decidedly odd between you. You are under no obligation to tell me, but I do hope you know I shall listen, and, if you wish for it, offer my advice."

After two or three false starts, Elizabeth looked at her aunt and, with a heavy sigh, said, "I hardly know what to say."

Mrs Gardiner waited, her expression compassionate and calm.

At length, Elizabeth spoke. "My husband and I had an argument, a horrible one. At the end of December, before he came to London, two weeks or thereabouts before he went to Gracechurch Street."

"About what did you disagree?" Mrs Gardiner asked when Elizabeth remained silent.

Elizabeth shook her head. "It is not so simple to explain. You know, of anyone you best know it has not been easy for me since I married Mr Darcy. He was not happy to marry me. I was not happy to marry him, either, although I must say he and his family have acted as though all the advantage was on my side. They all seemed to forget that I did not wish for this marriage any more than he did, but because he is rich, and his family is an ancient—" She stopped and let out an exasperated breath. "I know he has looked upon me with contempt."

"The man I have seen these past weeks is not one who dislikes his wife!"

Elizabeth regarded her aunt for a long moment, opening and closing her mouth three times before words came out. "If you had seen him after that morning, you would not say that."

Mrs Gardiner inched closer to Elizabeth on the settee and placed a hand on top of her niece's.

"And before that day? I thought from your letters that the two of you were managing rather well, considering the newness of your marriage and the difficult beginning to it."

Elizabeth would not meet her aunt's eye. She knew the answer to her aunt's question—that Darcy had not displayed any disdain towards her—but was reluctant to admit it. She had questioned his feelings, but a day or two before that morning she had believed that perhaps he had come to care for her, at least a little, and that her new family was beginning to accept her. "You cannot... We had so many guests with us, he could hardly..." But it was not only when they were with other people that he treated her with kindness. When they were alone, he had been... Elizabeth did not know what he had been. At one time she told herself that his gentleness might be a mark of acceptance and perhaps even a little bit of affection, but after the quarrel, she decided it was her ignorance that had allowed her to think so.

"And since then?" Mrs Gardiner gently prodded. "I know it is difficult to talk about, and I shall not insist you tell me more because I do not believe I have any right to such information, especially if you hesitate to give it. A husband and wife will argue, and that is, by and large, a matter for them to resolve."

She took a deep breath. "Lizzy, I assure you the gentleman I have seen does not dislike his wife. I am happy to repeat it as many times as you need to hear it. I would say that his feelings are rather the opposite. I do not know what it was like between you before you argued, but something that was said ended with him coming to see me and your uncle. Would you agree that was true?"

After a slight pause, Elizabeth nodded.

"Whatever happened," Mrs Gardiner went on, speaking softly and gently, "seems to have led to some agreeable change. Is this true?"

Elizabeth nodded again. She hesitated less before doing so this time.

"All married people disagree. Your uncle and I do, and we especially did when we were first married, I am afraid. I sometimes think the world would be a much better place if that were freely admitted. The early months of marriage can be very difficult. There is a great deal of adjustment that must be made, particularly by the female half of the partnership. This is true of all couples, even those who begin married life under the best of circumstances, and you and Mr Darcy certainly did not have that advantage."

"No, we certainly did not." Elizabeth's voice was very quiet, and her eyes remained focused on anything other than her aunt.

"This disagreement you and Mr Darcy had was now about three months ago?"

Elizabeth nodded and, for the first time in some minutes, looked at her aunt.

"I am going to share with you one very good piece of advice which I was so fortunate as to receive before I married. My aunt Mrs Jenkins—do you remember her?"

Elizabeth nodded. "Yes."

"She told me I should expect to quarrel with my husband. It is not unnatural and what is more significant is what happens afterwards. Lizzy, whether you believe the fault was entirely Mr Darcy's or not, you must both find some remedy for it. I know you were very concerned about finding happiness in your married life. Whatever your husband believed when he married you, however he acted then, if you still wish to have a good marriage, you are going to have to think not of the past, but of the future. Decide what you have to do to have it be what you want it to be, and then do it."

Elizabeth covered her eyes with one of her hands and bowed her head. A single sob overcame her control, and she felt her aunt's arms around her, pulling her close.

"I tried so hard," Elizabeth cried, but she could not continue without letting loose a torrent of tears and heartache. In an instant she felt all the pain and loneliness that had marked her introduction to marriage. She had never shared it with anyone, except that which had escaped the morning she had confronted Darcy in December.

"Oh, my dear girl," Mrs Gardiner soothed.

She said nothing more for several minutes, allowing Elizabeth time to compose herself. She then encouraged Elizabeth to tell her more about the argument. Elizabeth did, speaking of how difficult she had found it to be on her own in Derbyshire with a husband she did not believe liked or respected her and a sister-in-law who clearly did not. Without saying exactly what had happened between her and Darcy, Elizabeth explained that she had told him something of her unhappiness and his part in creating it.

Mrs Gardiner listened in silence before saying, "I believe you know what I am going to say."

Elizabeth nodded and wiped away a stray tear.

Holding Elizabeth's hands between hers and in a tone meant to rally courage, she said, "Whether it is right or wrong, I am afraid that if you wish to have a happy marriage, you are going to have to try again."

ELIZABETH THOUGHT ABOUT HER AUNT'S ADVICE A GREAT DEAL. SHE admitted the soundness of it but trying again to make her marriage happy would not be easy.

"It seems less impossible now than it did a month ago, does it not, Lizzy?" she asked her reflection just before going down to breakfast the next morning.

On the brink of returning to Pemberley for several weeks, Elizabeth had to acknowledge that a great deal had changed since the three Darcys had travelled to London in February; it left her feeling much more optimistic. There was still a chasm between her and Darcy, but perhaps work on the bridge to traverse it had begun. Darcy was making an effort. As for herself, well, there was no more she could do. Had she not done everything possible in the weeks and months leading up to their argument?

She sighed and shook her finger at her mirror-image. "You should rather say you have not yet decided how you can do more. It does not matter whether I should have to exert myself. I do if I am to have some measure of contentment in this life."

It would require a delicate balance, some way she could allow herself to once again do everything she possibly could to make the best of her situation and yet protect herself. She would endeavour to be more open with her husband, perhaps even enjoy his company upon occasion, yet not fall into the trap of caring about him or minding whether or not he cared for her.

Seeing Mrs Northmore on the way to the breakfast parlour, Elizabeth learnt that Georgiana would not be eating downstairs. It was thus no surprise when she arrived to find only Darcy in the room. He said good morning while she sat down.

Elizabeth said one or two little things, to which Darcy did not respond. He was very distracted, but Elizabeth would not immediately accuse him of ignoring her. More likely his distraction was due to Georgiana. Elizabeth had not joined them for an early trip to the Park that day; she had gone shopping with several other young ladies.

"Fitzwilliam?" She had to repeat his name before he looked at her.

"I beg your pardon." He took a sip of his coffee while waiting for her to reply.

Elizabeth regarded him. His mood was low and uncommonly sombre, which for Darcy was saying something.

"I wondered about Georgiana. Mrs Northmore told me she would not be coming down for breakfast—" She stopped speaking when he sighed in exasperation. *As I suspected.* "'Twas not important." She could not expect him to confide in her, especially if the subject was his sister. *That is not just, Lizzy! He has asked you more than once how she has acted towards you, or what you think he and Tom should do.*

"You want to know why she is not here after I made such a point about her eating with us."

He shook his head and sat up straighter, looking and sounding more like the confident Mr Darcy she saw him as. *But he is more than that. This situation is very hard on him.* She must endeavour to understand him better.

"I apologise. During our ride, she—" He shook his head.

She debated silently for a moment before saying, "If you wish to talk about it..." She hung between regret and expectation until he replied. She could not anticipate any discussion about his sister, but encouraging him to share his thoughts would be a step towards making their relationship better.

Darcy pressed his eyes closed for a moment, and she prepared herself to hear something particularly dreadful.

"When Georgiana and I were riding this morning, she tried to say she realised now that she had not behaved as well as she could have. She was very sweet, but it took no more than one or two questions to discern that she was not sincere. She shows no understanding of the seriousness of what she has done, no willingness to admit she has been very, very wrong. I hardly recognise this person she has become... I know she has been spoilt, but... I was spoilt. I see that now. As a child, my parents encouraged me to care for none beyond my own family circle, to think meanly of the rest of the world, even to think meanly of their sense and worth compared with my own."

His voice became harsher as he continued. "But I was never taught to lie or be so blatantly... And I do not recall ever expecting that I could put on a pretty face and get what I wanted regardless of whether or not I deserved it."

Elizabeth's attempt to stifle a laugh failed, and she felt terrible when her husband startled at the sound of it.

"I apologise. Nothing you said was in the least bit amusing, except," she took a moment to regain her composure, "it was the thought of you putting on a pretty face to get your way. It struck me as very—"

"Ridiculous?" He guffawed and rolled his eyes.

"I have to admit that it caused a rather...interesting image to appear in my mind."

"I can well imagine."

"But," Elizabeth said, her tone properly sombre, "you were saying that Georgiana...?"

He groaned. "I am ashamed to admit that I can understand some of her opinion. I can understand how she, why she—"

Elizabeth saved him from his attempt to find the right words. "I believe I take your meaning. You have some understanding of her feelings, but...?"

He gave her a look she wanted to believe was one of gratitude. "What she has done, I cannot understand. The way she has lied, the fact that she was prepared to elope. Even knowing that Wickham can be very pleasing where he wishes to be, even accepting that she is young and naïve, I do not understand. I find it troubling that she is so unwilling to admit she has behaved poorly, and that she thinks she can manipulate me or Tom so readily."

As they spoke a little longer about Georgiana, Elizabeth reminding him that he was taking several very positive steps to help his sister receive the attention she needed, she thought about the difference between the siblings. Fitzwilliam had been willing to admit his faults and change his behaviour, something Georgiana was unwilling to do. That was very much in his favour. He was also dedicated to doing his best as a guardian, even when faced with such a difficult charge, and Elizabeth admired him for it. Surely such realisations would help in her quest to find the trust she needed to try once again.

*C*hapter 37

*W*hen Rebecca next called, Elizabeth was determined to be kinder. She liked Rebecca and now knew that Darcy had been correct when he told her that the two women could be friends. Elizabeth suspected that they could be very close, if she only allowed herself to accept the possibility, which, she hoped, she had now done.

"The visit with your sister and her friends went well?"

"Yes, very, I would say," Elizabeth answered with a laugh in her voice. "They are pleasant."

"And the particular gentleman?"

"Mr Hawarden." Elizabeth smiled. "I must naturally believe any man who appreciates my sister is very sensible and worthy of regard, but even so, I did like him very much."

"Do you think they will make a match of it?"

Her excitement at the prospect gratified Elizabeth. "It looked very promising. Jane has gone with them to Cheshire to meet his family. I hope when they return, there will be more news. What do you and your parents do for Easter?"

"My father and Freddie have gone to see friends, and my mother and I remain in town. But tell me more about the visit. That is far more interesting!"

After exhausting the subject of Jane and her friends, they spoke about Elizabeth's impending departure for Pemberley.

"I anticipate seeing what spring has brought to the landscape. I hope we have some pleasant weather. I do long for the country whenever I am in town."

"As do I!" Rebecca cried.

"How have you enjoyed your weeks in London thus far?" Elizabeth asked after they had spoken at length about the pleasures of the country.

Rebecca scowled. "Not very much, I am afraid. Oh, Lady Romsley's ball was lovely, as was your dinner party, but I would rather have stayed in Norfolk. However, I could not and can only hope to make it through the Season unscathed."

"Unscathed?"

Rebecca scoffed. "My mother is determined that I marry, and she is introducing me to every single man of her acquaintance, regardless of their age or character. Not that she wants me to marry a gentleman who is unkind, but she thinks nothing of whether I would like them or if we would suit. She cannot believe I shall be happy if I do not marry, but I disagree. I have enough money of my own, and I know that Freddie will always give me a home. Even should his wife, whoever she may be, not like to have me around all the time, I have enough relations with whom I could spend part of the year."

"Including me. We would always welcome you at Pemberley."

Rebecca smiled and pressed Elizabeth's hand. "I will not marry simply for the sake of being married! I will only marry where I know I am loved and can love in return, and where I know I can be happy and have the sort of marriage I want."

In the last day or two, Elizabeth had considered what she would say if the subject of marriage or Sterling came up. She wanted Rebecca to know that she, Darcy, and Tom had deduced there was something out of the ordinary between her and the viscount. With some hesitation, she asked, "And you cannot have that with Sterling Fitzwilliam?"

Rebecca started and looked away.

"I am sorry. I should not have asked."

Rebecca shook her head and turned back to Elizabeth. "I did not know it was that obvious."

"You do not have to—"

Rebecca shook her head again. "I have had no one in whom I can confide. He...he has asked me to marry him, but I cannot."

She hung her head, and Elizabeth took one of her hands.

"His first marriage was arranged, as I suppose you know, and they did not love each other. That was well known, but no one thought anything of it. A man in his position does not choose to marry where his affection lies. He marries a suitable woman, one whose family connexions and fortune are seen to match his. He...was not faithful. I do not say that Lady Cassandra minded; she did not, and I do not believe she meant to be any more faithful to him than he was to her once she had given him an heir. I could never be happy in such a marriage. I want a husband who loves me and only me and who will not...when we argue, he will not run off and..."

These were feelings Elizabeth understood very well. "And you do not feel Sterling could give you that."

"No, and I do not know what he wants with me, or why he cannot accept that I shall not marry him. He asked me months ago, almost a year. He said that since we both should be married, we might as well marry each other. It was the stupidest—Every opportunity he gets, he talks about it. I feel as though I have to spend each day I am in London avoiding his company."

"Do you care for him?" Elizabeth asked gently.

Rebecca pressed her eyes closed, and Elizabeth was afraid her question would make Rebecca cry.

"The heart can be remarkably stupid. I will not let either of us be miserable by asking of him that which he cannot give."

Elizabeth was at a loss. She did not know what to say, and so she sat, still holding one of Rebecca's hands.

ONCE REBECCA HAD CALMED HERSELF, THE LADIES SPOKE ON EASY topics for about twenty minutes before Mallon entered the room,

trailed by none other than Viscount Bramwell. After announcing Sterling, the butler retreated.

Rebecca jumped out of her seat. "I must go. I had no idea how late
it was."

"Rebecca, Elizabeth," Sterling said at the same time.

Elizabeth felt as though she were living in a farce. Of course, Sterling would, somehow, manage to turn up just when Rebecca was
there. How did he always know where she was?

"I am so sorry, Elizabeth, but I must." Rebecca refused to look at
Sterling. "My mother will be expecting me. We are... Well, I-I
must go!"

Elizabeth smiled kindly at her friend. She went to the door and
asked that Rebecca's carriage be brought around.

Sterling glared at one lady then the other. "Elizabeth, may I
request a moment alone with—"

"No!" Rebecca cried. Her cheeks were bright pink. "You will not
mind if I wait outside, will you?"

Elizabeth shook her head and briefly clasped Rebecca's hand as
she left the room. Elizabeth closed the door and stood in front of it,
preventing Sterling, who now approached her, from following
Rebecca.

"I find I no longer remember what I wanted to say to you," Sterling said. "I shall bid you good day."

Elizabeth shook her head again. "I will not let you leave until I
know Rebecca is away."

"Really, Elizabeth!"

"She does not wish to talk to you, and if you think anything you
say or any stern look you shoot my way will convince me to move
away from this door, you are very much mistaken!"

They glared at each other. After a moment, Sterling threw up his
hands, let out a barely restrained growl, turned his back to her, and
walked into the room.

"This is none of your concern."

"It was none of my concern when Georgiana was meeting with
Wickham, but I did not let that stop me. And this *is* my concern. I
could hardly let you importune any young lady who was here as my
guest."

Sterling turned and glared at her. "You do not understand!"

Elizabeth fixed him with a look. "I think I understand well enough."

Acting on the impulse of the moment, she commanded him to sit. To her surprise, he did, and appeared willing to listen, if only so she would let him leave.

Elizabeth wondered when she had become so invested in other people's matrimonial prospects and promised herself it would stop after she did Rebecca this service. As soon as Rebecca admitted that Sterling had proposed almost a year earlier, Elizabeth had wondered if they were trapped in a misunderstanding. Given Sterling's persistence —if he simply wanted a wife, he could easily find one—she suspected they were. Whether that meant the couple could find their way to the altar was another matter altogether.

"I do not know if I do the right thing or not," she said, "but I believe I have information which you should hear. Mind, I only do it for Rebecca, so that you might, finally, act in her interest, not your own!"

"Everything I do is with her in mind," he retorted.

"I can see how well that is working. Every time I have seen you two together, she is unhappy."

Sterling grumbled. "Say what you have to say and be done with it." He picked up his hat and played with it, keeping his eyes on his hands.

"I know why Rebecca refuses to marry you."

Sterling shot a surprised look at her that was almost desperate. Elizabeth thought both about laughing at him and hitting him; he must have done a remarkably poor job of proposing if Rebecca, who had all but admitted to being in love with him, could continue to refuse him.

"Rebecca knows what she needs to be happy."

"Which is…?"

"She is aware of the nature of your first marriage."

Sterling scoffed.

"It is not the sort of situation in which she could be happy. In short, she wants two things from her husband, neither of which she believes you can offer her: love and faithfulness."

Sterling, a decidedly strange look on his face which Elizabeth could not understand, leapt out of his seat and took a step towards the door.

"Sterling," Elizabeth begged him, "if you cannot give her what she needs, please, leave her in peace."

He kissed her on the cheek, thanked her and left the room. Elizabeth prayed she had done the right thing.

THE FOLLOWING MORNING, ELIZABETH WAS OVERSEEING THE preparations for their removal to Pemberley with Mrs Northmore when Mallon interrupted them.

"Miss Rebecca Darcy wonders if you might be available, Mrs Darcy."

"Of course. Mrs Northmore, we can finish our conversation later."

Elizabeth could only suppose that Sterling had gone to see Rebecca after their conversation and that Rebecca's unexpected call had something to do with it. Elizabeth hoped she had not ruined her chance of being friends with Rebecca. While she waited, she paced.

Rebecca entered the room, carelessly tossed her reticule and bonnet onto the nearest chair, and threw her arms around Elizabeth.

"I had to come and tell you as soon as I could!" Rebecca grinned. The joy she radiated washed away all Elizabeth's concerns.

"Tell me what?" Elizabeth asked, feigning confusion.

Rebecca took Elizabeth's hands in hers and pulled her towards a sofa. The ladies sat, hands still clasped.

"Sterling came to see me yesterday. After leaving you, I suppose. He said, oh, he said so much, and we talked and talked, and-and…we are engaged!"

Elizabeth made Rebecca tell her everything and apologised for interfering as she had.

"How can I possibly want you to apologise?" Rebecca cried. "I am so happy! Sterling is so happy. He is a complete… Well, he does not always think about what he says, and, would you believe it, in all these months, he never so much as thought to assure me that…well, that he loves me. We talked about, oh, everything! Really, I think I might have agreed to marry the stupidest man in England! What was I thinking?"

They laughed and spoke for a little longer before Rebecca took her leave.

"You must come and stay with me when we return to London," Elizabeth said. "I would be very happy to have your company, and, although I am yet untested, I believe I shall make an excellent chaperon. I can avoid hearing what other people are saying, even if I am the only other person in the room with them, and I am frequently in need of having a word with my housekeeper. I can be quite clumsy, too, and rarely am I able to catch people unawares if I were to, for instance, enter a room after having been absent for a quarter of an hour."

Both ladies laughed, and Rebecca threw her arms around Elizabeth again.

THEY LEFT LONDON EARLY THE NEXT DAY. BEFORE THEY DID, Elizabeth asked Darcy to come to her sitting room for a minute and told him about Rebecca and Sterling's betrothal. "I ought to have told you yesterday, but we were so busy, I did not recollect."

Darcy fell into a tufted ivory chair and regarded her for a moment before saying, "She accepted him?"

Elizabeth smiled and nodded reassuringly. "It appears their miscommunication has been satisfactorily resolved. In short, she believes they will be very happy together. No one else knows just yet. Her father is away from London, and they will not tell her mother or Lord and Lady Romsley until Sterling can speak to Frederick."

Darcy only stared at her in confused disbelief. Rebecca and Sterling did seem like an odd match to her, but Elizabeth accepted that she did not know either of the parties particularly well yet.

"I knew it was unlikely we would have a chance to talk privately once we are underway. I did not wish to speak of it before your sister, but did not wish to remain silent until we reached Pemberley." Since he seemed undecided in his reaction to the news, she said, "Rebecca seems very happy and says Sterling is, too, so I am happy for them."

Darcy slowly nodded.

"I shall be ready to depart very soon."

"I shall see how Georgiana has progressed with her preparations. I would like to be off." On reaching the door, he turned back to her. "I am very glad you and Rebecca are friends. I assume you are, given her desire to confide in you."

"I believe we are. I asked her to stay here after we return." She had asked on the impulse of the moment and had not thought then, or indeed at all, about what Darcy would think. Fortunately, he seemed pleased.

"Good. She is very kind. Very genuine. Mad to accept Sterling, but…"

"They love each other and have agreed to be happy." Elizabeth shrugged, and Darcy did likewise.

"I imagine she would very much like Jane. You should consider introducing them."

"I shall."

Elizabeth stared at the door after he left the room. He was probably correct that Jane and Rebecca would like each other, and for him to suggest they meet showed… She was not certain she knew what it meant, but she was pleased he thought well enough of Jane to propose introducing her to more of his family.

THE WEATHER ON THEIR JOURNEY NORTH WAS FAR MORE AGREEABLE than what they had encountered on their journey south almost two months earlier. It was unseasonably warm, and riding would have been very pleasant, but Darcy refused to leave the ladies to themselves in the carriage. He did what he could to be good company to Elizabeth.

They could not talk every moment, and when they did not, Elizabeth spent her time in reflection. She thought about marriages and Rebecca's engagement and Jane's hopes. She loved Jane dearly, and knew she would be able to say the same about Rebecca soon, and wished them both the very happiest of marriages. Mr Hawarden appeared to be a wonderful match for Jane, in temperament and wishes for the future. Sterling was an interesting character, but he was clearly devoted to Rebecca, and Elizabeth was willing to believe his love was sincere. She prayed that Miss Haddon found a gentleman who would love and value her and with whom she, too, could look forward to a good, fulfilling future. It was not Tom. Given his doubts, which Elizabeth had so distressingly overheard him discussing with Darcy, it was just as well he had withdrawn his attention. Perhaps Mr Llewellyn would catch Miss Haddon's interest. It was clear he liked her.

No, Lizzy, you promised yourself you would not matchmake after your little intervention with Rebecca and Sterling. It could have been a disaster! Thank Heavens it was not, but do not tempt fate again. Devote your attention to your own marriage.

She was much more content than she had been in the winter. There were even moments of joy, such as when she saw Jane and the Gardiners. Her relationships with the Fitzwilliams and Darcys were more civil, and, with some of the cousins, even friendly. Elizabeth had opened her heart to the possibility of finding true friends among her new family and acquaintances, which could only add to her future comfort and happiness.

And Fitzwilliam. What a great change she had seen in him! It was almost shocking.

Could he truly be so changed for me? Dare I believe it?

He was sitting across from her looking out of the coach's window, and she watched him. She must put her faith in him. She had always known it would take a great effort for them to have anything approaching a good marriage.

*All those months in the summer and autumn, I did everything I could to show him I wanted to be a good wife and then...*Then they had quarrelled.

When he returned to Pemberley, and she admitted she did not need to fear him, she had...what? *Given up. That is what you did, Lizzy, and you know it was wrong. It was wrong at the time, and now, after he has shown you time and again that he wants to do better, that he wants you to be happy, it is especially wrong.*

All her misery had poured out of her that December morning. Was it possible some of what she said then was exaggerated, that her despair had made her say more than she ought to have said? *You thought not long afterwards that every word of it should have remained unsaid. Now it is a matter of whether* some *of it was exaggeration? My, my, how everything has changed! I suppose I should not think that day an evil if good has come of it.*

Whether or not she would ever remember their argument with anything other than abhorrence was not of immediate concern. The idea that perhaps she had gone too far in some of her assertions was foremost in her mind, and she tried to remember, wondering if there was something she could learn from it just as Darcy had evidently done.

She did not immediately understand why it was so, but her declaration that he was disgusted by her family remained with her, irritating her mind for hours as they stopped to partake of a nuncheon, and as she and Darcy spoke about this and that for some time after returning to the carriage. He had looked upon the Bennets with contempt. There was no denying that, and Elizabeth had no wish to give him more credit than was his due. What had he said to her—that he had not known them? That was true, but it did not excuse his incivility when he met her mother and younger sisters.

And how did they act, Lizzy? The picture that came to mind was not pretty. Elizabeth remembered arriving at Longbourn and introducing Darcy and Georgiana to her mother. Mrs Bennet's behaviour had been mortifying. It had been the same at the wedding. Mrs Bennet had practically thrown Jane at Sterling and had indiscreetly spoken about how little Elizabeth deserved to make such a good match. Her younger sisters were no better, being in turn rude, silly, and ignorant. As for Mr Bennet, he had acted as though he were the injured party in the whole affair, as though Elizabeth had erred in going to Georgiana's assistance, which was something Elizabeth would never regret. His petulance had caused Elizabeth to suffer.

I was embarrassed by their behaviour—all of them save Jane. How can I blame Fitzwilliam for thinking ill of them when they did so much to show he should?

Elizabeth did not believe he had been justified in thinking ill of her because of the Bennets' behaviour, but she could not blame him as much as she had in the past.

Have you not judged him by the example of his family? Yes, there was much in his behaviour you could rightly censure, but he was not responsible for Lady Romsley's rudeness or even, really, for Georgiana's cruelty. As her guardian, he must bear some responsibility, but not all of it, not when she is fifteen.

There was one matter upon which she could not think without even greater shame. Had she not said or implied that she never wished for him to share her bed? That had not been just. The situation was by no means as easy as such an assertion would suggest. He had made no outright demands of her, and she had derived some comfort from their marital relations. Had she wanted to become intimate with him in that way? She could not remember, not after so long and given how confused her feelings had been.

Since then he has not hinted that he wishes to resume relations. There have not even been the sorts of hints he gave in the autumn, have there? The most he has done is kiss my hand two or three times. Why? Elizabeth could think of many possible reasons, but only her husband could tell her the correct one. Perhaps one day they would discuss it, but it seemed unlikely.

Chapter 38

The quiet hours in the carriage inevitably left Darcy with time to reflect, and his thoughts turned to his wife and sister. He was thankful that Elizabeth's mood was so much improved, and resolved to stay on the path he had embarked upon in January. It was remarkably easy, and he felt happier knowing he was becoming a better man.

The greater part of my happiness comes from seeing Elizabeth so much happier. I am, I trust, becoming a man who can please a woman such as her, a woman whose approbation is not lightly given and is thus a rare gift. She has taught me so much about myself and what it means to be a true gentleman, and for that I am forever in her debt.

He would never look upon his past behaviour with anything but abhorrence, particularly when it came to their families. *How could I have censured her family when mine has shown her so much incivility? They did not all treat her with contempt or suspicion, to be sure, but neither did all her family behave improperly. The Gardiners and Miss Bennet have greeted me and Georgiana with kindness, even after my poor showing last summer.*

In thinking meanly of her family, he had denied her the comfort Jane could have given her after their wedding. It had never even occurred to him to suggest Jane stay with them.

I do not know how she can forgive me, as she seems to be doing, but I thank God she is willing to overcome her disgust of me.

It was a sort of sweet torture to indulge in his feelings for Elizabeth knowing he had no right to expect a return of them. She was so lovely and caring, and he was very fortunate to have her as his wife. He could not forget that, better mood or not, she did not wish to hold that position, and the pain that realisation caused him was severe. Every day it seemed Elizabeth did or said something that showed him how truly blessed he was to have her of all women by his side. *What I would not give to have her one day think the same of me.*

Then there was Georgiana, again sitting as though she did not wish to acknowledge that Elizabeth and he were in the carriage with her. *With luck, it will not be very long before we find a companion whom we can trust. We cannot ask my aunt to bear the responsibility for long; it is not fair to her. The close attention of some other person must help Georgiana.*

Darcy had come to believe there was more to Georgiana's contempt for Elizabeth than she had yet acknowledged, including jealousy. Unless his sister discovered what it was, she might never be able to treat Elizabeth with civility. *If there is no progress with Georgiana, say, by the end of the summer, what do I do? How do I help my sister and fulfil my duty to her and do the same for Elizabeth? Should I move Georgiana out of Pemberley, again place her in a separate establishment so that Elizabeth and I have a chance to be happy? Could I possibly trust Georgiana not to make foolish decisions or spread lies about Elizabeth in such a situation?*

His thoughts circled around this question endlessly, defying his attempts to set it aside and to not worry about it until he had to. The end of the summer was a long way off, and much could change by then.

ELIZABETH HAD KNOWN FOR SOME TIME WHEN GEORGIANA'S birthday was, and, as soon as the arrangements had been made for their removal to Derbyshire—placing them at Pemberley for the occasion—she had written to Mrs Reynolds to request a celebratory dinner of all Miss Darcy's favourites. She and Darcy had discussed other arrangements for the day as well.

"Happy birthday, Georgiana," Elizabeth said when her sister-in-law entered the breakfast parlour the morning after their arrival.

Georgiana glanced in Elizabeth's direction and took her seat. Elizabeth had not expected more from the girl and found that Georgiana's continued petulance had little effect on her. Darcy caught her eye, and Elizabeth could see that he questioned her reaction to Georgiana's manner, so she shrugged just enough for him to see. She meant to tell him that it mattered not.

"Elizabeth was just telling me that she and Mrs Reynolds will be busy today, is that not right?"

"Yes. There is much to do to prepare the house for the warmer season, and much was done in our absence that I would like to review."

"Pemberley is fortunate to have you," Darcy said.

Elizabeth allowed herself to feel pleased with his praise and smiled.

Darcy turned to Georgiana. "As Elizabeth will be occupied, I thought you and I could go riding. It is a lovely day."

"Yes, Brother."

"After breakfast, Elizabeth and I have a few gifts for you." He turned to his wife, "I think it would be appropriate to give them to Georgiana now rather than at dinner. What do you think, Elizabeth?"

"I agree." She, Darcy, and Tom had discussed appropriate gifts for Georgiana, and Elizabeth had sought out several novels she had read and found sensible, as well as enjoyable. Whether or not Georgiana would like them as much as the more sensational stories of misunderstood heroes and reformed rakes was another matter entirely, and not one about which Elizabeth or Georgiana's guardians would worry. Despite Georgiana's continued stubbornness, they did wish to provide her with appropriate ways in which to amuse herself and wanted to show her that, if she continued to behave and attend to her studies, she would be allowed more liberties.

"Elizabeth has arranged a special dinner in honour of your birthday."

"Mrs Reynolds assures me that the menu includes many of your favourites."

Georgiana made no reply, as expected.

Elizabeth introduced the topic of the renovated guest chambers, and Darcy expressed a desire to see what had been accomplished in their absence, saying he was certain Georgiana would like to see them as well. A plan was made to undertake a tour after breakfast, and after Georgiana had opened her gifts.

GEORGIANA WAS NOT DISPLEASED WITH WHAT HER BROTHER AND TOM had decided were appropriate presents. Elizabeth's name was mentioned as one of the givers, but she did not believe she had had any role in selecting them whatsoever. The gifts were new paints and pencils and several novels, none of which she had read.

It was a better day than any other Georgiana had had since that awful morning when her tendency to exaggerate had been exposed. Dinner was a quiet, but not unpleasant affair. It was a delicious meal, Elizabeth said very little, and Georgiana had the pleasure of thinking back on a day well spent. She and Fitzwilliam had taken a long ride. She had not had to look into one of her dreadful serious books all day and had instead spent the morning drawing and reading one of her new novels. It was not quite as amusing as some of her disallowed favourites, but it would do.

The day was pleasing enough that Georgiana began to hope her life at Pemberley would not be nearly as horrible as the last few weeks in London had been. Aunt Horry did not return to Derbyshire for several more days, and Georgiana intended to convince Fitzwilliam that it was not necessary to tell their aunt about Ramsgate or her exaggerations. Her aunt would be much more manageable if she did not know the whole of it, and Georgiana was certain that once her brother and Elizabeth returned to London, her aunt would allow her a few liberties. She would have to do enough to satisfy her guardians, but it would be easier to do so if she could spend the better part of her days in activities she found more agreeable.

THE WEATHER THE NEXT DAY PROVED TO BE JUST AS PLEASANT, AND Elizabeth and Darcy took a walk together before dressing for dinner. Elizabeth was happy to be at Pemberley again, which she found a little surprising. She preferred the country, but being in London meant being able to see Jane and the Gardiners. Yet now she was confident that she would see them again soon. That was the essential difference. When she had last been at Pemberley, she was very unhappy and had had no great expectation of seeing Jane and none whatsoever of Darcy allowing her to see the Gardiners, even though he had called on them.

Everything is different now. She stole a glance at the tall gentleman walking by her side. *Well, not everything perhaps, but it is improving.*

"I do not expect we shall see many people while we remain in the neighbourhood," Darcy said.

Elizabeth murmured an agreement or a question—she was not sure which she meant.

"Few of our acquaintances will have returned from London. It will be quiet, especially after how busy we were in London."

"I do wish to call on Miss Pratt soon, and some of the families of the neighbourhood. Mr Llewellyn will return next week, I believe."

Darcy nodded. "We shall see him before we leave again. There is no need for you to make your calls immediately, although I know you will not wish to delay for long. Potter keeps an eye on the families in need, and Llewellyn told me himself, when we last saw him, that Miss Pratt was well. It will make no difference if you take a day or two to see to things here. Mrs Reynolds is keeping you busy."

Elizabeth laughed. "She admitted to me just this morning that she is happy Pemberley has a mistress again. I presume it is so she has someone to talk to about spring cleaning and renovation and what should be done with the curtains in the red reception room."

"She is happy to have an intelligent, sensible mistress who is interested in household management."

Elizabeth blushed. It was gratifying to hear such sentiments, and it did much to bolster her belief that what she had done since becoming

Mrs Darcy had made a difference and that she and her husband would find their way.

Darcy gently took her elbow to steer her away from a patch of mud that she had almost stepped in; she was distracted by a few early spring flowers just starting to bloom.

After a minute or two of silence, Darcy said, "If the weather remains fair tomorrow, I shall ride out to see some tenants in the north of the estate. I expect we shall soon see the end of this mild weather, but not until we have a chance to enjoy a day or two more, I hope."

"Another day or two would suit me very well!"

Chapter 39

*D*arcy left after breakfast the next morning. The weather remained unseasonably mild and fair, which made it a good day for the excursion. The head gardener had told him that morning that the weather would break soon.

"All the more reason to take advantage of it while it lasts," Darcy had said to Elizabeth and Georgiana at breakfast.

Elizabeth agreed. "I certainly will."

"You should take some exercise as well, Georgiana. It will help you work better. We can discuss what you have learnt about China upon my return."

"Yes, Brother."

Elizabeth reflected that it truly was a shame that Georgiana had no wish for her company. She had loved reading about different countries when she was younger—still did, truth be told—and they could have had very interesting conversations about what Georgiana was studying. As things were now, it was difficult to believe they could ever be friends, let alone think of each other as sisters.

Should Georgiana ever wish for such a thing, Elizabeth thought as she went about her duties. *At the moment, it seems difficult to believe the day will come when she does not hate the very sight of me.*

It was two or three hours after breakfast when Elizabeth happened to notice that what had been a lovely blue sky with a few wispy clouds had become white with patches of grey. *I hope Fitzwilliam gets home before it rains. If it rains.*

Elizabeth continued with her day, feeling no great concern. She wrote letters, and, after another hour or so, she realised she was feeling a little chilly. She was not so cold that she would bother to have the fire built up, but she was uncomfortable enough that she decided to fetch her wrap.

When Elizabeth's maid heard her in the bedchamber, she hastened to join her mistress and enquired after her needs.

"I was looking for a shawl. I felt a little chilled."

While retrieving the garment, Drewe said, "One of the footmen told me it has become much colder out since this morning. He says it will feel more like a Derbyshire spring soon, but I did not half believe the stories he told about how terrible it can be."

Elizabeth laughed, as she knew Drewe expected, and they spent a few minutes sharing what they had been told about the local climate before Elizabeth returned to the rose parlour.

I hope Fitzwilliam does not get a chill. I am not sure he was properly prepared for it to become so much colder while he was out. Fortunately, she reminded herself, he was in excellent health, and a little exposure to cold weather was unlikely to cause him serious harm. She turned her attention to the household accounts, refusing to give in to needless anxiety.

She almost leapt out of her seat when a loud burst of thunder seemed to shake the room. It was immediately followed by the sound of a great deluge of water hitting the sides of the house and the ground outside. Elizabeth rushed to the window. Her eyes confirmed what her ears had heard—a storm had begun. Great walls of rain were falling from the sky, and it had become far darker than it should be for the time of day. Looking at her watch, Elizabeth saw there was still an hour before she should go dress for dinner.

He should not be on his way back yet, she thought, although she was not convinced she was correct. She knew Darcy might have set out to return home at any time, and that, if he were to be back in time for dinner, he should be on his way. Her forehead furrowed, and she felt a moment of apprehension.

"No," she reprimanded herself. "I will not worry until there is reason."

She returned to her task, although it was increasingly difficult to attend to her work as the sounds of the storm, which seemed to be growing worse, raged outside. Finally, deciding it was close enough to the dinner hour, she rang the bell and asked for Mrs Reynolds, who confirmed that Darcy was not yet returned.

"Then it is unlikely he will make it back before dinner. If he was already on his way home when the storm started, he would be here by now. If he was not close by, I trust he would have had enough sense to stay where he was, or to seek shelter. We should not hold dinner. He would not wish it when his return is uncertain. Have hot water at the ready. Should he have been caught out in this rain, he will want a bath."

"Yes, Mrs Darcy. I am sure there is no cause for alarm. No doubt as soon as he felt the first drop of rain, he found somewhere dry and warm to wait it out."

Elizabeth nodded and tried to force a feeling of foreboding into submission. She reminded herself, repeatedly, that there was no sense in worrying when she had no particular reason to do so. Wherever Fitzwilliam was, he was safe and would return either later that evening, if the weather cleared before dark, or in the morning.

Elizabeth explained the situation to Georgiana when they met for dinner.

"He would have sought shelter as soon as it began to rain if he were not still at his last destination. The Thorns, I believe. There is no sign of the storm letting up yet," Elizabeth said. She looked out of a window and thought that, if anything, it seemed a little stronger than it had an hour earlier.

Schooling her features so Georgiana would not see her anxiety, Elizabeth turned away from the window. "We are unlikely to see him until the morning, I am afraid."

Dinner was very quiet. When they had eaten all they could and left the dining room, Georgiana turned towards the stairs to return to her chambers.

Elizabeth did not bother to mask her impatience. "We will take tea together. Do not make me remind you why."

Once they were in the withdrawing room, Elizabeth went immediately to the window and pushed aside the curtain. It was so terribly dark; there would be no moonlight tonight. They could not expect that Darcy would appear. Wherever he was, he would remain until daybreak.

Elizabeth sat upon a sofa near to where her book and needlework had been placed. After several minutes, the butler entered the room. Hudson had not come to deliver the tea tray, however. He looked at Elizabeth as though he had to say something, but very much wished he did not.

"Hudson, what is it?" Elizabeth asked.

"I do not wish to cause alarm, Mrs Darcy, but Maudsley has sent word from the stables that the master's horse has returned. Alone. He sent several of his men out to look for signs of Mr Darcy, but I am afraid there is little they can do tonight. The storm continues, and it has grown full dark."

There was a short pause before Elizabeth replied. "No, of course not. Please do bring tea, and I need not say that should you learn anything, tell me immediately."

With Hudson gone, Elizabeth could not hide her agitation, which had grown substantially. She stood and went to the window again. There was the occasional flash of lightning and the sound of now-distant thunder. The draught which came in from around the window and the coolness of the glass when Elizabeth laid her hand on it confirmed how cold it had become. It still rained, and Elizabeth thought that perhaps it was starting to turn to snow, or it soon would.

Where was he? Why had his horse returned without him? Elizabeth closed her eyes and sent out a silent prayer that her husband was safe and sound.

DARCY WAS ON HIS WAY BACK WHEN THE RAIN STARTED. HE FELT THE cold through his riding clothes and thought longingly of sitting in front of a fire and sipping a glass of wine before dinner. There were some very dark clouds in the sky, which created a little anxiety. They had not been there when he had started for home. He was calculating how long it would take to reach the house when he felt the first drop of rain hit his face. More drops soon followed, and he suspected that it would become quite heavy before it was finished.

The only thing to do was to urge his horse on and discover if there was anywhere nearby where he could stop and wait out the rain. He knew of nothing on his land, but he was not very far from the border of his property, and there might be something on his neighbour's estate. He did not need much—just shelter from the rain until it slowed or stopped long enough for him to make it to Pemberley house.

Without warning, the few drops turned into a deluge, and there was a flash of lightning shortly followed by a loud crack of thunder. His horse reared, but Darcy stayed in the saddle.

Finding shelter became an urgent matter. The lightning and thunder were fierce, the rain heavy, the wind strong, and the temperature rapidly falling. Keeping close control of the animal, he veered to the west, crossing onto the neighbouring estate. In a few minutes, he spied some sort of structure during a flash of lightning. When he reached it, Darcy discovered that it was the remains of what had once been a wood and stone cottage. He would never have allowed such ruins to stand on Pemberley's lands, but at the moment he was very glad to know his neighbour was not so fastidious. One side of the cottage was almost entirely gone, which suited Darcy. It meant he could easily get his horse under what was left of the roof; he hoped it did not leak very much. He prayed the building was sound enough to survive the storm.

As he led his horse under the protection of the partial roof, an exceptionally loud crack of thunder scared the animal, who pulled the reins out of Darcy's hands and bolted. Darcy's inarticulate cry was drowned by the pounding of the rain. Within a minute the horse was lost to his sight, and all that was left for him to do was hope that the animal found his way safely home.

As for Darcy, he would have to make do where he was until the storm abated and possibly until morning. He could not risk losing his way, especially on foot. He made a quick survey of his surroundings. There was precious little to comfort him, but he found a dry corner which would afford him shelter from the wind. Sitting upon the hard ground, he pulled his coat tightly around him. It was cold and uncomfortable, but he was safe. His thoughts drifted to Elizabeth and Georgiana, hoping that they would not become unduly alarmed by his absence.

IN THE COMFORT OF THE WITHDRAWING ROOM, IT WAS HARD NOT TO feel anxious. As much as Elizabeth told herself that she should not fret, she could not shake off her alarm.

The ladies drank tea without exchanging a word. When she was finished, Elizabeth continued her restless vigil. She paced the room now and again and looked out of the window, although that provided no comfort. She was certain the rain turned to snow as the hour grew late. Attempting to compose her mind, she tried to attend to her needlework, picking it up only to put it down after a few minutes. She did the same with her book.

Some half an hour later, Georgiana began to play the pianoforte. She was not supposed to play, but Elizabeth did not care under the circumstances. It did not disturb her, and no doubt Georgiana was anxious about her brother. If playing gave her comfort, so be it.

They passed almost three hours in this way before the room fell silent. Elizabeth glanced at Georgiana to see that she had returned to the sofa and was absently playing with the hem of her shawl. Georgiana let out a mighty sigh. Elizabeth took it as a mark of how concerned the girl was for her brother. In this, at least, they shared similar feelings.

"You should not worry too much about Fitzwilliam, Georgiana. It is by far the most likely outcome that he is well and will turn up or be found somewhere safe in the morning."

"You do not know that!" Georgiana cried.

Elizabeth felt the heat grow in her cheeks. Why, she wondered, had she bothered to say anything? Despite this thought, she could not stop herself from saying more. "No, that is very true, although it is what I choose to believe. If, however, it is not so, you should remember that you would hardly be alone. There are so many others who love you and would care for you, see you through any difficulty —Tom, Lord and Lady Romsley, all your Darcy relations."

"And what would you do? None of them would want you," she retorted.

"I am sure I would—" Elizabeth stammered, involuntarily beginning to respond, before turning away from Georgiana. The girl's words were intended to injure her, but Elizabeth did not wish to admit anger, not at such a time. She had no desire to speculate on what would happen to her should something dire have befallen Darcy. It was not concern for her well-being; it was fear for his which she did not wish to contemplate, not until—unless—it was necessary to do so.

A stab of resentment that Georgiana had used this moment to say something spiteful added heat to Elizabeth's voice when she spoke again. "We should not think this way at all." She stood and began to pace again. "I will believe he is well, but you should remember that, unlikely as it might be, if he is not, there are people who care for you."

"Care?" Georgiana demanded. "What do you know about it? You do not care about him or any of us, no more than we do you!"

This was going too far. Elizabeth stopped and glared at Georgiana, her feelings of resentment and anger boiling over. "If you think I truly could not care that someone—*anyone*—is missing under such circumstances, let alone the man to whom I am married, the man with whom I have lived all these months, then you really do not understand me at all.

"What have I ever done to make you think I could be so heartless? Why do you think I went to help you that night in Ramsgate? I did not know you or who you were, whether you were highly born or not, how rich you were. None of it would have mattered to me, even if I had had a moment to think about it. I saw a girl who was frightened, and so I helped, without stopping to think whether I should or not, because I *do* care.

"Do you know what is especially sad? I would do the same again, regardless of the outcome for me, and if you think that I rejoice in what my life has become, you are very wrong. I had to marry a man I did not know, and I am so very, very fortunate he is a good man, because if he were not my life would be," she paused only long enough to swallow a sob, "I cannot even imagine how miserable my life would be. Perhaps as awful as your life would have been as Mrs Wickham.

"It does not matter now. Not now. You can continue to dislike me as much as you want tomorrow, after Fitzwilliam is home. Once we know he is safe, then you can nurse your antipathy for me all you like. Until we *do* know he is safe, until we know he is home where he belongs, or until it is morning and I can do something to help find him, we have only each other for company. If you cannot bear my presence, by all means go to your rooms. I shall wait here alone if necessary."

Speaking only to herself, she said, "I shall not rest until he is home." She walked away from Georgiana, returning to look out of a window again. "It does not matter now. Not now." Georgiana's pettiness was unimportant compared to Fitzwilliam being missing.

Chapter 40

Georgiana had been puzzled by Elizabeth's disquiet from the moment she joined her before dinner and learnt her brother was not returned. It was unwarranted unless there was something Elizabeth had not told her. If there was not, then there truly was no reason to furrow one's brow and stare out of windows, especially when it was too dark to see anything. Georgiana had no great apprehension. Her brother knew what was best to do and was perfectly safe wherever he was. The news that Fitzwilliam's horse had returned without him created an anxiety Georgiana had not felt earlier, and having to witness Elizabeth's agitation did not lessen her disquiet. She would very much have welcomed news of her brother's whereabouts. Playing the pianoforte had helped for as long as she could bear to do it. At least then the time passed more quickly, and she did not have to witness Elizabeth's nervous activities, which only increased her own anxiety.

Elizabeth stood at the window for a very long time. As she did so, Georgiana watched, and her feelings softened just a little. It truly seemed that Elizabeth was anxious about Fitzwilliam, which was interesting and unexpected. Ought it be so surprising, though? Elizabeth *had* come to her assistance that dreadful night in Ramsgate. Georgiana had been grateful for it because once she said she wanted to tell her brother about their engagement, Wickham's behaviour had caused her great alarm.

Her aunt had had a great deal to say about what her life would have been like had she eloped with Wickham, and even believing that Lady Romsley exaggerated, Georgiana knew she would have been very unhappy. Last summer it was so easy to become caught up in the romance and excitement of it all, but ideas of romance and excitement had quickly faded when faced with Wickham's anger. She had seen his true nature at that moment and could only be relieved that no marriage had taken place.

But a marriage had taken place. Her brother's.

And Elizabeth's, Georgiana remembered a moment later. Elizabeth had not suffered by marrying Fitzwilliam, but still, it had not been Elizabeth's choice. As Elizabeth had herself said, she was fortunate that Fitzwilliam was a good man. Wickham was not; Georgiana had been completely taken in by him.

Georgiana could feel some small measure of sympathy for that reason. And, she supposed, more than a little gratitude that Elizabeth had cared enough to come to her assistance that ghastly, humiliating night in Ramsgate.

AROUND MIDNIGHT, HUDSON BROUGHT IN A TRAY OF TEA AND ONE OF bread, cheese, cake, and fruit. He told Elizabeth that most of the servants had been sent to their beds, but he, Mrs Reynolds, and Cook remained awake. He had insisted that Drewe and Quinn retire as well, so that they would be rested when needed by the master and mistress.

"Thank you, Hudson. You should retire for the night. There is no good to be done by having all of us lose sleep in this manner."

"Begging your pardon, Mrs Darcy, but I will not, not until we have news of the master. Neither will Mrs Reynolds, but Cook will drift off in her chair soon enough, and we shall leave her be. The men will go out once day breaks, and if there is no sign of him soon, we will spread the word that more help is needed to search."

In the early hours of the new day, Georgiana fell asleep. Elizabeth tried to rest as well, but could not. There was such a commotion in her mind, and she struggled with her emotions. She heard Georgiana's words again and again.

How could she accuse me of not caring? She was vexed, even disappointed, that Georgiana was determined to think so little of her after everything that had happened since the summer.

Thoughts of Fitzwilliam were naturally foremost in her mind. It was pointless to tell herself that her anxiety was too much for the occasion. She had tried to do that, and it had done nothing to control the degree of her apprehension. She sought some explanation for it, hoping she could use logic to calm herself. The reason, once she looked for it, was simple.

How could I ever think that I could do this without caring?

She did her best to stifle a sob. She had no wish to give into despair, especially since there was, as of yet, no just cause to do so. Covering her mouth with one hand, she rested her forehead against the cold glass of the window at which she stood.

Elizabeth was a caring person. She always had been. It was she who commonly nursed her sisters and her father when they were ill. It was an admirable part of her nature, one which she knew others valued, and one of which she could not be ashamed. It was that which had made her fly from the window of her bedchamber in Ramsgate to go to the assistance of an unknown girl who had put herself in great danger.

Elizabeth realised it was wrong to deny this essential aspect of her character and useless to say she would guard her heart against her husband and her new family and acquaintances. How could she ever hope to be happy if she did? It had not worked. It *could* not work, not without turning her into someone she did not want to be—a cold, unfeeling, miserable person.

No matter how much she had tried to protect herself from disappointment, she *did* care. How could she ever have thought she could prevent herself from caring about Fitzwilliam when she lived with him, saw him every day? When she gave herself to him? It was easier to maintain some sort of barrier when she could reasonably tell herself that he thought nothing of her, but these last weeks, when he had been so kind, so considerate, how could she ever have thought she could prevent herself from caring about that man? Had he not shown, through his changed manner, that he had heard and accepted the awful accusations she had thrown at him in December?

She did care. Of course, she cared. She was frightened for him because she cared about him, and because he had become an important part of her life. He was, after all, her husband. She could not deny that she liked Fitzwilliam. It was even reasonable to think he had come to like her. Everything he had done since his return to Pemberley in January showed that he did like her, at least a little. Suddenly, everything he had done took on new significance. Staying by her side throughout the Fitzwilliams' ball and at other parties, asking after her comfort again and again, befriending the Gardiners—it was because he cared about her happiness and well-being.

It is not unreasonable to suppose that that is the truth, Elizabeth thought. She remained by the window, looking out into the darkness. A glance over her shoulder showed her that Georgiana was still sleeping. *We are husband and wife, and he does want us to...care for each other, to be friends. He may not have wanted it when we were first married, but he does now. It is not wrong to believe he wants us to be happy, to make the best of our situation that we can. It is not wrong to suppose that he...that he* does *care about me, and that I can allow myself to care for him.* But after so much—the months of unhappiness and disappointment—it was difficult to trust that it was safe to allow herself to open her heart to Fitzwilliam. Especially when his whereabouts and safety were in question.

It was just before dawn when Georgiana awoke with a start. She looked around in some confusion, and when her eyes fell on Elizabeth, Elizabeth shook her head to say there was no news.

Finally, as dawn was breaking, and as Elizabeth looked upon the snow-covered ground from her place at the window, Hudson returned to the room. His customary reserve was displaced by relief and fatigue.

"Mrs Darcy, a runner has just come in from the search. Mr Darcy has been seen. He is walking towards the house and will be here soon."

Somehow, Elizabeth was able to keep her composure and thank him. "Alert Quinn," she ordered. "Hot water. Be sure there is enough for a bath. And have someone prepared to go for the apothecary if needed. Food, too. He will be hungry. Have a tray prepared with something to eat and something hot to drink. He will certainly have taken a chill."

Hudson nodded and went to see to her orders. With his departure, Elizabeth looked at Georgiana and saw she was softly crying, her hands covering her face.

"He is returning, and under his own power." Elizabeth's voice shook. "That means he is well, Georgiana, and uninjured." *Not so badly that he cannot walk, at least.*

At last, Fitzwilliam appeared before them. Elizabeth, who had been pacing impatiently, stopped when she heard the door open, and remained where she was, staring at him. Georgiana flew into his arms, and he returned her embrace.

"I am so glad you are here," Georgiana cried.

He said something to his sister. Elizabeth did not hear it, though she could not say whether it was because it was too quiet or because of how overwhelmed she felt. She was prepared to accept that she could allow herself to care for him and believe that he could genuinely care for her in return, but it was still a new idea for her. Between the newness of her realisations of the last hours, relief, and exhaustion she did not know how to act or what to say.

Darcy disengaged Georgiana's arms from around his neck and led her to a sofa. "Have you two been up all night?"

"Yes," Georgiana said. "I could not rest, not knowing where you were."

"Where were you?" Elizabeth asked, her voice sounding hollow to her ears.

He relayed the story of his ride home, the beginning of the storm, his search for shelter, and his horse's flight. He glanced at Georgiana periodically as he spoke, but mostly he kept his eyes on Elizabeth.

"As soon as it was light enough to see clearly, I began to walk back to the house. I did not know where I was yesterday, but it was easy enough to tell this morning."

"Thank God you found a place to wait out the storm," Elizabeth said. "I-we had thought as much, hoped as much. You should go upstairs. You must change and get warm. There will be hot water for a bath, and Quinn is waiting." He looked cold, despite the thick blanket wrapped around his shoulders, and he was wet.

"That sounds wonderful," Darcy admitted. He sent Georgiana off to bed, telling her to remain there as long as she liked.

Once they were alone, Elizabeth said, "I shall have Mrs Reynolds prepare a tray for you."

"Thank you. I do long to be dry and warm again, and I am hungry. You should get some sleep."

Elizabeth nodded. "I shall once I speak to Mrs Reynolds. I must make certain that no alarm has been raised. There was talk of alerting the neighbours and tenants to search for you." Elizabeth smiled and encouraged him to go to his rooms. "I shall retire in a minute."

It was close to a half an hour later when Elizabeth was able to go to her chambers. She had spent some time with the servants, who were now all awake, assuring them their master was well, then making arrangements with Mrs Reynolds and Hudson for the day. Drewe quickly had Elizabeth out of her gown and into a robe with her hair plaited and ready to climb into bed to try to sleep for at least a few hours.

DARCY GRATEFULLY SHED HIS DAMP CLOTHING AND TOOK A HOT BATH. He had emerged from his long, sleepless night wet, chilled to the bone, and desperate to see Georgiana and Elizabeth.

Elizabeth. It had been impossible to tell what she was thinking. By all appearances she had been stoic, but the way she kept her eyes locked on him, the way she held herself, the expression on her face, all of it had suggested she was struggling with her feelings. His attempts to gain some hint of her thoughts had failed. Most of the night had been spent thinking about her, and he longed to hold her, and to tell her…well, there was a great deal he longed to say to her, but that was nothing new.

Because he had been listening for it, Darcy knew when Elizabeth was in her room. Wanting to make sure she was well before he got into his bed, he knocked on the door which separated their rooms, and entered when she called out.

"Fitzwilliam, is everything well?"

She stood before him looking so lovely it was all he could do to refrain from going to her and wrapping his arms around her so that he could feel her warmth. He could not, however, not without knowing it was what she wanted, and he was rather certain she did not want him in the way that he very much wanted her.

"I wished to ask you that. I was...concerned about you when we were downstairs."

Elizabeth let out a short, humourless laugh. "I was not the one missing all night in a violent storm."

"I was never in any danger." She had been worried about him. He was oddly joyful about that.

"We could not know that, could we? We were left to wait and wonder where you were, if you were injured or safe, when we would see you again, what would become of our lives if— "

Her voice broke, and she lowered her head, hiding her face from him. Her last words reminded him of a subject he had thought about a great deal during the long hours of the night—what would happen to Elizabeth should he meet his end. They had never spoken about it, and he did not know if her father had told her about the marriage settlements.

"You would be well taken care of if anything happened to me." His exhaustion and her upset augmented the difficulty he often felt in talking to her. "You are provided for should—"

Looking at her stopped his speech. She looked at him, and even though he stood six or seven feet away, he could see the tears in her eyes. The sorrow on her face—her beautiful, beautiful face—cut through him, and her voice, trembling and full of passion, was almost enough to knock him to his knees.

"Do you think so little of me that *that* is what has occupied my mind? After everything? That I c-care about-about money or—"

"No! No, no," he repeated, his voice becoming softer each time he repeated the word, begging her to believe him.

Elizabeth stared at him, her chest rapidly rising and falling, her eyes showing...what? Confusion perhaps, or hesitation—as though she wished to believe him, but was not confident she should—and something else he could not name. He did not know how to reassure her and apologise for his choice of words. It would be difficult at any time, but now, with exhaustion clouding his mind, it was impossible. He stood there stupidly, shaking his head, and imploring her with his eyes.

To Darcy's astonishment, Elizabeth quickly bridged the chasm between them, threw her arms about his neck, and kissed him soundly. He moaned as he wrapped his arms around her body and pulled her as close to him as possible, returning her kiss in equal measure. It was a kiss of desperation and uncertainty, longing and hope. Darcy never, ever wanted it to end.

MUCH LATER, AS EXHAUSTION CLAIMED THEM, THEY LAY ON THEIR sides, Elizabeth's back to Darcy's chest, one of his arms wrapped around her, their fingers entwined.

She said, almost too quietly for him to hear, "I was afraid I would never see you again."

He could not speak, but he could kiss her, and so he did, two or three times. He buried his nose in her hair and pulled her just that little bit closer before falling asleep.

Chapter 41

*D*arcy woke up and immediately realised he was not in his bed. It took no more than an instant to remember where he was and why. Elizabeth was fast asleep. She was lying on her stomach, one arm on her pillow, and her back partially uncovered. He had never seen it thus, although he had felt it many times—most memorably earlier that morning when they had so unexpectedly been intimate. Her face was turned towards him, and he took a moment to appreciate how beautiful she was, the delicacy of her eyelashes on her cheeks, the way her soft, rich hair lay in a tangle around her head.

She was lovely, and he loved her. When his feelings had progressed from admiration and affection to love he could not say, but he could easily fix the day when he knew. It was the moment she came to him that awful morning and so gently laid a hand on his arm to stop him from continuing his lecture to Georgiana. Elizabeth had been unhappy for weeks and had no reason to think well of him—and certainly not of Georgiana—and yet she had acted so kindly, so compassionately. That she could soothe him with just a touch—turn all his anger and disappointment and disgust aside—showed how much power she had over him. It was even possible to say that every-thing he had done the last several months proved how much in her power he was. Her words that morning in December would not have affected him so greatly if he did not care deeply for her. He would not have been driven to examine his character, to understand how he had failed, for one who was less worthy than Elizabeth.

If he were to act on instinct at the moment, he would caress her, feel the softness of her back, kiss her shoulder and cheek until she woke up and then...

No, he should definitely not continue that line of thought. He slipped out of bed, covering Elizabeth with the thick woollen blanket so she would not become chilled, and searched for his dressing gown. He collected Elizabeth's robe and chemise and placed them at the end of the bed so they would be nearby when she awoke.

Going into his bedchamber, he rang for Quinn, asking for a tray. The food that had been sent up early was spoilt, and he was very hungry. No doubt, Elizabeth would be, too. Dismissing his valet, Darcy returned to Elizabeth as quietly as possible. He did not want her to wake up and find him gone, although that might be what she preferred. He could not guess at her wishes. He would, however, remain close by until he knew the breakfast tray had been delivered. He could go eat, leaving the door between the rooms ajar so that, should Elizabeth awaken during his absence, she would know where he was, and it would not seem as though he were avoiding her.

He drew a chair closer to Elizabeth's bed and sat.

What exactly had happened? Why had it happened? He admon-ished himself. Had he not vowed that he would never be with her again without knowing it was what she wanted, not what she felt she owed to him as her husband? Despite that oft-repeated promise, what had he done? What he had not done was stop to think. He had so longed for her that the second they kissed, and he had felt her in his arms, he had lost all reason. He did not think, he just took. He supposed she had been the one who initiated their intimacy, even step-ping away from him to let her robe and chemise fall from her body as she never had before, but that did not mean he had been right to allow them to proceed as far as they had, not without first making certain it was, truly, without reservation, what she wanted.

He felt a sudden surge of sadness. He had wanted her. His desire was not strictly physical. He wanted her regard and affection and forgiveness, and, if it were at all possible, her love. How many times had he told himself that he had no right to any of them? It must have been at least once a day and more likely six or seven. When he had held her in his arms and felt her response to him, everything had seemed possible.

But now he doubted. Was it simply because he had been missing? Elizabeth was incapable of not being alarmed under such circumstances. He prayed she had been especially worried because it was him, that she truly had been afraid for him, and that it meant she no longer despised him. She had been different. The way she acted, what passed between them. But perhaps it was only he who was altered. He thought he felt acceptance and a shared passion, but it could be that it was only because it was what he wished to feel.

He could not know until she awoke, and he could observe her. More importantly, he must ask, and they must talk. No good would come for either of them if he simply continued to speculate. If he were fortunate, this could be the new beginning he had prayed she would one day be willing to grant him.

After a few minutes, she began to stir. He sat, very carefully, at the edge of her bed. Her eyes opened then closed as she yawned, covering her mouth with her left hand. Her wedding ring caught his eye, and he hoped that one day she would not hate what it represented.

When he again looked at her face, he saw that she was watching him. There was a brief awkward pause before she spoke.

"What time is it?"

"About eleven, I believe," Darcy replied.

"Have you been awake long?"

He shook his head. "Just long enough to ask Quinn to bring up a tray. It should be here soon."

Elizabeth nodded, and smiled shyly. "I am hungry."

"As am I." Darcy forced a small smile onto his face.

She sat, clutching the counterpane to her chest. "If you would excuse me for a minute?"

"Of course." He stood. "I shall see if Quinn has brought breakfast."

He handed her robe to her before walking back to his room, closing the adjoining door to give her privacy.

Elizabeth had to attend to her body's needs and wished for a moment to order her feelings. When she had opened her eyes to find Fitzwilliam beside her, she felt the awkwardness of their position, especially hers. She was undressed, and she knew her hair was frightfully messy. Far beyond that was the memory of how she had thrown herself at him and acted the part of a seductress.

Dear God, please let it not have been a mistake. I could bear it if—

When he had said something about her being well provided for, it was as though he thought she had been worried about herself and how she would live, how much money she would have, should something dreadful befall him. *I thought he believed me mercenary, that he did not,* could *not like me if he could think so meanly of my character.*

In that moment, there had been so much pain. Elizabeth had allowed herself to hope, even to believe that they could be happy, which is what she had prayed for from the moment she accepted they would have to marry. His words had robbed her of it and exposed her to more disappointment and misery than she had felt since that dreadful morning in December. How could it not be worse now when Elizabeth understood that she could never truly keep herself from caring about him, not without becoming a person she hated?

But then…

Then, such a simple word. But it was not his denial. It was the way he looked at me almost as if…

Perhaps it had been relief, perhaps it had been her exhaustion, and the joy of knowing he was at home and well, perhaps it was all of that and more, but she had allowed her impulsiveness to take control. She had given herself to him, taken him once again as her husband, this time not out of obligation or a desire to show that she would be a good wife, or out of loneliness. This time, it had been for her and Fitzwilliam alone.

She prayed she was not wrong, and that he had come to care for her, at least enough to say that he liked her and wanted them to have a good marriage—to be intimate friends, as she believed a husband and wife should be. What she feared most of all—even beyond learning he did not have the same hopes she did—was having to live day-to-day without knowing. Some understanding of the terms under which they would live would mean so much to her. All she needed was enough courage to ask.

She approached his room with hesitation.

When Darcy saw her, he announced, "Breakfast has arrived."

Elizabeth slowly stepped further into his bedchamber. She had never been in it and said as much, adding, "Very nice." The dark furniture and deep azure striped wallpaper were rather masculine, but still very attractive. She gave him a weak smile.

They ate in silence for a while. Elizabeth commented on their breakfast and on the snow that was slowly falling. When Darcy did not answer, and even seemed not to hear her, Elizabeth's anxiety grew precipitously.

"Fitzwilliam?" She had to repeat his name before he looked as though he heard her. "You are...are you—? You are very quiet. Is-is-is something...?" She faltered.

Given their state of hunger when they sat down to eat, they had both made short work of breakfast, and by this time were largely finished.

He shook his head, stood, and held out a hand to her. "Come," he whispered.

Not releasing her hand, he led her to a small sofa. They sat, and Elizabeth waited for him to speak. His eyes were lowered, and he caressed her hand with his thumb.

After a false start, Darcy said, "I need to know if-if what happened was what you wanted, not...not what you thought you had to do or-or—"

Elizabeth was surprised by his words, and, despite having rallied her courage, she felt her cheeks burn. "Could you not tell?" She had not only offered herself to him, she had truly wanted him in return. That must have been obvious.

Darcy started to say something, but ended up closing his mouth, and shaking his head before the words came. "I have been wrong before. In December, before I went to London—which I ought not to have done—you said... I cannot bear the thought that you feel you have to give yourself to me regardless of your wishes."

Elizabeth clutched his hand between both of hers. "I am very sorry for what I said then."

Darcy shook his head again and gave a rueful laugh. "You need never apologise for speaking the truth."

"It was not entirely true. Not...not when I said, or implied, that I did not..." It was very difficult to discuss such a matter, especially when they were not accustomed to sharing their feelings with each other.

"What you said to me then, I deserved. I did," he insisted. "I cannot think of my behaviour without abhorrence. I treated you terribly, but of all the things you said to me, of all the ways I failed you, the thought that I had demanded this of you, that I failed to tell you I would never expect—" He covered his eyes with one hand and bowed his head. "You should rightly hate me, yet here you are."

"I never thought you would take what I said so—"

"Of course not," he interjected. "You thought me devoid of any consideration for you, understandably so. I had done nothing, all those months, to show you otherwise."

"I was angry and disappointed when I spoke. I cannot say that some of what I said was not...not true, but Fitzwilliam, when I said that, I did not—" She growled. "It is hard to say what I think I ought to say, to tell you what I feel. I do not know if you will be angry or-or disgusted."

"Just tell me. I want to know what you are feeling."

Elizabeth hesitated. "There are things not easily discussed with anyone. For us... I am afraid of ruining the easiness we have started to find."

He again encouraged her to speak freely.

Elizabeth could not look at him. She had never considered telling him what she was about to divulge, and only did so now because she could think of no other way to ease his mind about the matter of their intimacies. She did not want them to have it hanging over their heads. "I must confess to doing something I know I was not supposed to do.

When I returned to Longbourn from Ramsgate, I wrote to my aunt, and told her the truth of our engagement."

He was surprised but did not withdraw his hand.

Elizabeth quickly went on. "I did not do it unadvisedly. I knew I could trust my aunt and uncle completely. They would never betray my confidence or use what I told them in any way other than to be of assistance to me should I need it. And I did. I was so lost, so... I do not know a word strong enough. I was, in less than a month, to be married to a man who was a stranger to me. I knew they would never allow any hint of what happened to spread, not only because it would cause me, as your wife, injury, but because they would never purposely harm another person. Neither would they judge you or Georgiana harshly, not on the basis of what happened then, during that one small part of her life."

Seeing that her husband was appeased, she went on. "I told my aunt because it is she I most trust to advise me. I knew that from her I could expect the understanding and comfort I needed. I asked her what I could do to be a good wife, especially under the circumstances we faced."

After Fitzwilliam nodded, she continued, her eyes again lowered. "In our letters, she gave me much to think about, and, indeed, the hope I so needed." Elizabeth told him about Mrs Gardiner's advice. "She encouraged me to believe that what happens between a husband and wife could be pleasurable and comforting, even in a marriage such as ours. It is necessary to produce children, of course, but beyond that, it could be a way to forge a bond, a way to create and strengthen the partnership two people have as a married couple. I kept my aunt's words always close to mind. During the early months, I felt... I felt very much alone."

"Elizabeth..."

She shook her head and begged, "Please, let me continue."

He nodded.

"It was a difficult time, but there were moments when I no longer felt so alone, not at first, but after we came to Pemberley."

"When?"

He spoke with evident foreboding, and Elizabeth tried to be gentle as she explained, "We would be together, and you would touch me or kiss me. Those moments when your attention was on me, I did not feel as alone or unhappy." Her voice broke, and she took a moment to compose herself, pressing his hand in an unspoken request that he stay silent. "I allowed myself to forget, for a time at least, everything that made me discontented. I would tell myself at all other times that it did not signify anything in particular, that I was relieved you were not still so disgusted by my presence that you could not be in the same room with me, or that what you sought was an heir, and even that I was glad it was me to whom you came to…fulfil your needs. I wanted you to know you could do so."

"So I would not seek another?" Fitzwilliam asked.

Elizabeth nodded. She would not look at him.

"I would not. We took vows, and I could never be that sort of husband, no matter why we married."

"I know that now, but, Fitzwilliam, what I want you to understand is that I did not accept you into my bed because I felt I had to, not only for that reason. It was not that simple. I did not dread those times, not really. I welcomed them."

"Even if you did not absolutely feel you had to accept me… Elizabeth, you should not have felt at all that you had to. I never would have wished that. I should have made you understand."

"We were both in a very difficult situation."

He lowered his head and shook it. "You much more so than me. I made it difficult for you, while you did everything you could to make it easy for me."

"I think perhaps we have a great deal to talk about. Things I said that morning, what I understand so much better now."

Fitzwilliam nodded mutely for a moment then spoke, almost without volition. "I am sorry. I am so sorry. That day, the things you said to me, not just about—"

"I should not have spoken—"

"What did you say of me that I did not deserve?"

"Fitzwilliam—"

"No!" He sighed and pulled her hand to his mouth and kissed it. "You should not excuse any part of how I acted. I had ample opportunity to think about what you said, and why you said it, when I was alone in town. I did not give credit to your words at first. I admit that.

I was angry. But then, I thought about what you said, the months of our marriage, and even the month or so of our engagement. I treated you infamously."

He stopped and pressed his eyes closed. "I cannot think of how I behaved towards you—who did not deserve it—without revulsion. I was thoughtless and worse than that."

"You are being too hard on yourself," Elizabeth cried. "I made no allowance for your feelings after what happened with Georgiana."

"I deserved everything you said of me. I am rightly ashamed of how I behaved towards you. Trying to excuse any part of my behaviour because of what happened at Ramsgate, or for any other reason, will not do. I should have acted better towards you—towards my wife—for no other reason than because you *are* my wife. I was selfish and arrogant. Even once I began to see so much in you to admire, I did not acknowledge it. Not to you, hardly to myself."

"I entered into our marriage not expecting you to like me," Elizabeth admitted. "I do not believe I fully understood that at the time— just how convinced I was that you, that none of you, would like me. I knew you were disgusted by the prospect of marrying me, and as much as I struggled to do everything I could to find happiness, I am not convinced that I really believed it was possible. I do not know, not yet. I do know that I thought very meanly of you, even before we were married. I gave no thought to how much you had suffered at Ramsgate, or that you must confront the consequences in your own way, and that that way may not be the same as mine."

Darcy shook his head.

Elizabeth was determined to make him understand. "Jane even said it to me once. I believe I had just received one of your letters."

"Which I resented having to write. Not that any of them were more than a line or two."

"Yes, that is true. I am not trying to say that you could not have acted differently. I wish you had. But when I was upset about it, Jane told me I should consider what you were experiencing. You had Georgiana to tend to, and your own disappointed hopes. I never gave credence to it. For all I know, there was a lady you were fond of, who you hoped to mar—"

"No," he interrupted her to say, "there was no one."

Elizabeth smiled at him. It was oddly reassuring to know that, whatever else he had given up by marrying her, it was not another lady for whom he had had a *tendre*.

"But do you understand what I mean? I expected very little," she said.

"And that was certainly all I gave you. I cannot, and will not, think of those months without disgust, at myself alone, for giving so little thought to what you were thinking or feeling. You deserved better from me."

Elizabeth placed a hand on his face. It was a caress of sorts and an acknowledgement of his words. He kissed her palm.

"I do not deny that you were at fault, but I did not say anything about how I felt."

"It would not have mattered if you had."

"We do not know that." Elizabeth struggled with what to say. "What I suppose I am thinking is that, perhaps if I had acted a little differently, if I had accounted for how shocking the situation was for you, then maybe things would have unfolded differently. It might have spared us that dreadful morning. I did not try to understand why everyone was so apprehensive, and I allowed myself to be easily offended. I was unhappy, but I never showed it. We cannot know what would have happened had I taken a different approach, adopted a different manner from the very beginning."

She bowed her head, hiding her remembered pain from his view. He caressed her, softly running a hand over her hair. She could almost feel the ache in her heart easing, her spirit lightening as she calmed.

After a moment, she looked at him again, and spoke. "This marriage may not have been what we chose, but we can still perhaps...move forward instead of standing in this place or clinging to the past, which would be horrible. The situation is not going to change. We are not going to become unmarried." Her voice sounded small and tentative to her ears, but her future, and Fitzwilliam's, was in question.

"I would not wish it even were it possible."

Elizabeth smiled, blushing just a little. They were handsome words, if an exaggeration. "Maybe now we can be...friends, husband and wife with a better understanding of each other and...more trust."

"You are too generous, but yes, that is what I hope for."

Elizabeth slipped her hand from his and put her arms around his torso, laying her head on his shoulder. She had the sensation of breathing easier than she had in weeks, months even. *It will be well. Truly, now, everything will be well.*

Chapter 42

*E*lizabeth was a marvel. That she could forgive him and even seek to lessen his guilt and self-reproach was extraordinary.

How could I have not seen how fortunate I was for all those months?

The feeling of having her so close to him, and the promise of a new beginning, made Darcy happier than he knew he had a right to be. But part of him felt like crying. He understood her last words well enough. She wanted them to trust each other, to be a true husband and wife, and to have a good marriage—but she did not love him. He had considered telling her of his feelings, but to do so now would be wrong. She had given him so much, and he could not, even implicitly, suggest she must also give him her love.

After a minute, Elizabeth sat back, withdrew her arms from about his body and slipped her hands into his. "I have to admit that I am a little afraid." She laughed, short and nervous. "I used to think I had a prodigious amount of courage—ready to face any attempt to intimidate me—but I think I over-estimated it."

"The way you have conducted yourself since the day we met tells me you have not only a great deal of courage, but also intelligence and sense. I told Georgiana she could do no better than to take you as a model of the woman she should be."

This made Elizabeth laugh again, and she shook her head. "I am sure there are far worthier examples for her to follow. But I am… apprehensive. So much has changed, even in the last half day, let alone the last month or two."

"Trust me," he implored. "I promise you will not regret it."

She stared at him for a long moment. "I have always wished for a marriage such as the Gardiners have. They are the best of friends, as well as husband and wife and parents."

"That is what I want for us." He wished he knew the words to make her believe him.

"I have to admit that, in the early months, I was afraid of being whoever it is that I am, certain I had to guard every action, become a wife and mistress and sister you could respect, and who you would not always despise. Even now, I am afraid I do not know how I am supposed to be."

"I want you to be yourself. Elizabeth Darcy, Elizabeth Bennet Darcy. Do you remember that day in London, when Jane first came to see you? When Tom and I entered the room, you were laughing like I do not believe I have ever seen you laugh. I want you to be able to do that with me. And, Elizabeth, I have seen who you really are—your curiosity and your kindness." He caressed the side of her face, and at last, she met and held his eye. "You do not have to pretend to be someone you think you should be. I am confident, extremely confident, that the person you are is more than worthy of being Mrs Darcy. And most of all, I want you to be happy."

At length, Elizabeth nodded and smiled faintly. "I would like that. I am not formed for unhappiness." She laughed, and this time the sound was lighter. Her voice had just enough teasing in it to be noticeable, and it eased his heart. "At least I do not think I am."

Darcy smiled in return, and, when she leaned just slightly towards him, he very gladly opened his arms to allow her entry. They sat, embracing each other silently, for several very long, very peaceful minutes.

WHEN THEY SEPARATED, ELIZABETH SMILED AT HIM, PREPARED TO take her leave to return to her room so that she could dress and get on with the day. Darcy's words stopped her.

"Elizabeth," he called, "what changed? It could not be just that I was missing."

Elizabeth looked off to the side, her eyes unfocused for a moment before she explained. "It was. In part, at least. After Lady Romsley's ball—Was that really only three weeks ago? It feels so much longer. But I suppose it was before that. I could see you were altered, and I began to feel we could be comfortable together. It was easier to believe that was possible once I saw my sister and the Gardiners, and once I began to accept it was what you wanted."

She hesitated, and to Darcy her countenance seemed to show a measure of apology. In a moment, she told him about her last conversation with Mrs Gardiner and accepting that she had to find the courage to try again.

"Yesterday," Elizabeth said, her voice trembling, "when it started to storm, I was worried—more than I could account for—long before Hudson told us about your horse. After he told us, while we waited for news, I…I understood something about myself."

"What?" Darcy whispered.

Elizabeth's eyes fell, and she took one of Darcy's hands in hers. "I told myself long ago that I had to guard my heart. I could not expect you or Georgiana or anyone I met in my new life to care about me, and so I would not let myself care about any of you."

He could only feel wretched to hear her admit this.

"It was a foolish decision, and it prevented me from seeing any good in other people, and even from trusting you once everything began to change. And I realised I could never be happy if I did not allow myself to care."

He caressed her cheek and smiled. *Perhaps in time I shall have her love. It would make her happy to love her husband, as long as he is worthy of her. I shall simply have to show her that she is more important to me than anyone or anything else and…and what? How does one convince a lady such as Elizabeth to love them?* "How was Georgiana?"

"Very worried about you, I believe."

"How was she towards you?"

Elizabeth hesitated.

"I do wish you would tell me." He spoke gently, but it was impossible to keep a hint of his frustration from his voice.

Elizabeth nodded and pressed his hand. "I know, and I shall. We have a great deal to talk about, but perhaps we need not do it all today?"

"If that is your wish."

"Georgiana might be awake by now. She would like to see you and reassure herself that you are truly well."

Darcy nodded although he did not speak.

"I shall go down and talk to Mrs Reynolds. I have been using the rose morning room since the refurbishment of my sitting room is not yet finished."

"I shall see Georgiana and join you when I can."

Elizabeth leaned forward just an inch or so and it was all the invitation he needed to do likewise. Slowly, thus, they moved until their lips met, and they shared a soft kiss.

THE BROTHER AND SISTER SHARED A BRIEF, LIGHT EMBRACE BEFORE sitting down together.

"Did you sleep well?" Fitzwilliam asked.

Georgiana nodded. "And you? I hope that you were able to rest. You are not ill or injured?"

Her brother shook his head. "I am perfectly well. I would not wish to repeat yesterday's experience, but I have taken no harm from it."

His words brought her some comfort. Georgiana could not look at him knowing how awful she had been of late. She had thought perfectly dreadful things about him. She suspected she had said some of them, too, but could not recollect which or how often. She knew that she ought not to have harboured, let alone voiced, disrespectful or cruel feelings towards him, but she had been so angry. He and Tom were treating her very harshly, and she wished they could extend some understanding and compassion for what she had had to contend with since the summer.

But last night had been awfully frightening. In her heart, she had known that Fitzwilliam would be well, but even the thought that something evil might have befallen him had left her feeling almost completely undone.

It was even possible, just perhaps, that she had not been entirely fair regarding Elizabeth. She could not like her, but Fitzwilliam wanted her to be more accepting of Elizabeth, and, for his sake, she supposed she could try.

Georgiana glanced at him, then lowered her head again. "I am glad to hear it. It was very upsetting yesterday."

"I am perfectly well."

Georgiana furrowed her brow. "Elizabeth was worried, too. I think." She lifted her chin and looked at him, waiting for his reaction. A smile, whose meaning she did not understand, flickered across his face.

"Yes, of course she was."

Georgiana nodded, but said nothing further.

It was a moment before Fitzwilliam asked, "What have you been doing?"

His question alarmed Georgiana. Was she supposed to be studying? It had not entered her mind to attend to her books. "I am still very tired, I own, and have a bit of the headache. From not sleeping, I suppose."

"Of course, you are tired. We all are today. You should rest until dinner."

Her brother saw the book she was reading. It was one of the novels Georgiana had been given for her birthday. He asked her about it, and they spent an agreeable half an hour discussing the book. Georgiana had not been so easy in his company in months and prayed that it was the beginning of a better time for them, one in which, at last, there would be less discomfort and discord.

DARCY JOINED ELIZABETH JUST AS MRS REYNOLDS WAS LEAVING.

"Is everything well?" he asked. "What news does Mrs Reynolds have?"

"She has not heard of anyone being seriously injured or of any serious damage from the storm."

"Good."

"Georgiana was well?" Elizabeth glanced at him, but found something of interest in the hem of her wrap.

"Yes. She will rest until dinner. Perhaps you should as well."

His hand reached out, almost of its own accord, and he touched her cheek, his fingers tracing the shape of her jaw. Being free to do so, after so many weeks of wishing he could, but knowing he should not, was wonderful. That his action seemed to calm Elizabeth made him especially glad.

"I doubt I could if I tried. It is best to get on with the day, what is left of it."

Feeling disinclined to part, they decided to tour the picture gallery which contained family portraits. Darcy told her stories he knew about this ancestor or that, and about how much he had hated sitting for the portrait which had been done of him when he came of age. He realised they needed to have her likeness done as well, insisting that it was absolutely necessary when she demurred. It was a very companionable and diverting way to pass the time.

Dinner was a quiet affair. They spoke of the likely delay in Horatia Darcy's arrival, as well as the news that had come in from the neighbourhood regarding storm damage. Georgiana watched and listened, but said little.

After tea, Georgiana said good night as soon as she could.

Once they were alone, Elizabeth went to the window. Darcy joined her. It was already growing dark.

"I think it is snowing."

Darcy glanced outside, but preferred to watch her. "Just lightly."

Elizabeth admitted that she could not remember what he said about where he had passed the night and asked him to tell her again.

He did, assuring her that he had never been in any danger. "I was not comfortable, but I was safe."

"I was so worried. I remember standing by this very window, wishing there were some way to know you were safe. You cannot imagine."

"I think I can."

Her eyebrows arched in silent question.

"I can imagine how I would feel if it were you missing. I would be frantic."

A smile which could only be called mischievous appeared on her face despite her best attempts to prevent it from forming. He found it charming.

"Would you do something terribly romantic, but very foolhardy, and rush out despite the dark and the storm to try to find me?"

Darcy was unaccustomed to being teased by her and did not know how to respond. "I would be sorely tempted to."

Elizabeth giggled. "I apologise. I was teasing, and I shall blame my tiredness. I would hope that you would have more sense than to do something so imprudent, although I must own, I wanted to. Fortunately, almost as soon as dawn broke, Hudson came to tell us you were on your way home. It was such a relief."

He wrapped his arms around her waist, and they looked out into the night, each lost in their own thoughts. It was tranquil, so much so that at least one of them was in very great danger of falling asleep. When Elizabeth failed to stifle a yawn, he escorted her to the door, and once there, kissed her hand.

"I shall have a word with Hudson before retiring," he said. "You go on. I shall see you in the morning."

Elizabeth smiled at him and squeezed his hand. "Sleep well."

GEORGIANA DID NOT SEE HER BROTHER AND ELIZABETH AGAIN UNTIL breakfast. She remained silent, contemplating the step she must take while they chatted. Towards the end of the meal, Fitzwilliam informed Elizabeth and Georgiana that Horatia would arrive that day and they could expect to see her on the morrow.

"Georgiana, we should meet in my study as soon as you are ready. It is time to resume your work."

"Yes, Brother." After a momentary pause, she said, stumbling over her words, "I-I wonder if I might speak with...with b-both of you first."

Georgiana saw him exchange a look with Elizabeth, but would not admit they seemed surprised and wary. She could not, not if she wanted to keep her composure during the upcoming interview.

"Of course, Georgiana."

They went into a small parlour. Once there, Fitzwilliam and Elizabeth stood together, faced Georgiana and waited. Georgiana stood with her chin so low it almost touched her chest. It was easier that way. She had spent a great deal of time the night before and that morning thinking about the situation in which she found herself. She was not happy, not with the constant discord with her brother, Tom, and the rest of her family. She accepted that Elizabeth was now part of that family, and knew she would have to make peace with Elizabeth if she wanted to be on easier terms with Fitzwilliam, Tom, and her aunt and uncle. It would also be necessary if she were to avoid living under the strictest of guards until the day she married— although how she would ever get out into society in order to decide whom she wanted to marry if she was imprisoned forever she did not know. In short, it was in her best interest to apologise to Elizabeth. She took two or three deep breaths before launching into her speech.

"I wanted to say to Elizabeth that I regret that you and my brother had to marry. I know you have put a great effort into learning your duties and being a good wife, and I was not as welcoming as I should have been. I hope that now we can…begin anew."

Georgiana glanced at her companions. She did not know what she expected to see on their faces, but both of them looked at her as though expecting her to say more. Tom and Fitzwilliam had told her so many times that she should be grateful to Elizabeth, and that she had to acknowledge that she had not been fair to Elizabeth, and on and on, so her brother at least must be pleased she had finally done so. Now everything could return to the way it should be. Elizabeth would be there, but now that everyone understood that Georgiana did not like her, and that that would not change, Elizabeth would stop expecting them to be on friendly terms, and they could all go on with their lives in a much more agreeable manner.

After a moment her brother asked, "And are you sorry, Georgiana, for the way you have treated Elizabeth?"

Georgiana did not fully understand what he was asking. She had said what they wanted her to, had she not? "Y-yes." She wished she had managed to sound more convincing.

Fitzwilliam sighed and shook his head.

"Are you truly?" There was not a hint of kindness in Elizabeth's expression. "I am afraid I find myself doubting your sincerity. You have shown nothing but contempt for me unless you were required to do better because someone else was with us. Even as recently as two days ago, as we sat in the withdrawing room, not knowing when or even if we would see your brother alive again, you could say nothing kind to me.

"I have often wondered if you blame me for intervening that night in Ramsgate. Perhaps in your heart you wish you had been able to elope with Wickham."

"No!" Georgiana's cheeks burned, both because of what Elizabeth said and how she said it.

"Why then do you have such antipathy towards me? I have never understood it. I know very well that you and many others have thought I did not deserve to be Mrs Darcy, but you have always treated me with such antagonism, such contempt—disgust even—far more than I could explain to myself. Do you understand it?"

Georgiana bit her lower lip, holding it between her teeth, to prevent it from trembling. She would not look at Elizabeth or even Fitzwilliam. She could not, not while being confronted with Elizabeth's outrageous questioning. She had no answers and could only hope that her brother would intervene.

When a full minute had passed in silence, Elizabeth said, "I am afraid that until you say or show me that you do understand what prompted your terrible behaviour towards me, I cannot trust that you are sincere in your desire for us to have a better relationship, and I cannot trust that it will not happen again. I am sorry."

When Elizabeth's tone changed, Georgiana peeked at her to see that she was now facing Fitzwilliam.

"I am sorry," Elizabeth repeated, sounding far kinder, even sincere.

Her brother nodded and smiled at his wife, touching her arm in what looked like a caress. It was disgusting that that was Elizabeth's reward for speaking so meanly to her. Georgiana did not blame her brother. She blamed Elizabeth for casting some sort of spell over him. Elizabeth was hateful. She had just proven that, but for some reason, Fitzwilliam simply could not see it.

Without looking at Georgiana again, Elizabeth left the room.

Chapter 43

Georgiana threw herself upon a settee and began to cry.

"Georgiana." Darcy sighed, feeling exhausted with the situation.

Without lifting her head more than was necessary to be heard, Georgiana cried, "You heard her! She will not accept my apology!"

"What apology?" He spoke sternly, which had the effect of halting Georgiana's tears. A little less harshly, he went on. "Self-pity will do you no good. You said you were not as welcoming as you could have been. There was no expression of regret for everything you have done, and what you have done went far beyond not being welcoming."

Darcy took a deep breath, seeking to cool his anger. When he spoke again, his voice remained firm, but his temper was moderated. "Georgiana, I think the best I can do for you at the moment is to tell you some of my own experience. I hope it will help you to understand how you have erred, and what you will have to do if you truly wish to improve the conditions under which you—all of us—are forced to live."

It took a few moments and he had to say her name again, but at last Georgiana sat properly, and, he prayed, was prepared to listen. Darcy spoke at length of the ways he had failed during the early months of his marriage. He spoke of selfishness and responsibility and arrogance and character. Georgiana said nothing, but at least gave the appearance of attention.

When he could think of nothing more to say, he sent her to her books and went to find Elizabeth. She was sitting in the rose parlour, a handkerchief in one hand. Going to her side, Darcy saw that her eyes were red and a little puffy, although her cheeks were dry. The look she gave him was not confident, and he imagined she feared he would be upset with her, so the first words out of his mouth were ones of reassurance. She made him relate the whole of his interview with Georgiana. He again apologised for not seeing how his sister was behaving towards her sooner, and she again apologised for not being more open with him earlier.

"Will you tell me now what she has done and said to you?"

Elizabeth nodded, and after a sad, quiet laugh, started by saying, "I had hoped to be a sister to Georgiana, and that she could be a sister to me. I thought that, because I knew what she had experienced in Ramsgate, I could help her, and at the same time, I would be so much easier if I had a friend here. My father had forbidden Jane to come with me, even if you would have allowed it, and I was used to having my sisters about. But soon after we came into Derbyshire, I knew my hopes would be unanswered. Every time I asked Georgiana if she would like to do something together, she ignored me, or said she had no wish to be in my company."

"That morning in December, what happened?"

Elizabeth averted her eyes, and an expression which showed the anger and pain that had led her to speak so candidly to him flashed across her face, as did one of regret. He waited as patiently as he could until she was prepared to speak.

"You have to understand that I hoped, all along, that if I showed you, Georgiana, everyone in your family, that I would do everything I could to be a good wife and mistress—and sister— that, with time, you would learn to accept me and perhaps even…like me."

"Eliz—" Darcy stopped because Elizabeth shook her head and pressed his hand.

"When the Fitzwilliams were here, it seemed as though everything was improving. Their visit, Christmas, it was…pleasant. I thought perhaps everything I hoped for was coming true, and sooner than I had dreamt it would."

She told him about overhearing him discussing Miss Haddon's lack of suitability as a bride with Tom, and Darcy saying that he never would have considered her. "You agreed that she has far more to recommend her than I ever did. You might have said more, I do not know, but I had heard enough to tell me that it was ridiculous of me to think you would ever accept me, or cease to think of me as an evil."

"I do not think that!"

"I know."

He accepted her reassurances with some reluctance.

She went on to tell him that she had retained a little optimism, and, seeking a sign that she was right to hope, she had, unfortunately, asked Georgiana to tour the rooms she planned to redecorate, "While your family was here, she had been quite nice to me, and I wanted to believe it was more than pretence." Two bright pink spots appeared on her cheeks.

"What did she say to you?"

"That if I thought she or you or anyone else liked me, I was mistaken. You were all pretending to do so, just as we had known would be necessary in order to make everyone believe ours was a marriage of choice, not need. I would never belong. She had no interest in spending time with me, as I have said." She sighed and shook her head. "I do not believe her words would have affected me so severely if she had not voiced my own fears. You know what happened after that. I was angry, but most of all I was disappointed, and every morsel of optimism I had was gone."

Darcy was angry with himself and Georgiana and again apologised.

"It is in the past. That day and every other slight, even what happened when you were missing. I admit her words that night caused me a little pang, but only a little. She cannot affect me the way she did in the winter. Now," she said in a much brighter tone, "I am, dare I say it, full of hope and optimism for the future. I have learnt a great deal about myself these last few weeks, and I trust I shall put my new knowledge to good use, and we shall both benefit from it."

"Shall we?"

"Yes! I am determined to be happy, and I would not be a very nice person if I could be happy when you were not, so you will have to resolve to be happy as well."

He looked at her hand, so small in his, almost undone by the mere thought that she was offering him so much, and the knowledge that he wanted yet more. *Perhaps, in time, she who is so caring might come to love me as I do her.*

AFTER DINNER, DARCY TOLD ELIZABETH AND GEORGIANA THAT Horatia would call the next morning.

"She will have heard about my mishap. She likes to know the news of the neighbourhood, as she calls it, and has a housekeeper who is happy to collect and supply it."

Elizabeth chuckled. "My mother is the same way."

"Ah." He never would have thought to compare the ways in which Mrs Bennet could be like any of his relations. It might help him to learn to tolerate being in her company, something he was determined to do. "I shall explain the situation to Horatia. I do not believe either of you need be present."

"Oh, please do not tell her!" Georgiana cried. "Please! It will be horrible. I cannot bear for her to know! She will never let me forget. I-I promise to do whatever you want, I will study—" A sob prevented her from saying more, and tears ran down her cheeks as she kept her imploring eyes on him.

When she stopped speaking, Darcy took a moment to think about his response. He was not insensible to his sister's distress, but they could not go on as they had been. With each word or act of contempt Georgiana aimed at Elizabeth, it was more and more unlikely they would ever become comfortable together, let alone learn to love each other. It would always be a source of discontent for Elizabeth, for him, and even possibly in time for his sister. "I am sorry, Georgiana, but I do not believe you have left me any choice. There is no one else

I trust who can undertake the task of watching you. After everything that has happened, the person responsible for you must know what you are capable of doing."

Georgiana's face crumpled, and her chin quivered. She made an inarticulate noise of wretchedness and fled the room.

Darcy sank into the sofa and closed his eyes. He felt a gentle hand on his arm and Elizabeth's presence by his side.

He sighed and looked at her. "Did I make the right choice?"

Elizabeth moved closer to him. "Yes, I believe so."

He held her as she rested her head on his shoulder. After some minutes of silence, she stood, tugging at his hand to encourage him to do likewise.

"Come. We have been entirely too serious, and I am afraid that to be so solemn so close to the end of the day will only guarantee a very poor night's sleep. I shall play for you."

At the pianoforte, she bade him sit beside her. "What would you like to hear? You know my talent is meagre, so do choose wisely if you wish to be entertained."

She smiled so archly, and with just a trace of pleading in her eyes, that he was soon smiling in return. Tomorrow would be a taxing day, and they might be able to face it better for having an hour or two of cheerfulness tonight.

HORATIA BUSTLED INTO THE ROOM AND WENT IMMEDIATELY TO Elizabeth's side, her voice drowning out that of Hudson, as he attempted to announce her arrival.

"Oh you poor girl!" Horatia sat and began to pat Elizabeth's hand. "You must have been frantic with worry. I can see that my nephew is well, and I received many assurances that he was, or you may be sure I would have come to the house yesterday upon my arrival, regardless of my fatigue."

"I was worried, too," Georgiana said.

Jealous even of this, Darcy thought, but held his tongue.

Horatia huffed. "I have lost a brother, and I have lost a husband, and so I speak from experience, Georgiana. Unless he is very disagreeable, it is far worse to lose a husband. Now, Fitzwilliam, you must tell me what happened."

Darcy did what he could to satisfy his aunt's curiosity. This way she would have the facts, and not just gossip upon which to draw when she inevitably wrote to his relations about his mishap.

Once Horatia had all the information she required, he invited her to go into his study for a private conversation. "Georgiana, I believe it would be best if you returned to your rooms. I shall send for you if you are needed."

Georgiana stood, curtseyed, and left without speaking.

Elizabeth excused herself, which resulted in Horatia turning a startled expression on her nephew. "What in heaven's name is the matter?"

Forgoing a removal to his study, and as delicately as he could, Darcy explained the events of the last nine months. Horatia's shock was great.

"Elope? With George Wickham? Georgiana was going to elope with the steward's son?"

When Darcy admitted that the early months of his marriage had been difficult, she huffed and proclaimed, "Well naturally they were! And here all of us were thinking you had lost your head over a pretty face!"

There was more still to dismay Horatia when Darcy laid before her everything he knew about Georgiana's treatment of Elizabeth.

"Lied? She lied about your wife, and said all those dreadful—? Treated your wife—? She never did!"

"Yes, I am afraid she did." He went on to explain that he and Tom were searching for a new companion for Georgiana, and that they did not believe it was wise for his sister to remain in town. "Elizabeth and I must return to London, and there are few we would trust to ensure Georgiana behaves appropriately until more permanent arrangements can be made. I hope we can rely on you."

"Of course, you may," Horatia said. "There will be none of that sort of thing while I am in charge of her!"

Darcy impressed upon her the necessity of secrecy and answered a great many questions.

When she was satisfied, she announced that she would speak to

Elizabeth. "She can give me a lady's view of Georgiana's behaviour, which, think what you like Fitzwilliam, is crucial in such cases. Oh, that poor, poor girl! What she has been through, having to marry— And all of us— Well, the less said about that, the better."

Darcy could only shake his head in wonder knowing that the combination of his mishap and learning the truth about Georgiana had turned Horatia into Elizabeth's greatest champion—apart from himself—for better or worse.

THE EASTER HOLIDAY WAS CELEBRATED AS IT CUSTOMARILY WAS. THE weather was not conducive to outdoor activity, although they did make it to church. Georgiana kept to herself and said little when with her brother and Elizabeth. Not that Fitzwilliam noticed or cared. He was too much occupied with Elizabeth. They did who-knew-what in the house, and, when the weather improved, they made a few calls, and once went into Lambton to enjoy what diversion it could offer. They talked about what they did and what they wanted to do ceaselessly.

In her own way, Georgiana was pleased for her brother. She did not understand why he wished to be friends with Elizabeth, but it was just as well someone at Pemberley was happy, because she could not be. She attended to her books and remained as silent as she could, afraid of offending Elizabeth, and thus angering Fitzwilliam. Her outward manner towards Elizabeth may have improved, but days of listening to Horatia lecture her, and having to witness Elizabeth's good cheer while she remained miserable, only added to Georgiana's dislike.

She was taken aback one day after dinner when she heard Elizabeth say her name. She and Fitzwilliam had been talking about visiting tenants and whether Darcy should go with her or attend to his estate business. Elizabeth had teased him, which was shocking enough, but her brother, rather than being upset, laughed!

"No more of that, if you please, Mrs Darcy," he said.

"Very well, sir. Now, I believe you were going to write a letter, and so was I. Perhaps Georgiana might like to play while we do. Music would sound much better than the scratching of our pens."

This was a very pleasant surprise for Georgiana. It had been weeks since she was allowed her music, except for a short time on her birthday.

Fitzwilliam asked, "Would you care to play for us, Georgiana?"

"I would." She nodded like a fool, but it was so unexpected and pleasing that she could not help it.

"Then you may. Elizabeth, Aunt Horry, and I have seen that you are doing as we asked in other regards, and we agreed that you have earned this. For now, you will be restricted to playing after dinner and for one hour during the morning."

"Thank you! Thank you, Elizabeth," she added, quietly and tentatively, knowing it would please her brother.

Elizabeth glanced at her and nodded, smiling faintly—as did Georgiana—before turning to her letter. Georgiana did not care about Elizabeth's dismissiveness; she even preferred it to Elizabeth's earlier attempts to befriend her. She could no longer be bothered trying to make out her brother's odd behaviour. All that mattered at that moment was music, and the thought that Fitzwilliam had come to understand that he should be kinder to her. If it was Aunt Horry's doing, she would bless her every day for the next year.

Chapter 44

The following day, Elizabeth received letters from Jane, Rebecca, and Miss Haddon. She shared the little news they contained with Darcy while they took a walk, and proposed inviting Miss Haddon to Pemberley for a week or two in the summer. "If it is possible. I do not know what we shall do, or where we shall be."

"It is a splendid idea, if you will enjoy it."

"I would."

Darcy directed them to a bench, and took Elizabeth's hand in his, staring at it for a moment while he played with her wedding ring. "I have imagined that part of our time after the Season would be occupied visiting Hertfordshire. You said last month that you did not wish to visit your family. Was it because of me? Are you afraid that I shall behave as dreadfully as I did last summer?"

Elizabeth shook her head, and, after almost a full minute had passed, admitted, "I am concerned about how my sisters and mother will behave. You will not be comfortable, and I cannot like that. But I do not anticipate such a visit because of, well, because of my father.

You would not know it, but people have long spoken of me as my father's favourite."

This surprised him, but he remained silent, seeing how difficult it was for Elizabeth to talk about Mr Bennet.

"I had always thought it was true. I am certainly not my mother's favourite. Her behaviour made that plain when you were at Longbourn. It was pleasant to think I was my father's. That changed last summer, the very night you and I met."

"Are you saying that your relationship with your father suffered because of what you did for Georgiana?"

Elizabeth, with some reluctance, nodded. "I do not blame Georgiana, and you should not either. My father alone is responsible for his actions." She spoke for some time before saying, "He felt I should have left Georgiana to her fate. I could not have done so, regardless of everything that has happened since then. Even should Georgiana and I never love each other, or be like sisters, or even friends, I will not ever regret going to her assistance that night."

Her tale of Mr Bennet's anger and dismissiveness shocked and disgusted Darcy. He kissed her hand, not knowing what words would repay her generosity or comfort her about her father.

"He did not feel I had much chance of finding happiness. I would be miserable, and he did nothing to decrease the likelihood that that would be my fate. Jane believes he was simply worried for me, but I do not credit it. I have not heard from him since I left Longbourn— not a letter, not a line added to one of my mother's or sisters' letters. It is almost as though he has dismissed me from his life. Once I became Elizabeth Darcy, I would never again be the Lizzy he knew, and so he would rather forget me altogether."

Darcy doubted that very much. He pulled her to him and encouraged her to rest her head on his shoulder as he held her, seeking to ease her distress. "We cannot avoid them forever," he said after a few minutes.

Elizabeth made a dismissive noise.

"You have agreed to put my errors in the past."

Elizabeth shook her head. "It is not the same. You have sought forgiveness. He has not. You, I must live with. Him, I do not."

She smiled archly, but he would not be put off by her teasing.

"Will you be happy if you do not reconcile with him, if we never go to Longbourn? What about when Jane marries? Do you not wish to see your other sisters and your mother? Is avoiding your father worth—"

"Must you be so logical?" Elizabeth laughed, although the humour was strained. "Very well, Mr Darcy. You have convinced me. We shall visit Longbourn when a good opportunity to do so arises."

He kissed her soundly. "Good! And, before we visit, I would like you to tell me more about your family. It will help me to know them better."

THE REMAINING DAYS OF ELIZABETH AND DARCY'S STAY AT Pemberley passed quickly. The weather became pleasant, and they took the time to enjoy the spring whenever they could. While walking or riding or driving, they talked again about their past, learnt more about each other, and began to plan for the future. Mr Llewellyn returned to the neighbourhood, and he and Miss Pratt came to dinner. Elizabeth enacted her scheme to involve Miss Pratt in the community to allow her to see that she still had value, despite the fall in her fortunes. Georgiana attended to her books and did whatever Darcy required of her. She took no interest in the proposed school or caring for those less fortunate, which Darcy regretted, hoping to leave Pemberley having seen some greater improvement in his sister. Elizabeth was satisfied that Georgiana was being civil. Darcy wanted more.

"What will it take?" he groaned.

"My absence," Elizabeth said.

Darcy looked at her, alarm in his eyes. She met it with a happy smile.

"I do not mean I should go away for good, Fitzwilliam. I meant that Georgiana might benefit from not having to see me for a while. With luck, she will learn that she does not have to dislike me or be envious of me before we return. I think you were correct—and do not expect me to say that very often—when you said Georgiana is jealous. That, along with thinking too well of herself and her place in the world, and too poorly of mine when I was Miss Elizabeth Bennet. I suspect I remind her of last summer, too, and she dislikes it, thus me."

"That is very...perceptive of you," he said, sounding uncertain.

Elizabeth laughed. "Or perhaps I have spent too much time thinking about it! My conversations with Horatia have given me a great deal to think about, and, I shall own, a great deal of time to do so. Your aunt does like to talk!"

They laughed together at that, something they were doing more and more, to their mutual pleasure.

Tom wrote to Darcy, and Rebecca to Elizabeth, to announce that Lord and Lady Romsley and Frederick and Julia Darcy had been informed of Rebecca and Sterling's engagement. By all accounts, neither family was entirely happy.

"Shall we be returning to an epic battle?" Elizabeth asked. "I cannot believe that Frederick is so opposed to the match!"

Darcy greeted this with a shrug. "Frederick has never liked Sterling. Julia will settle him down. She will be satisfied that Rebecca is getting married, and care little to whom."

"How awful!"

"Yes, well, she is hardly the only mother who thinks that way. Lord and Lady Romsley may not like it, but in the end, I believe they will be pleased Sterling is remarrying. They simply need time to accustom themselves to his choice. So, no, my l-dear, I do not believe it will be an epic battle. Perhaps a minor skirmish." He hoped she had not noticed that he almost said love rather than dear. One day, perhaps even soon, he would tell her that he loved her.

The day before Darcy and Elizabeth left Pemberley, Darcy spent as much time with Georgiana as he could. To his delight, she showed none of the anger or stubbornness she had in recent weeks. She readily discussed her progress with her studies and participated willingly, if not eagerly, in deciding what she would do until Tom's arrival. Upon being asked, she admitted that, if she could, she would like to spend more time drawing and painting, something she had not been allowed to do very much in recent weeks. Darcy agreed and also gave her permission to spend more time at the pianoforte, provided their aunt was happy with her progress with her books.

Georgiana thanked him. She looked uncomfortable, and he dreaded what was to come, but waited in silence for her to speak again.

"I wanted to say that...that...I have seen that you and Elizabeth are..."

"Please speak freely, Georgiana."

Georgiana nodded. "I believe you and Elizabeth are...happier."

"Yes, that is true."

Georgiana nodded again. "I am glad. It is a very good thing that you can l-like each other. It would have been upsetting had you and she not been able to...be friends."

"I am very fortunate that Elizabeth is such a kind, sensible woman."

"I-I know that she exerted herself to be a good mistress, and that speaks well of her."

"She has, and it does. Thank you for saying so."

It was something, he told himself. Not much, perhaps, but a little was better than nothing.

ON THE EVE OF DARCY AND ELIZABETH'S DEPARTURE, ELIZABETH found herself reflecting on how much had happened since their arrival less than three weeks earlier. While she would not claim to be perfectly happy, she was far happier than she had believed possible when her marriage began.

Given how this all began, perhaps eight or nine months to reach this point is reasonable. She laughed a little at the thought, but it soon turned into a sigh. *Perhaps in eight or nine months longer I shall truly be able to laugh at how wretchedly our marriage began!*

The pain and disappointment were still too strong for her to see humour in it, but, resolving to be optimistic, she forced herself to remember how much Darcy had changed for her. She truly believed that the seeds of the good man she now saw in him were there all along. He had shown it when, instead of fleeing Ramsgate and leaving the Bennets to suffer from the brewing scandal, he had stayed and done everything he could to ensure that they, along with himself and Georgiana, emerged from it unsullied.

She did not love him in the way that a woman ought to love her husband, and she did not believe that he loved her. It did not hurt her to admit this. In many ways, they hardly knew each other, but they were taking steps to rectify that, spending as much time together as possible. Perhaps one day they would love each other. At the very least, she was pleased with how far they had come, and confident that their relationship would continue to improve.

"In short, Lizzy, you were wrong. Being Mrs Darcy does not mean being unhappy!"

Chapter 45

*E*lizabeth and Darcy's return to London marked what would be a very busy six or seven weeks. Tom came to see them before breakfast the morning after their arrival, bringing with him news that could lessen one source of anxiety for them all. He had found an excellent candidate for Georgiana's companion.

Upon meeting Mrs Annesley the following day, Elizabeth and Darcy's impression was very favourable. Tom and Darcy decided to offer her the position. They arranged a subsequent interview to discuss the particulars of the post and to disclose the tale of Georgiana's failed elopement and her poor behaviour since then. They could not allow Mrs Annesley to accept their offer without fully understanding the circumstances so that she could judge whether she was willing and able to do the job properly.

Mrs Annesley took the news of Georgiana's behaviour calmly. Tom and Darcy explained everything that had happened and what they required of a companion as clearly and unemotionally as they could. Mrs Annesley requested a private audience with Elizabeth, who assured her that Georgiana had not surrendered her virtue to

Wickham, and that, whatever Georgiana's faults, Elizabeth did not believe she would repeat her folly of the previous year.

"She does not need a guard," Elizabeth said, "but she would benefit from having someone to talk to. We hope that someone sensible can help her understand herself and what she has done."

Mrs Annesley requested time to consider their offer, but the next morning they received the happy news that she accepted the post. She would make arrangements to travel to Derbyshire with Tom.

THREE DAYS AFTER THEIR RETURN TO LONDON, DARCY AND Elizabeth went to Fitzwilliam House for a family dinner. It did not take long to realise that Lord and Lady Romsley were not yet reconciled to Sterling's engagement. Neither was Rebecca's father, Tom confided to them; Frederick continued to delay reaching an agreement on the marriage contract. It was wearing on the couple, as evidenced by Sterling's bad mood.

Lady Romsley made plans with Elizabeth to prepare for her presentation and finalise the arrangements for the ball Elizabeth and Darcy were hosting to mark the occasion. "I took the liberty of making an appointment at the dressmakers for Thursday, as I told Elizabeth," Lady Romsley said when Darcy joined them after the separation of the sexes. "And we have much to discuss regarding the ball."

"I am sure I speak for both of us when I say we are very grateful for all your assistance," Darcy said. "After the presentation and ball, perhaps we shall not need to rely on you so much."

Darcy spoke kindly, and his words, combined with those of Elizabeth who echoed his sentiments, succeeded in halting his aunt's fretting.

"It is true that my attention will be needed elsewhere soon." Lady Romsley looked at Sterling and sighed. "Since he has elected to marry a lady who was not born to expect such a position, she will need a great deal of my assistance."

"Oh, really, Mother."

"You know my feelings on this, Sterling. Rebecca is respectable and comes from a good family—none of us would say otherwise—but as the heir to an earldom..." She shook her head. "You could have done much better."

"I think it is a brilliant match for Sterling," Elizabeth announced, startling every person in the room. Her cheeks coloured. "He and Rebecca love each other, and a man ought to love his wife, if he can. Rebecca is kind, thoughtful, intelligent, and I know that she loves Sterling. She will be an excellent wife to him, and they will be very happy."

"I agree with Elizabeth," Darcy said.

Elizabeth turned to look at him and smiled rather brilliantly, in his opinion. Her words about a man loving his wife gave him hope that she would not think it was impertinent of him to admit to loving her. He would have to soon. He came close to blurting out the words when they were in bed together, and that was no way to tell your wife that you loved her for the first time.

"Thank you, Elizabeth." Sterling spoke in an exaggerated tone. "It is always nice to know that one member of your family is happy for you."

"Really, Sterling," his mother said, while his father called him to task. Tom walked over to him and punched his shoulder.

ELIZABETH RECEIVED MANY CALLERS, INCLUDING REBECCA, THE following day. They spoke about Rebecca's engagement and the problems she and Sterling were having with their families.

"Sterling told me what you said to Lady Romsley. Thank you. It is such a comfort to know that you and Fitzwilliam are pleased for us."

"Very pleased. But do not fear Lady Romsley. She has been kind to me, especially knowing that she wished a better sort of wife for her nephew."

"There could be no better wife for my cousin!"

Elizabeth smiled and nodded. She had forgotten herself for the moment. Rebecca did not know the truth about her marriage.

Before parting, they spoke about a party Elizabeth was arranging. Weeks earlier, Darcy had mentioned having the Gardiners to dinner, and, upon their return, the scheme had been revived. Elizabeth was determining whom to invite, knowing that some people would object to meeting her aunt and uncle because of their ties to trade. Rebecca assured Elizabeth that she had no objection to meeting Mr and Mrs Gardiner, and that she would convince Sterling that he felt the same.

"They are your dear aunt and uncle, and that is all I need to know," Rebecca said.

The ladies also arranged that Rebecca would stay at Curzon Street for a week beginning the following Monday.

LATER THAT WEEK, ELIZABETH RECEIVED A NOTE FROM JANE informing her that she was in town and asking if Elizabeth could come to Gracechurch Street. As Elizabeth had left some hours free to do just that, anticipating very good news, she and Darcy arranged to go after breakfast.

Elizabeth and Darcy had no sooner entered Mrs Gardiner's parlour then Jane threw her arms around Elizabeth and cried, "Oh Lizzy, I am so happy!"

"Do come and sit down, Mr Darcy," Mr Gardiner said. "My nieces will be insensible to the rest of us for the next ten minutes."

Mrs Gardiner and Elizabeth laughed. Jane blushed.

Darcy offered his congratulations, adding, "Mr Hawarden is a very fortunate man."

Jane blushed further and smiled.

Elizabeth said, "Go talk to my aunt and uncle, if you please. I would like to hear what Jane has to tell me."

Jane gladly told Elizabeth about Mr Hawarden's proposal and how warmly she had been greeted by his family. Elizabeth rejoiced in her sister's happiness. To be married to a man you loved, and who returned that love, was just what she had wanted for Jane. The couple would marry in September.

"You will be settled at such an easy distance from Pemberley. Everything could not have worked out better!" Elizabeth said.

Darcy asked Jane about her time in Cheshire and said, "Perhaps you will be able to stay at Curzon Street before you leave London. I know that Elizabeth would be happy to have you. We both would."

Elizabeth could have kissed him for such words and would have if they were not surrounded by their relations.

"Thank you. Perhaps in a few weeks. Mrs Linnington and my aunt have so kindly agreed to help me shop for my wedding clothes, and they tell me I must attend to it immediately."

"And Mr Hawarden will need much of your attention, I assume?" Elizabeth teased.

"I suppose he might wish for a little of it."

Elizabeth's joy increased when she saw the four Gardiner children, who ranged in age from five to twelve years old. Spending time with them made her anticipate having a child of her own, and she prayed that she would not have to wait much longer. Whereas once she wanted a child so that she would not be so much alone—and so that Fitzwilliam and his family would see that she was a good wife—now she simply wanted to be a mother and make a family with the man she had married.

Before they left, Mrs Gardiner found a moment to speak privately with Elizabeth.

"My dear niece, I can see that everything is much, much better between you and Mr Darcy. I am so very happy for you!"

"I do not believe that Mr Darcy and I would be how we are now without your wise advice, so thank you, my dear aunt."

On the way home, Darcy asked about Jane's brief stop at Longbourn on the way back to London. Mr Hawarden had wanted to seek Mr Bennet's permission, and Jane had wanted to tell her mother in person about the engagement.

"She said that both my mother and father talked of us visiting. I told her that perhaps we would on our way to Pemberley in June."

Fitzwilliam took her hand in his, pulling it to his mouth for a kiss. "That is a fine idea. I truly believe you will be happier if you can resolve things with your father."

Elizabeth shrugged, but did not disagree.

THE DAY BEFORE THE BEGINNING OF REBECCA'S SOJOURN AT CURZON Street, Sterling came to see Elizabeth and Darcy just before the breakfast hour. He told them that he was uncomfortable with Rebecca not knowing about Ramsgate.

Visibly embarrassed, he explained, "I promised to be honest with her, and she talks about how happy you are, and that you did not allow convention to prevent you from being together, despite anything the family had to say about it."

"And you want her to know the truth," Elizabeth said. She understood. Rebecca's fervent support of their supposed love match often left Elizabeth uncomfortable as well.

"I am glad you understand. You can tell her when she comes to stay with you."

Elizabeth looked at him, her eyes round with surprise. "Me?"

"You know me well enough by now to know that I would make things worse and not better if I do it." The viscount grinned at her.

"You somehow managed to convince her to accept you," Elizabeth retorted.

"She will want to talk to you about it anyway, so you might as well." He leapt to his feet. "Must dash. Until tomorrow." As he reached the door, he turned back to Elizabeth. "Oh, yes, and thank you!"

When Rebecca arrived for her stay, Elizabeth took the earliest opportunity to dispense with the unpleasant task of telling her about Georgiana, Wickham, and all that had followed. Rebecca's shock was severe, and Elizabeth had to reassure her that she and Darcy were happy, even if they had not been at the outset. With such a beginning, the ladies were soon sharing their deepest secrets, from Elizabeth's struggles with Georgiana, to Rebecca's doubts about one day being a countess.

The week of Rebecca's visit passed quickly and was the most enjoyable one Elizabeth had experienced in London. Becoming intimate friends with Rebecca was wonderful. They were very busy with this salon or that party, and although it was invigorating at times, it was also exhausting. Sterling was with them as often as possible, and Elizabeth allowed the engaged couple time alone, which earned her their gratitude and affection.

THE FOLLOWING SUNDAY, REBECCA RETURNED TO HER PARENTS' house. After saying their farewells, Elizabeth and Darcy stood facing each other. Elizabeth put her hands on his waist, and he put his on her neck, his fingers extending to her nape.

"I am very glad that you and Rebecca are such good friends."

Elizabeth smiled. "As am I. You were going to say, 'but…'"

Darcy smiled and silently chuckled. "But I am a selfish being."

Elizabeth grinned. "And?"

"I prefer to have you to myself."

Elizabeth laughed and rested her head on his chest. He wrapped his arms around her, and she felt him sigh. Something was disturbing him, but she did not know what. When she asked, he admitted that he did not always enjoy the many engagements they had, although he understood why it was important that they be seen this year of all years. Elizabeth suspected that there was something more to it. She could only suppose it was anxiety about Georgiana and how she was faring with Mrs Annesley, and that he was hesitant to discuss it as it might upset her.

She gained further insight into his private thoughts a little over a week later. They had had a busy evening, between promenading in the Park with one group of friends, having dinner with another, attending the theatre, then going on to a ball. Elizabeth was in high spirits, and she admitted that, for the most part, she was enjoying the activity of the Season. She liked to meet new people, and although there were the occasional whispers or hints about the gossip that had surrounded their betrothal and marriage, no one was unkind to her. Most people dismissed the speculation as jealousy or disbelief that Darcy had chosen an unknown as his bride, and the few who persisted in believing there was more to it were easy to ignore. Elizabeth even heard a number of people say that marriage agreed with the previously staid Mr Darcy, and it pleased her to feel that she made him happy.

Elizabeth remained energetic and laughed repeatedly in the carriage on the way home as she and Fitzwilliam discussed their various entertainments. It had been a very long day, and, upon reaching the house, they immediately went to their chambers. When they reached the door to Elizabeth's apartment, she made sure that no one would witness her actions before she reached up one hand, curled it around the back of his neck, and pulled him down. The kiss she initiated was deep and passionate and meant to convey a very particular message. She did not know why, but she felt such an overwhelming need to be with him. They had married without love, or even a wish to join their lives together, but now, ten months after meeting, they were more united than she ever would have supposed possible. She could not say how exactly it had happened, but, somehow, they had truly become husband and wife.

It made Elizabeth almost indescribably happy. After the months of darkness in the autumn and winter, to emerge to the promise of a future of friendship and comfort and joy was wonderful. The feeling translated, in part, into a longing for her husband that at times felt like hunger. She needed him and wanted him, and, because it was not wrong to feel this way, she allowed herself to enjoy the experience without restraint.

They lay together afterwards relishing a period of closeness before Fitzwilliam returned to his bedchamber.

"I am so tired," he said after a few minutes.

"Have I kept you up past your bedtime?"

He kissed the top of her head. "The day I choose sleep over being with you, you will know I have gone mad."

Elizabeth laughed.

"The west wing of Pemberley is quite pleasant. If you have to lock me away from the world, make it there. Quinn will, I am certain, remain loyal."

She laughed again. Her husband was not often prone to being silly, and she found his words, combined with his deep, tired voice, excessively amusing.

He kissed her head again. "Laugh like that oh, once an hour or so, my darling Elizabeth, and it will protect me from insanity."

Elizabeth kissed his chin then his lips. She gazed down at him, a smile on her mouth. "I promise to do my very best. I would much prefer to have a husband who is sane."

She rested her head on his chest again, and they fell silent. Fitzwilliam held her as he usually did at such times, often remaining until she fell asleep. She suspected that at times he fell asleep in her bed, stumbling back to his during the night.

This is good, she thought. *This is better than good. We are confi-*

dants and lovers who respect and like each other. It is so much more than I hoped for last summer or even two months ago. We shall be happy, now and forever, because it is what we both want.

It had been very hard for Elizabeth to let herself trust him and try again to make their marriage a good one. She was thankful that she had found the courage to do so. Now, she believed, she had fully destroyed the barriers she had erected to protect herself from disappointment and hurt. She would never need them again.

Darcy gently turned, laying Elizabeth down onto the bed. She smiled at him, and he gave her a soft kiss.

"I am going to fall asleep," he said.

She smiled and slowly ran her fingertips across his cheek, enjoying the slight roughness of the stubble.

He stared at her for minute before lying down next to her, resting with his mouth close to her ear. "Elizabeth, that morning in December, you said that you had been taken away from everyone who loved you and cared about you. You should know—"

"I know that you care," she interjected, keeping her voice soft and reassuring, "that you like me, and do not hate that I am your wife."

"No, Elizabeth, you do not under—I do not only care about or like you, I *love* you. I love you, and I am so, so happy that you are my wife. I could not imagine anyone else making me feel so much or being so...so perfect for me. I wanted you to know that you are loved, and valued, and cherished by me."

She lay, incapable of saying or doing anything.

He kissed her shoulder and said, "I should let you sleep."

His arm started to slip away from her, and she clutched at it. Rolling onto her side, she held onto him, her fingers wrapping around his.

"Stay with me," she managed to gasp. "Stay with me."

Fitzwilliam tightened his hold on her. He said nothing further and, after a few minutes, his body relaxed as he fell into sleep.

Chapter 46

$\mathcal{D}$arcy woke up to find that he was still in Elizabeth's bed. Daylight showed at the edge of the curtains. He should return to his bedroom, but he did not want to. It would be so much more pleasant to remain and look at Elizabeth. She was such a beautiful sight, and his heart ached. She was lying on her back with the counterpane pulled up under her arms, and one hand tucked beneath her pillow. She looked peaceful, yet he suspected he had discomposed her with his confession. He could no longer bear to keep his secret, especially as she had asked him two or three times if something was worrying him. He was convinced that it was right to tell her. He had felt so close to her, so connected, and the words were right there, in his mouth, knocking at his teeth demanding freedom. Now he must leave it.

She knows, and if she can love me, she will. She must know it would be safe for her to do so, just as she came to realise that it was safe to trust me.

Oh, how he prayed that one day she would love him, but he accepted that she might never return his feelings with the same ardency. She might love him as one does a dear friend without being able to return the romantic, passionate love he felt for her. One did not love or not love someone because they wished to, not entirely at least, and even if she wanted to return his love, she might not be able to.

Darcy pushed back the blankets. Just as he swung his legs over the edge of the bed, Elizabeth stirred. She yawned and opened her eyes halfway.

"Shh." He kissed her shoulder. "It is still early. Go to sleep again."

Elizabeth rolled onto her side, turning her back to him. Darcy covered her with the blankets, kissed her head, and left.

ELIZABETH'S PRESENTATION AT COURT WENT AS WELL AS COULD BE expected. Lady Romsley was pleased by her performance and reception, and Elizabeth was pleased it was behind her and she could anticipate more pleasurable entertainments for the remainder of their time in town.

Elizabeth and Darcy's ball that night was a great success. Jane was in attendance, along with Mr Hawarden and the Linningtons, and Fitzwilliam made a point of introducing them to his family. The earl and countess did not embrace Jane, but they were polite, and Elizabeth was satisfied.

I am so very fortunate, Elizabeth thought as she and Darcy danced the waltz. *He is a good man. If he had been a lesser one, my lot would be terrible. Everything he has done to make me happy once he understood that I was not! It is no evil thing to have the love of a man such as him, and a man ought to love his wife if he can.* She considered him for a minute. *And a wife ought to love her husband if she can.*

At the start of their journey together, Elizabeth had never expected that love would be a part of it, certainly not romantic love. For so long, it had seemed impossible that even the love of friendship, or that of belonging to the same family, would be possible for them. But now…

A mischievous smile formed on her face as an impertinent thought sprang to mind. *He is also handsome, which a man ought to be if he can manage it. It is no hardship to have the love of such a good-looking man!*

"What makes you smile?"

"I am enjoying myself. Even more than I thought I would."

Darcy smiled a special smile which Elizabeth recognised as one only for her.

The middle of a ball is not the time for such deep thoughts! You cannot make yourself love or not love someone, Elizabeth thought. *I must remember that and let what happens, happen. Not stop it because I am afraid or...untrusting.*

ELIZABETH AND DARCY WERE CAUTIOUSLY RELIEVED WITH TOM'S news when he returned from Derbyshire in early June.

"I am optimistic. It took some time, but Georgiana is becoming more comfortable with Mrs Annesley. My aunt spends time with them, although not so much as to interfere. Mrs Annesley is new to the neighbourhood, however, and Aunt Horry intends to introduce her around, take her to the shops in Lambton, that sort of thing. I believe they were concocting schemes for Georgiana as well. They hope to help her understand the world better—what it can be like for girls who are not as protected and fortunate as she is—but also amuse Georgiana and themselves while the weather is so agreeable."

Darcy accepted this with a slow nod. "I shall be hopeful that when we return to Pemberley, we shall find Georgiana much improved."

They spoke about their plans for a little while. Elizabeth and Darcy would return to Pemberley at the end of the month, after a brief stay in Hertfordshire; it was the most Elizabeth would agree to for their first visit. Tom expected to go into Derbyshire again in a few weeks. He would be busy with his military duties for most of July and August and wished to see Georgiana once again before then.

The Darcys received an unexpected invitation to stay at Netherfield when they went into Hertfordshire. Upon questioning, Jane admitted to Elizabeth that she and Mrs Gardiner had concocted the scheme, and Mrs Linnington readily agreed to it.

"Then you would not need to be concerned with anything," Jane explained. After a pause, she cried, "Oh Lizzy! I know you do not anticipate seeing Papa again, and they were so—when Mr Darcy was there. And at your wedding! You know what I mean."

Elizabeth knew this was as close as Jane could bring herself to criticising their parents and younger sisters.

"Truly, I think you should stay at Netherfield. You will be more comfortable there. This time, at least. I shall talk to Mama and Papa and make them understand. Once this visit is behind you and you and Papa can talk, I hope…that is, I trust…everything will be easier."

It was a kind thought, and after some discussion, Elizabeth and Darcy accepted Mrs Linnington's invitation.

With all her busyness during the early weeks of the month, Elizabeth hardly had time to think, which, with the upcoming visit to Longbourn, was perhaps just as well. She knew if she thought on it overlong, she would be in a fine state of nerves and anger.

Her mood was not improved when she realised one morning that it was a year since she, Jane, and Mr Bennet had gone to Ramsgate. It left her feeling a little low. What had started out as an enjoyable holiday to improve Jane's health had turned into the start of the worst months of Elizabeth's life. But once she sternly told herself several times that everything had turned out well, she began to recover. Soon she would have been to Longbourn, and, one way or another, the visit would be over, and she would no longer have to worry about it. There was still the matter of Georgiana, but Mrs Annesley's letters were promising, and Elizabeth looked forward to a better, if not intimate, relationship with her sister-in-law.

ELIZABETH AND DARCY LEFT LONDON AFTER SPENDING TWO DAYS AT the Ascot races, one with family and one with friends. As much as Elizabeth could not anticipate seeing her father, and was a little anxious about how her mother and younger sisters would behave, she was glad they were finished with the Season; its amusements and busyness were beginning to wear on her, and she knew that Fitzwilliam had long ago tired of it, too.

They planned their departure so that they would reach Netherfield in time for dinner. Their stay would be just two days, upon which time they would travel on to Derbyshire. On the second night of their stay, they would attend a dinner party at Longbourn so that Elizabeth could see more of her former neighbours, as well as her aunt and

uncle Philips. Nothing Elizabeth could do enti~
dation, and Fitzwilliam did his best to comfort ~.
assured him that, whatever happened, she would be we.

"Nothing my family does can take away our happines~
pered before kissing him. She wanted to thank him, to tell
she appreciated and treasured the care he took of her, but lack~
words to say all that she felt. They had travelled so far together f~
the day he took her away from Hertfordshire to today when he was
bringing her back. The life they had made was so important to her,
each day more so than the last.

As they approached her old neighbourhood, her face was impassive, and she only occasionally glanced out of the carriage window. It
was impossible for Elizabeth not to remember the last time she was
on these roads. She had been glad to have the wedding finished,
relieved to know she would not have to see her father again for
months, and afraid, oh so afraid, of what would come next. *That is all
behind you now. We do not go to Longbourn today. Nothing Jane says
to my mother and father will be enough to explain our staying at
Netherfield or not visiting until tomorrow, but I cannot let it
worry me.*

The Linningtons welcomed them warmly. Elizabeth made the
best of the evening, but knew she was not good company. Her
thoughts were on the morrow when they would take breakfast at
Longbourn. Not knowing what else to do, she retired as soon as it
was polite.

As they approached Longbourn house the next morning, Elizabeth
saw that Darcy was again looking at her anxiously. She smiled and
tightened her grip on his hand.

"I have you with me, and so I have no fears."

The family was waiting for them outside, and Elizabeth was
reminded of returning from Ramsgate. She heard her mother's voice
before the carriage stopped. To her surprise, she heard Fitzwilliam's
deep chuckle.

"Your mother is very excited. It is good that we are here. Whatever else may be said, we should remember our visit is bringing your
family pleasure."

Elizabeth nodded and prepared to exit the safety of the carriage.

"Oh Lizzy, my dear girl!" Mrs Bennet exclaimed. "Let me look at you!"

"Let us have a turn, too, Mama!" Lydia cried. "You do look very nice, Lizzy. You are so fortunate to have such pretty things!"

The greetings with Jane, Mary, and Kitty were quieter, and they hardly had time to say words of welcome when Mr Bennet spoke, his tone crisp.

"Come, girls. Come, Mrs Bennet. Let us go into the house. I welcome you, Mr Darcy." Although he looked at Elizabeth, he said nothing to her.

Elizabeth took Darcy's arm, smiled at her sisters as they took their positions behind her—a courtesy she had hardly expected them to adhere to, as they were her sisters and it was just the family—and walked into her childhood home.

They went immediately into breakfast, which was a loud, boisterous affair as most meals were in the Bennet home. Elizabeth sat beside her father, although her attention was on her sisters, who wanted to hear about the Season, Derbyshire, and her life as a married lady. She said enough to satisfy them while also eating her food. Mr Bennet did not speak to her, but she knew that he spent breakfast studying her and looking frequently at Darcy. She promised herself that she would not let her father's behaviour spoil her enjoyment in seeing her mother and sisters again.

After breakfast, Elizabeth had to repeat and expand upon her stories about London. It was a lively conversation, and Mr Bennet, after sitting by himself and watching her for a while, moved closer so that he could better hear what she said. Jane and Darcy sat apart from them; Elizabeth was glad Jane was occupying him.

"You have been very busy, Elizabeth," Mr Bennet said after a few minutes.

"Yes, very. But that is the way of the London Season."

"For those who like to preen and display themselves for other people to gawk at, I suppose it is."

"Oh, Mr Bennet!" his wife cried. "How can you say so? Our Lizzy has been to dinner with dukes and was presented to the queen!"

"My Lizzy had enough sense to care nothing for such things!"

Elizabeth ceased to hear her parents and sisters. Her father had not just disparaged the world in which she now lived, but also her. When he referred to her as 'my Lizzy', she wanted to scream at him and tell him that she was not his and had ceased to be his—not on the day she became Mrs Darcy, but on the day he withdrew his care and support from her when she most needed it.

When Elizabeth saw Darcy walking towards her a moment later, her distress lessened.

"Oh Mr Darcy," Mrs Bennet cried, "you must not mind anything Mr Bennet says. He likes his little jokes, but he means nothing by them."

"Of course, Mrs Bennet. Has Elizabeth told you about her presentation at St James's yet?"

As he spoke, he rested a hand on Elizabeth's back, and she leaned into him, not caring how her father glared at them.

Elizabeth watched with great appreciation the effort Fitzwilliam was making to know her family and his patience with even their silliest behaviour. It made her want to throw her arms around his neck and tell him…something, although she did not know what, exactly. Perhaps how much she admired his strength of character, or how hopeful she was for the future, a sensation she had not expected to feel as lately as March. Or perhaps how much she cared for him, and how that feeling grew each day as she knew him better, and as the pain and fear of the past slipped further and further into history.

When the scheme of an outing arose, Elizabeth was among those championing it. The five sisters and Darcy decided a walk around the gardens would have to do, given the hour and how hot the day had become. They would go into Meryton, something Elizabeth particularly wished to do, the following day.

"Jane," Elizabeth whispered, "will you see that my husband is well-occupied? I think I should speak to my father, and Mr Darcy will be uneasy."

"Of course, Lizzy, if you think it is wise."

"I think I must."

When Elizabeth told Darcy what she proposed to do, he expressed his opposition.

"I have to talk to him, if only to make him see that he must stop staring at us and acting so peevishly. It is distressing to my mother, to say nothing of making you and me uncomfortable. Please, trust me to know what is best."

Although reluctant, he agreed, but only after obtaining her promise to tell him everything that she and her father said to each other.

"I will join you in the gardens soon," she said.

"I do not like it." He pressed a finger to her lips when she opened them to respond. "But I do understand why you must do this."

She kissed his finger. "Go. The sooner I begin, the sooner it shall be over."

Chapter 47

"How kind of you to take the time to visit with your father, Elizabeth Annabelle," Mr Bennet said once they were alone. "Ten months it has been, or near enough."

She retorted, "Ten months, and you have said nothing to me. Not a letter or a note, not a line added to one of my sisters' or mother's letters, to say nothing of your behaviour to me before I left Longbourn. It seemed to me, and would to any reasonable person, that you had no interest in seeing me. Was I to think otherwise?"

"I would have been very happy to see my daughter, but you are correct. I have no interest in seeing Mrs Darcy."

"Shall I leave?" Elizabeth's tone was even, but angry. "I am Mrs Elizabeth Darcy, formerly Elizabeth Bennet. You cannot separate the two."

Mr Bennet scoffed. "What has happened to you, Elizabeth? Is it the excitement of being rich and of having whatever you take a fancy to? Fine clothes, jewels..."

Elizabeth's cheeks burned with indignation. "I should not have expected better of you. Why were you so angry with me, why did you blame me, act as though I had done something so terrible? How can you justify the way you treated me last summer, and even today?"

"You should not have helped her. She was a stranger to you, and she should have remained thus. If you had not acted so—"

"If all you have to say is what you did then, I have no interest in hearing it. I saw a young girl, alone and afraid, and I did the only thing I could do. That she was unknown to me was irrelevant. I helped her the way I pray someone would help Lydia or Kitty or Mary if they were in peril."

Mr Bennet threw up his hands.

"Afterwards, when we decided that Mr Darcy and I would marry, why did you treat me so-so cruelly?"

Mr Bennet stood, prepared to walk away from her.

"Why, Papa? You owe me an explanation."

"I owe you an explanation?"

"Yes, you do."

He made an angry, almost disgusted noise. "You, through your own stupid, impulsive actions had to marry that man. I know what people like him are like. Rich and high-born, believing they are better than everyone else, not caring a thing about anyone or anything other than their own pleasure. It was obvious to me that you would have to become one of them, or you would be crushed by living with him. Either way, I lost my daughter through no fault of my own."

His ignorance—did he truly think there were no kind, decent people among the *ton?*—and small-mindedness were disgusting to Elizabeth.

"Why did you refuse to allow the Gardiners to come to Long-bourn? Why did you decide that no one could visit me for six months?"

"As for the second question, you know very well why. How else could I stop your mother's tongue? That man you married would never have allowed her or your sisters to visit. As for the Gardiners, the last thing we needed were two more people in the house. You would have been tempted to tell—"

"I did tell them," Elizabeth interjected. "I wrote to my aunt almost as soon as we returned to Longbourn and begged her for advice. Any assistance I needed, any comfort, I got from them, not from you.

"It was wrong of you. Everything that you did, the way you spoke to me, the way you dismissed me, refusing to allow me to see the Gardiners or have one of my sisters with me, your silence all these months—it was wrong. You made the whole situation so much harder for me and for no good reason."

"Elizabeth—"

She spoke on. "You thought of yourself, never of what I—I was so alone, and instead of offering me consolation or advice, or even the company of someone who could help me through those dreadful early months—and they were terrible—you isolated me. Simply because your world was made more difficult. You did not like it, and so you acted like..." She shook her head. "It does not matter. I will not let you take away my pleasure at seeing my mother and sisters again. I do not believe I can ever forgive you, especially when you will not admit that you were at fault. I shall do my best, for their sakes, but you and I can never be what we once were."

"Are you quite finished?"

Elizabeth turned away from him and prepared to exit the room.

"Do not think I shall ever permit you to talk to me like that again," Mr Bennet said to her back.

Elizabeth turned to look at him. "Do not think I shall ever again be tempted to say more to you than the minimum courtesy requires."

"You are changed, Mrs Darcy. I knew you would be ruined by marriage to that man."

Elizabeth laughed sadly, shook her head and walked out of the room and out of the house. She soon found Jane and Darcy in the gardens. Mary, Kitty, and Lydia had wandered into another part of the grounds. Jane slipped away as Elizabeth joined them.

"I can see from your expression that it did not go well," Darcy said.

Elizabeth shook her head and put her arm through his. "I am glad I had an opportunity to tell him that his behaviour was hurtful. I will try to forgive him for my mother and sisters' sake, or at least tolerate his company. I hope he will treat us with respect. I expect nothing more."

"And I will accept nothing less."

Elizabeth smiled at him, pleased by his defence. "I shall tell you everything when we return to Netherfield. Let us join my sisters for now."

DINNER WAS A QUIET AFFAIR WITH JUST THE FAMILY AND MR AND Mrs Linnington. The Netherfield party left soon afterwards, Elizabeth and Darcy promising to return in time for breakfast.

Fortunately, Mr Bennet spared them his conversation at dinner, and he remained just as quiet at breakfast. Darcy, Elizabeth, and her sisters had an agreeable outing in Meryton. Elizabeth's heart felt full of joy and something she could not name seeing her husband with Mary, Kitty, and Lydia. He was more than polite. He took an interest in them, and she could see how much her sisters liked him. With Jane, it was evident that he was comfortable, and she could foresee a time when he loved Jane as a sister almost as much as she did.

When they returned to Longbourn, Mrs Bennet required a private word with Elizabeth, and they went to her room. Mrs Bennet began to question her, and, despite the great deal of fussing that was involved, Elizabeth knew that her mother was attempting to be kind.

"I know I am not clever like you are, Lizzy, but I have been a married woman for a great many years, and I have had five children. Even you may find my advice worth having."

Elizabeth found that it was not difficult to be patient with her mother after such a long absence. "Of course I would, Mama. I am not certain that I have anything to ask advice about at the moment, however."

Mrs Bennet examined her through narrowed eyes for a moment before sighing. "There is no indication that you are with child?"

"No, Mama."

Mrs Bennet shook her head. "Are you sure? You may not know what to expect."

"I am certain."

Mrs Bennet was very disappointed, and Elizabeth prepared herself to hear a great deal of unwanted advice, and perhaps a few suggestions regarding how she was to blame for the unfortunate situation. She was surprised, therefore, to see that her mother only quietly shook her head.

"Jane assures me that you and Mr Darcy are happy."

"We are."

"My sister Gardiner said that you are, and I know that she and Jane have seen you a great deal more than I have. But we shall not speak of that at the moment."

Elizabeth said a silent prayer of thanks.

Mrs Bennet sighed again. "I do hope you will soon have a child, Lizzy, for your sake. A man wants a child, and a man such as Mr Darcy, with such a fine estate, will want one even more. I pray you are more fortunate than I was and will have sons. You do not know what it is like to know that you are a disappointment to your husband. I would not wish that for any of my girls."

"Mama, please do not fret. Mr Darcy and I are happy even though I am not yet with child. Naturally, I do hope to give him a son, but the situation with Mr Darcy's estate is not the same as it is with Longbourn." Darcy had insisted on explaining the particulars of the marriage settlements, his will, and the disposition of his estate to her.

"Whatever do you mean?"

"Pemberley is not entailed, Mama. Mr Darcy is free to leave it to whomever he likes, and he has assured me that should we only have daughters, our eldest daughter's son will inherit."

Mrs Bennet stared at her. "And should you have no child?"

"Then Mr Darcy's eldest cousin on his father's side will inherit Pemberley. His cousin is a very amiable, very kind gentleman, and he will soon be married to a lovely lady. The marriage settlement is such that I would be independent, and I would be able to take care of you and any of my sisters who remained unwed. With son-in-laws such as Mr Darcy and Mr Hawarden, you need not worry for the future."

"I must say that is a much more sensible way to arrange things. I never could understand why Longbourn is left in such an awkward way, and it is no use trying to explain it to me again. You never have been able to before, and you will not today, and that is the end of it. Are you absolutely certain you understand the situation?"

Elizabeth reassured her mother. After going over it all once more, Mrs Bennet at last seemed satisfied. It did not prevent her from spending a half an hour offering advice on how best to fall with child and several techniques which were supposed to increase the chance of bearing a son.

"For although they did me no good, you might be more fortunate than I was!"

THANKS TO JANE'S INTERFERENCE, THE GUEST LIST FOR THAT EVENING'S dinner party was restricted to particular friends and family; Mrs Bennet had wanted to invite half the neighbourhood, and, as it was, spoke of what she would do when next the Darcys came to Longbourn. Mr Bennet was polite to his guests, but said nothing to Elizabeth and Darcy. Elizabeth saw that he watched them now and again but she chose to ignore him. She and Fitzwilliam remained after everyone else had gone, and, when the time for parting came, Elizabeth warmly embraced her mother and sisters and was able to say with perfect sincerity that she looked forward to making a longer visit in the autumn when they returned for Jane's wedding.

Thursday morning, Elizabeth and Darcy set out for Pemberley. They would be two nights on the road. For the first time, Elizabeth felt a genuine longing to be home.

Pemberley is my home now. I want to be there and see how the gardens look in the summer. I want to wander the grounds with Fitzwilliam and hear how the servants and tenants are. I want to see how the renovations have turned out and visit with Mrs Morris and Mr Llewellyn and Miss Pratt. I am happy to be going home with Fitzwilliam.

Home, where they would together share in the mundane as well as the joy and sorrow that were part of every life. Elizabeth was happy, hopeful, and confident. She smiled without realising it and her heart beat just a little faster.

THE MORNING AFTER THEIR SECOND NIGHT ON THE ROAD, DARCY slipped into Elizabeth's room at the inn, telling Drewe that her mistress would call her when she was needed. Elizabeth was still asleep; he sat down upon the bed, and whispered into her ear. "Happy birthday."

Elizabeth's eyes flew open.

"Shh," Darcy said, "it is only me. Happy birthday, my lo-darling." He did long to call her 'my love' and tell her that he loved her over and over again, but he would not allow himself that pleasure. She might consider it a burden, to be reminded that he loved her when she did not return his sentiments. He kissed her forehead.

Elizabeth made a sleepy, happy noise, and mumbled his name.

"How very unfortunate that we must spend your birthday in a carriage." He brushed aside the stray strands of hair which were across her forehead and cheeks.

Elizabeth smiled, and shook her head. "We shall be home today, which is just what I most want."

"Your birthday should be celebrated. You did so much for me in March. It meant a great deal to me," he admitted. "I knew how little I deserved it, and it showed me what a wonderful woman you are and how fortunate I am that you are my wife."

"Fitzwilliam," Elizabeth whispered.

He gave her a kiss. "I have something for you." He pulled a box from the bedside table where he had placed it upon entering the room. Once she sat up, he put it into her lap.

"Shall I guess?" she asked.

Darcy smiled at the mischief in her eyes. "No. Open it."

Elizabeth gave him a kiss and turned her attention to her gift. She undid the ribbon and opened the box to reveal a necklace of pearls—her birthstone—and sapphires, with a matching pair of earrings. "Oh, how beautiful!"

"Do you really like it? I was not certain, but your aunt and Rebecca thought you would."

"Did you really ask them both?" She giggled.

"I did, and I thank you for not mocking me. I wanted to give you something special."

Elizabeth kissed him again. "It is perfect, and I adore it. Thank you."

In a minute or two, Elizabeth chased him from the room, saying that she would dress quickly so that they could resume their journey home. There, she promised, she would thank him again, and show him how much she appreciated the effort he took to make her birthday begin so pleasurably.

IT WAS CLOSE TO FIVE O'CLOCK BY THE TIME THEIR CARRIAGE CAME to a stop in front of Pemberley house. Elizabeth was so happy to be there that she hardly managed to keep from bouncing up and down in her seat. Georgiana, Tom, and Mrs Annesley were waiting to greet them, and the couple stepped out to words of welcome and birthday wishes.

Georgiana said a shy happy birthday to Elizabeth, and, keeping her eyes lowered, added, "We should go in. It is growing quite hot. Th-there are refreshments waiting in the blue saloon, if you would care for…"

Elizabeth was averse to saying anything directly to Georgiana, too accustomed to receiving her sister-in-law's slights, and not wishing to have the homecoming spoilt. Almost unconsciously, she looked at Mrs Annesley and Tom, as did Darcy.

Tom grinned and nodded.

"I would like something cold to drink," Darcy said slowly. "Elizabeth?"

"Yes. That would be lovely. Mrs Annesley, tell me, how do you find Pemberley?"

GEORGIANA WAS SATISFIED WITH HOW THE DINING PARLOUR LOOKED. It was nicely decorated with flowers, the silver candlesticks she had insisted be moved from the red withdrawing room for the occasion gleamed in the light cast by the beeswax candles, and Elizabeth's favourite china was laid out on the table.

"You did not think a few happy birthdays would be the only way we marked the day, did you, Elizabeth?" Tom said. "Georgiana arranged everything."

"Did you really, Georgiana?" Fitzwilliam asked.

Georgiana did not speak, but she did nod. Her brother's question and Elizabeth's silence were enough to tell her they found it difficult to believe she had done this for Elizabeth.

"She did," Tom insisted. "The menu was planned by Georgiana, although I do know that Mrs Annesley and Mrs Reynolds assisted her with other arrangements."

"Thank you, Georgiana. It was very kind of you." Elizabeth spoke evenly, if not warmly. "This truly is a very agreeable surprise."

Georgiana glanced at her and happened to catch her eye. Elizabeth gave her a quick smile before asking Mrs Annesley about her family. It was, Georgiana supposed, a promising beginning.

WHEN DARCY ENTERED ELIZABETH'S BEDCHAMBER SOME FIVE minutes after she succeeded in banishing her maid, she was pacing, which was unusual. She sighed when she saw him, held out a hand, which he took, and led him towards an armchair, where she insisted he sit.

"Elizabeth?"

She pulled her bottom lip between her teeth and stared at him. It was a moment before she spoke. "There is something I wish to tell you. I have been thinking about it for-for days, I suppose, but now that I can, I do not know how to say it."

"Elizabeth, are you—? Do you think that you—?"

"No, it is not that." She gave a little laugh and smiled broadly. "It is good news, though. At least I believe you will think so." There was a slight pause before she said, "I love you, Fitzwilliam."

Darcy stared at her, hardly knowing if he had heard what he thought he had. It was his fondest wish that she might love him, but he had hardly ever allowed himself to believe she would, and certainly not that she would so soon. To add to that, he was not certain what she meant by it. There were many different ways of loving someone, and he knew she cared about him, even that she cared a great deal about him. But he, whose heart was so full of love for her, wanted a particular type of love.

Elizabeth continued to speak, her voice a soft caress. "I hardly know when I realised that what I felt was love, that I had fallen in love with you…"

Darcy let out a groan of relief, thankfulness, and joy at these words. Taking her face between his hands, he pulled her down onto his lap and kissed her, pouring everything he felt into it. Elizabeth wrapped her arms around his chest and pressed her body into his. They broke apart, but just a little, when she began to smile, a gurgle of laughter escaping.

"I take it that I was right. It makes you happy."

Darcy could hardly reply, so full of emotion was he. Out of habit, he struggled to school his features, and blinked his eyes repeatedly at the tears which, unaccountably to him, formed. He nodded. "I love you," he said, his voice rough. "I love you so much, Elizabeth. I know I do not deserve…"

Elizabeth shook her head as she inched closer to him. "You do, and I do. We both deserve to be happy, and since it is apparent that neither one of us could be happy unless the other was—"

She stopped speaking because it was next to impossible to speak when someone was kissing you as fervently as he kissed her. He did not have the words, not at the moment at any rate, to tell her what he felt, but he could show her.

Chapter 48

Georgiana had been conflicted about Mrs Annesley's arrival. She was growing weary of her aunt's company, yet she expected her new companion would be little different. There would be more lectures about her horrible behaviour, more endless praising of Elizabeth, and another person watching her every move, censuring her every word, and refusing to understand Georgiana's view. She had learnt to want her brother's good opinion, and had tried to create a good impression during their last conversation before he left Pemberley—going so far as to acknowledge Elizabeth's efforts to be a good mistress—but she could not anticipate being urged to like her sister-in-law, or follow her example.

It was therefore surprising to find that Mrs Annesley was rather nice. She listened to her. She asked Georgiana about this and that, and, somehow, Georgiana found herself talking about Ramsgate. It was so good to just talk and talk and know that she could say what-ever she liked and there would be no scolding.

One day, their conversation had ended with her crying on a bench in the gardens. It was because of Elizabeth. Some question or other of

Mrs Annesley's had made Georgiana understand something she had not before. That awful night in Ramsgate, she had been so indescribably relieved that someone who knew what to do had appeared just when she most needed them. Elizabeth had stood between her and Wickham, literally shielding her from him. Elizabeth had held her hand, and she had felt safe and protected, and she had known that everything would be well.

The next time Georgiana was at church, she thanked God for sending Elizabeth to her that day. She could imagine few fates worse than to have married Wickham.

Although she had been reluctant to talk about Ramsgate again, Mrs Annesley encouraged her to do so, claiming a desire to understand what had happened after that night. The feeling of discomfort grew and grew as Mrs Annesley made her talk about what it was like to have Elizabeth as a sister. Mrs Annesley said very little. It was just a sentence now and again, such as when she joked that Elizabeth had learnt so much about every servant, whereas Mrs Annesley expected she would never know, let alone remember, all their names.

Georgiana realised she could not name most of the servants herself, and knew very little about any of them—even Mrs Reynolds who had been there for as long as she could remember.

There was always more. Whenever they went out, they would meet with someone who asked after Elizabeth, and not just to be polite! The servants asked about her, the tenants and neighbours and shopkeepers asked about her. They asked because they liked Elizabeth and knew they could trust her to care about them, and to do well by them.

Could Georgiana not also trust Elizabeth to care for her? Had Elizabeth not shown she cared at Ramsgate and at Longbourn and that dreadful night Fitzwilliam had been missing?

"And how have you repaid her?"

There were so many voices asking that question—Fitzwilliam's, Tom's, her aunts', and, belatedly, her own. The answer was too awful to contemplate, although Georgiana forced herself to do so. Elizabeth had done so much for her, and, in return, she had done so little for Elizabeth. No, the truth was worse than that. She had made the situation so much more difficult for Elizabeth because…

Why?

She did not like Elizabeth, but surely whether or not she liked Elizabeth was immaterial. Not liking her was no excuse for acting as she had.

But then, Georgiana wondered, why had she been so awful?

TOM, DARCY, AND ELIZABETH HAD A LONG CONVERSATION ABOUT Georgiana and her improved demeanour, which, Tom insisted, was genuine.

"I am not saying she has made a complete turnaround, but she is doing well. She has acknowledged to me that she behaved very poorly, and that she wishes to make amends. I cannot say that she will apologise to you today or tomorrow, but I am more hopeful than I have ever been that it will not be very long in coming. Aunt Horry agrees, as she shall readily tell you when next you see her."

When Elizabeth spoke with Mrs Annesley later in the day, she, too, expressed satisfaction with how far Georgiana had progressed. Mrs Annesley explained to Elizabeth that all she had done was listen to Georgiana and ask the occasional question to nudge Georgiana's thoughts along the line she wanted them to go.

When Elizabeth asked what she recommended they do next, she said, "Continue to treat her fairly, without being too harsh or too easy. She is old enough to accept your honest response to her behaviour and your reluctance to trust her. I shall continue to be someone to whom she can speak without fear of censure. Miss Darcy is not a stupid girl, even if some of her actions have suggested otherwise."

"She is very young, is she not?"

"She is, but she will mature. She is spoilt and needs more guidance than many other young ladies her age do, but I believe she has been taught sound principles. She simply needs to remember and act on them. We are making good progress, Mrs Darcy."

Elizabeth did her best to take comfort from Mrs Annesley's words, and for Darcy's sake—as well as her own and Georgiana's— she would keep an open mind.

TWO DAYS AFTER ELIZABETH AND DARCY'S RETURN, TOM DEPARTED, and they settled into a quiet, busy existence. Darcy spent time with his sister each morning, and, on the fifth morning of easy, if banal conversation, he was surprised when Georgiana said, "I-I-I wanted to say that I am sorry that I...about last summer. I apologise for trusting *him*, and for not telling you that he was in Ramsgate."

"Why did you not?"

There was a slight pause before Georgiana spoke again. "Because it was exciting. Because he made me feel like I was not a child any longer. Because he told me what I liked to hear. It was very stupid of me, very foolish, but," she lowered her eyes, but not before he saw them fill with tears, "it was like something from a novel. An adventure. I know that sounds remarkably silly, and it was. I can see that now, but at the time, I did not think about it at all. Mrs Annesley has helped me to understand things, and-and I was so stupid. If Elizabeth had not—" She let out a sob.

Darcy put an arm around her shoulders and kissed her head. He let her cry for several minutes before pressing a handkerchief into her hand.

In as kindly a voice as he could muster, Darcy said, "I am very happy to hear you say this much, Georgiana. I know it can be difficult to admit when you have been wrong. I do not hold you entirely to blame for last summer. I am convinced that Wickham and Mrs Younge used your naïvety to their advantage. However, you must accept your part, just as Tom and I regret whatever part we played."

"I do not understand what you mean."

"Georgiana, Tom and I are responsible for you. It is natural that we would feel that we failed you. We did not see what Mrs Younge was. We let you think too highly of yourself compared to other people. It does not diminish your responsibility, however.

"I am very, very glad Elizabeth was in a position to help you that night. It makes our subsequent treatment of her—yours, mine, our family's—unconscionable. It would have been in any case, but after she had done so much good for us, we owed her our thanks. Instead, I was inconsiderate and unfeeling. I shall not say it was unforgivable, only because she has forgiven me, and we are happy now."

"And I was much worse," Georgiana whispered. "I know I should have been kinder to her even if...even if we could not be friends."

Darcy suspected that Georgiana clung to her antipathy for reasons that were still unknown to her. He would regret it if she truly did dislike Elizabeth, but as long as she was kind and respectful, he would be satisfied.

A moment later, Georgiana said, "She is not what I expected. Everywhere we go, people ask after her. Even here, in the house, she always seems to know what to say and do."

There was a wistfulness in her voice which reminded Darcy of his belief that Georgiana was jealous of Elizabeth. He wondered how much Georgiana compared herself to Elizabeth, and if, in doing so, she found herself wanting. "Elizabeth has an abundance of good sense which she uses well. She is also five years older than you are, and when she and I married, she felt it was her responsibility to become a good mistress. She did not find it easy."

Georgiana nodded. She bit her lower lip and furrowed her brow. "At breakfast, Elizabeth mentioned going to visit your tenants, and making charity calls. D-do you think that...would she take me with her?"

Darcy kissed Georgiana's hand, pressing it gently. "Yes, she would take you with her. It is a fine idea."

Darcy insisted that Georgiana ask Elizabeth herself. When he warned Elizabeth that the request was coming, she greeted the news with equanimity. Georgiana approached Elizabeth after dinner while he watched, ready to intercede if needed.

"Elizabeth, I-I wondered if perhaps, when you go to visit my brother's tenants next, I might go with you? Or-or when you...do things like that. I feel that I should. I could help, and learn what I should do when, one day, I am mistress of an estate. So that I can be a good one."

"If you truly wish to, yes, of course you may. I thought to visit some of the villagers tomorrow, if the weather is agreeable. It might rain, but if it is not too wet, I shall go. There are some tenants I shall wait to see until I can ride. You will enjoy that."

Georgiana nodded. "Thank you."

No more was said of the matter, although Elizabeth and Darcy exchanged hopeful smiles.

The next morning was overcast, but not rainy, and, at an appropriate hour, the ladies departed Pemberley. Georgiana said hardly a word to Elizabeth or to anyone they visited, but Elizabeth much preferred that to her insolence. They made several calls of charity before going to see Miss Pratt. Georgiana acted in much the same way when, two days later, Elizabeth took her to visit several tenants.

They saw a fair bit of Mr Llewellyn at Pemberley during the month of July, and he was very pleased when Elizabeth told him that Esther Haddon was coming to stay for a fortnight at the start of August. Elizabeth sternly lectured herself about becoming a match-maker, yet all she had done was inform Mr Llewellyn of Miss Haddon's visit—she had not invited Miss Haddon because of Mr Llewellyn. And if Elizabeth happened to have a particular need to see him during her friend's visit, or he happened to have a particular reason to call at Pemberley, well, these things could not be helped, could they?

The middle of the month was the anniversary of the day they met. Elizabeth and Darcy briefly discussed it, reminding each other how happy they were, and how little the past mattered in comparison. Seeing Georgiana's distressed looks at breakfast, Elizabeth encouraged Darcy to spend time with her, which he did. It was a sombre day, but was a little improved when, after dinner, Elizabeth insisted they read aloud from a very silly book she had found in London.

It was during one of Elizabeth and Darcy's excursions two or three days later that they spoke about another upcoming anniversary. They had ridden out to a very pretty lake, bringing with them a small picnic.

"It is so beautiful here," Elizabeth said.

"I thought you would like it."

He had removed his jacket, and was sitting beside her, leaning back on his elbows with his long legs stretched in front of him. She had her bonnet off, her face lifted to the sky.

"I have an idea," Fitzwilliam announced. "Next month is another anniversary."

Elizabeth felt very stupid that it took her a moment to understand what he meant. "Oh."

He brought one of her hands to his mouth for a kiss. "I was so unhappy last summer, and on that day in particular as, no doubt, were you. I want to take you away, somewhere we can be alone, and I want it to be then. It was not a joyous occasion last year, and we cannot erase those memories, but we can make better ones this year."

Elizabeth smiled, and her first response was to give him a proper kiss. "I would like that very much, to be alone with my darling husband, and to make wonderful new memories. What more could a lady wish? But where? Have you any ideas?"

"Not the seaside."

Elizabeth laughed at the disgusted sound in his voice. "No, definitely not the seaside!"

"I do have one idea, one I think my geology-loving wife would like. The Lake District."

A broad smile overtook her face. "The Lakes? I promise to love you forever if you take me to the Lakes, Mr Darcy."

He grinned. "Oh, you do, do you, Mrs Darcy?"

"Absolutely. I will be completely devoted to you and make it my life's work to see you happy."

"I do very much like the sound of that," he said, laughing.

Chapter 49

As July approached its end, Elizabeth was greatly surprised to see a letter from Mr Bennet among her post. They were at breakfast, and a soft exclamation escaped before she could stop it.

"Elizabeth?" Fitzwilliam asked, concern etched on his countenance.

She smiled, although it was forced. "'Tis nothing. Simply a letter I was not expecting to receive."

She was gratified that he understood her wish not to discuss the matter until they could go to her sitting room after the meal. Once they were alone, she explained, "My father."

Darcy's eyebrows arched high on his forehead, and his mouth set into a grimace.

"I suppose I should see what he wants." Elizabeth read the letter aloud.

Lizzy,
As you might well imagine, four out of every five words spoken at Longbourn are about your sister's upcoming wedding, and

the other one is seldom anything of particular interest or importance. I have not heard a word of sense since you left unless it is from Mr Linnington. Jane informs me that you intend to be here for the wedding, and that you and your husband will stay at Longbourn. If this is not the case, pray tell your mother. In among her wedding plans are those to redecorate the guest rooms so that they are befitting her elegant daughter and son-in-law. You would save her a great deal of effort, and me a great deal of money, if your plans have changed or never were to be our guests. Jane also tells me that you must go into Worcestershire after being here, and that the Gardiners will go to Derbyshire in October. So much to-and-fro-ing. I am sure it is very good for the economy, but it sounds exhausting. I do trust that you will not be so much occupied that you will forget us in our little corner of the world. Your stamina, I know, can easily bear what I would find a trial.

Rest assured that we are all perfectly well at Longbourn, &c. As I have not heard differently, I assume the same is true of all of you at Pemberley.

Yours, &c.

Elizabeth folded the sheet of paper and set it aside. "Well, that was…unexpectedly civil."

Darcy looked at her as though she had spoken complete nonsense.

She chuckled. "If you were more accustomed to my father's manner, you would know I speak the truth, Fitzwilliam. Why, he even mentioned you three times, in a roundabout fashion." She took up the letter again and searched it. "Here, he wrote, 'your husband', let me see, 'son-in-law', and later, here it is, 'true of all of you at Pemberley.' That was handsome of him, was it not?"

Darcy stared at her.

Elizabeth sighed. "I expected nothing more. I could not conceive of a reason for his having written to me at all. You will have to trust my judgment on this. It was rather a friendly letter for him, given the

449

circumstances. He would have been more than capable of reprimanding me, or insulting me, by letter, if he had wished to. He will never outright apologise, or admit that he was wrong, and this," she shook the letter, "must be seen as a peace-offering."

Darcy took a deep breath and slowly released it. "I do not like it."

Elizabeth threw aside the sheet of paper and gave her husband a sound kiss. "I do not ask that you like it, and I do not ask even of myself that I like it. I shall, however, accept that my father hopes to be on easier terms with us. If he does, it will make visiting Longbourn much, much more pleasant."

JULY HAD ONE LAST SURPRISE IN STORE FOR THEM. GEORGIANA apologised to Elizabeth.

One morning after they returned from making calls, Georgiana asked to speak to Elizabeth privately. "I wanted to say that I am sorry I was not kinder to you. You were so good to me right from the beginning. That night, last summer...I am very, very glad that you came to my aid even though you did not know me. I was f-f-frightened, and I did not know what to do, but you did, and even then, even though I was so upset, I knew I was safe once you were there. I am very grateful, and I am sorry I did not tell you that before. I think you would say I owed you nothing, but I believe I did. At the very least, I could have tried to help you once you married my brother. I ought to have been kinder and I never, never should have..."

She faltered, and Elizabeth waited silently, believing that was what Georgiana would prefer.

"I should not have spoken so hatefully to you, or told Tom things that were not true. It was wrong of me, and I knew that."

Elizabeth did not know what to say. She had promised herself she would keep an open mind with respect to Georgiana. It was for Fitzwilliam that she would seek to trust Georgiana's sincerity. At length she said, "Thank you for saying so much. I do appreciate that you have, but I have to ask—why?"

Georgiana bit her lower lip. "I-I have thought about it, but I have to admit that I am not entirely certain I can explain. Yet. Not completely. But I think I know, or at least I am beginning to understand."

"I am interested in what you think. No one, least of all me, believes you can know yourself perfectly after so short a time, or at such a young age—if it is ever possible for any of us to always understand why we act the way we do. Please speak freely, Georgiana, and believe that your brother and I both appreciate how much effort you have made these last weeks."

Georgiana huffed, and Elizabeth could not hide her shock.

Two bright red spots appeared on Georgiana's cheeks and she spoke with more warmth than she had thus far. "You are so good, and it is…it is hard to live with someone who always knows how to act or what to do. It is not only that, but I hated that you knew what I was, how stupid I was last summer. I did not want anyone to know, but that you did was terrible! Then to discover you would be my sister, that my foolishness meant my brother had to marry you instead of the sort of lady he was supposed to marry. I hated it!

"I always expected you to say something, to remind me again and again about Ramsgate and that awful man, but you never did, and it was because you are so much better than I ever was! And I kept expecting that you would show everyone you were not like us, that you should not be Mrs Darcy, but you never did! Again and again, you always did just what you were supposed to do. I was so horrible to you, I made you have to marry Fitzwilliam, I was awful to you, and lied about you, and you were still so good! In April, when Fitzwilliam was missing, you were kind to me. How could you be kind to me when I was so stupid and hateful?"

Elizabeth did not know if Georgiana truly wanted an answer, but the answer was too close to what she had realised that night for her not to say it, although she spoke almost without volition. "I could not behave towards you in any other way, Georgiana, not without being someone I was not, or someone I would not like to be."

Georgiana huffed again, and this time it was combined with a sob. Tears slowly fell down her cheeks. Never, Elizabeth thought, had she heard Georgiana say so much that was sincere.

"You always knew what to do, and it was simply because that is who you are. When you became Mrs Darcy, you knew what to do, how to go about becoming a good mistress, and how to be a good sister to a foolish little girl like me. Perhaps I would have liked you more if you were less good, less kind, less capable. I know it was very wrong of me. You need not say it."

Elizabeth was vexed at the implication that she would say it. She gritted her teeth for a moment before trusting herself to speak. "I did *not* know just what to do. I simply tried my best, expecting to make mistakes—and I did make mistakes, with your brother most of all, perhaps, if not you. You do understand how difficult you made it for me in those early weeks and months? It was a dreadful time for me, and I had so hoped we would grow to love each other, to depend on each other, as I did my other sisters. It would have been easier for me, but I also believed I could help you after your disappointment."

"I hated that you were here," Georgiana admitted in a quiet voice. "It was a constant reminder of last summer. I thought if you were not here, then we could all forget about what I did. But that was impossible, and it was wrong of me to wish it."

"Yes, it was, because you could never have healed from the pain of what happened, or learnt from it, if you did not first accept it."

Georgiana nodded. "I know that now, but at the time, I wanted to pretend I had never even been to Ramsgate."

They sat in silence for a moment before Elizabeth said, "Thank you for your apology, Georgiana. I am very happy to think that we can begin to truly put the past behind us. That will make all of us—you, your brother, and me—much happier. You will see."

Georgiana nodded. "I-I shall go. Mrs Annesley will be waiting for me." She stood and left Elizabeth's sitting room as quickly as she could.

Elizabeth told Darcy about the conversation once he returned to the house and assured him that she was satisfied with Georgiana's apology. "I feel like I can breathe more easily," she exclaimed. "Everything will be better now, and we can all look to the future. I am absolutely convinced of that, and you should be, too. At last!"

ELIZABETH STOOD AT THE WINDOW OF HER BEDCHAMBER, LOOKING out on the beautiful Pemberley lawn. She could see stands of trees to one side and the lake at the other. It was now early August, and it had just occurred to her that it had been six or seven weeks since she had experienced a certain monthly occurrence.

Could I be? At long last, might I be…?

Unconsciously, she put a hand on her lower belly, hoping and praying there might be a child starting to grow within her. *I do not feel any different. Perhaps it is too soon. Oh, how I hope I am! I should so love to have a child, to give Fitzwilliam a son or daughter.*

Elizabeth could not remain where she was. She must go down for breakfast. Esther Haddon would arrive in a few hours and she and Darcy had promised to go for a walk before then.

I shall say nothing to him about this, not yet. I might be mistaken, and I do not wish to excite his hopes.

THE TWO WEEKS OF MISS HADDON'S STAY WENT BY QUICKLY AND very enjoyably. The weather was reasonably fine, and they took every opportunity to be outside. In addition to each other's company, they saw their friends for morning and evening parties every two or three days. Robert Haddon came to visit and remained several nights. During that time, they saw a great deal of the Morrises. Haddon's attentions to Miss Morris were even more pointed than they had been in London.

"They will marry, you know," she said to Darcy one night.

"Are you matchmaking?"

"No! But they will. Without any help from me. And they will be very happy."

"If I agree with you, can we talk about something else? I shall wait to congratulate Haddon until he tells me I need to, if you please."

"Very well, but only to oblige you. You may tell me how you liked your fishing this morning, if you like. I am sure you caught the most fish, or the largest ones, or more probably both."

Darcy threw his head back against the sofa, closed his eyes and laughed. "Teasing, teasing woman!"

Elizabeth laughed merrily. "You adore it when I tease you. You know you do!"

Darcy could not disagree and encouraged her to tease him further, but in a rather different way.

IT WAS CLEAR TO ELIZABETH THAT MISS HADDON LIKED MR Llewellyn. Even after telling herself that she would say nothing about it, she found herself doing just that. Miss Haddon had been saying that she did not understand why her brother had not yet proposed to Miss Morris, but they expected news of an engagement any day, and some story involving the parson had been part of it.

"He is a kind man. Am I correct that you enjoy his company?"

Miss Haddon nodded. "But I am not ready to...you understand?"

Elizabeth said that she did.

"I had once hoped—" Miss Haddon laughed ruefully. "You know what I once hoped. I hoped that another gentleman would follow his cousin's example and make a disinterested choice. He could not, and I am better off without him. He is a good man, but ours would not have been a good marriage."

"I own that I was afraid you were unhappy."

Miss Haddon shook her head. "I was for a time, but then I was angry." She laughed. "It is not very ladylike, but it is true. I would not be content with a man who liked me only because I have £10,000 and can say my family has long been friends with the Darcys of Pemberley, and I would not be content with a man who thinks that that is not enough for him."

"The man you accept should like you because of who you are, and value *you*, not whatever fortune or consequence you can add to his," Elizabeth asserted.

"I have come to the same conclusion. I am not prepared just yet to pledge myself to any man, however."

"But?" A mischievous smile took over Elizabeth's expression.

Miss Haddon blushed. "But I do very much like Mr Llewellyn, and I suspect that, if he can be patient, and is inclined to ask at some future time, I think we could be very happy."

"I believe you will find that he is inclined to ask, and that he can be patient. I hope so, for his sake as well as yours. I would like to see both of you happy and would be very glad to have a friend so close by."

When Miss Haddon smiled and nodded, but did not speak, Elizabeth knew that it was time to leave the subject. The heart needs time to heal after it has been injured, as Elizabeth knew only too well.

Once Miss Haddon returned home, Elizabeth and Darcy began to make final arrangements for their trip to the Lake District. Elizabeth's hope that she was increasing remained, and she intended to tell Fitzwilliam of her suspicions when they were on holiday.

The journey to the Lake District was, fortunately, not as long as that from London to Pemberley, but it did make Elizabeth dread all the upcoming travel they would do in the autumn. She often felt queasy during long carriage rides, but she felt especially poorly on this trip. As much as she did not like to feel ill, it made her more and more convinced that she was going to have a child.

The region's beauty and wildness left her breathless, and she could hardly wait to explore all of it, or at least as much as they had time and energy for. "Thank you for bringing me here!" Elizabeth threw her arms around Darcy and kissed him.

"If I had known I would get such a response, I would have done it sooner."

"This is the perfect time for us to be here, and I know that as our anniversary approaches in future years, I shall think of this year and not last summer."

As excited as Elizabeth was to be in a part of the country she had longed to visit, she could not fight her body's new demands. She was tired in the mornings and had to remain in bed longer than was usual for her. The morning after their arrival, it was easy to blame her fatigue on travel, but when she was equally as tired the next morning, Fitzwilliam asked her about it.

He perched at the edge of her bed where she was sitting up having just had toast and tea. "I am happy to hear you are feeling well now, but," he took her hand in his, "it is not the first morning you have been so tired, almost too tired to stay awake."

Elizabeth could not stop herself from grinning. She had reached the conclusion that she had to tell him sooner rather than later. She had considered waiting until their anniversary, which was at the midpoint of their holiday, but given her fatigue, queasiness when in the carriage, and her belief that her symptoms would get worse before they got better, she knew the time had come. "I did not want to tell you until I was confident, and I still am not, I shall not be for perhaps another two months—" She took his hand and laid it on her belly. "I think...I think I am going to have a baby."

He took a deep breath, and slowly released it. He looked at his hand on her stomach, over the place where their child might be growing, then into her eyes. "I had wondered, but I did not like to ask."

"Are you pleased?"

Her husband nodded. "Of course, I am pleased. Are you happy?"

Elizabeth whispered, "Happier than I knew possible."

"A baby." Fitzwilliam's voice was full of joy and wonder.

Elizabeth felt the sting of tears in her eyes. "I love you. And I am glad that it happened this way. That it only happened after we knew we loved each other, after we were happy to be married. Is that silly?"

He embraced her, burying his face in her neck, and shook his head. His voice rough, he said, "I love you, my darling wife."

ELIZABETH AND FITZWILLIAM MADE MANY WONDERFUL NEW memories during their holiday. None was more special, or would be remembered with more fondness and joy, than the one they created on the twenty-ninth of August—one year since they were united as husband and wife in Longbourn church. It was just past midday, and they were sitting at a very pretty site which gave them a glorious view of the wildness of the region.

"I wish I could ask you to marry me," Fitzwilliam said.

Elizabeth laughed softly. "Well, you can hardly do that, my love. I suppose you could, but we cannot be unmarried and re-married."

She was being teasingly obtuse. He knew it, and she knew he did.

He spoke again, still serious despite her initial response to his sentiment. "Still, I wish I could. I wish I could have met you, and courted you properly, enjoyed every moment of falling in love and making you love me, then asking you to be my wife."

Elizabeth smiled as he spoke. She touched his cheek, lightly running her fingers over it. She saw in his eyes not only his love, but also a sadness which she associated with the pain they had both felt in the past year, and his sense of guilt for having hurt her. It made her forget her playfulness. "What would you have said?"

"What would I say?" He spoke slowly and took a moment before continuing. "I would say that I love you more dearly than I knew it was possible to love another person. I would say that almost since I first knew you, I had come to respect your kindness and intelligence, your courage." He smiled. "Your sense of humour, your beauty, your passion."

Elizabeth kissed him.

He laughed. "I believe it would be prudent for a young lady to wait for a gentleman to finish his proposals before she kissed him."

"Perhaps it would be, if he were not already her husband."

He kissed her, then, when she sat back expectantly, continued. "I would tell you that I could imagine no greater honour than to have you as my wife, no greater happiness than to go through this life and the next with you by my side. I would tell you that I know I have not always been worthy of your regard or your trust, let alone your love, but that I would spend every day endeavouring to change that."

"You have," Elizabeth insisted, her voice at a whisper. She leaned in and pressed her lips against his, willing him to believe what he never truly, completely would—that he deserved her forgiveness.

"It would only remain for me to beg you to accept me, to tie your lot to mine, to make me the happiest of men. I would promise to never forget what a gift you give me."

Elizabeth thought that she had never loved him so well as she did at this moment. How could she not when he spoke so openly—which she knew was not easy for him—and so tenderly? She had already committed herself to him, in her heart as well as before God, but she would again today, and in different ways in what, she prayed, would be many, many years of marriage. "And I would say to you—no, not words of thanks for the honour you did me; they would take too long. I would only waste time with such words if I had no intention of accepting."

They both laughed, and Fitzwilliam brushed her cheek with the backs of his fingers.

Elizabeth took his hand in hers, and kissed it. "Instead, I would immediately tell you that I return your love, and that I could imagine no greater happiness than being Mrs Darcy."

ACKNOWLEDGMENTS

My heartfelt thanks to the community at A Happy Assembly for embracing and encouraging my writing endeavours over the years. Special thanks are due to the two women who acted as my betas as I originally wrote *Being Mrs Darcy*. You know who you are! I wouldn't be writing this if the wonderful people behind Q&Q hadn't contacted me, so thank you very, very much. I was in need of a new adventure!

ABOUT THE AUTHOR

Lucy Marin developed a love for reading at a young age and whiled away many hours imagining how stories might continue or what would happen if there was a change in the circumstances faced by the protagonists. After reading her first Austen novel, a life-long ardent admiration was borne. Lucy was introduced to the world of Austen variations after stumbling across one at a used bookstore while on holiday in London. This led to the discovery of the online world of Jane Austen Fan Fiction and, soon after, she picked up her pen and began to transfer the stories in her head to paper.

Lucy lives in Toronto, Canada surrounded by hundreds of books and a loving family. She teaches environmental studies, loves animals and trees and exploring the world around her.

Being Mrs Darcy is Lucy's first novel. Her second, titled Mr Darcy, A Man with a Plan will be released in summer 2020.

For more information about Lucy and other great authors, please visit www.QuillsandQuartos.com

Made in the USA
Monee, IL
31 July 2020

37328781R00270